A NOTE FROM MARY POPE OSBORNE ABOUT THE MAGIC TREE HOUSE Fact Trackers

When I write Magic Tree House® adventures, I love including facts about the times and places Jack and Annie visit. But when readers finish these adventures, I want them to learn even more. So that's why we write a series of nonfiction books that are companions to the fiction titles in the Magic Tree House® series. We call these books Fact Trackers because we love to track the facts! Whether we're researching dinosaurs, Pilgrims, sea monsters, or cobras, we're always amazed at how wondrous and surprising the real world is. We want you to experience the same wonder we do–so get out your pencils and notebooks and hit the trail with us. You can be a Magic Tree House® Fact Tracker, too!

Mary Pope Osborne

MAGIC TREE HOUSE® Fact Trackers

DINOSAURS

by **WILL OSBORNE**
and **MARY POPE OSBORNE**
adapted by **JENNY LAIRD**
with art by **JOMIKE TEJIDO**
color by **CAI TSE**

A STEPPING STONE BOOK™
RANDOM HOUSE 🏠 NEW YORK

Text copyright © 2000 by Will Osborne and Mary Pope Osborne
Cover art and interior illustrations copyright © 2025 by Jomike Tejido
Text adapted by Jenny Laird

All rights reserved. Published in the United States by Random House Children's Books, a division of Penguin Random House LLC, 1745 Broadway, New York, NY 10019. This work is adapted from *Magic Tree House Fact Tracker: Dinosaurs*, written by Will Osborne and Mary Pope Osborne and illustrated by Sal Murdocca, text copyright © 2000 by Will Osborne and Mary Pope Osborne and interior illustrations copyright © 2000 by Sal Murdocca. Published in paperback in the United States by Random House Children's Books, a division of Penguin Random House LLC, New York, in 2000.

Random House and the colophon are registered trademarks of Penguin Random House LLC and RH Graphic with the book design and A Stepping Stone Book and the colophon are trademarks of Penguin Random House LLC.

Magic Tree House is a registered trademark of Mary Pope Osborne; used under license.

Visit us on the Web!
rhcbooks.com
MagicTreeHouse.com

Educators and librarians, for a variety of teaching tools, visit us at RHTeachersLibrarians.com

Library of Congress Cataloging-in-Publication Data is available upon request.
ISBN 978-0-593-70585-8 (hardcover) — ISBN 978-0-593-70584-1 (trade)
ISBN 978-0-593-70586-5 (lib. bdg.) — ISBN 978-0-593-70587-2 (ebook)

Editor: Courtney Carbone
Designers: April Ward and Jules Buckley
Copy Editor: Stephanie Bay
Managing Editor: Katy Miller
Production Manager: Luke McCord

MANUFACTURED IN CHINA
10 9 8 7 6 5 4 3 2 1
First Graphic Novel Edition

This book has been officially leveled by using the F&P Text Level Gradient™ Leveling System.

Random House Children's Books supports the First Amendment and celebrates the right to read.

Penguin Random House values and supports copyright. Copyright fuels creativity, encourages diverse voices, promotes free speech, and creates a vibrant culture. Thank you for buying an authorized edition of this book and for complying with copyright laws by not reproducing, scanning, or distributing any part of it in any form without permission. You are supporting writers and allowing Penguin Random House to continue to publish books for every reader. Please note that no part of this book may be used or reproduced in any manner for the purpose of training artificial intelligence technologies or systems.

With special thanks to our scientific consultant
Dr. Thomas R. Holtz, Jr., Principal Lecturer in Vertebrate
Paleontology, University of Maryland, College Park, MD

Contents

CHAPTER 1: **A World of Dinosaurs** 1

CHAPTER 2: **Fossils**................................17

CHAPTER 3: **Dinosaur Hunters**..................27

CHAPTER 4: **Flesh-eaters**......................45

CHAPTER 5: **Plant-eaters**.....................62

CHAPTER 6: **Sea Monsters and Flying Creatures** ...78

CHAPTER 7: **What Happened to the Dinosaurs?** 92

CHAPTER 8: **Dinosaur Neighbors**....................104

Glossary..114

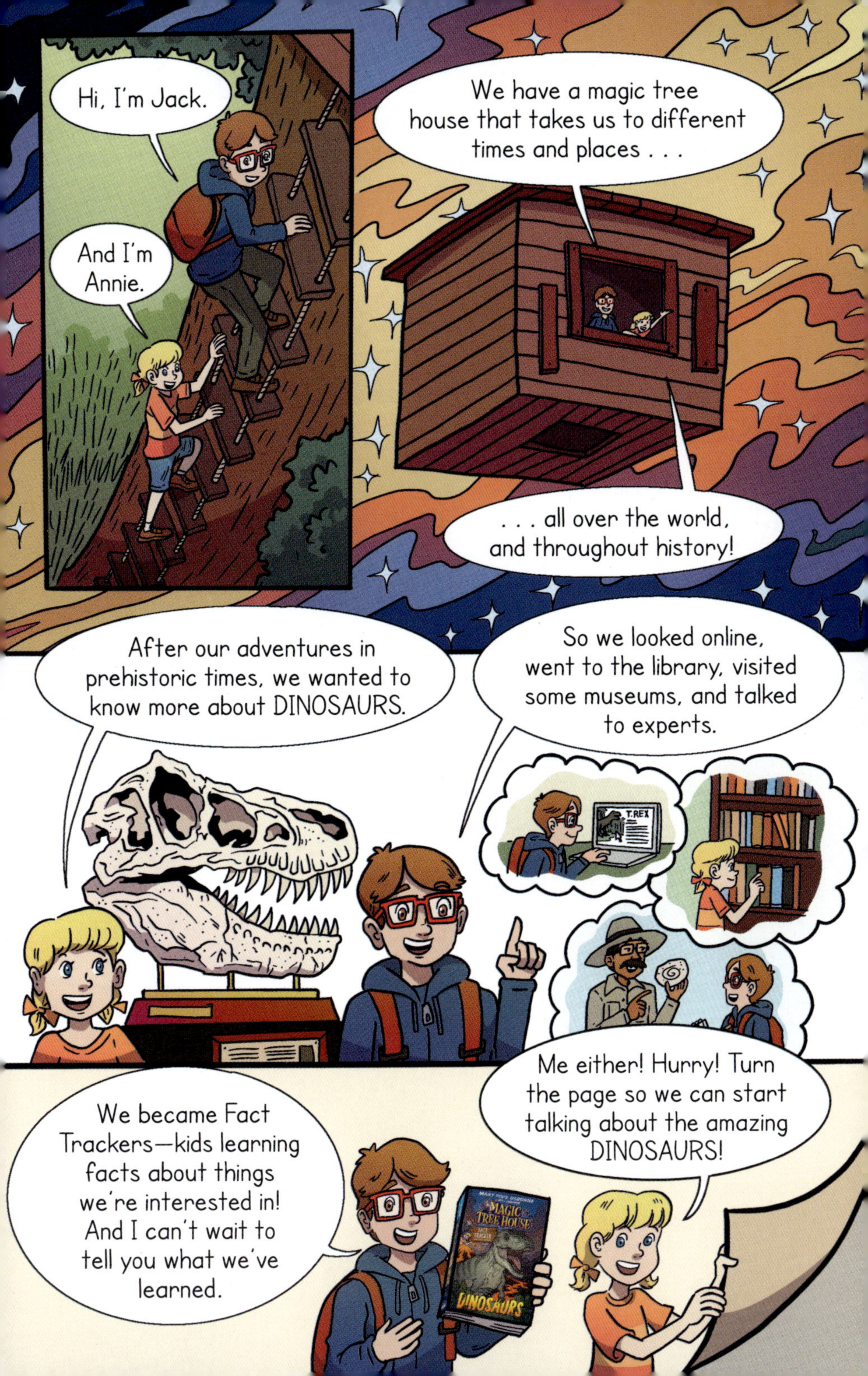
Hi, I'm Jack.
And I'm Annie.
We have a magic tree house that takes us to different times and places . . .
. . . all over the world, and throughout history!
After our adventures in prehistoric times, we wanted to know more about DINOSAURS.
So we looked online, went to the library, visited some museums, and talked to experts.
T. REX
We became Fact Trackers—kids learning facts about things we're interested in! And I can't wait to tell you what we've learned.
Me either! Hurry! Turn the page so we can start talking about the amazing DINOSAURS!
MAGIC TREE HOUSE
DINOSAURS

CHAPTER ONE
A World of Dinosaurs

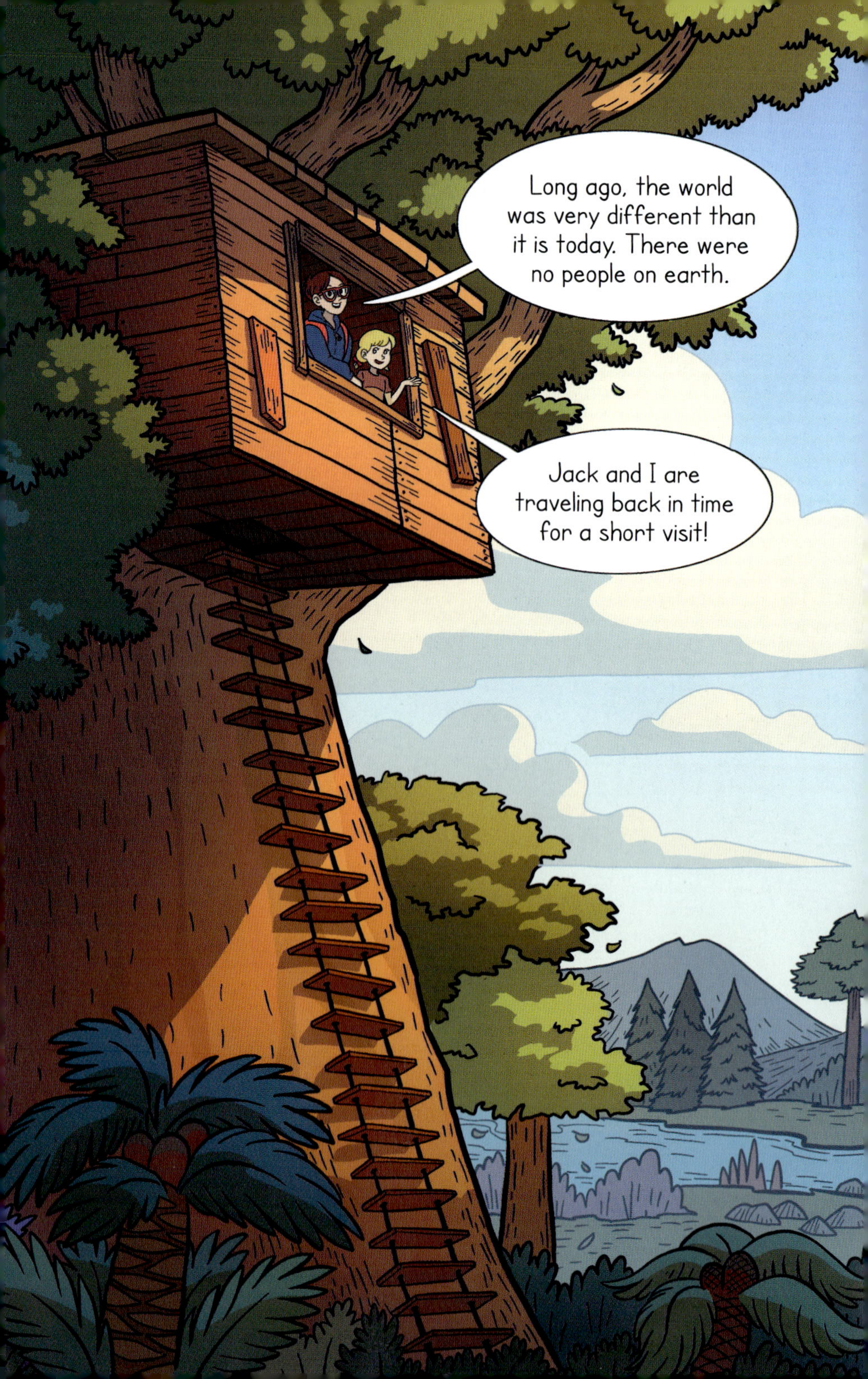
Long ago, the world was very different than it is today. There were no people on earth.
Jack and I are traveling back in time for a short visit!

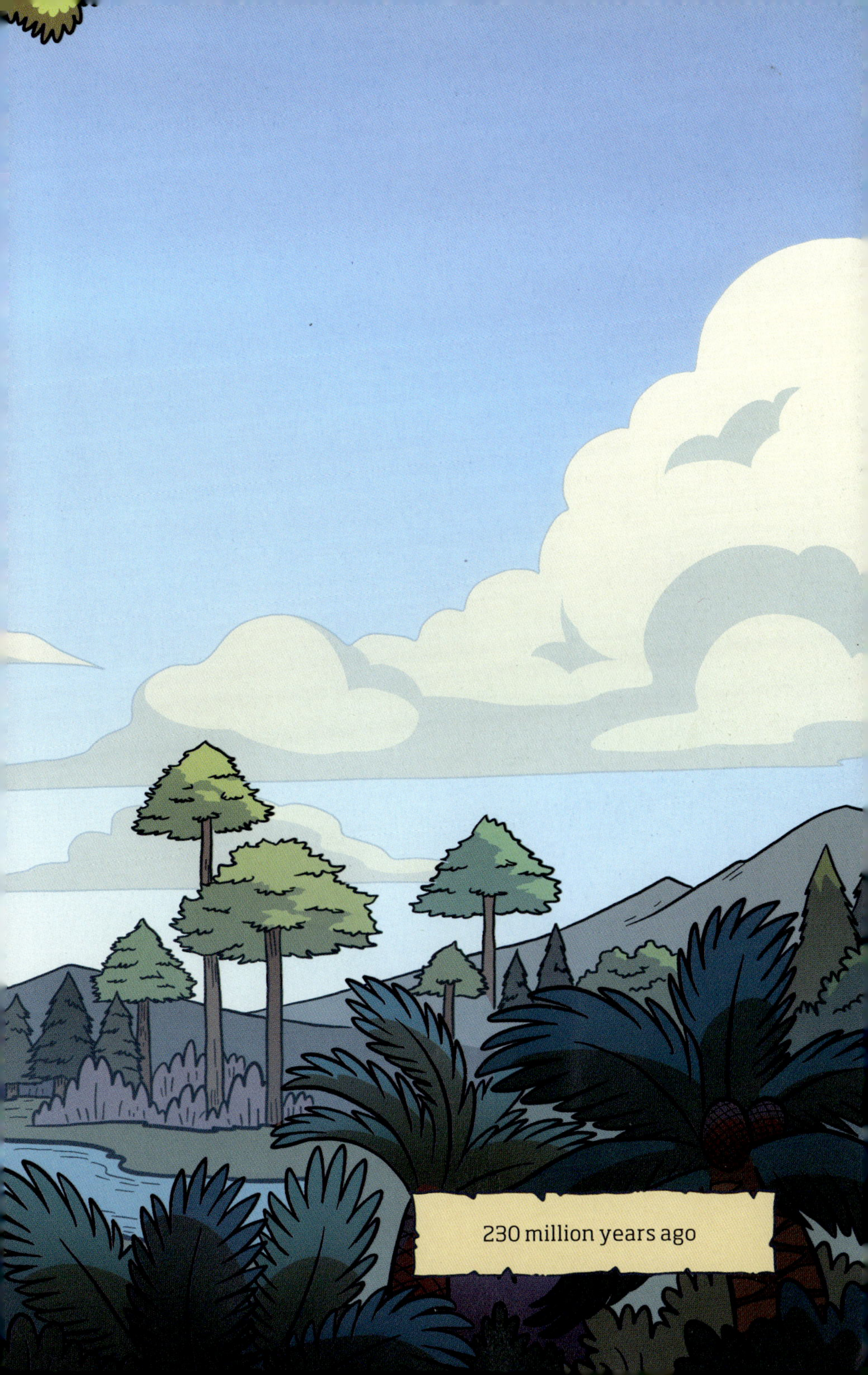
230 million years ago

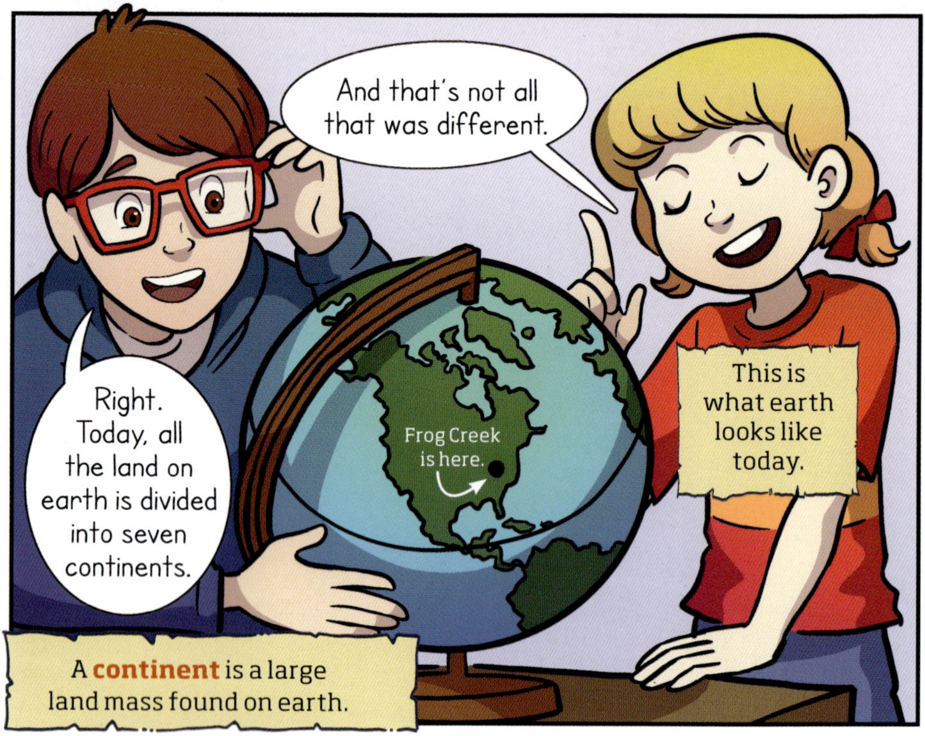
And that's not all that was different.
Right. Today, all the land on earth is divided into seven continents.
This is what earth looks like today.
Frog Creek is here.
A **continent** is a large land mass found on earth.

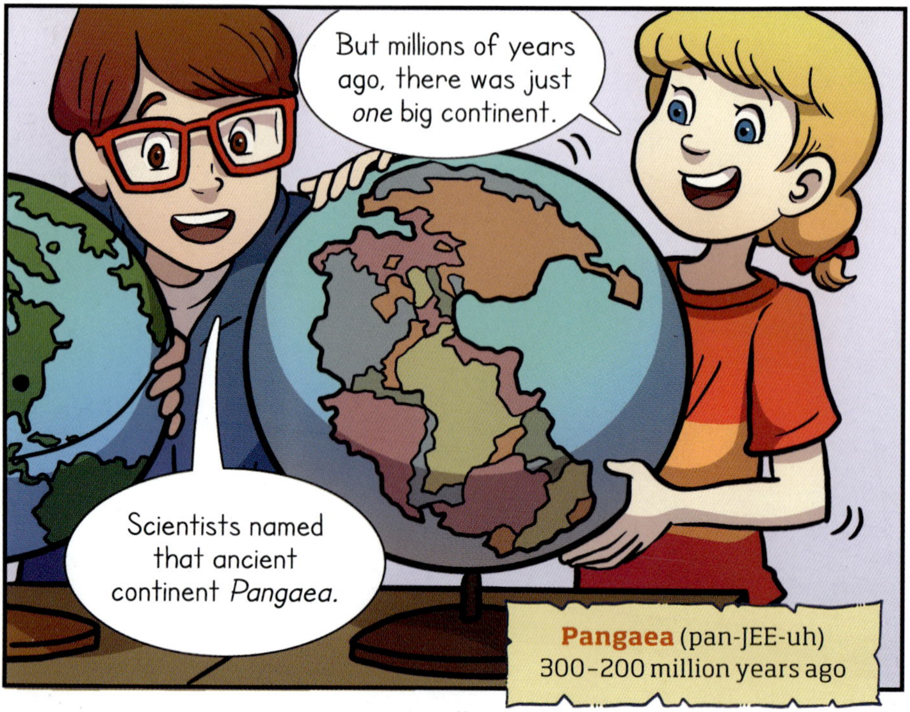
But millions of years ago, there was just *one* big continent.
Scientists named that ancient continent *Pangaea.*
Pangaea (pan-JEE-uh)
300–200 million years ago

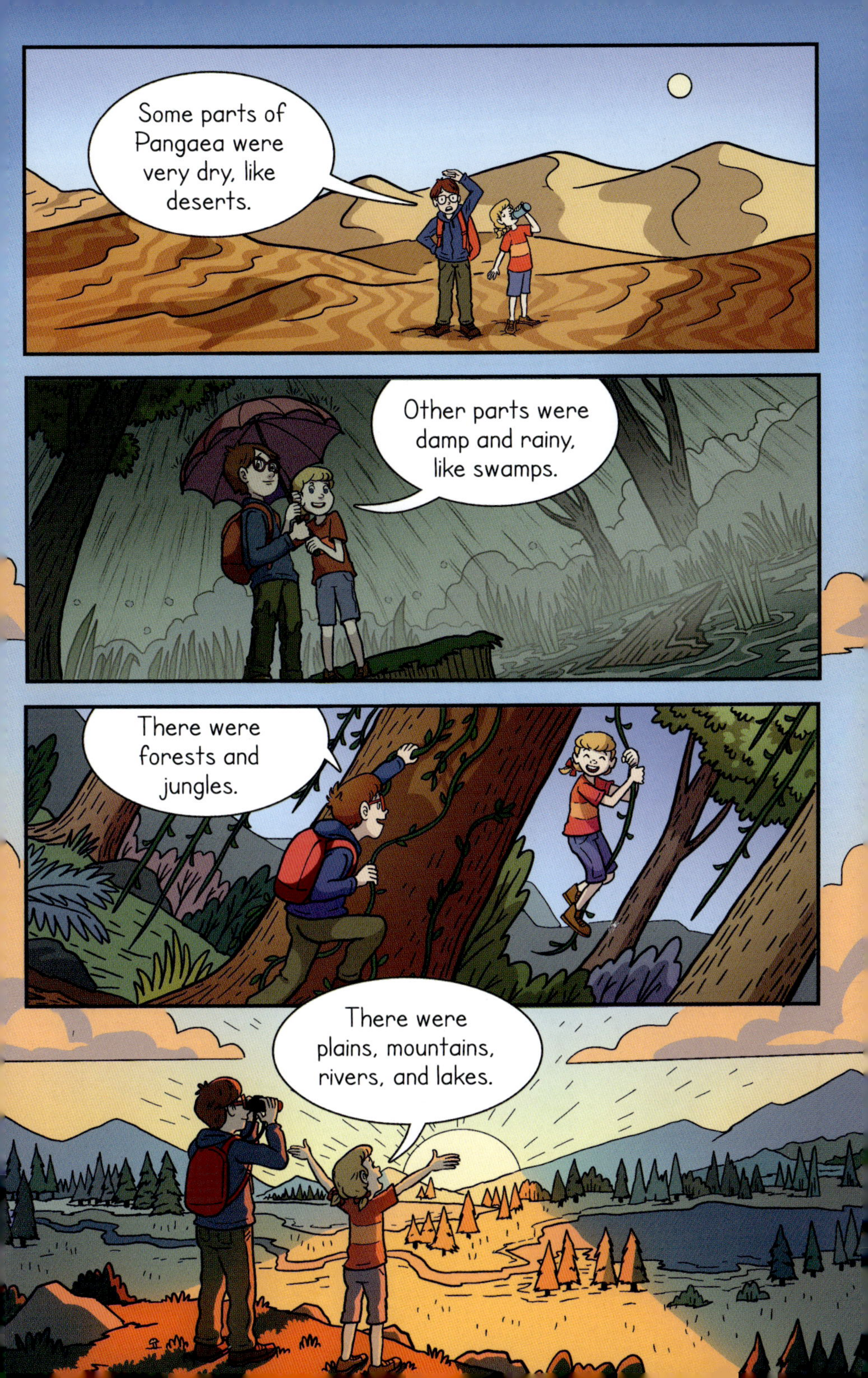
Some parts of Pangaea were very dry, like deserts.
Other parts were damp and rainy, like swamps.
There were forests and jungles.
There were plains, mountains, rivers, and lakes.

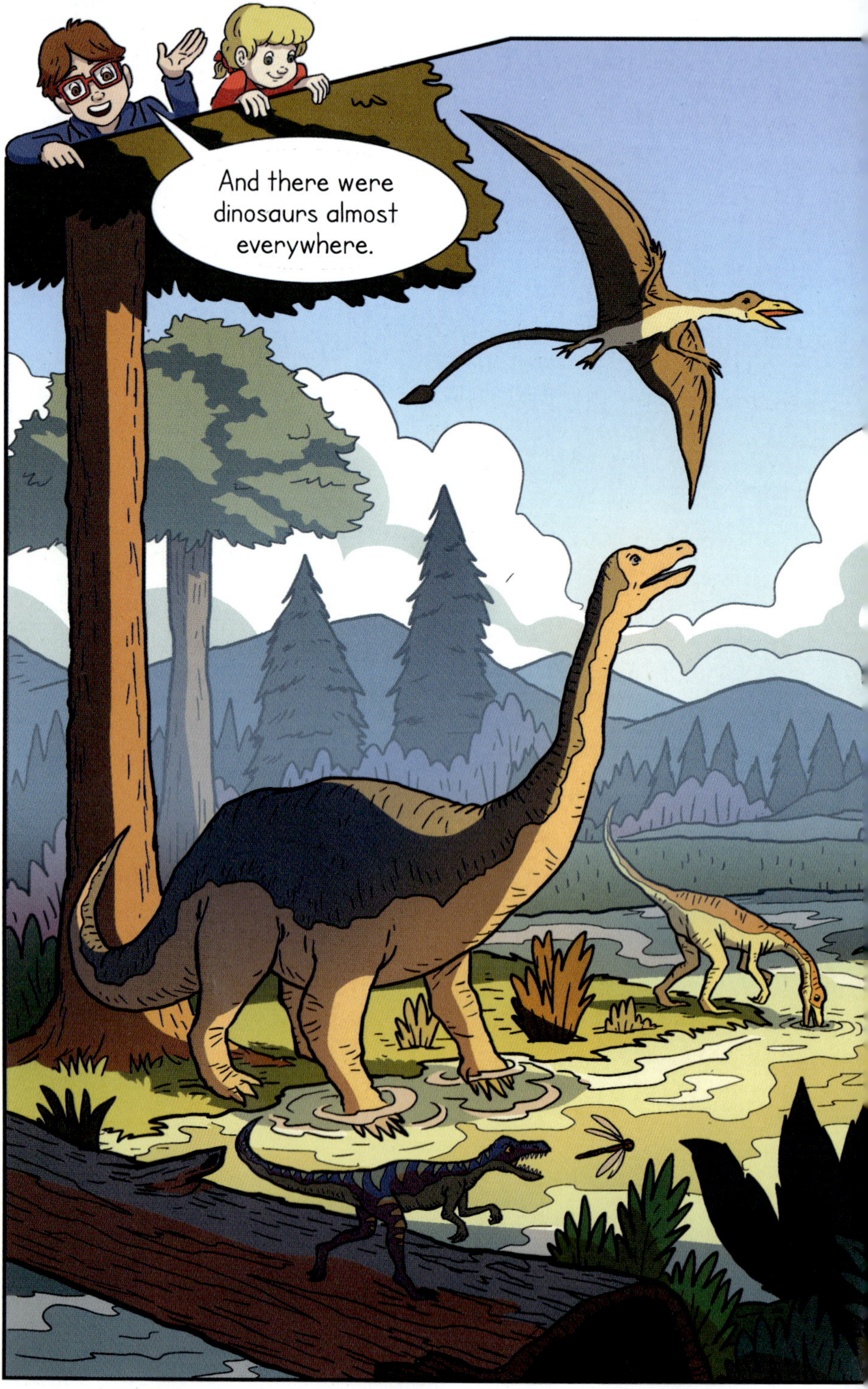
And there were dinosaurs almost everywhere.

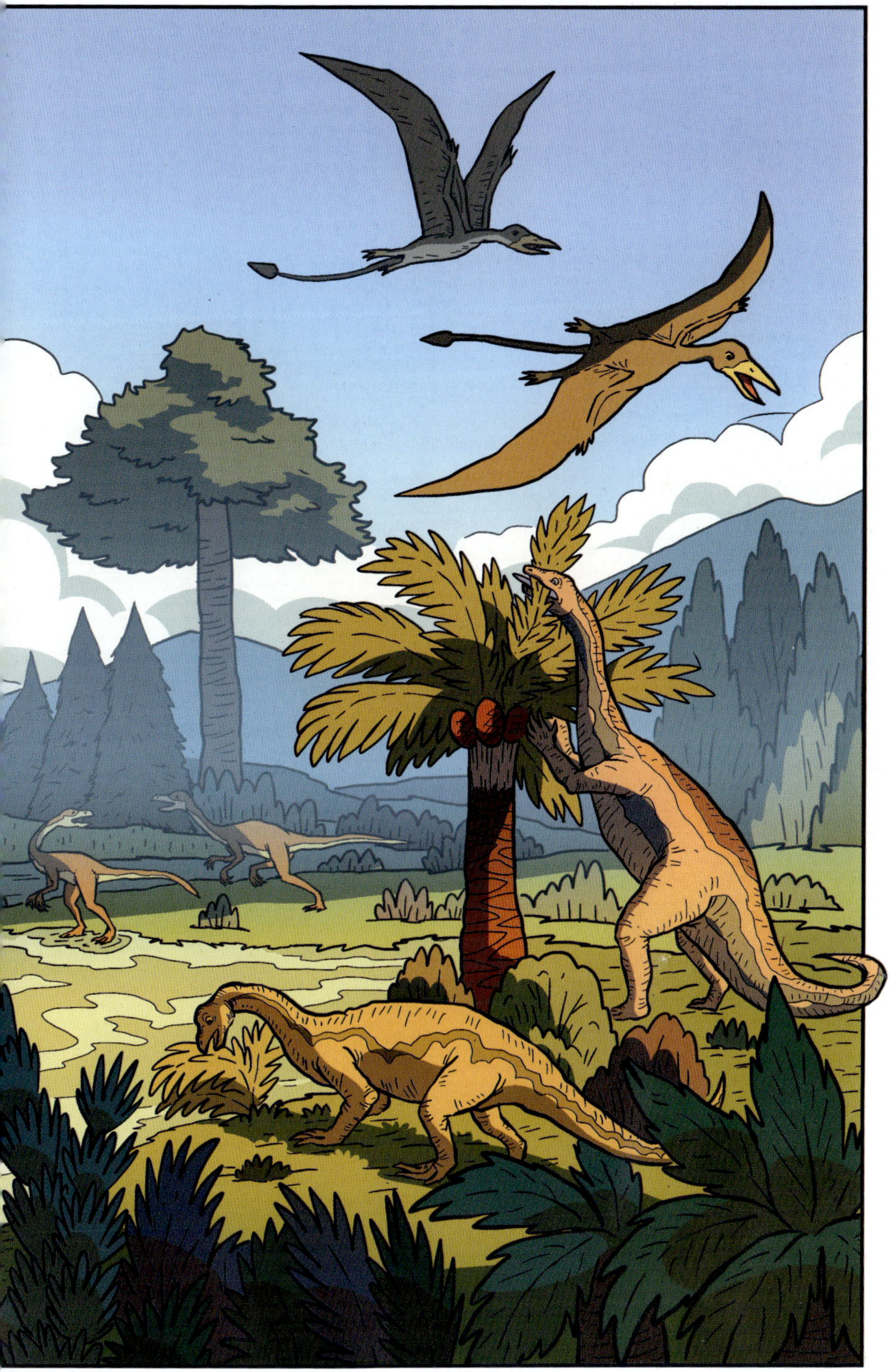

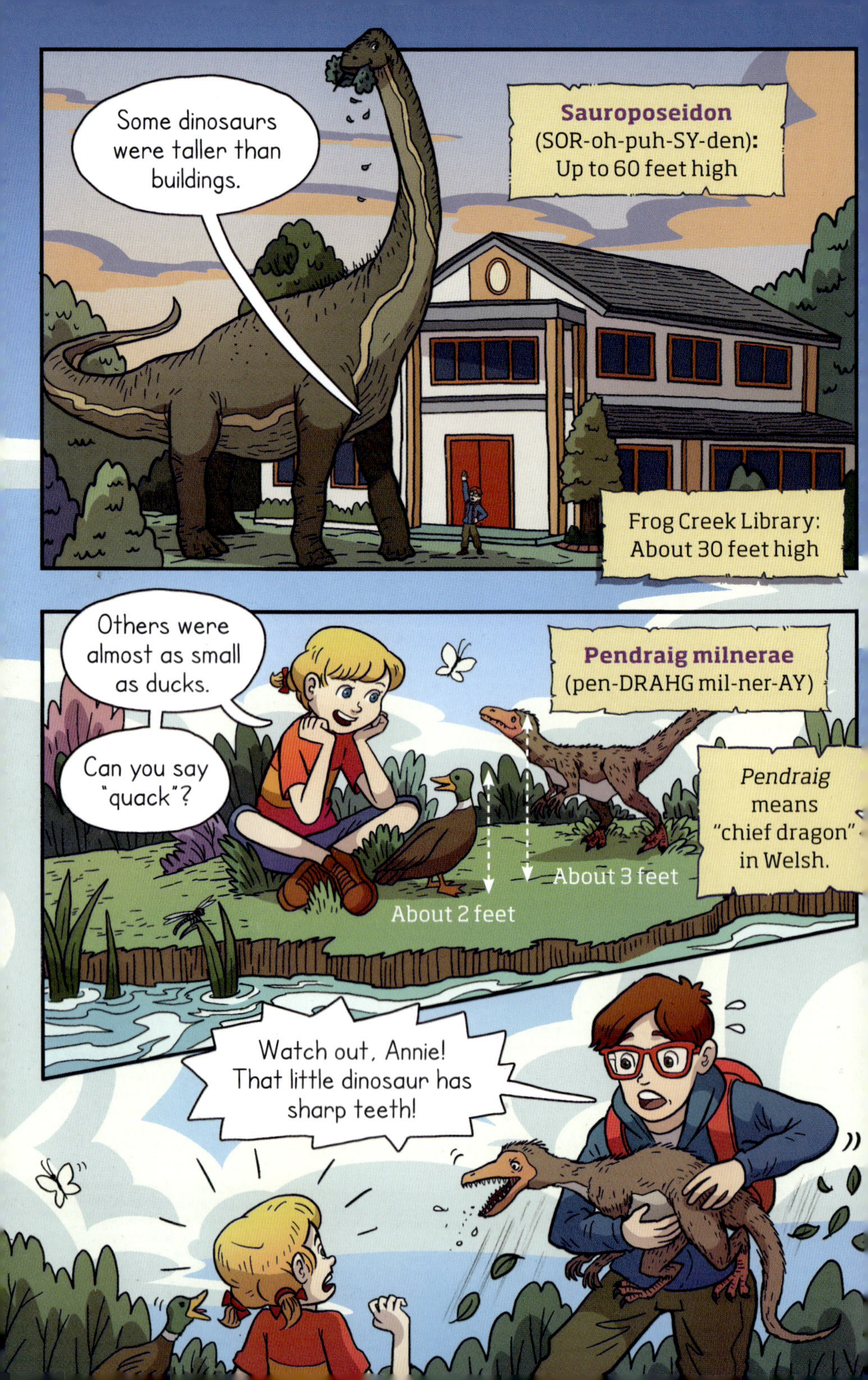
Some dinosaurs were taller than buildings.
Sauroposeidon (SOR-oh-puh-SY-den): Up to 60 feet high
Frog Creek Library: About 30 feet high
Others were almost as small as ducks.
Can you say "quack"?
Pendraig milnerae (pen-DRAHG mil-ner-AY)
About 3 feet
About 2 feet
Pendraig means "chief dragon" in Welsh.
Watch out, Annie! That little dinosaur has sharp teeth!

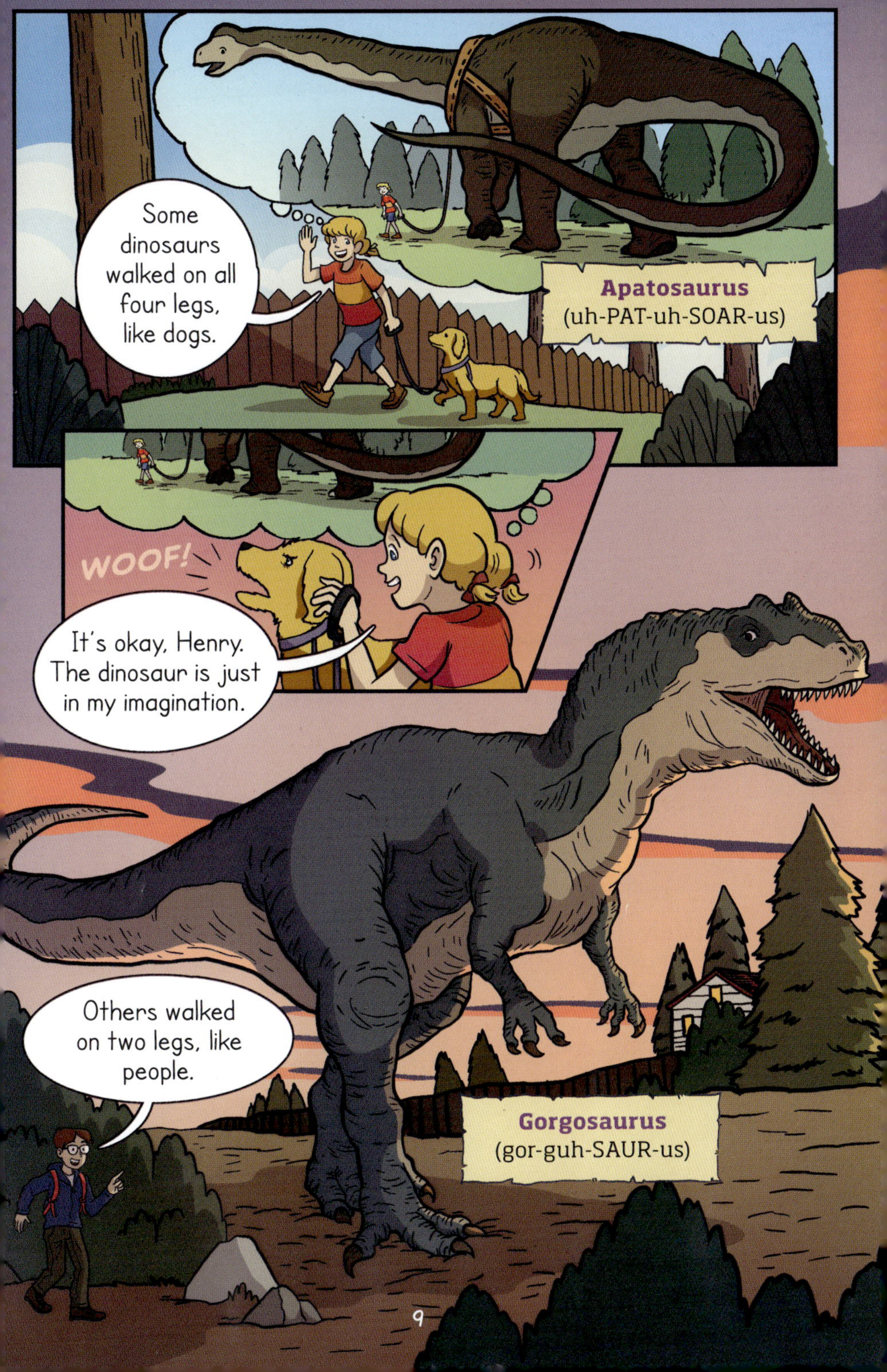
Some dinosaurs walked on all four legs, like dogs.
Apatosaurus
(uh-PAT-uh-SOAR-us)
WOOF!
It's okay, Henry. The dinosaur is just in my imagination.
Others walked on two legs, like people.
Gorgosaurus
(gor-guh-SAUR-us)

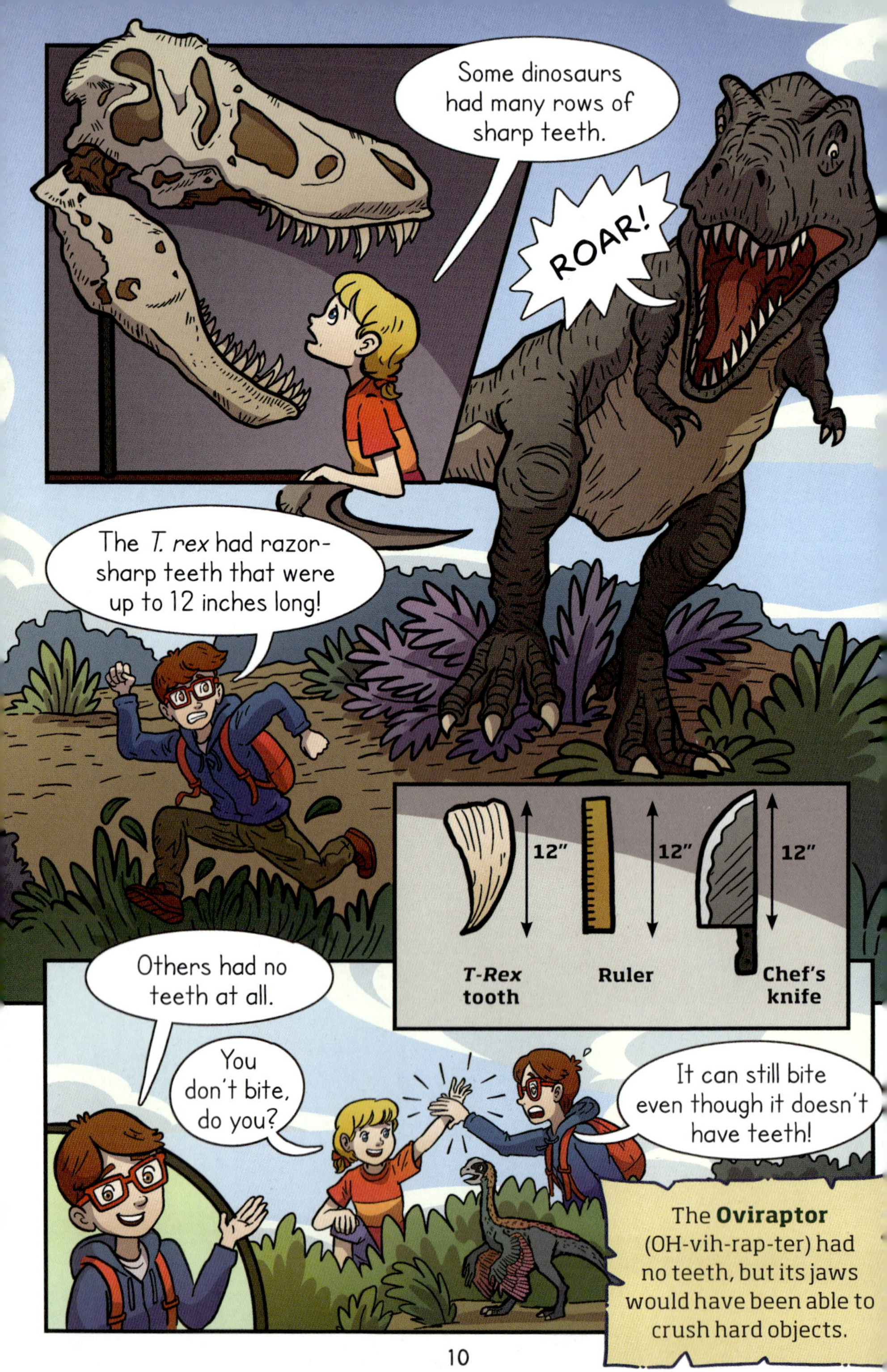
Some dinosaurs had many rows of sharp teeth.
ROAR!
The *T. rex* had razor-sharp teeth that were up to 12 inches long!
12"
12"
12"
T-Rex tooth
Ruler
Chef's knife
Others had no teeth at all.
You don't bite, do you?
It can still bite even though it doesn't have teeth!
The **Oviraptor** (OH-vih-rap-ter) had no teeth, but its jaws would have been able to crush hard objects.

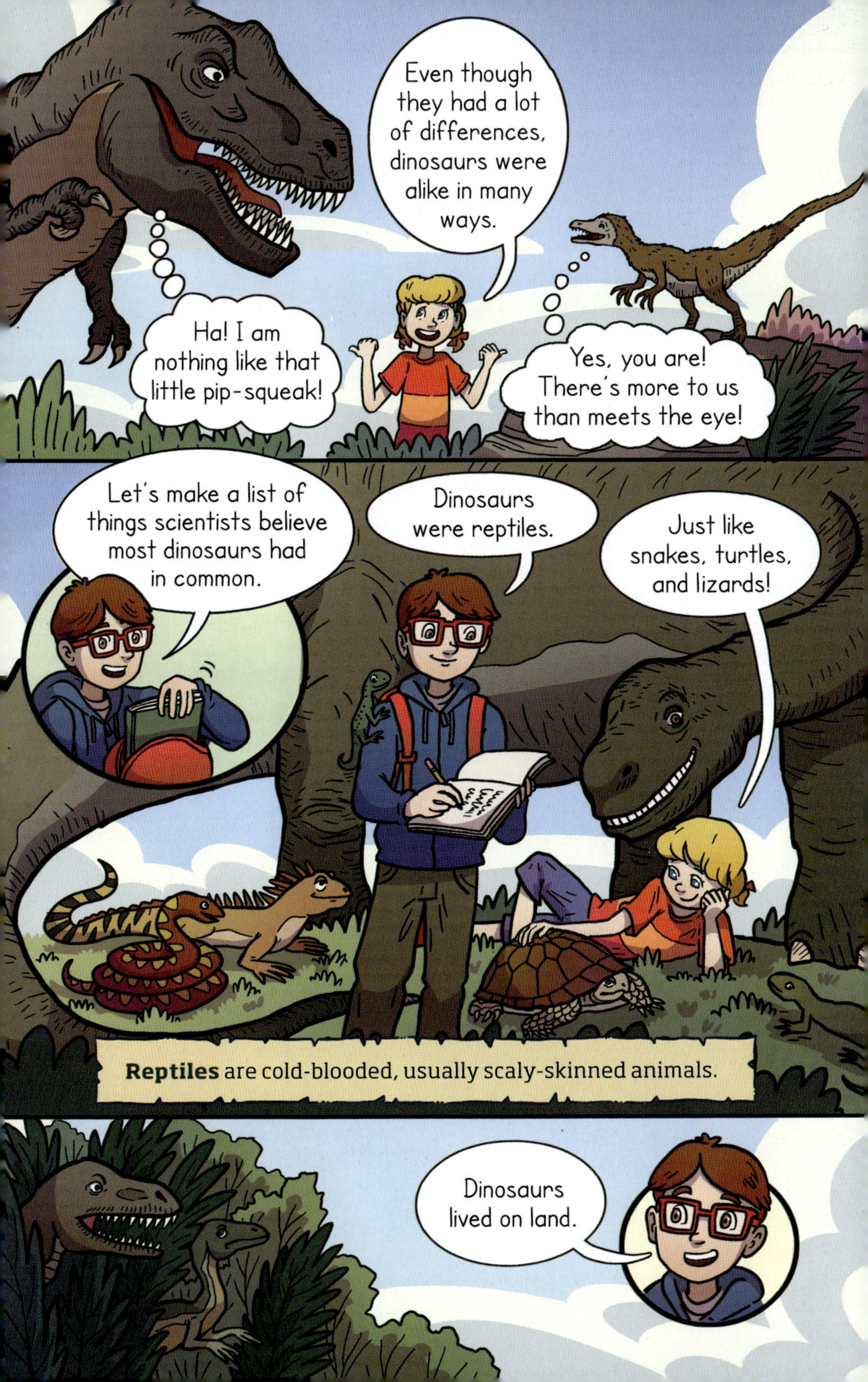
Even though they had a lot of differences, dinosaurs were alike in many ways.
Ha! I am nothing like that little pip-squeak!
Yes, you are! There's more to us than meets the eye!
Let's make a list of things scientists believe most dinosaurs had in common.
Dinosaurs were reptiles.
Just like snakes, turtles, and lizards!
Reptiles are cold-blooded, usually scaly-skinned animals.
Dinosaurs lived on land.

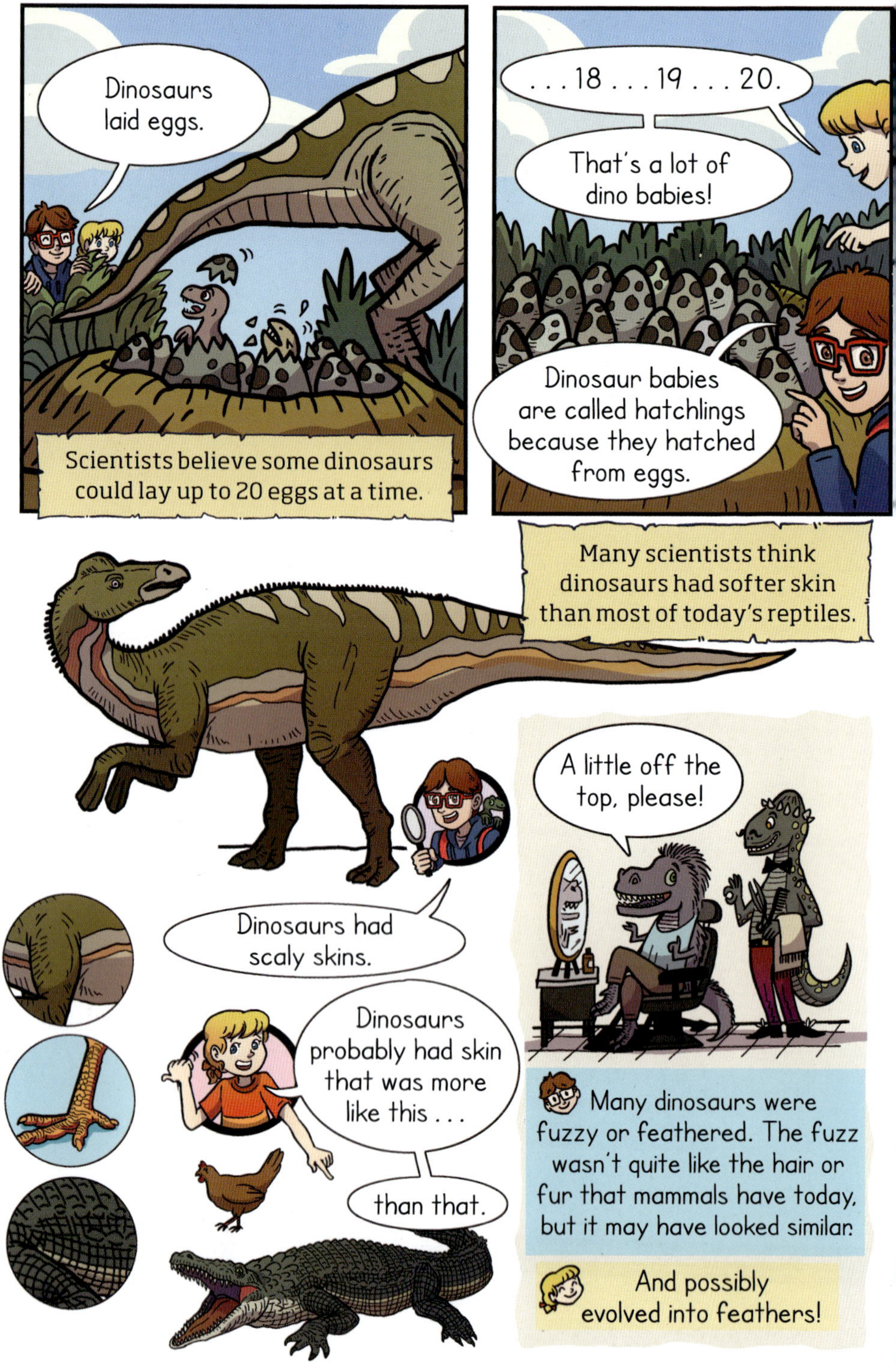
Dinosaurs laid eggs.
Scientists believe some dinosaurs could lay up to 20 eggs at a time.
. . . 18 . . . 19 . . . 20.
That's a lot of dino babies!
Dinosaur babies are called hatchlings because they hatched from eggs.
Many scientists think dinosaurs had softer skin than most of today's reptiles.
Dinosaurs had scaly skins.
Dinosaurs probably had skin that was more like this . . .
than that.
A little off the top, please!
Many dinosaurs were fuzzy or feathered. The fuzz wasn't quite like the hair or fur that mammals have today, but it may have looked similar.
And possibly evolved into feathers!

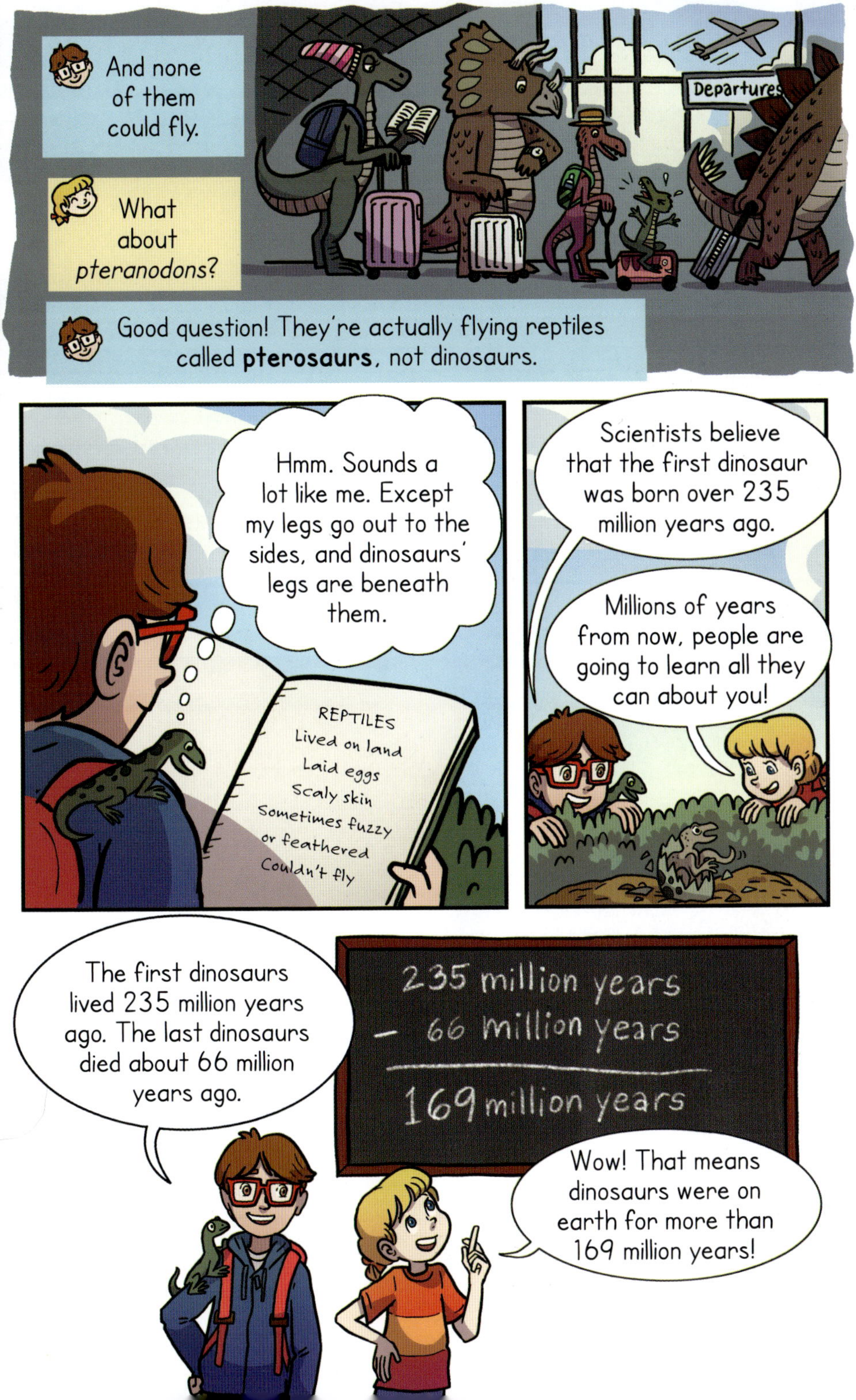

And none of them could fly.
What about *pteranodons*?
Departures
Good question! They're actually flying reptiles called **pterosaurs**, not dinosaurs.
Hmm. Sounds a lot like me. Except my legs go out to the sides, and dinosaurs' legs are beneath them.
REPTILES
Lived on land
Laid eggs
Scaly skin
Sometimes fuzzy or feathered
Couldn't fly
Scientists believe that the first dinosaur was born over 235 million years ago.
Millions of years from now, people are going to learn all they can about you!
The first dinosaurs lived 235 million years ago. The last dinosaurs died about 66 million years ago.
235 million years
- 66 million years
169 million years
Wow! That means dinosaurs were on earth for more than 169 million years!

The Age of Dinosaurs

Triassic (try-AA-sick) **Period**
252–201 million years ago
Dawn of Dinosaurs

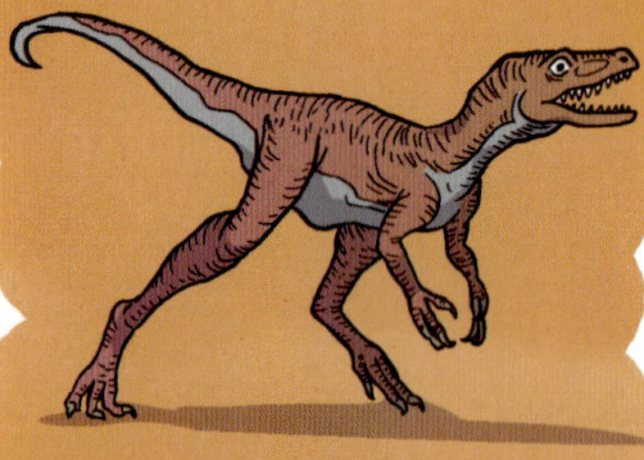

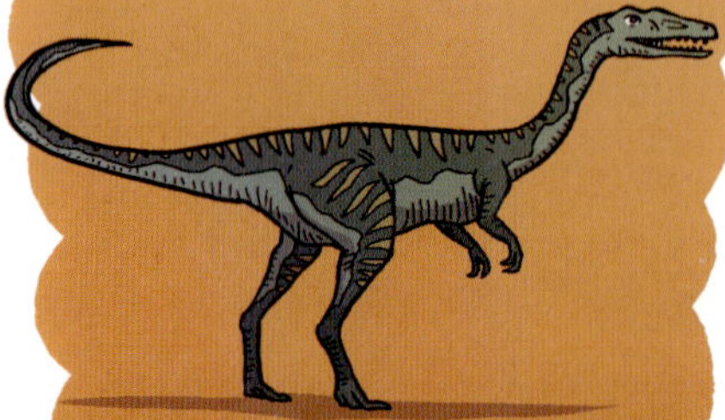

Jurassic (jur-AA-sick) **Period**
201–145 million years ago

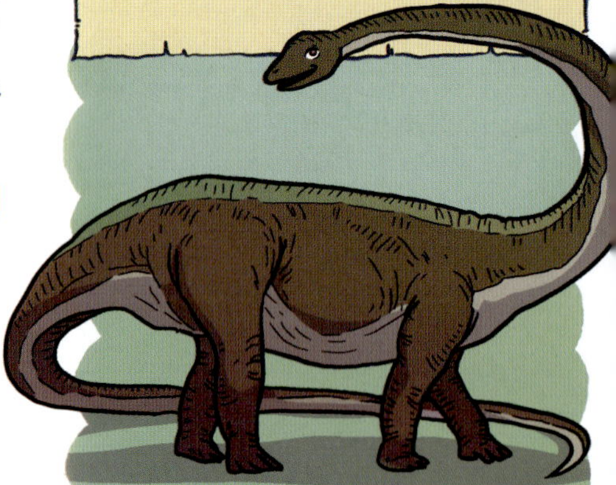

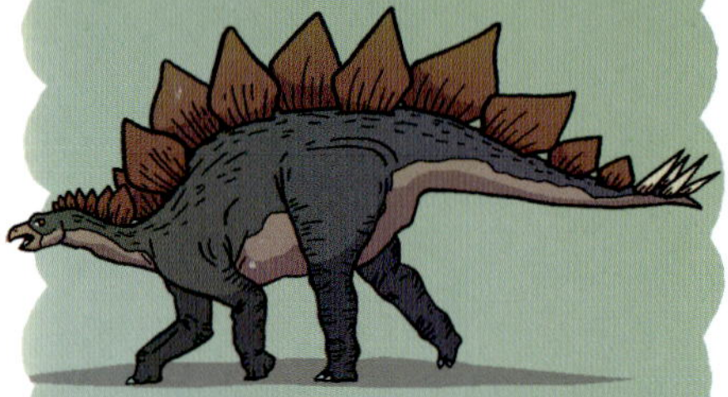

The Mesozoic (mez-uh-ZO-ick) Era

All the dinosaurs lived during what is called the Mesozoic Era. Scientists divide the Mesozoic Era into three parts, or periods.

Cretaceous (krih-TAY-shus) **Period**
145–66 million years ago

The first humans 350,000 years ago
Jack and Annie

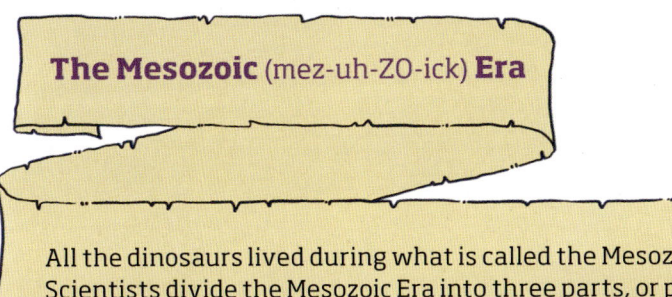

"Different kinds of dinosaurs lived during each period. The ones we know best today lived during the Jurassic and Cretaceous periods."

"That's over 60 million years before the first human was born!"

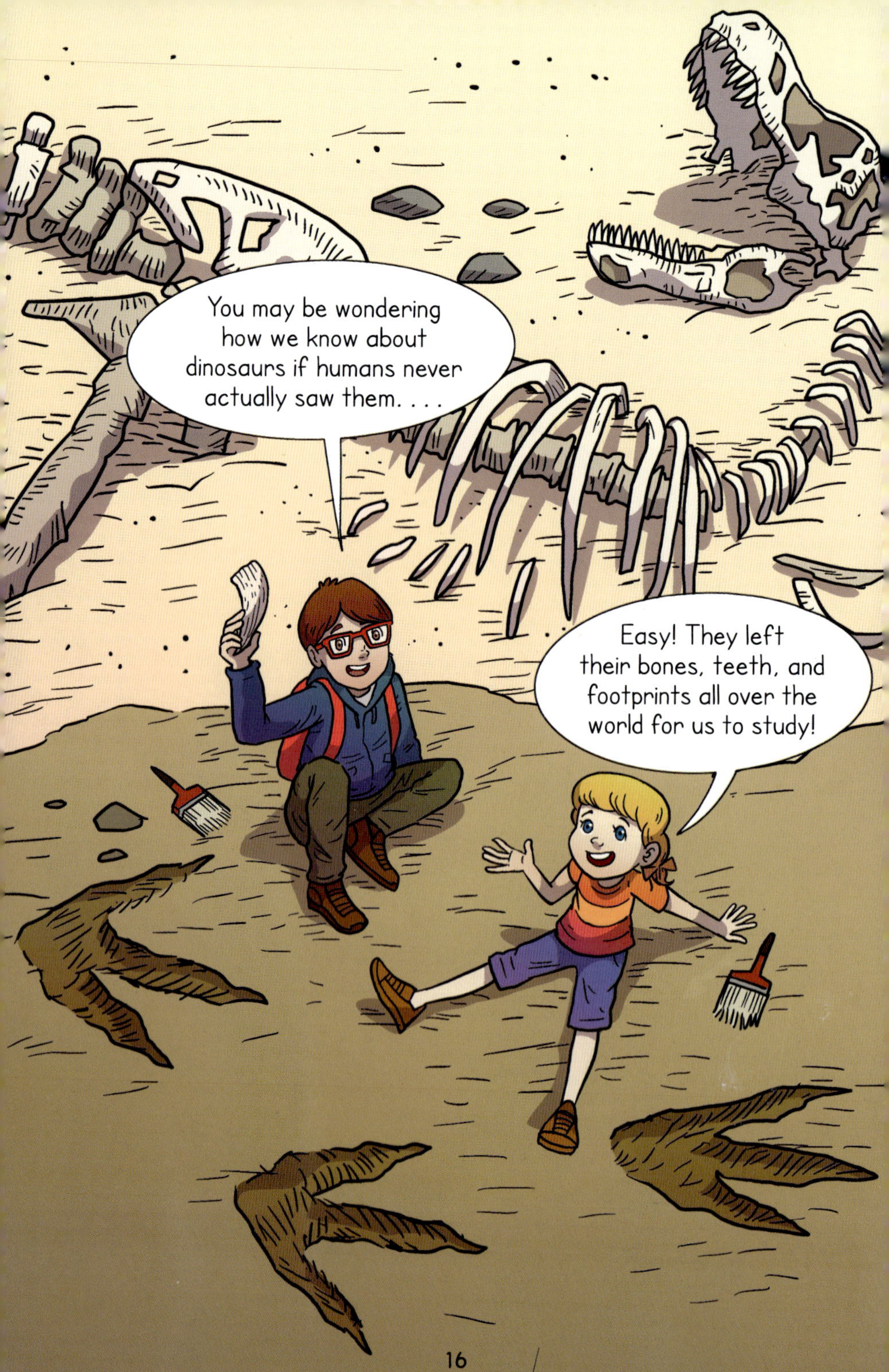
You may be wondering how we know about dinosaurs if humans never actually saw them. . . .
Easy! They left their bones, teeth, and footprints all over the world for us to study!

CHAPTER TWO
Fossils

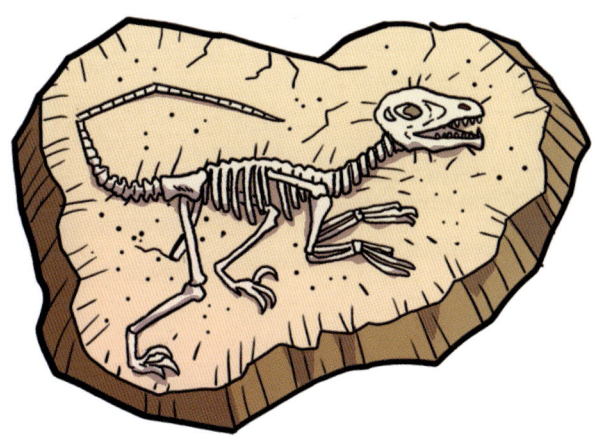

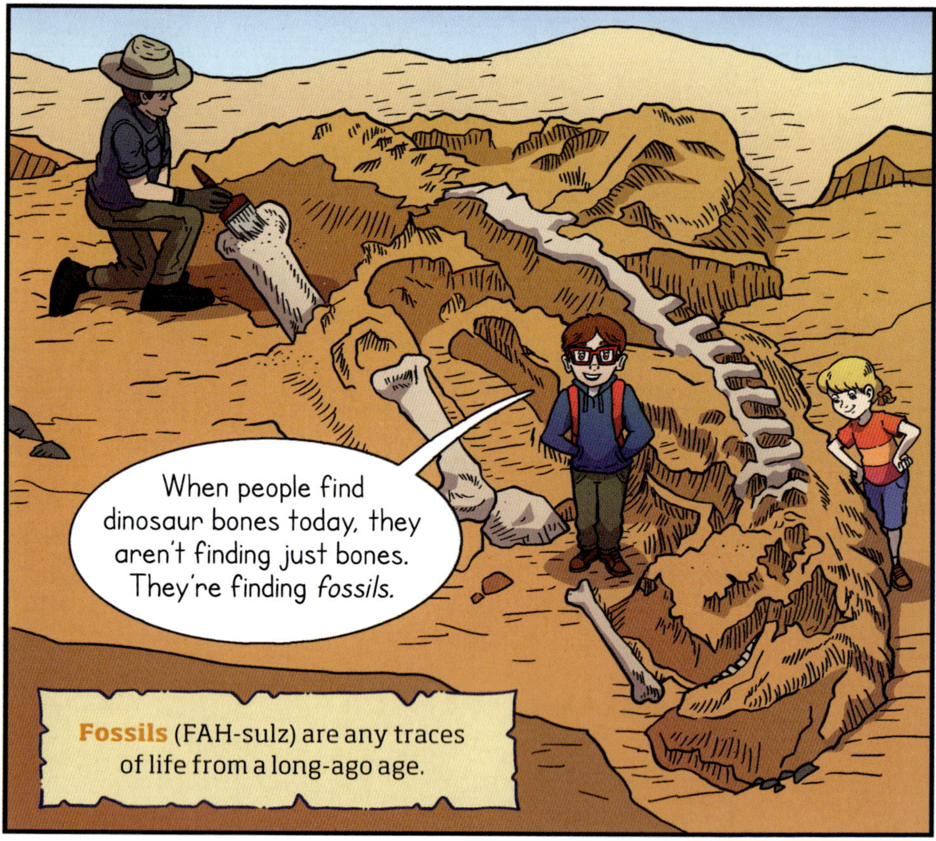
When people find dinosaur bones today, they aren't finding just bones. They're finding *fossils.*
Fossils (FAH-sulz) are any traces of life from a long-ago age.

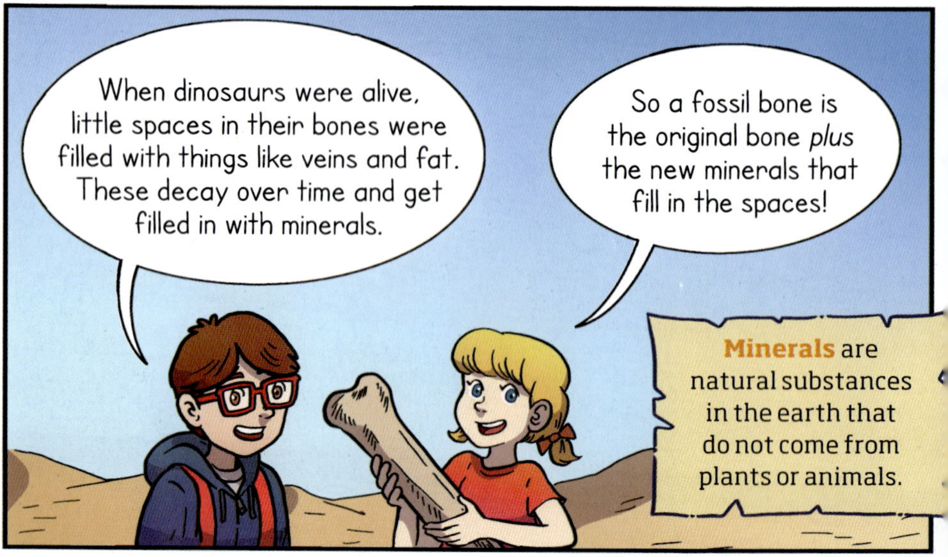
When dinosaurs were alive, little spaces in their bones were filled with things like veins and fat. These decay over time and get filled in with minerals.
So a fossil bone is the original bone *plus* the new minerals that fill in the spaces!
Minerals are natural substances in the earth that do not come from plants or animals.

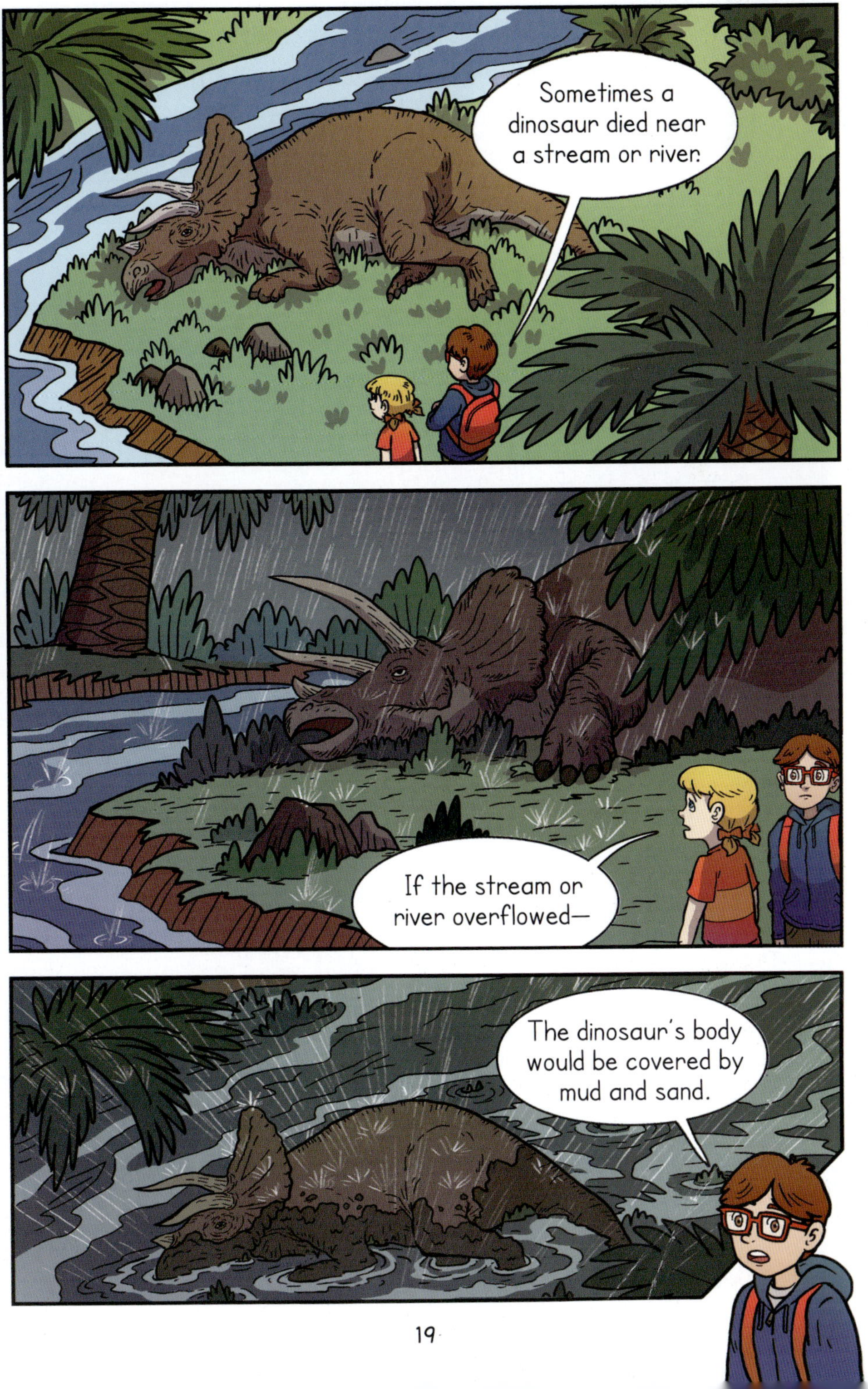
Sometimes a dinosaur died near a stream or river.
If the stream or river overflowed—
The dinosaur's body would be covered by mud and sand.

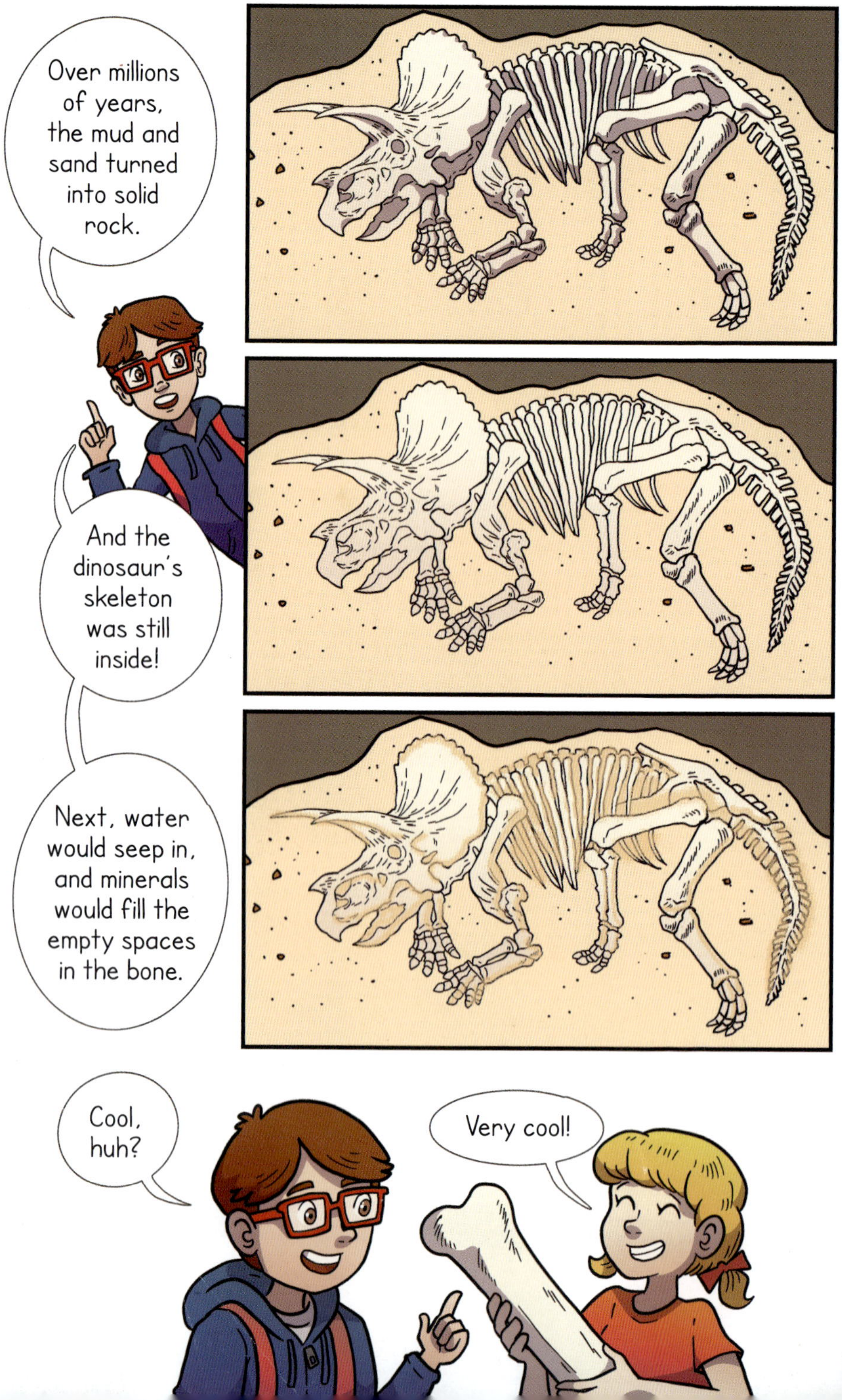
Over millions of years, the mud and sand turned into solid rock.
And the dinosaur's skeleton was still inside!
Next, water would seep in, and minerals would fill the empty spaces in the bone.
Cool, huh?
Very cool!

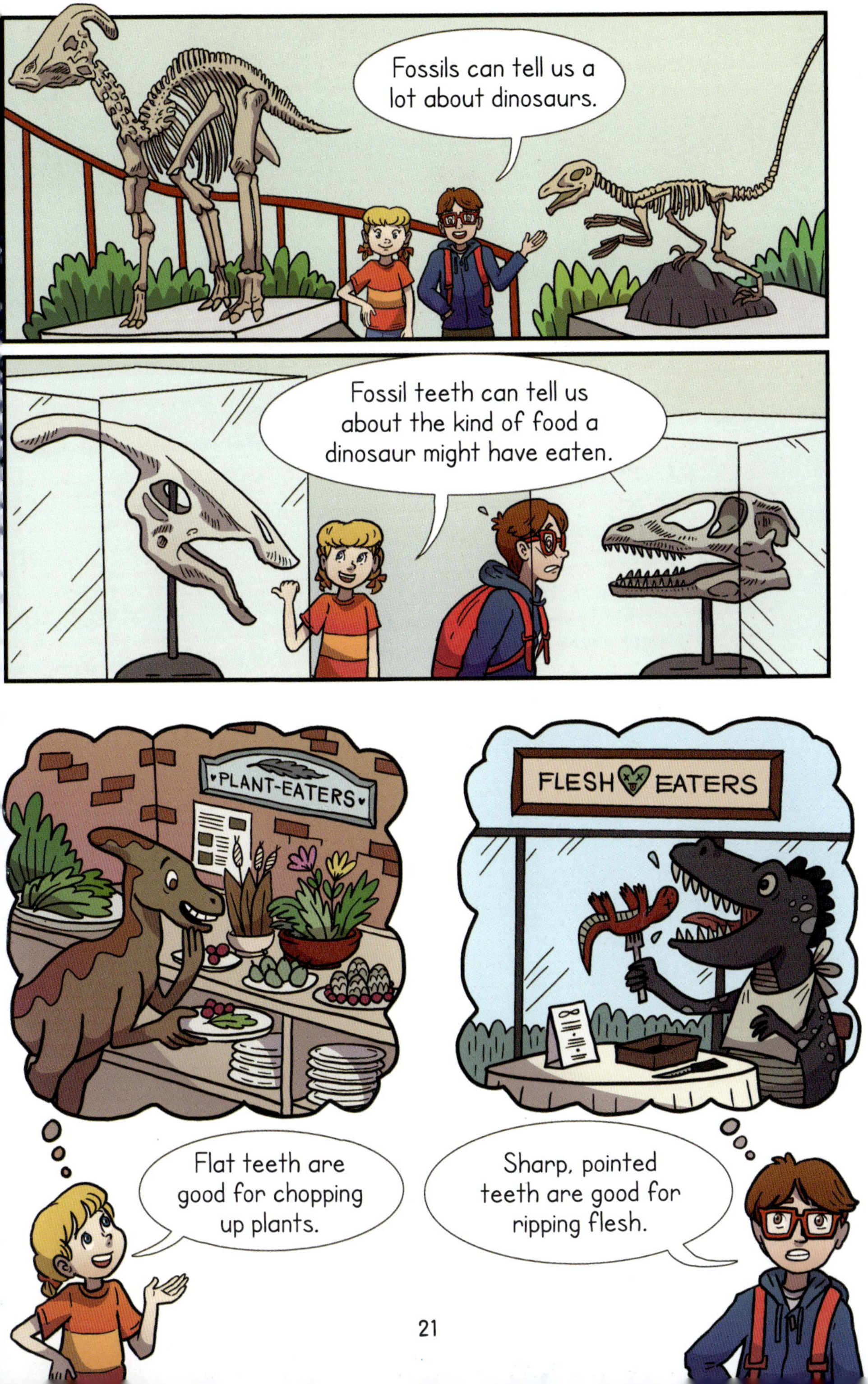

Fossils can tell us a lot about dinosaurs.
Fossil teeth can tell us about the kind of food a dinosaur might have eaten.
PLANT-EATERS
FLESH EATERS
Flat teeth are good for chopping up plants.
Sharp, pointed teeth are good for ripping flesh.

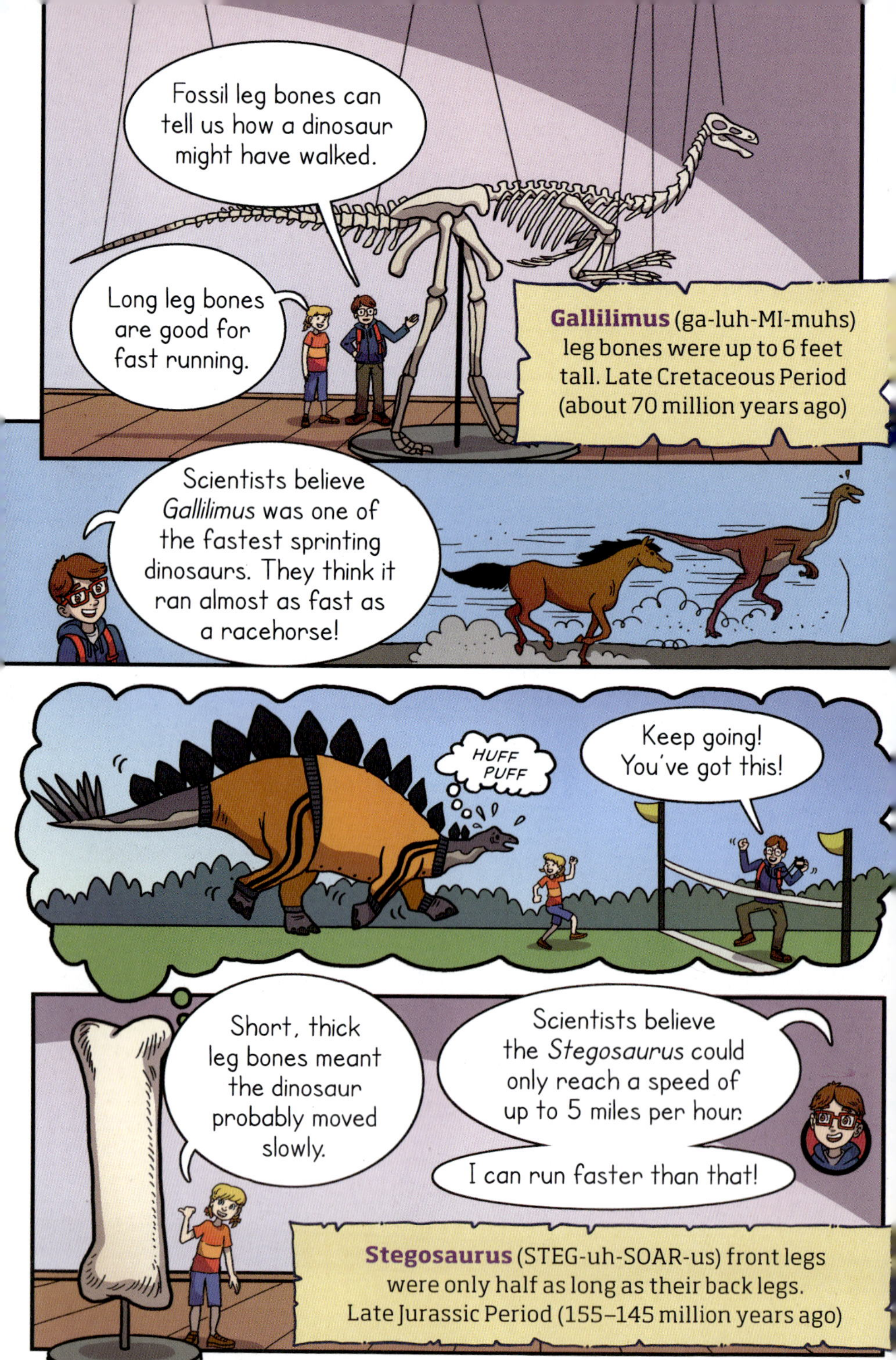
Fossil leg bones can tell us how a dinosaur might have walked.
Long leg bones are good for fast running.
Gallilimus (ga-luh-MI-muhs) leg bones were up to 6 feet tall. Late Cretaceous Period (about 70 million years ago)
Scientists believe *Gallilimus* was one of the fastest sprinting dinosaurs. They think it ran almost as fast as a racehorse!
HUFF PUFF
Keep going! You've got this!
Short, thick leg bones meant the dinosaur probably moved slowly.
Scientists believe the *Stegosaurus* could only reach a speed of up to 5 miles per hour.
I can run faster than that!
Stegosaurus (STEG-uh-SOAR-us) front legs were only half as long as their back legs. Late Jurassic Period (155–145 million years ago)

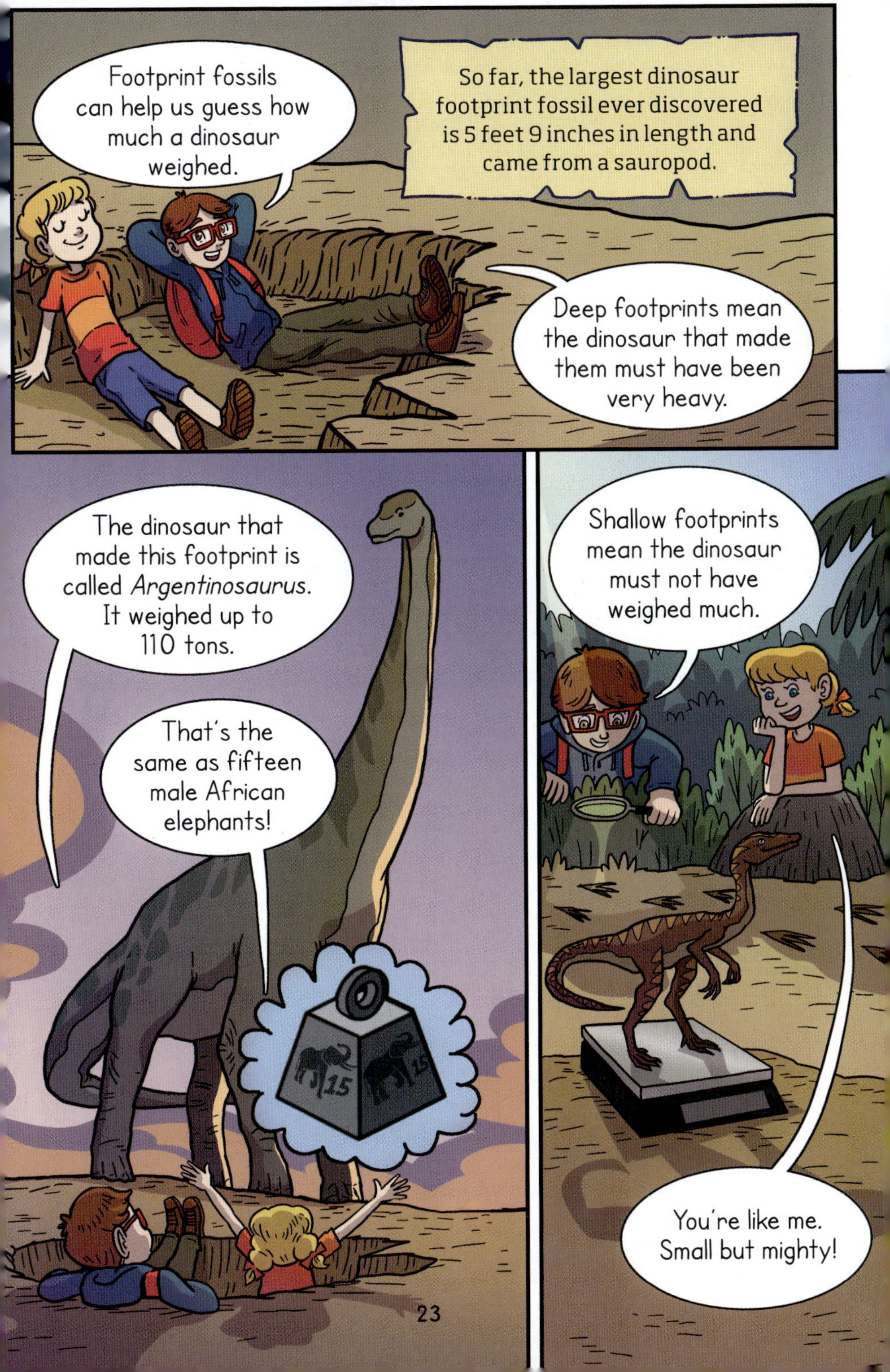
Footprint fossils can help us guess how much a dinosaur weighed.
So far, the largest dinosaur footprint fossil ever discovered is 5 feet 9 inches in length and came from a sauropod.
Deep footprints mean the dinosaur that made them must have been very heavy.
The dinosaur that made this footprint is called *Argentinosaurus*. It weighed up to 110 tons.
That's the same as fifteen male African elephants!
15
15
Shallow footprints mean the dinosaur must not have weighed much.
You're like me. Small but mighty!

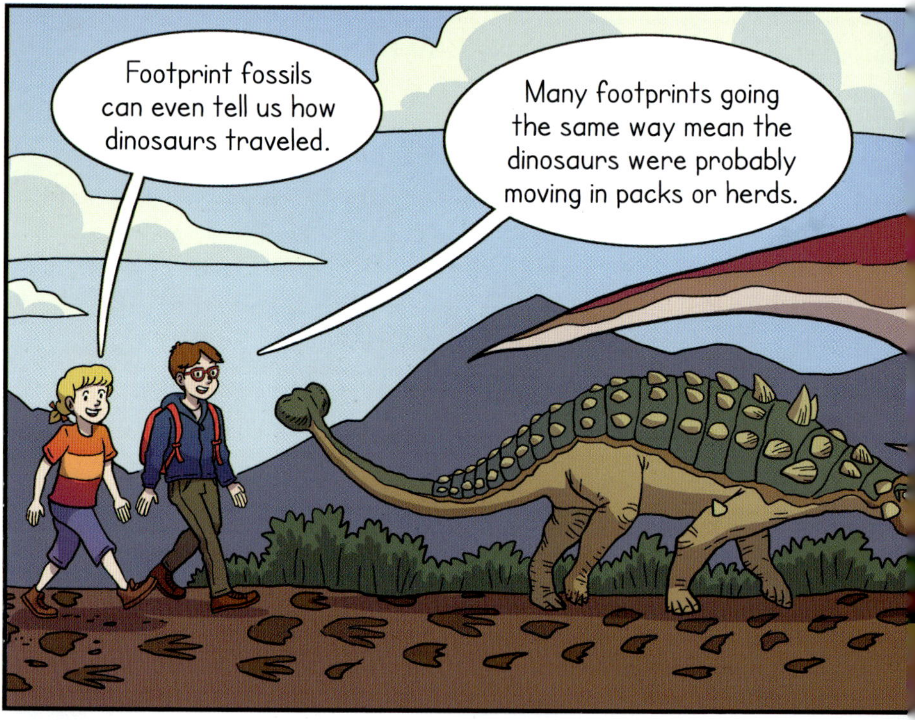
Footprint fossils can even tell us how dinosaurs traveled.
Many footprints going the same way mean the dinosaurs were probably moving in packs or herds.

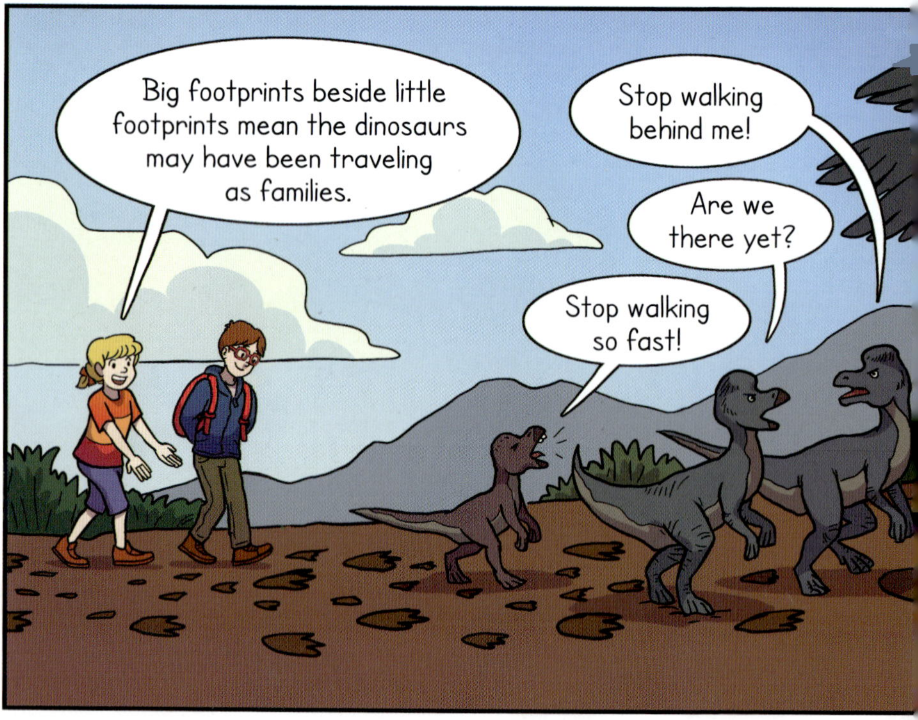
Big footprints beside little footprints mean the dinosaurs may have been traveling as families.
Stop walking behind me!
Are we there yet?
Stop walking so fast!

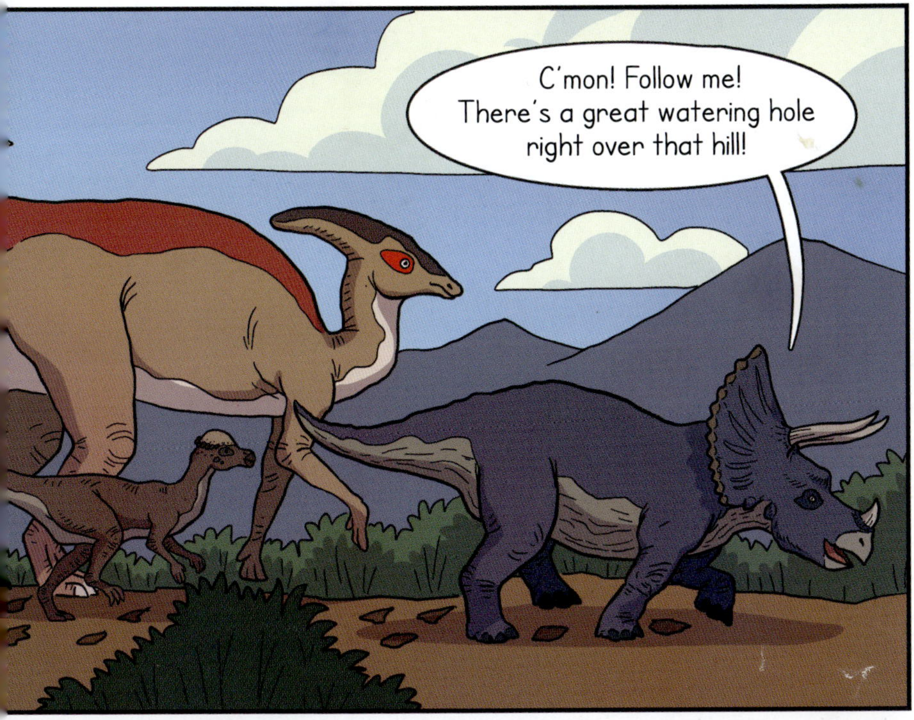
C'mon! Follow me! There's a great watering hole right over that hill!

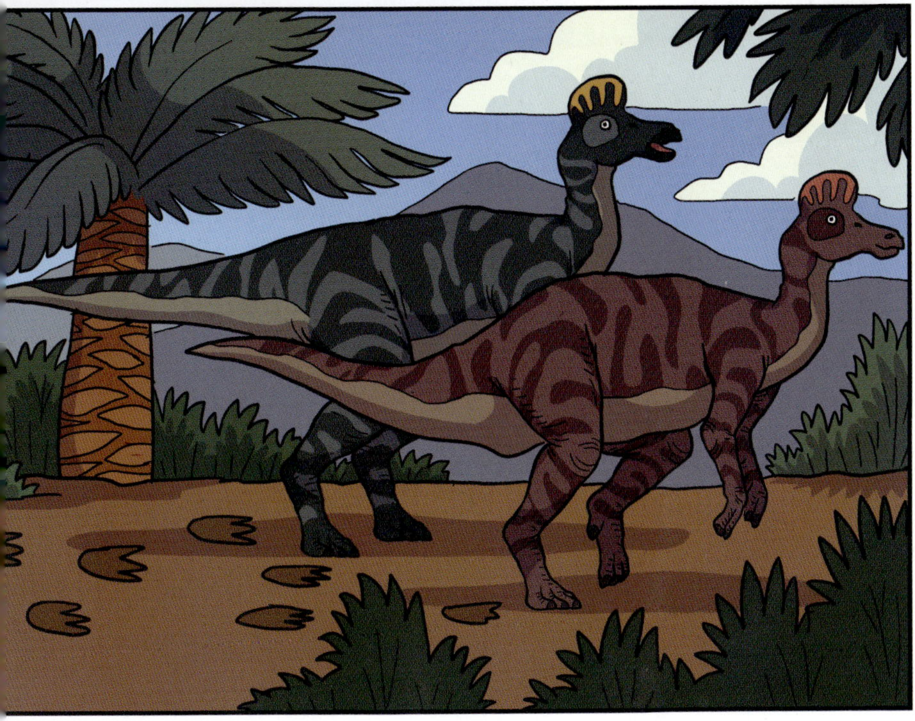

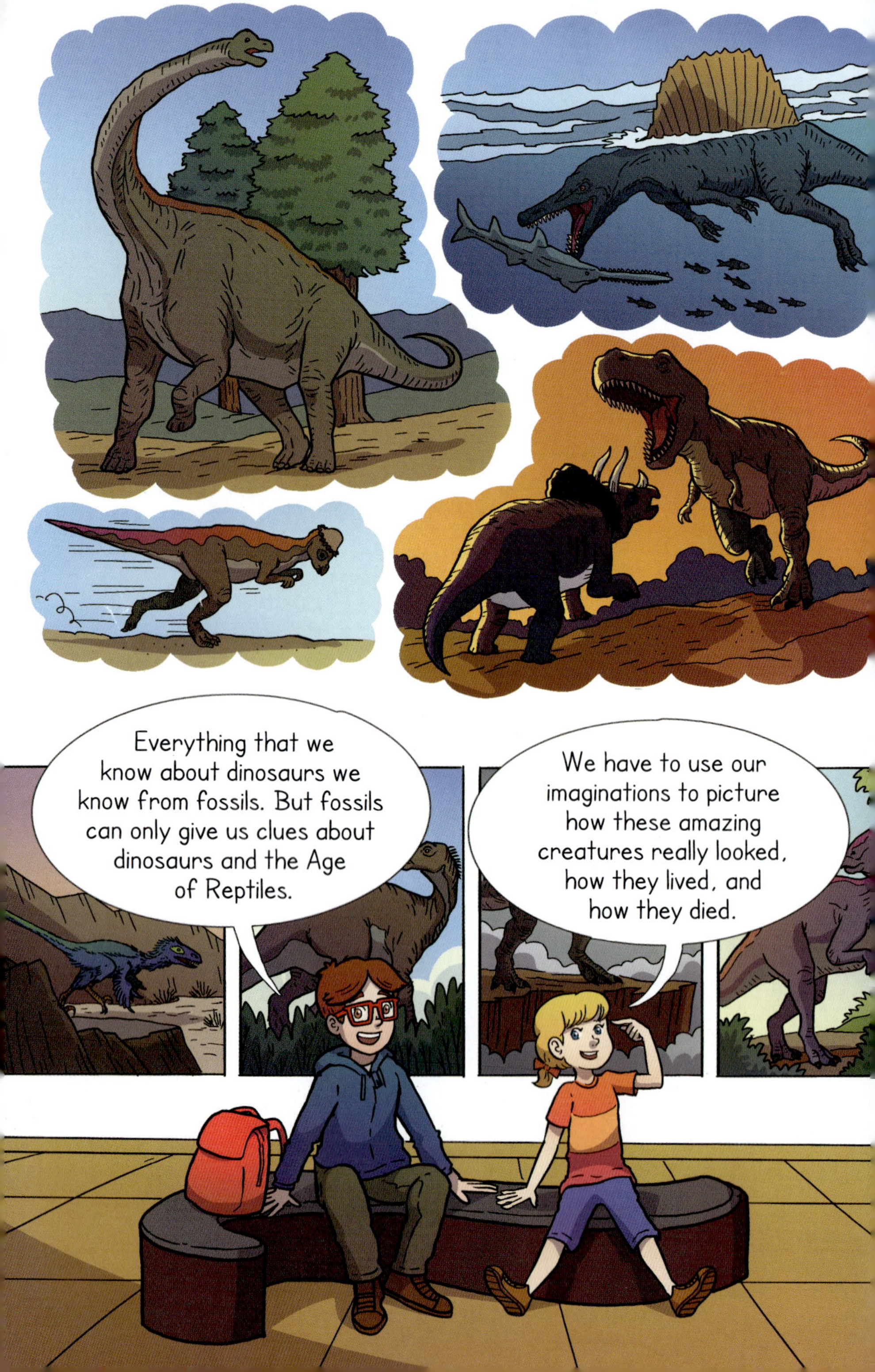
Everything that we know about dinosaurs we know from fossils. But fossils can only give us clues about dinosaurs and the Age of Reptiles.
We have to use our imaginations to picture how these amazing creatures really looked, how they lived, and how they died.

CHAPTER THREE
Dinosaur Hunters

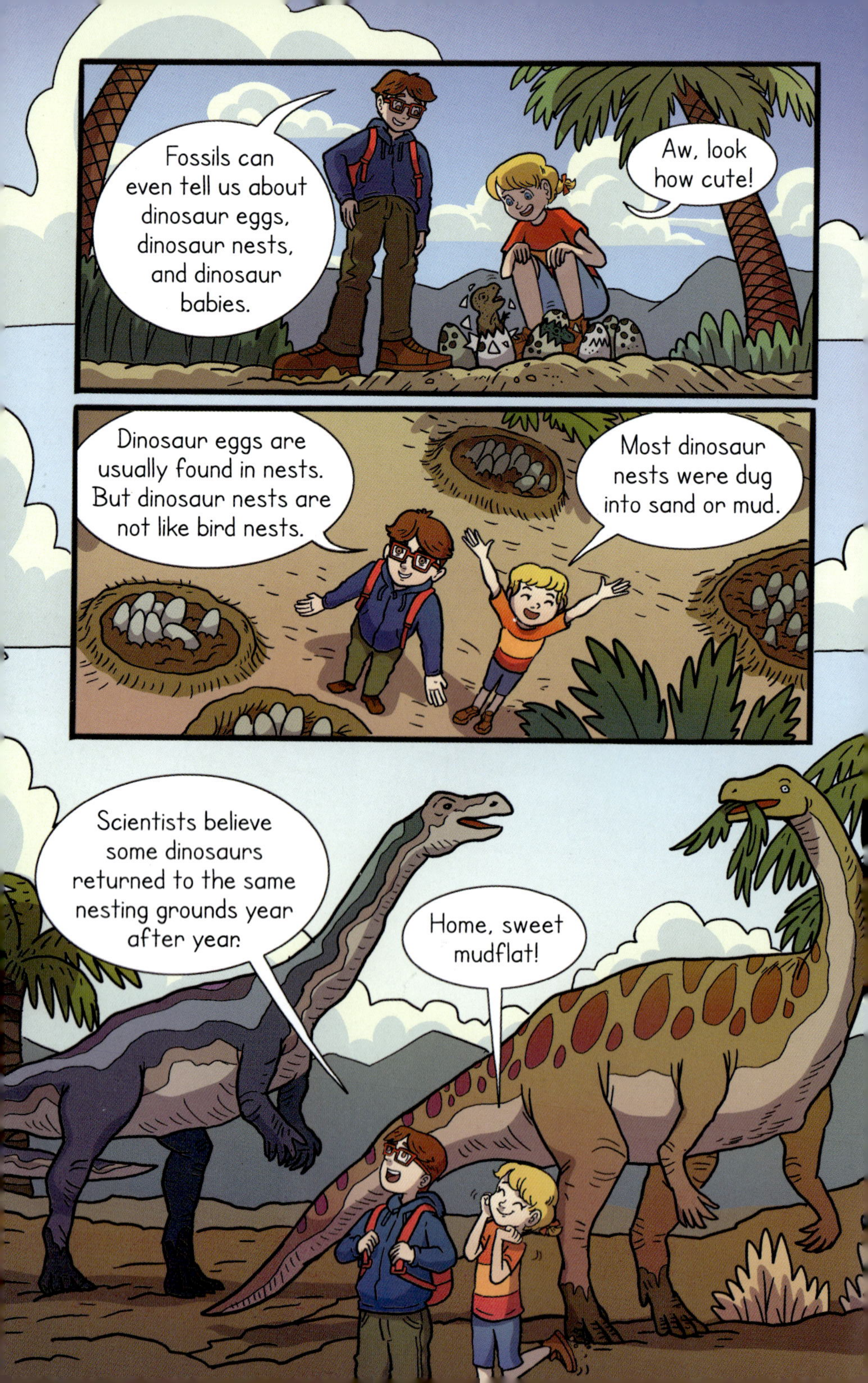
Fossils can even tell us about dinosaur eggs, dinosaur nests, and dinosaur babies.
Aw, look how cute!
Dinosaur eggs are usually found in nests. But dinosaur nests are not like bird nests.
Most dinosaur nests were dug into sand or mud.
Scientists believe some dinosaurs returned to the same nesting grounds year after year.
Home, sweet mudflat!

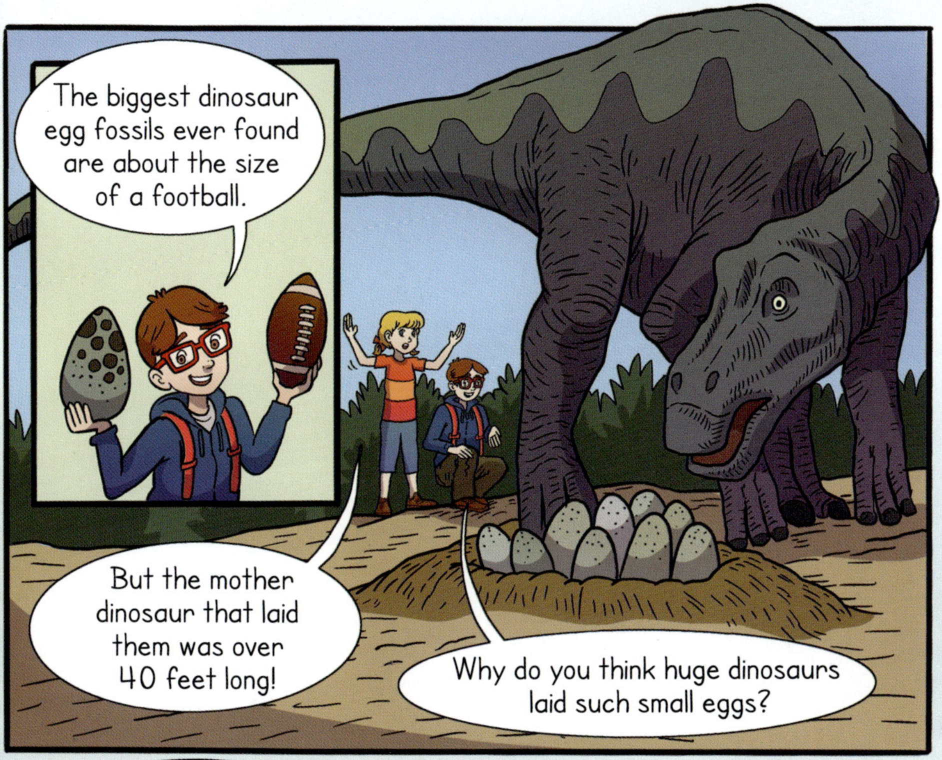
The biggest dinosaur egg fossils ever found are about the size of a football.
But the mother dinosaur that laid them was over 40 feet long!
Why do you think huge dinosaurs laid such small eggs?

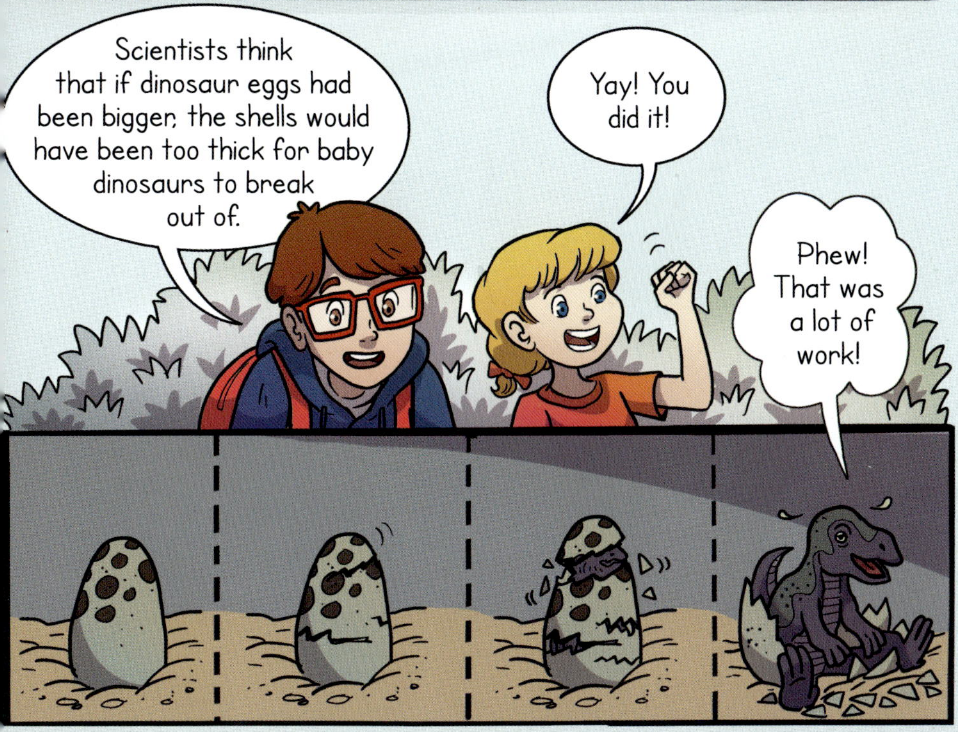
Scientists think that if dinosaur eggs had been bigger, the shells would have been too thick for baby dinosaurs to break out of.
Yay! You did it!
Phew! That was a lot of work!

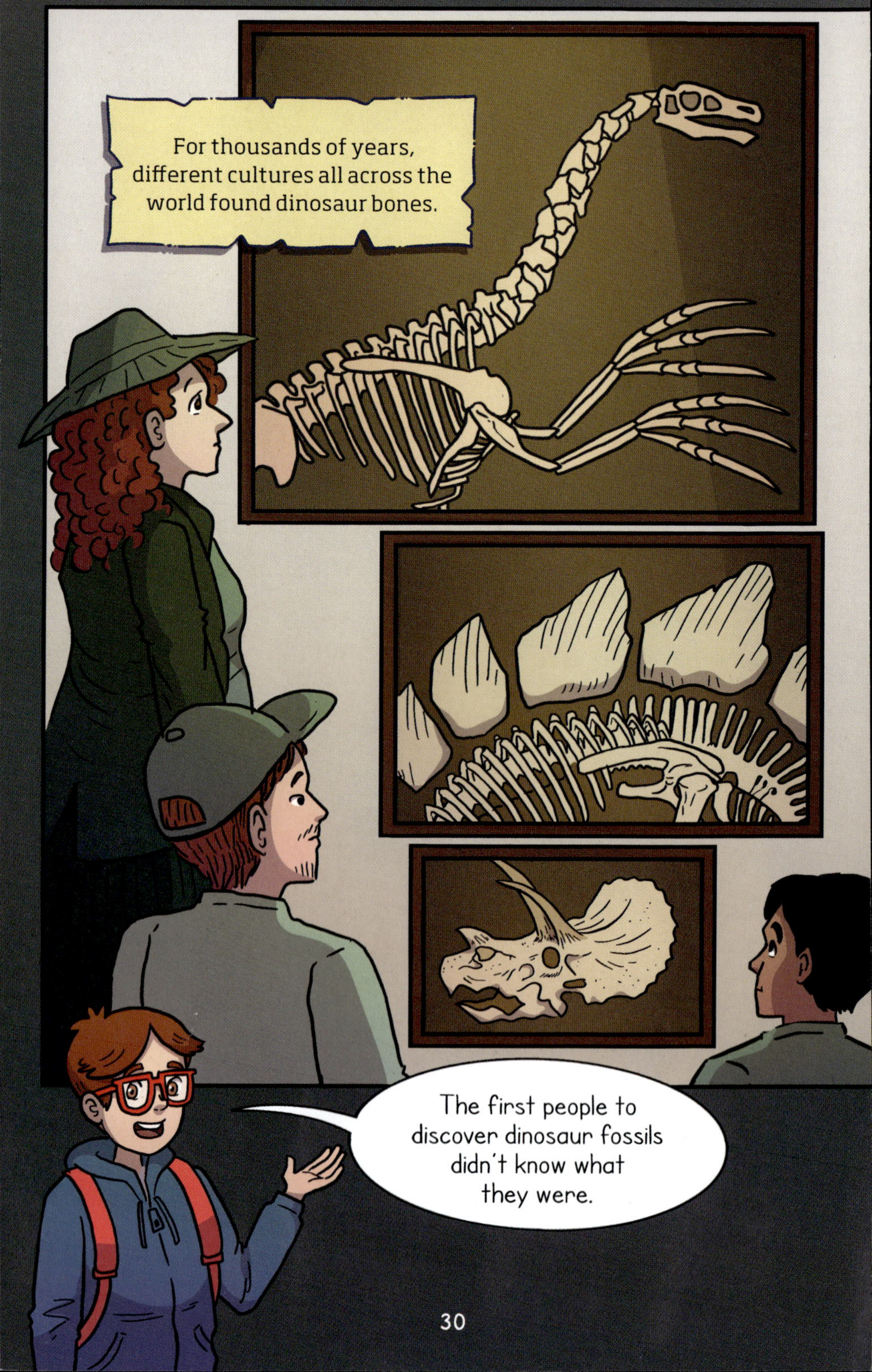
For thousands of years, different cultures all across the world found dinosaur bones.
The first people to discover dinosaur fossils didn't know what they were.

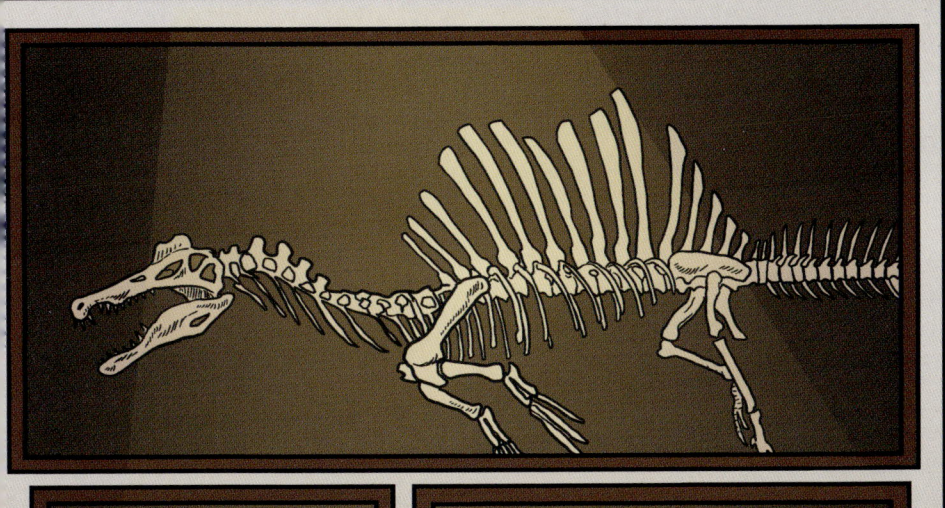

Different cultures believed dinosaur bones came from dragons, giant snakes, or even giant humans.

They had never come across animals with such large bones, so they could only imagine what they were seeing.

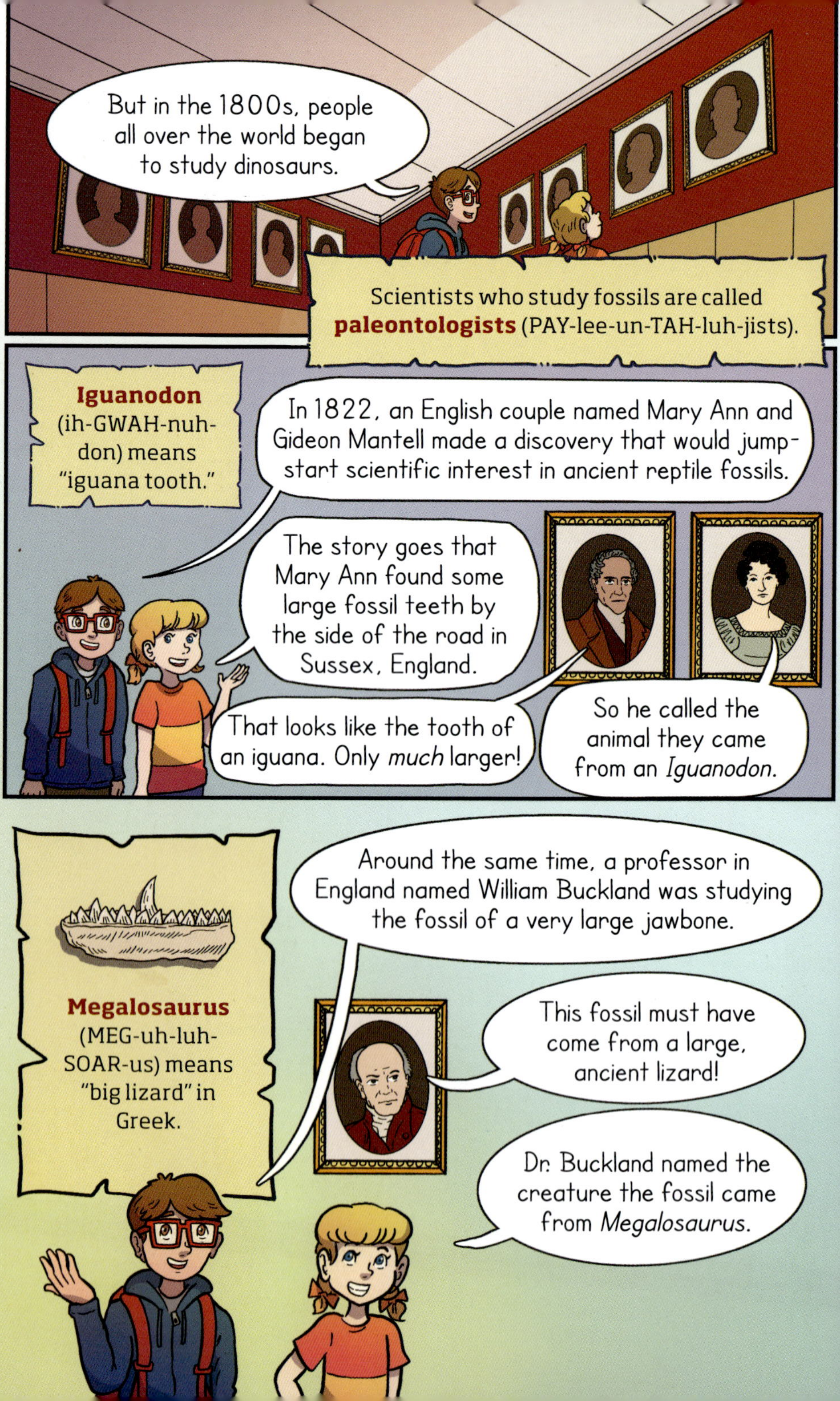

But in the 1800s, people all over the world began to study dinosaurs.
Scientists who study fossils are called **paleontologists** (PAY-lee-un-TAH-luh-jists).
Iguanodon (ih-GWAH-nuh-don) means "iguana tooth."
In 1822, an English couple named Mary Ann and Gideon Mantell made a discovery that would jump-start scientific interest in ancient reptile fossils.
The story goes that Mary Ann found some large fossil teeth by the side of the road in Sussex, England.
That looks like the tooth of an iguana. Only *much* larger!
So he called the animal they came from an *Iguanodon.*
Megalosaurus (MEG-uh-luh-SOAR-us) means "big lizard" in Greek.
Around the same time, a professor in England named William Buckland was studying the fossil of a very large jawbone.
This fossil must have come from a large, ancient lizard!
Dr. Buckland named the creature the fossil came from *Megalosaurus.*

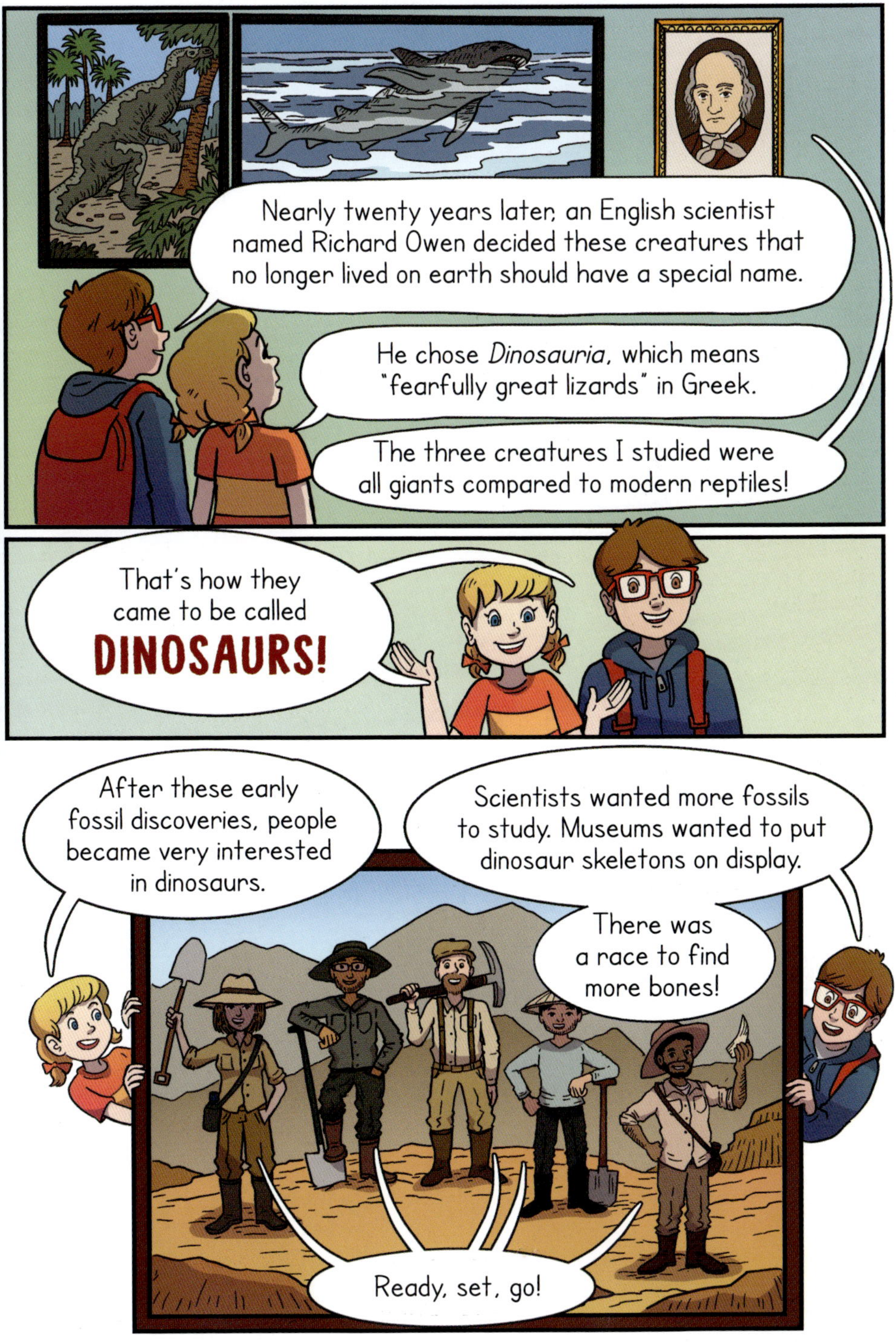

Nearly twenty years later, an English scientist named Richard Owen decided these creatures that no longer lived on earth should have a special name.
He chose *Dinosauria*, which means "fearfully great lizards" in Greek.
The three creatures I studied were all giants compared to modern reptiles!
That's how they came to be called DINOSAURS!
After these early fossil discoveries, people became very interested in dinosaurs.
Scientists wanted more fossils to study. Museums wanted to put dinosaur skeletons on display.
There was a race to find more bones!
Ready, set, go!

How Dinosaurs Get Their Names

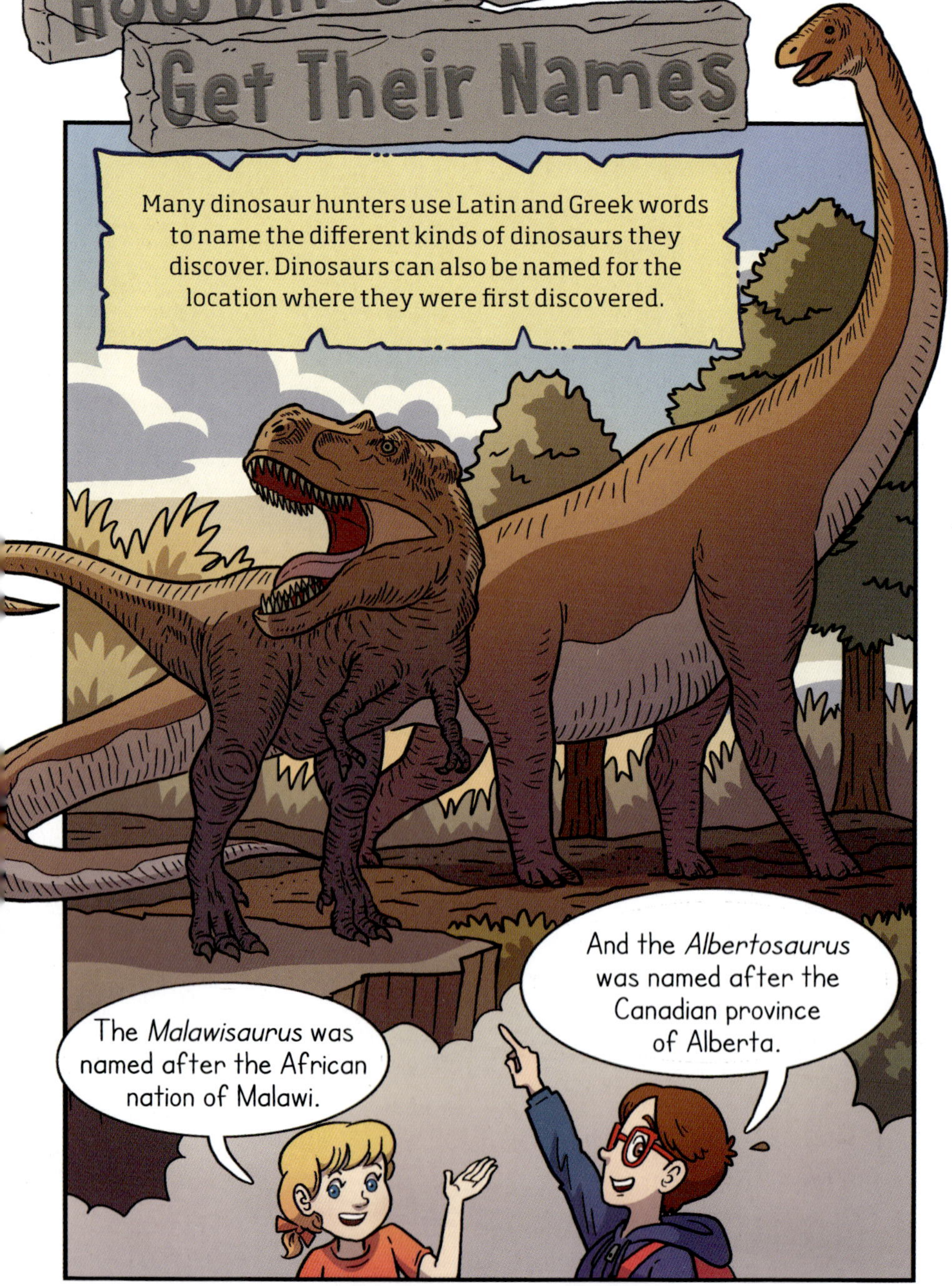
Many dinosaur hunters use Latin and Greek words to name the different kinds of dinosaurs they discover. Dinosaurs can also be named for the location where they were first discovered.
The *Malawisaurus* was named after the African nation of Malawi.
And the *Albertosaurus* was named after the Canadian province of Alberta.

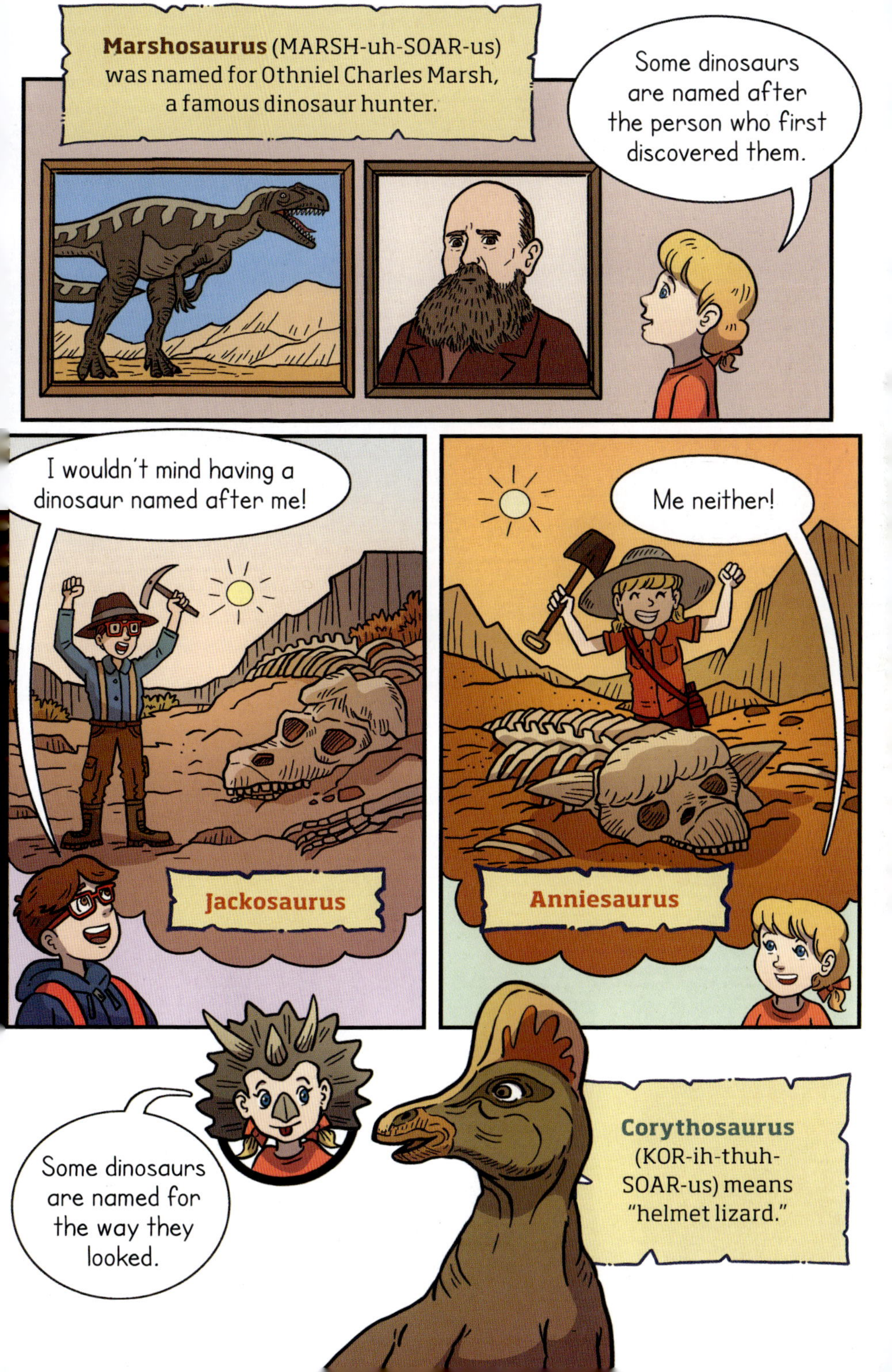
Marshosaurus (MARSH-uh-SOAR-us) was named for Othniel Charles Marsh, a famous dinosaur hunter.
Some dinosaurs are named after the person who first discovered them.
I wouldn't mind having a dinosaur named after me!
Jackosaurus
Me neither!
Anniesaurus
Some dinosaurs are named for the way they looked.
Corythosaurus (KOR-ih-thuh-SOAR-us) means "helmet lizard."

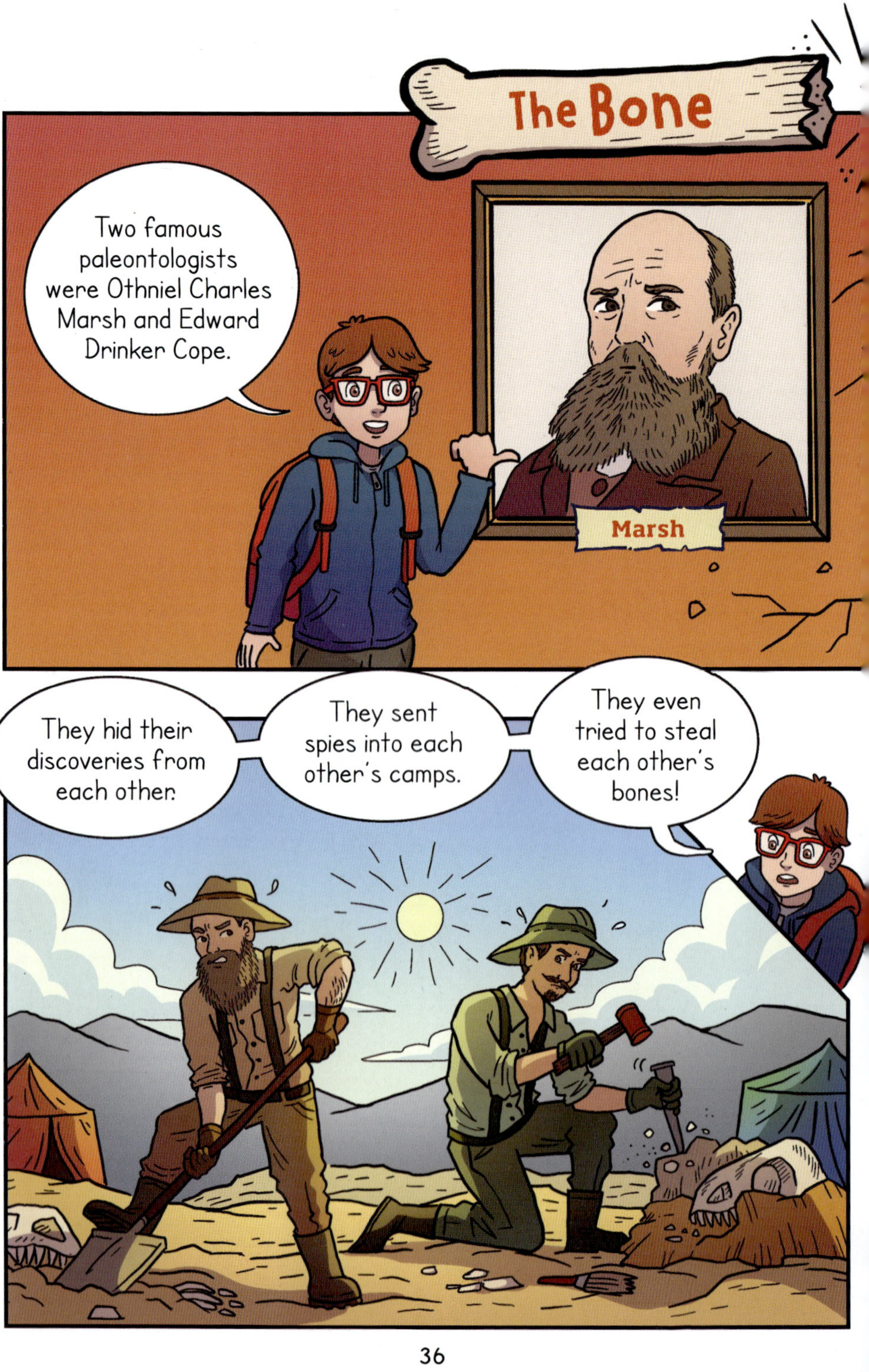
The Bone
Two famous paleontologists were Othniel Charles Marsh and Edward Drinker Cope.
Marsh
They hid their discoveries from each other.
They sent spies into each other's camps.
They even tried to steal each other's bones!

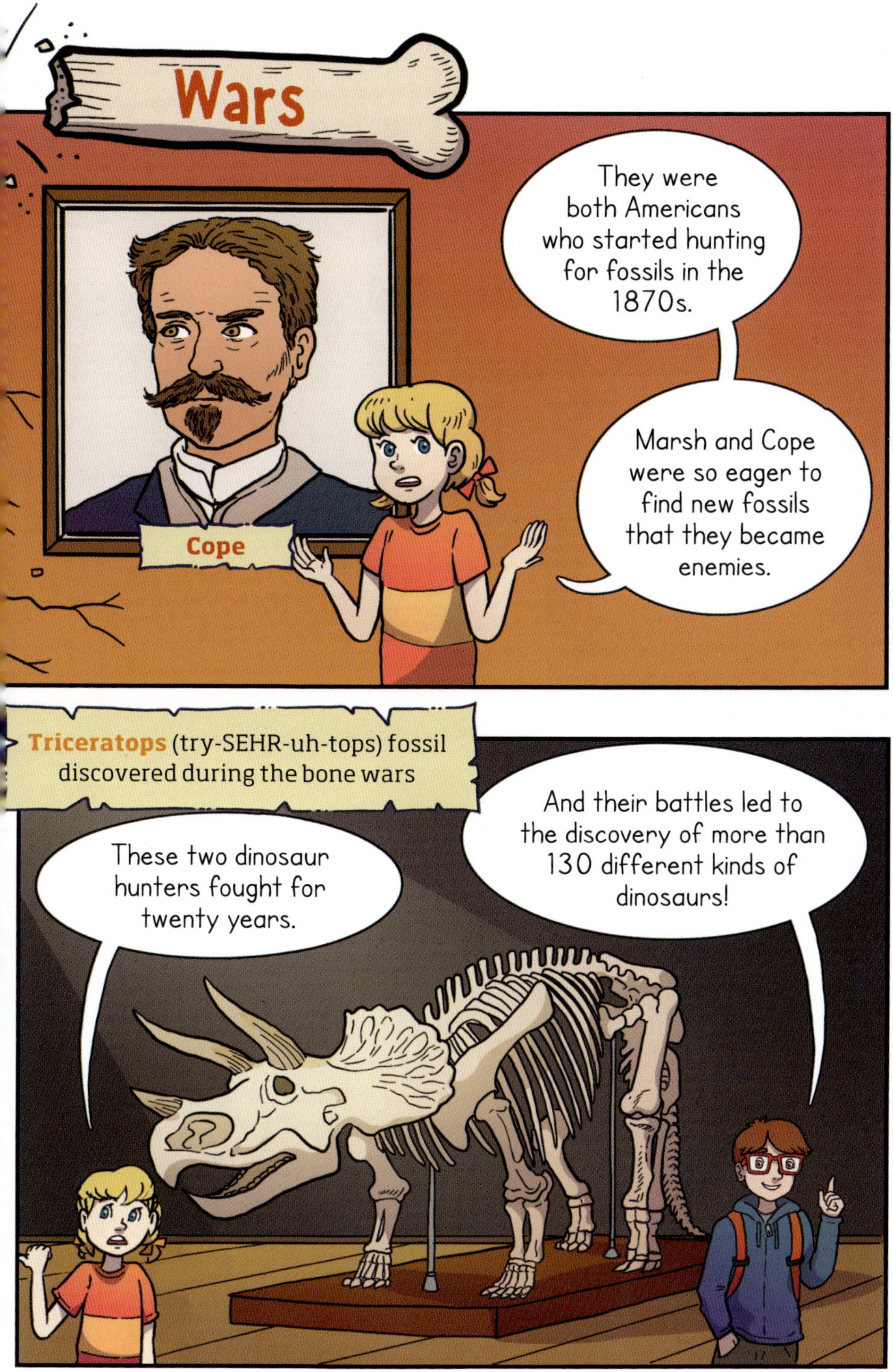
Wars
Cope
They were both Americans who started hunting for fossils in the 1870s.
Marsh and Cope were so eager to find new fossils that they became enemies.
Triceratops (try-SEHR-uh-tops) fossil discovered during the bone wars
These two dinosaur hunters fought for twenty years.
And their battles led to the discovery of more than 130 different kinds of dinosaurs!

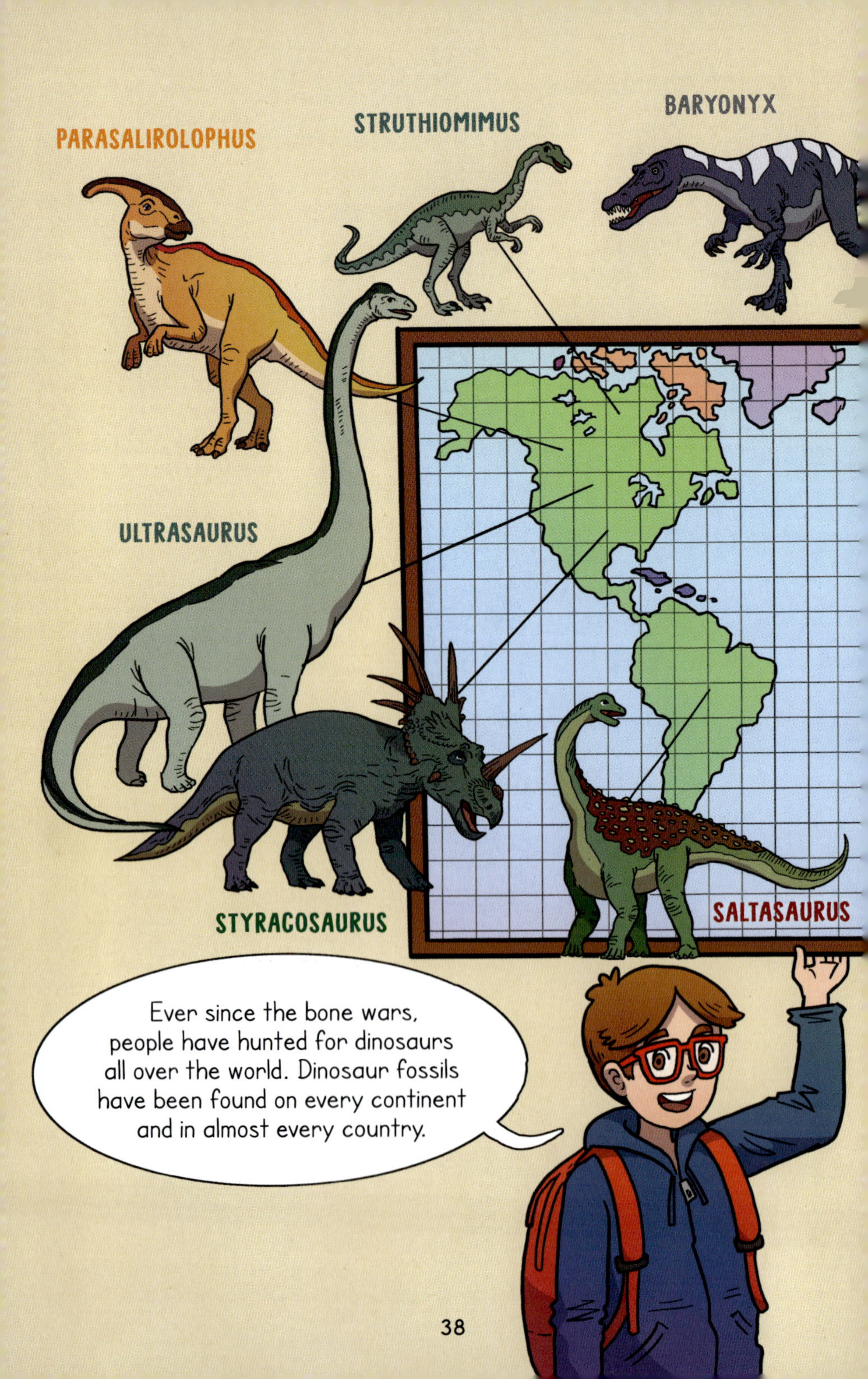
PARASALIROLOPHUS
STRUTHIOMIMUS
BARYONYX
ULTRASAURUS
STYRACOSAURUS
SALTASAURUS
Ever since the bone wars, people have hunted for dinosaurs all over the world. Dinosaur fossils have been found on every continent and in almost every country.

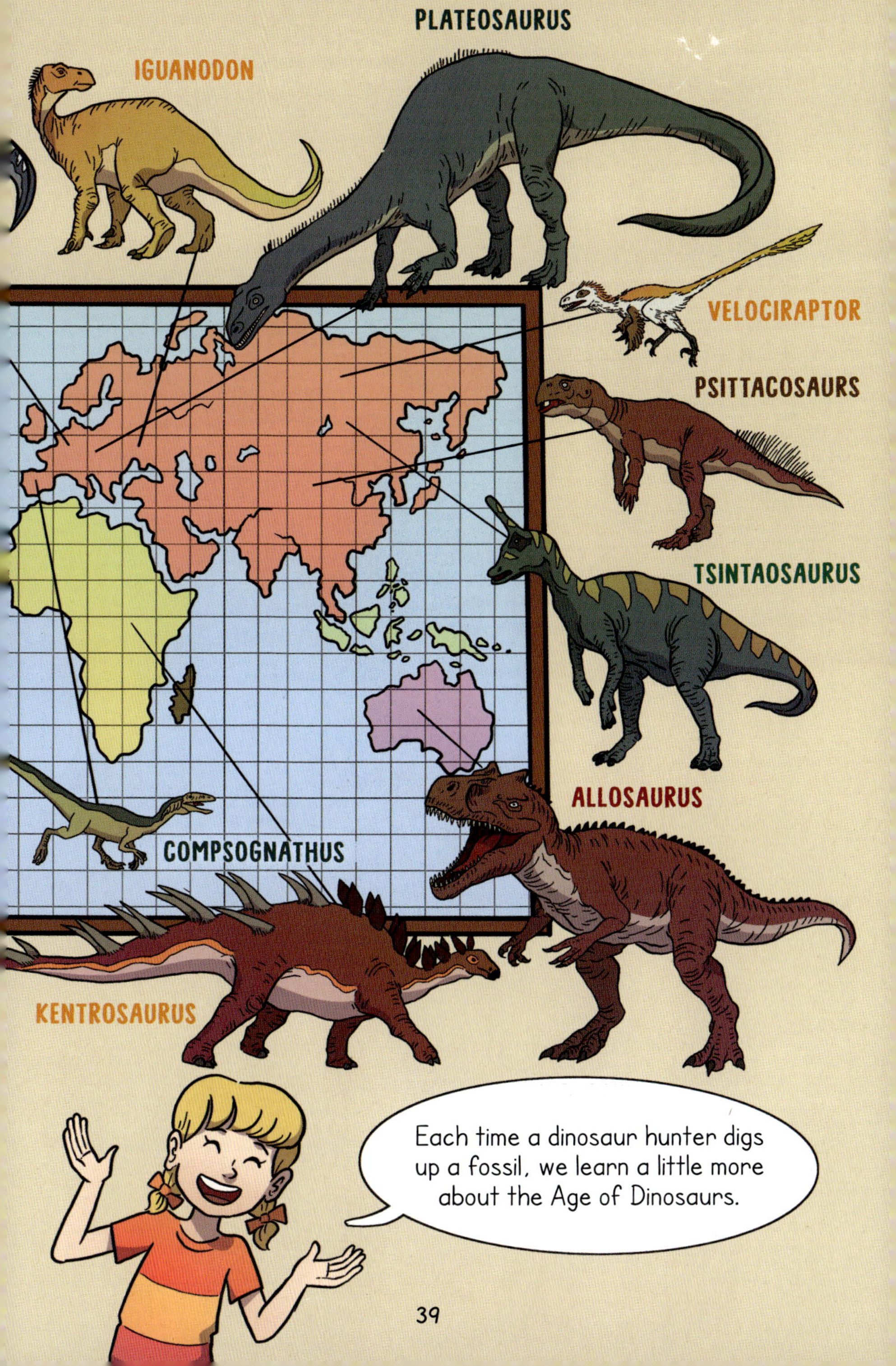
PLATEOSAURUS
IGUANODON
VELOCIRAPTOR
PSITTACOSAURS
TSINTAOSAURUS
ALLOSAURUS
COMPSOGNATHUS
KENTROSAURUS
Each time a dinosaur hunter digs up a fossil, we learn a little more about the Age of Dinosaurs.

Bone-Hunting

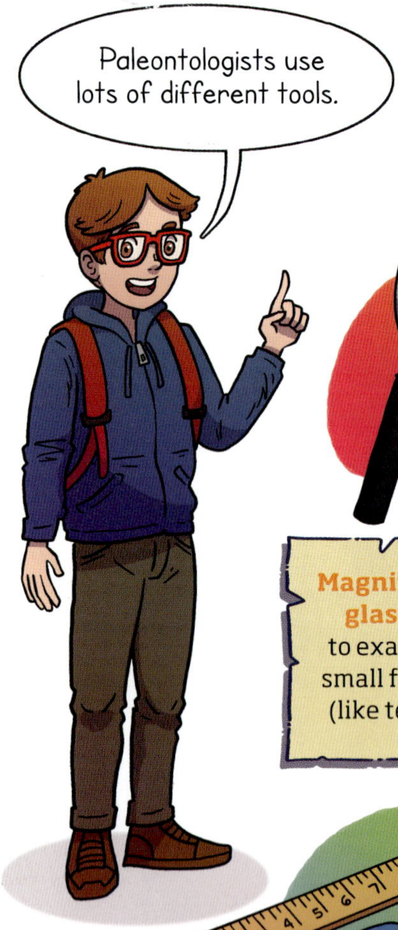
Paleontologists use lots of different tools.

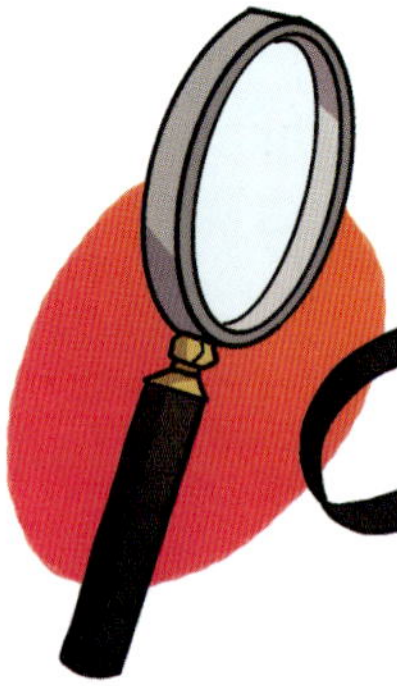

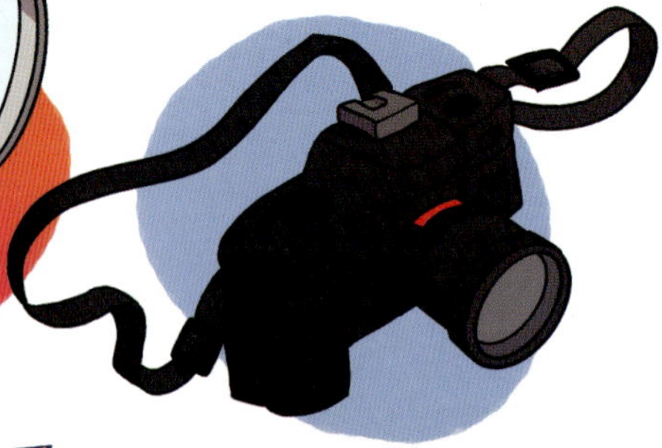

Magnifying glass—to examine small fossils (like teeth)

Camera—to take pictures of the site and the fossils

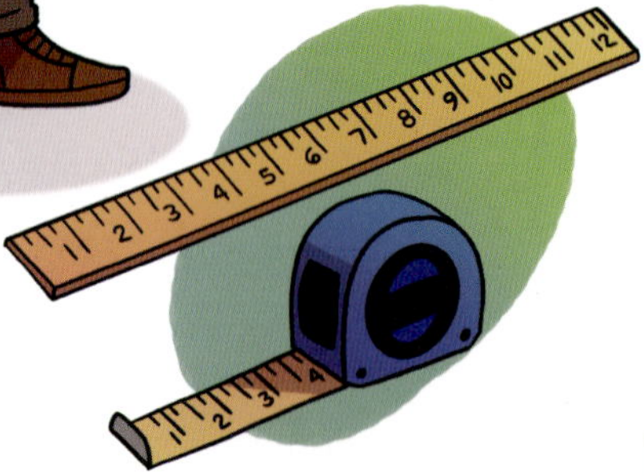

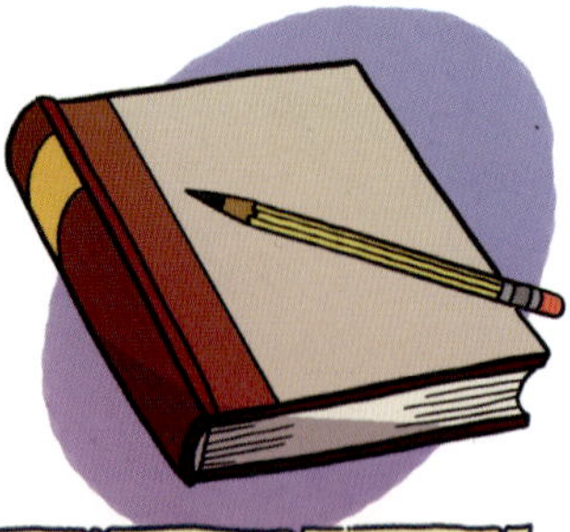

Tape measure and ruler—to measure the size of the bones

Field notebook—to keep a record of the bones

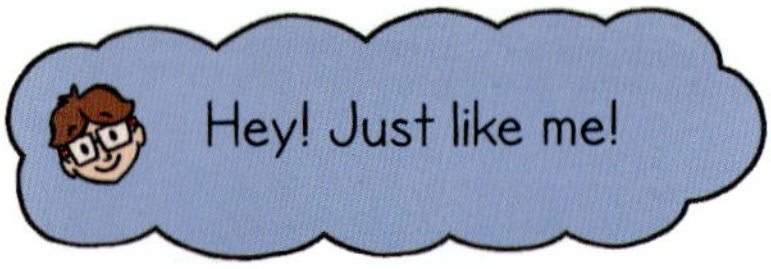
Hey! Just like me!

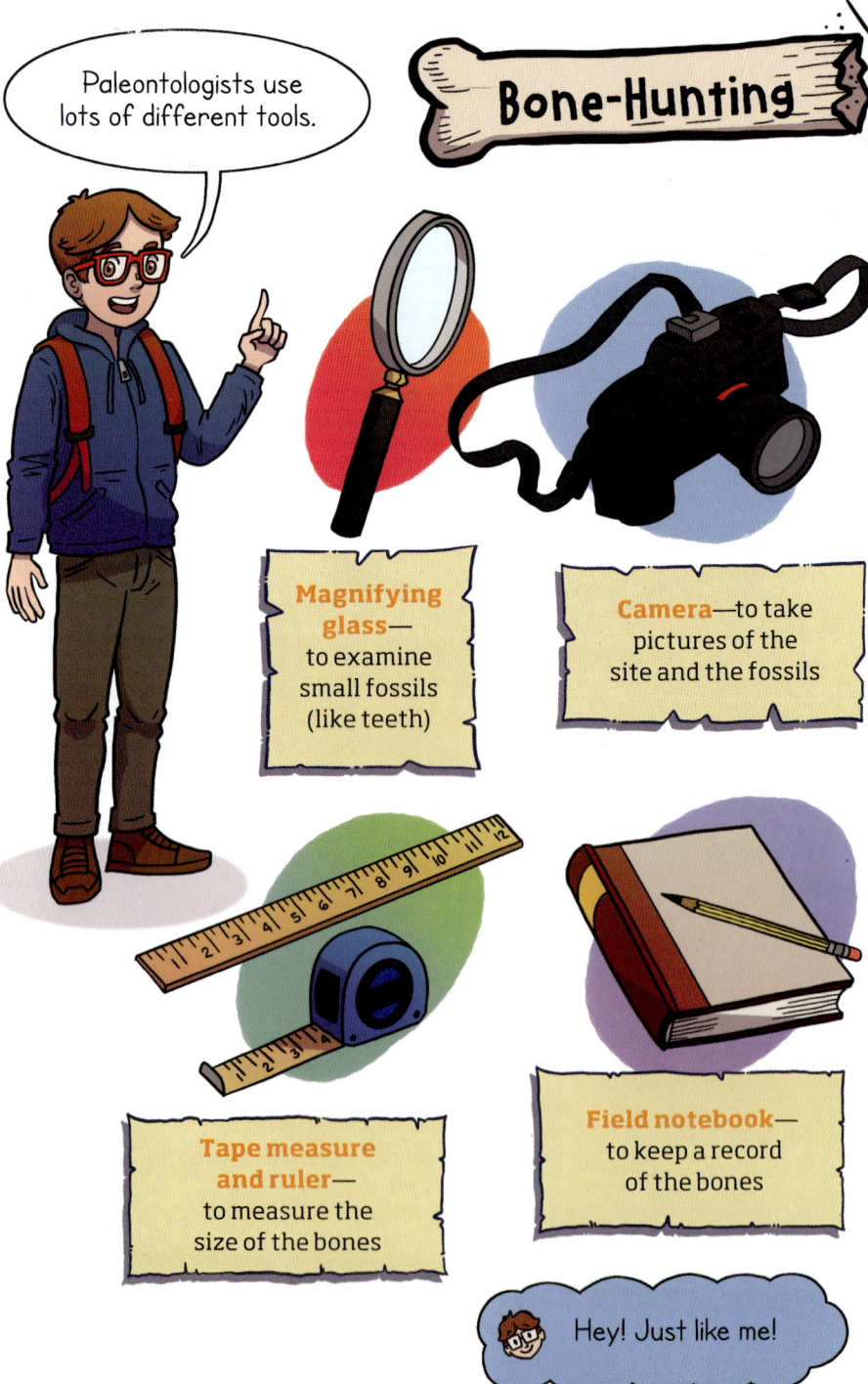

Tools

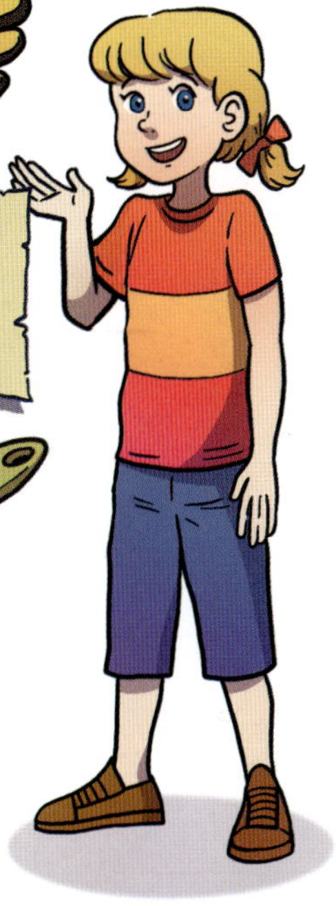
Here are some things they always take along when they go digging for fossils.

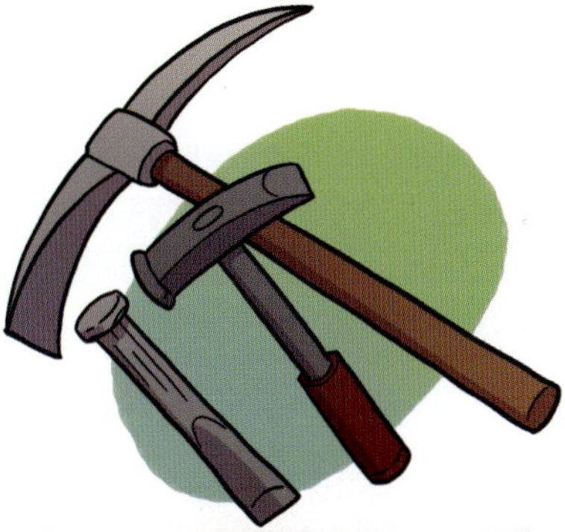

Hammer, chisel, and pick—to chip away the rock around the fossils

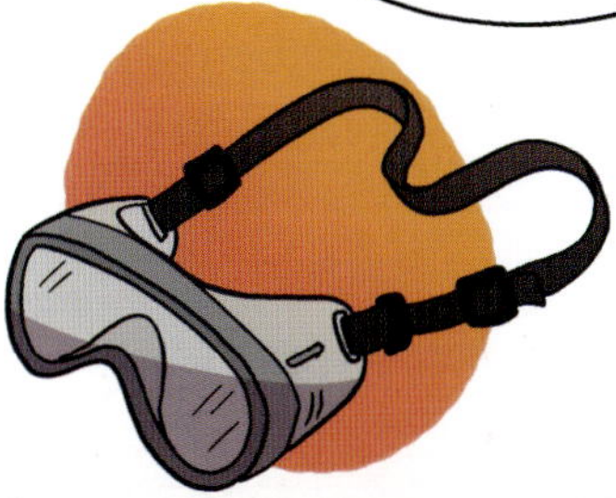

Safety goggles—to protect their eyes while working

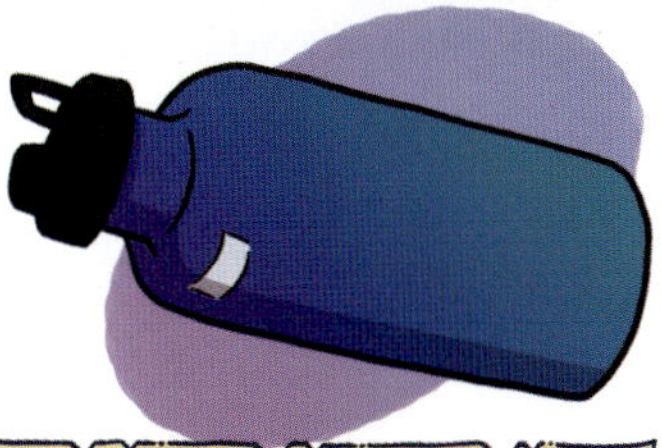

Water bottle—to stay hydrated while on a dig

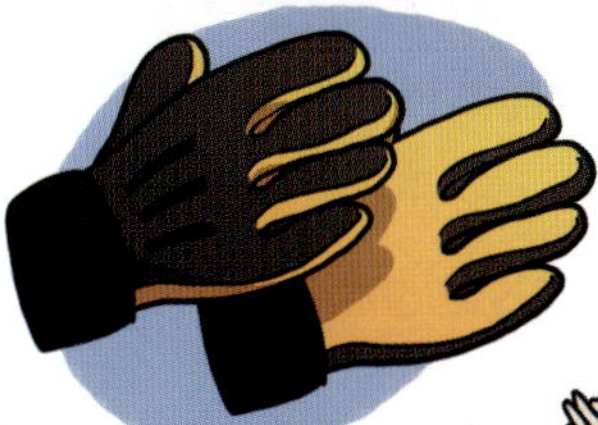

Work gloves—to protect their hands and the objects they are digging up

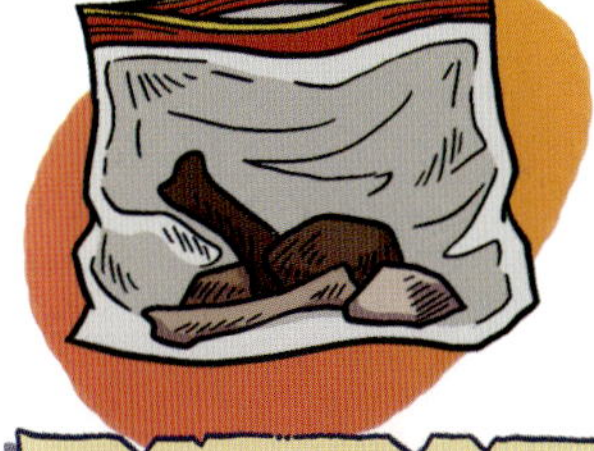

Sample bags—to collect rock samples and broken fossil pieces

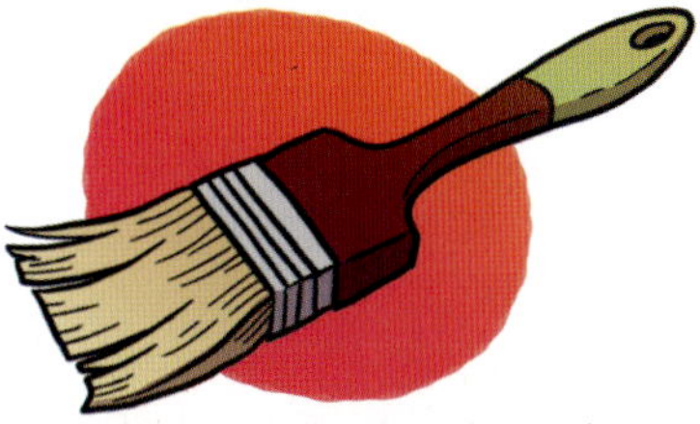

Brush—to brush away dirt and dust

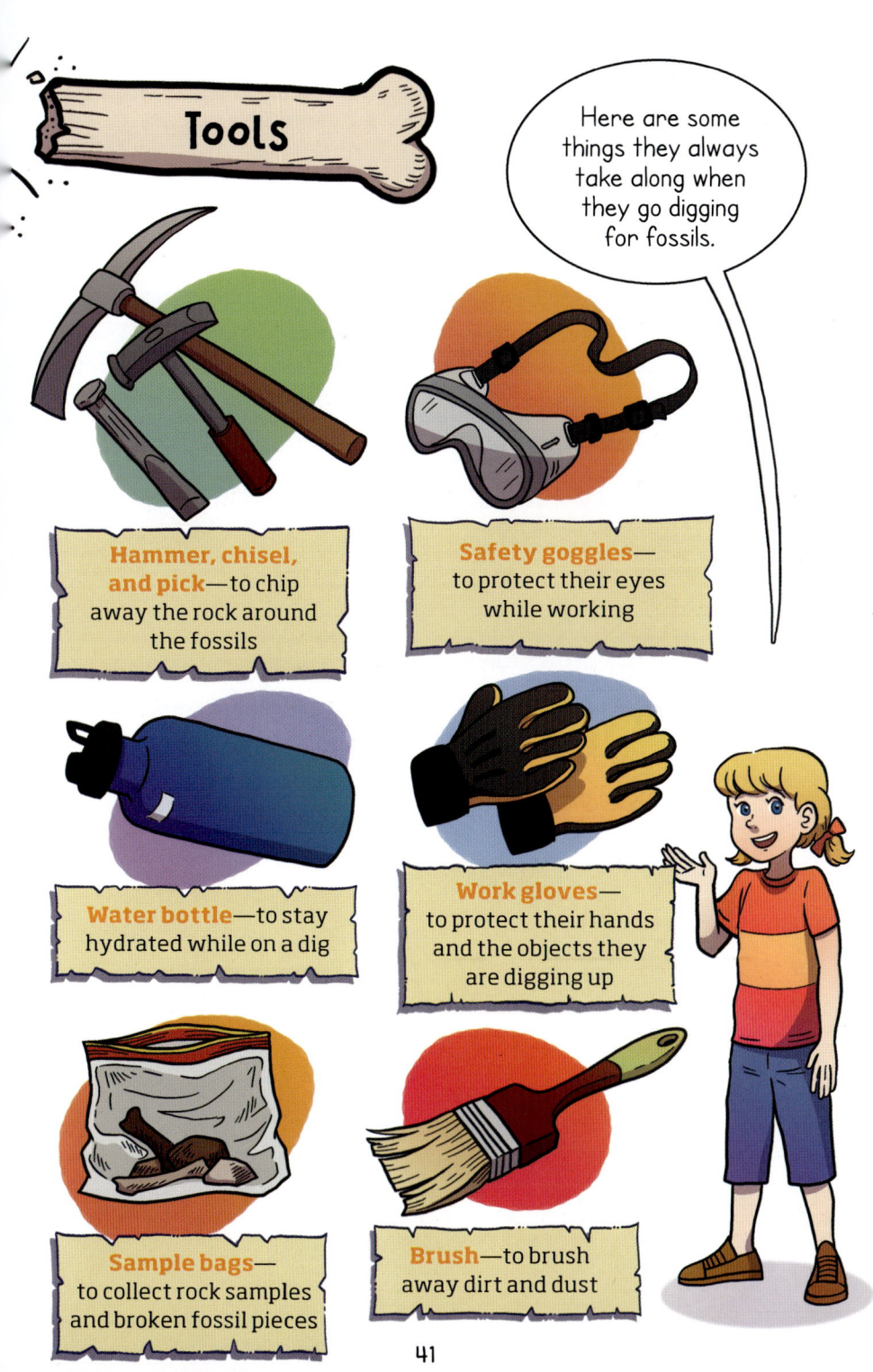

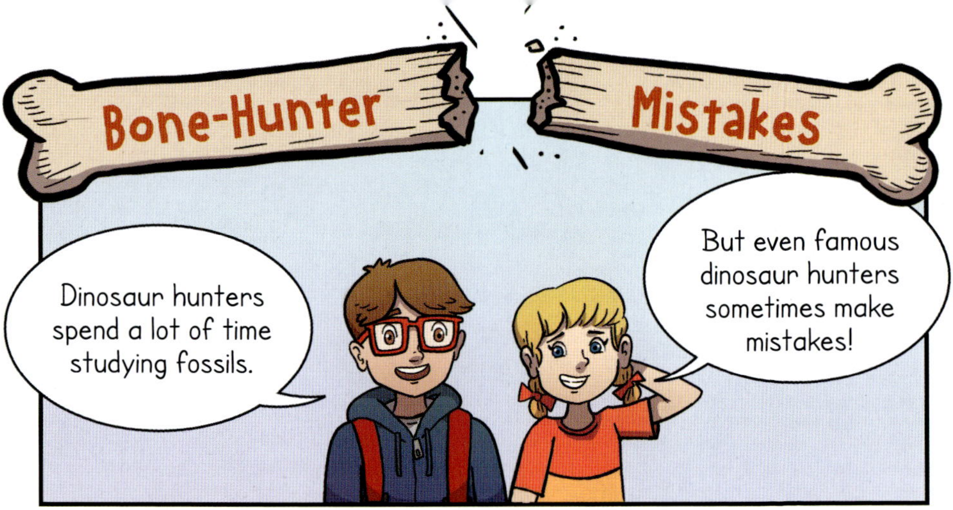
Bone-Hunter Mistakes
Dinosaur hunters spend a lot of time studying fossils.
But even famous dinosaur hunters sometimes make mistakes!

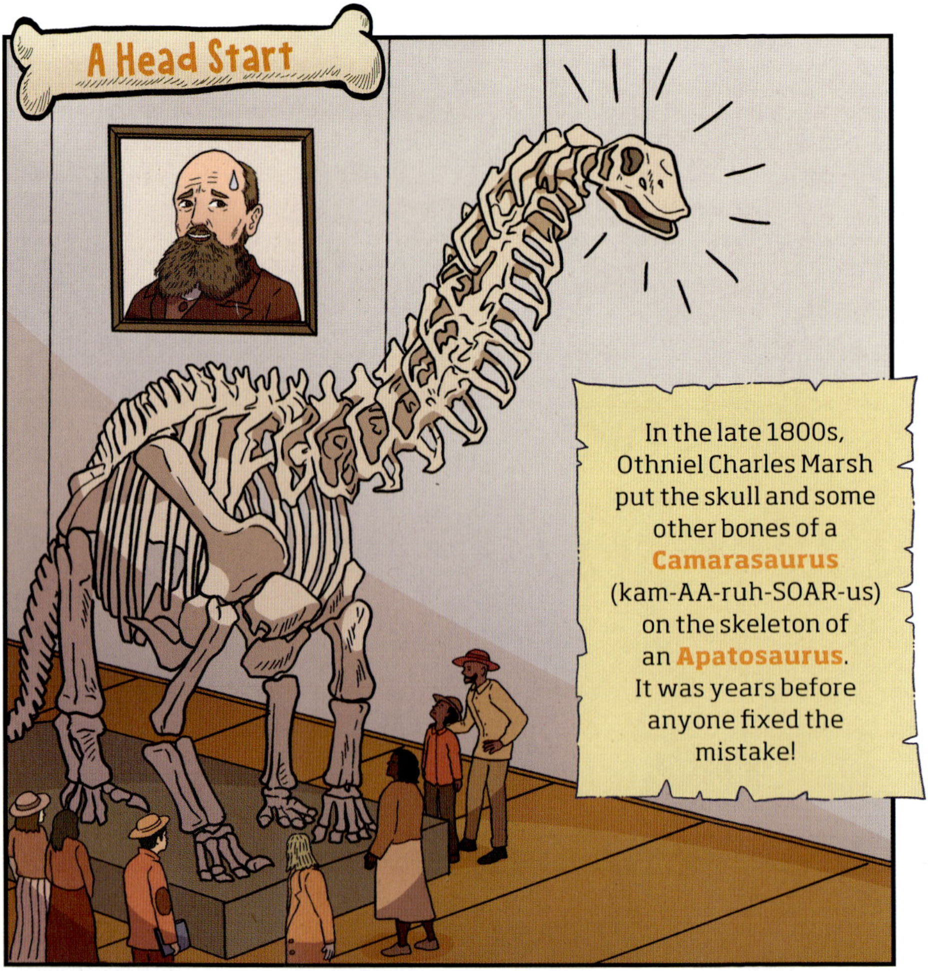
A Head Start
In the late 1800s, Othniel Charles Marsh put the skull and some other bones of a **Camarasaurus** (kam-AA-ruh-SOAR-us) on the skeleton of an **Apatosaurus**. It was years before anyone fixed the mistake!

The Wrong End

Early in his career, Edward Drinker Cope was trying to assemble the skeleton of a giant sea reptile. But when he put the bones together, he accidentally stuck the creature's head on the end of its tail!

Elasmosaurus
(ee-LAZ-muh-SOAR-us)

Horn or Claw?

When Gideon Mantell was studying **Iguanodon** fossils, he mistakenly thought the thumb claw was a nose horn. He drew a picture of an *Iguanodon* with a claw growing out of its face!

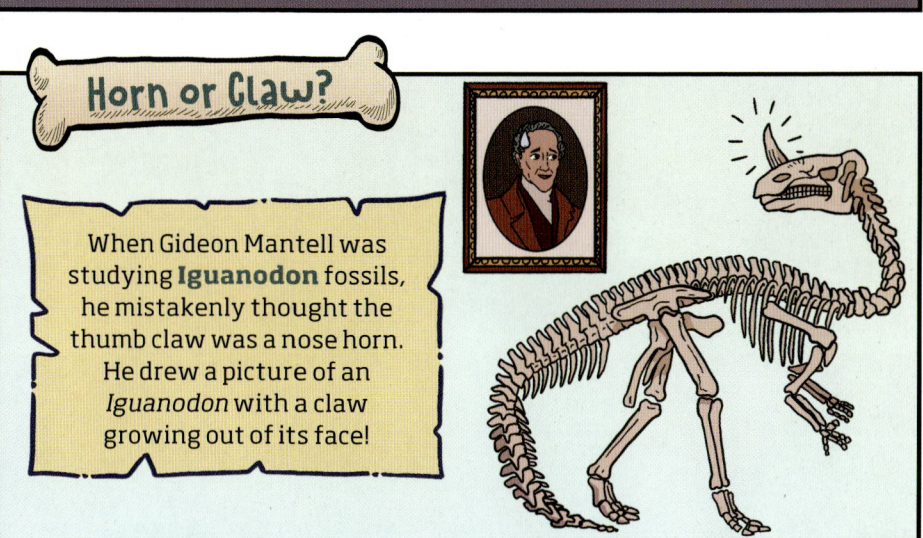

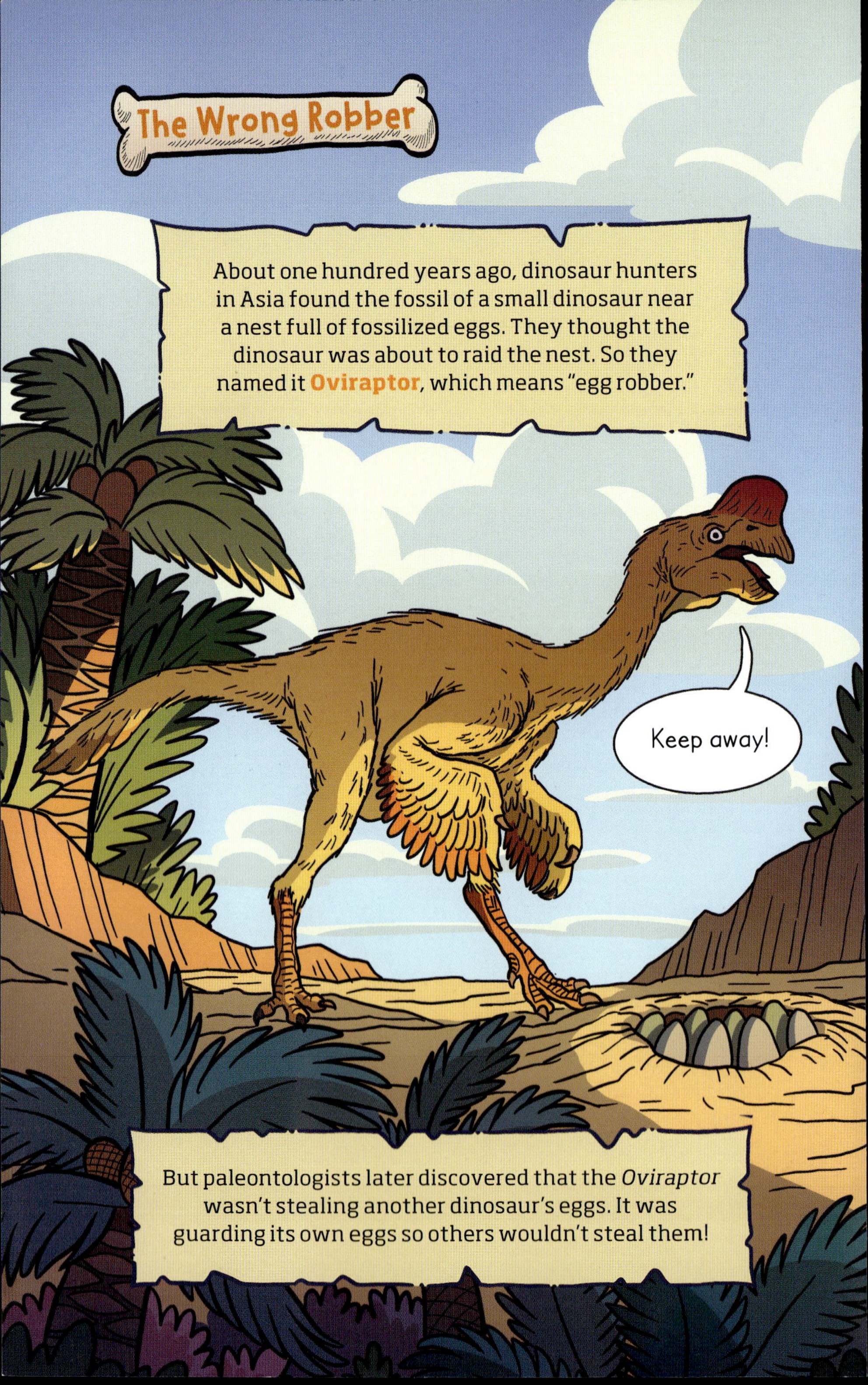
The Wrong Robber
About one hundred years ago, dinosaur hunters in Asia found the fossil of a small dinosaur near a nest full of fossilized eggs. They thought the dinosaur was about to raid the nest. So they named it **Oviraptor**, which means "egg robber."
Keep away!
But paleontologists later discovered that the *Oviraptor* wasn't stealing another dinosaur's eggs. It was guarding its own eggs so others wouldn't steal them!

CHAPTER FOUR
Flesh-eaters

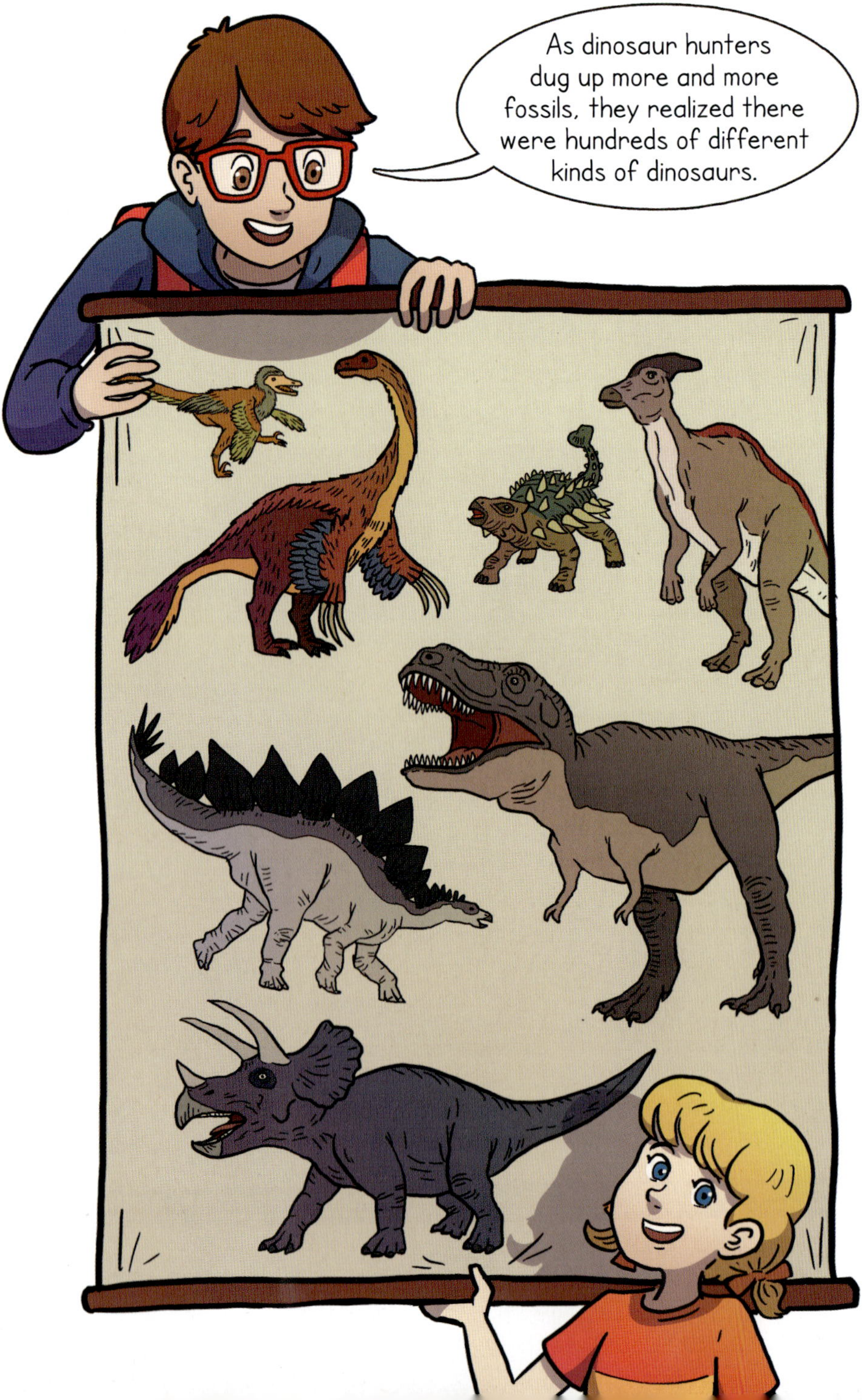
As dinosaur hunters dug up more and more fossils, they realized there were hundreds of different kinds of dinosaurs.

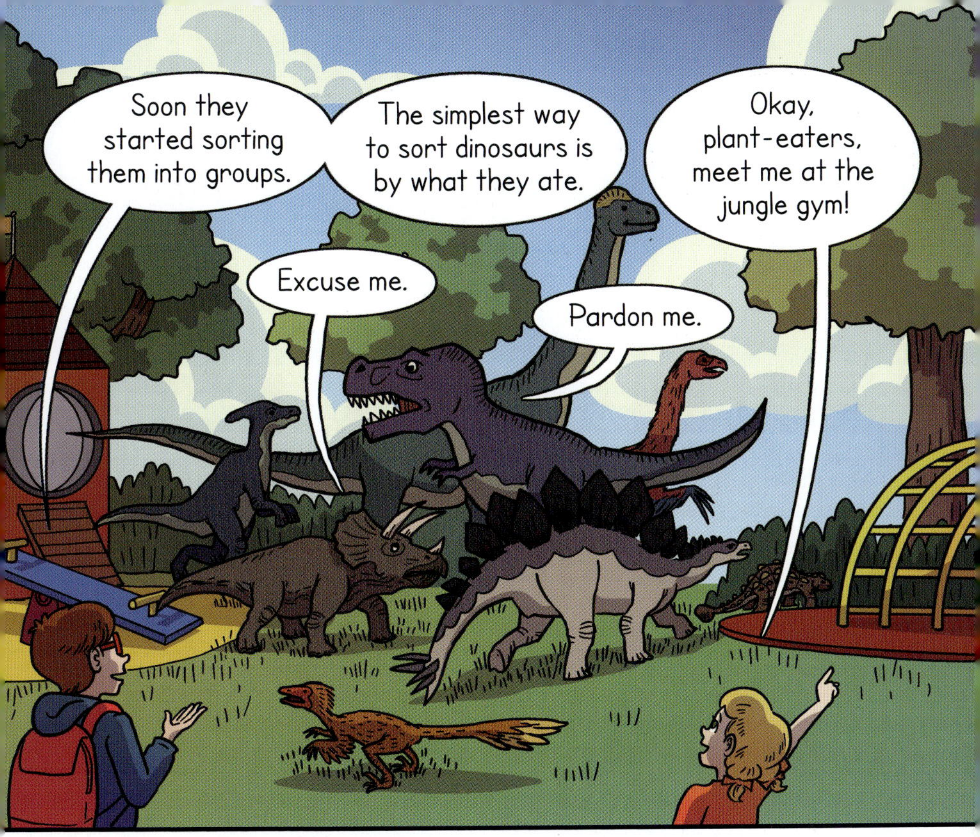
Soon they started sorting them into groups.
The simplest way to sort dinosaurs is by what they ate.
Okay, plant-eaters, meet me at the jungle gym!
Excuse me.
Pardon me.

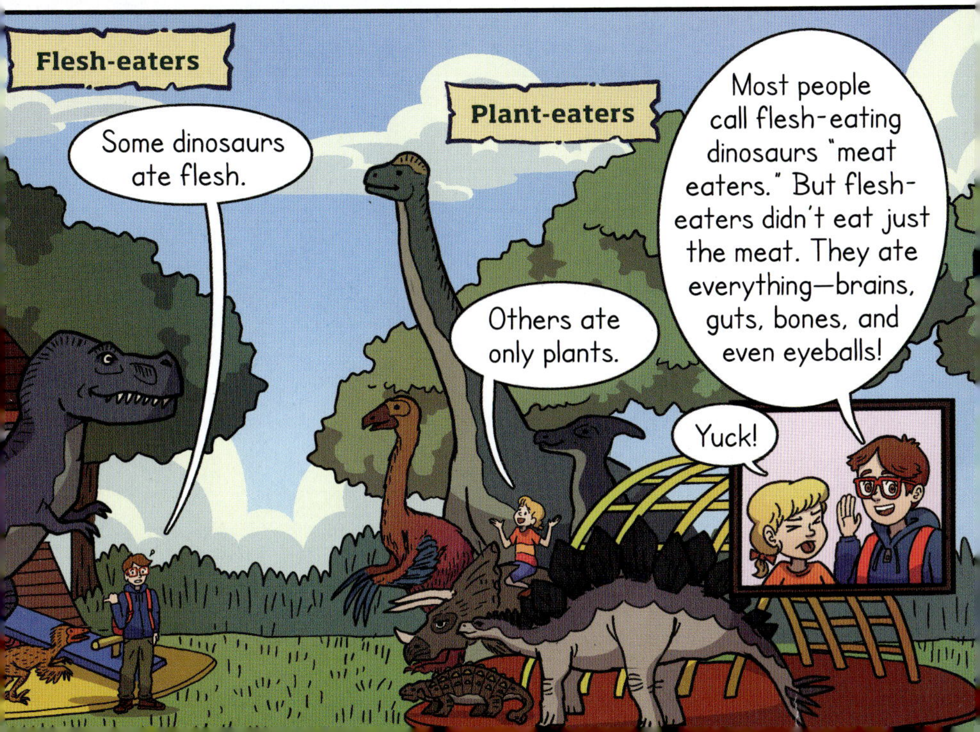
Flesh-eaters
Some dinosaurs ate flesh.
Plant-eaters
Others ate only plants.
Most people call flesh-eating dinosaurs "meat eaters." But flesh-eaters didn't eat just the meat. They ate everything—brains, guts, bones, and even eyeballs!
Yuck!

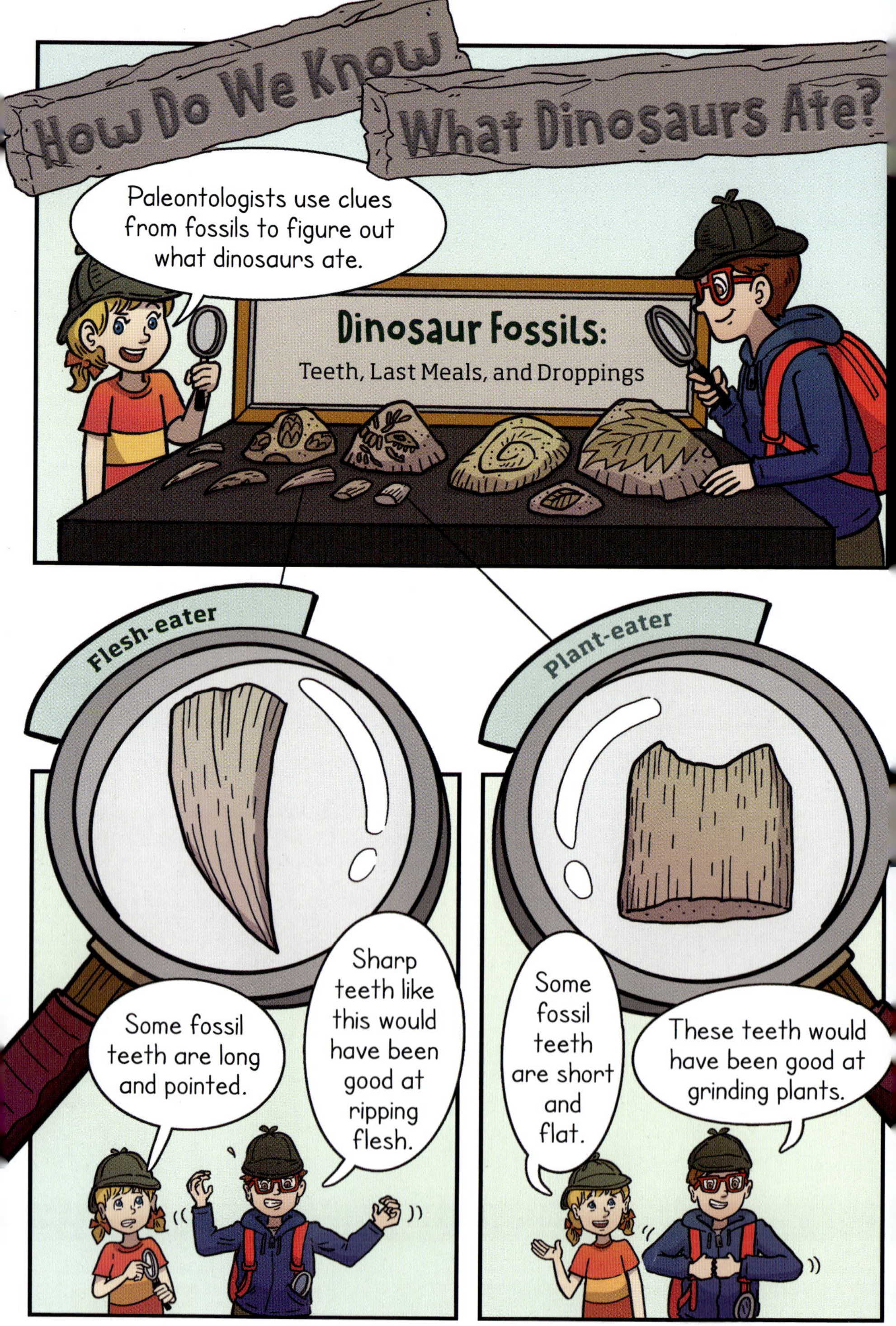
How Do We Know What Dinosaurs Ate?
Paleontologists use clues from fossils to figure out what dinosaurs ate.
Dinosaur Fossils:
Teeth, Last Meals, and Droppings
Flesh-eater
Some fossil teeth are long and pointed.
Sharp teeth like this would have been good at ripping flesh.
Plant-eater
Some fossil teeth are short and flat.
These teeth would have been good at grinding plants.

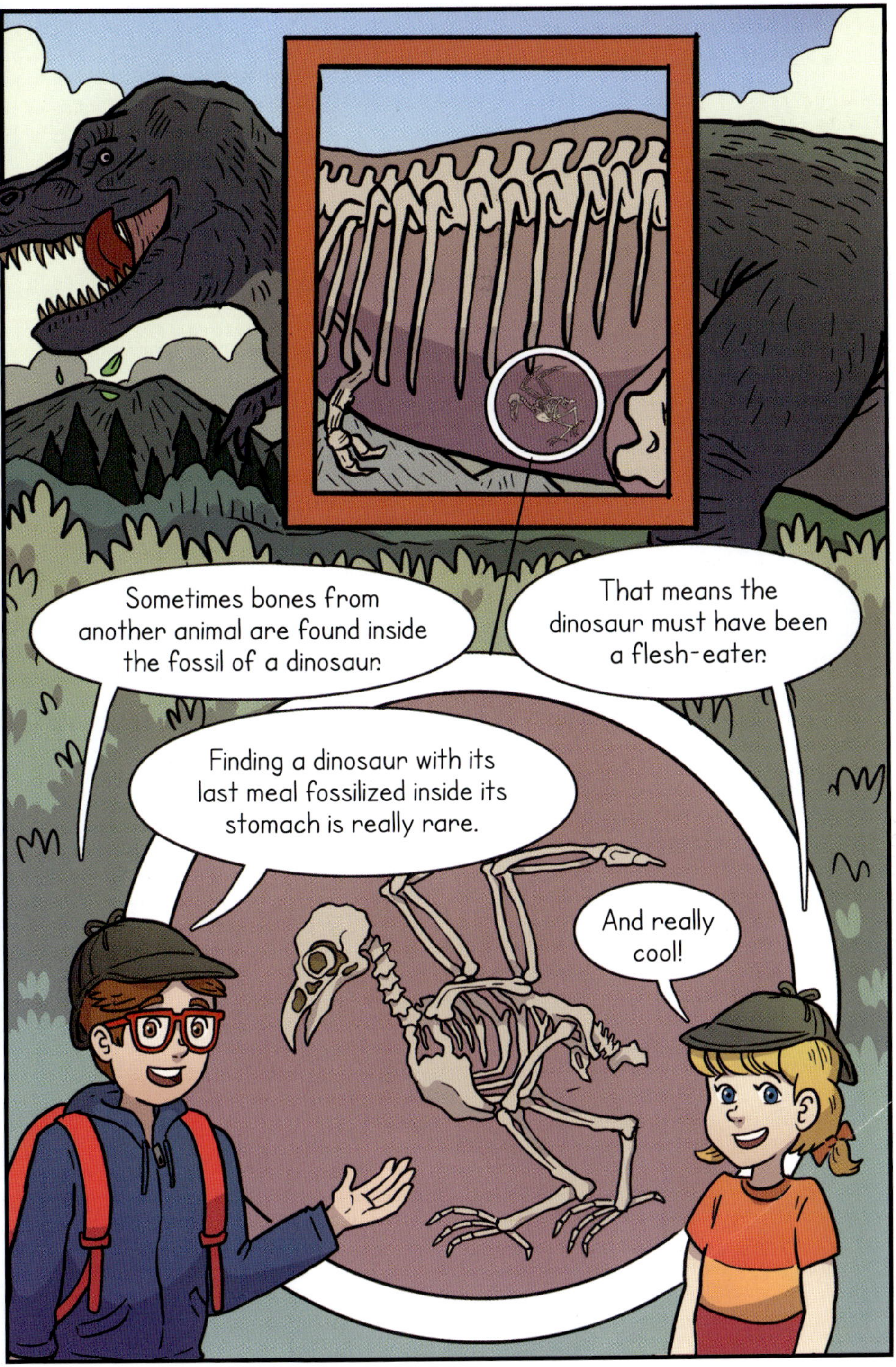
Sometimes bones from another animal are found inside the fossil of a dinosaur.
That means the dinosaur must have been a flesh-eater.
Finding a dinosaur with its last meal fossilized inside its stomach is really rare.
And really cool!

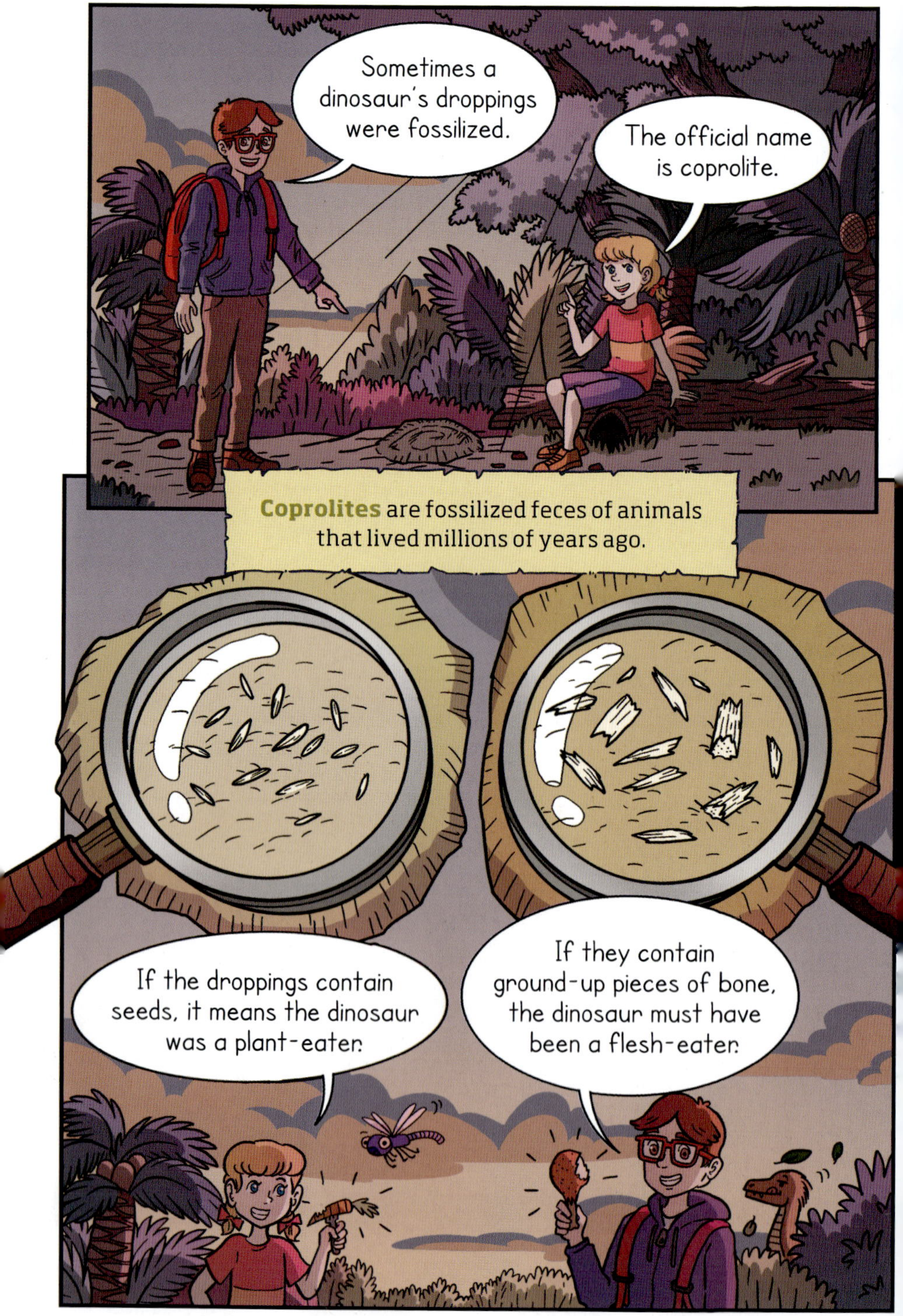
Sometimes a dinosaur's droppings were fossilized.
The official name is coprolite.
Coprolites are fossilized feces of animals that lived millions of years ago.
If the droppings contain seeds, it means the dinosaur was a plant-eater.
If they contain ground-up pieces of bone, the dinosaur must have been a flesh-eater.

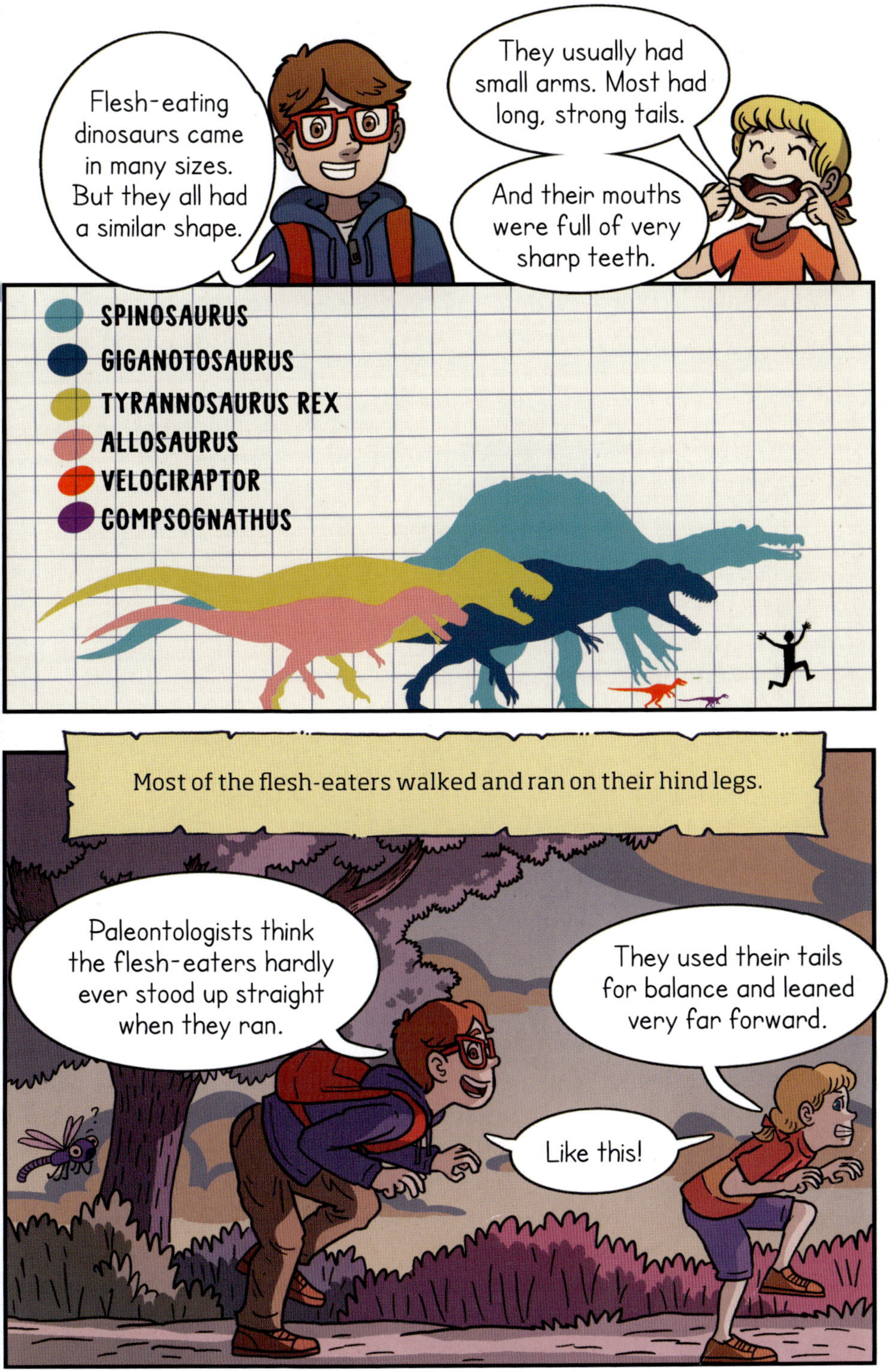
Flesh-eating dinosaurs came in many sizes. But they all had a similar shape.
They usually had small arms. Most had long, strong tails.
And their mouths were full of very sharp teeth.
SPINOSAURUS
GIGANOTOSAURUS
TYRANNOSAURUS REX
ALLOSAURUS
VELOCIRAPTOR
COMPSOGNATHUS
Most of the flesh-eaters walked and ran on their hind legs.
Paleontologists think the flesh-eaters hardly ever stood up straight when they ran.
They used their tails for balance and leaned very far forward.
Like this!

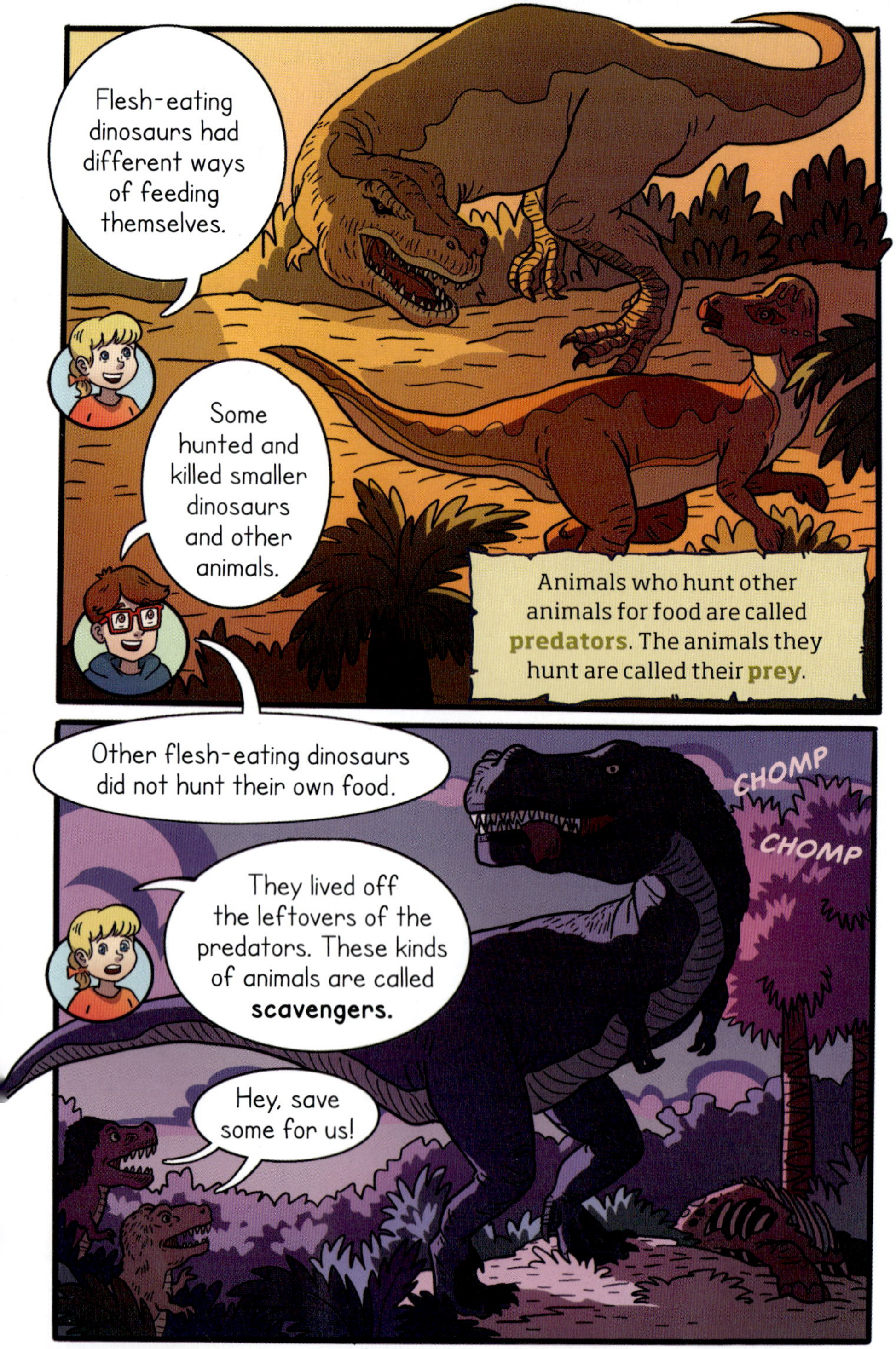
Flesh-eating dinosaurs had different ways of feeding themselves.
Some hunted and killed smaller dinosaurs and other animals.
Animals who hunt other animals for food are called **predators**. The animals they hunt are called their **prey**.
Other flesh-eating dinosaurs did not hunt their own food.
CHOMP
CHOMP
They lived off the leftovers of the predators. These kinds of animals are called **scavengers.**
Hey, save some for us!

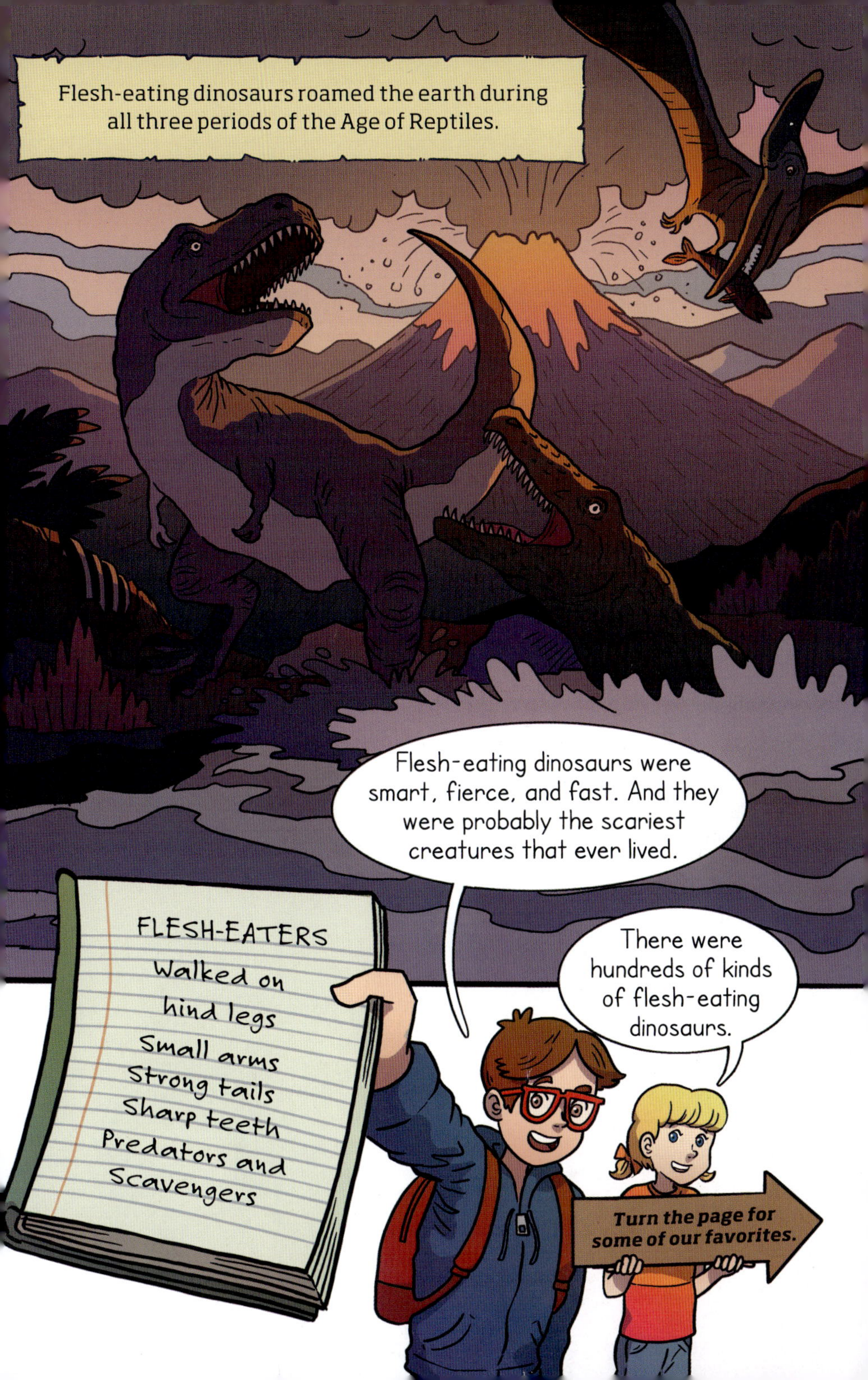
Flesh-eating dinosaurs roamed the earth during all three periods of the Age of Reptiles.
Flesh-eating dinosaurs were smart, fierce, and fast. And they were probably the scariest creatures that ever lived.
FLESH-EATERS
Walked on hind legs
Small arms
Strong tails
Sharp teeth
Predators and Scavengers
There were hundreds of kinds of flesh-eating dinosaurs.
Turn the page for some of our favorites.

Our Favorite Flesh-eaters

Coelophysis

(SEE-lo-FY-sis)

This name means "hollow form."

Coelophysis was one of the earliest dinosaurs.

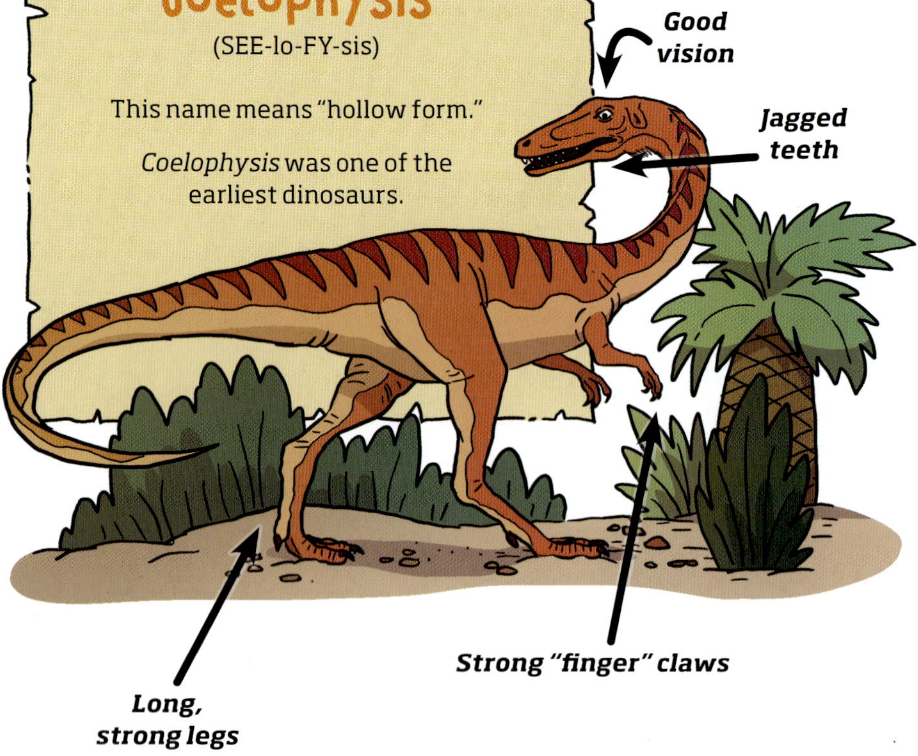

Good vision
Jagged teeth
Strong "finger" claws
Long, strong legs

Paleontologists think light bones and long legs made *Coelophysis* a very fast runner.

These pictures show our size next to the dinosaur's size.

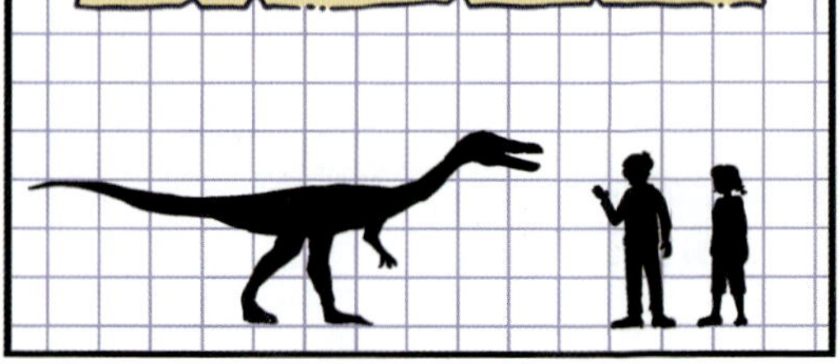

Troodon

(TRO-uh-don)

This name means "wounding tooth."

Paleontologists believe *Troodon* was the smartest dinosaur that ever lived. Its brain was very big for the size of its body.

Troodon's teeth were smaller than a human's, but they had jagged edges and *very* sharp points.

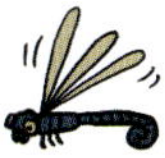

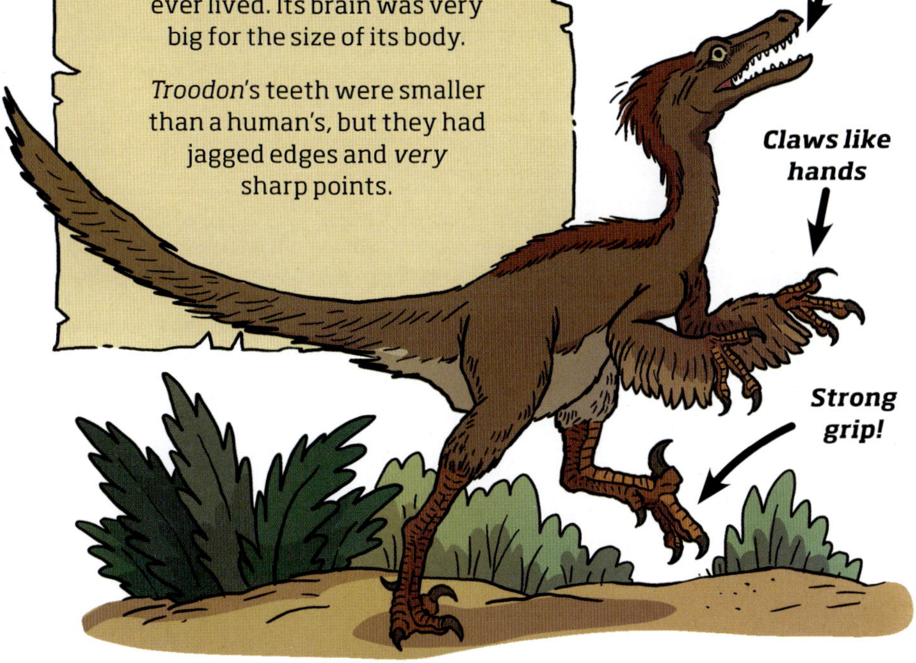
Small teeth—but sharp!
Claws like hands
Strong grip!

Troodon was fast! Paleontologists think it could run nearly 30 miles per hour. The fastest humans can run only about 23 miles per hour.

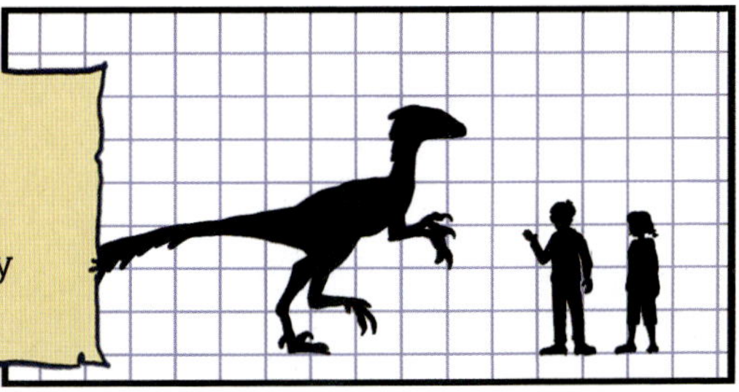

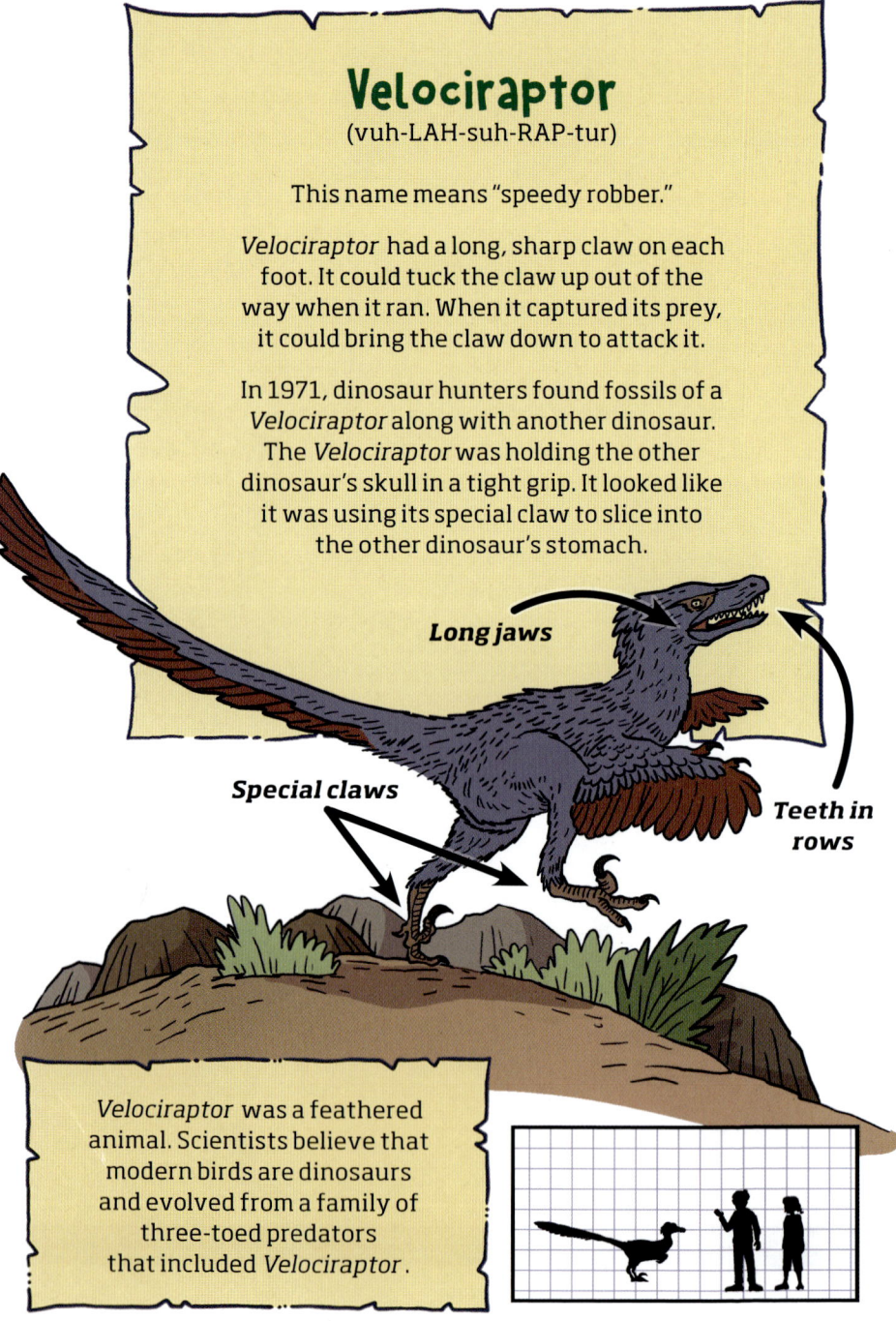

Velociraptor
(vuh-LAH-suh-RAP-tur)

This name means "speedy robber."

Velociraptor had a long, sharp claw on each foot. It could tuck the claw up out of the way when it ran. When it captured its prey, it could bring the claw down to attack it.

In 1971, dinosaur hunters found fossils of a *Velociraptor* along with another dinosaur. The *Velociraptor* was holding the other dinosaur's skull in a tight grip. It looked like it was using its special claw to slice into the other dinosaur's stomach.

Long jaws

Special claws

Teeth in rows

Velociraptor was a feathered animal. Scientists believe that modern birds are dinosaurs and evolved from a family of three-toed predators that included *Velociraptor*.

Baryonyx

(BAA-ree-ON-icks)

This name means "heavy claw."

Baryonyx had a snout like that of a crocodile.

It had twice as many teeth as most other flesh-eaters.

It also had a claw on each hand that was so long and sharp it was like a spear.

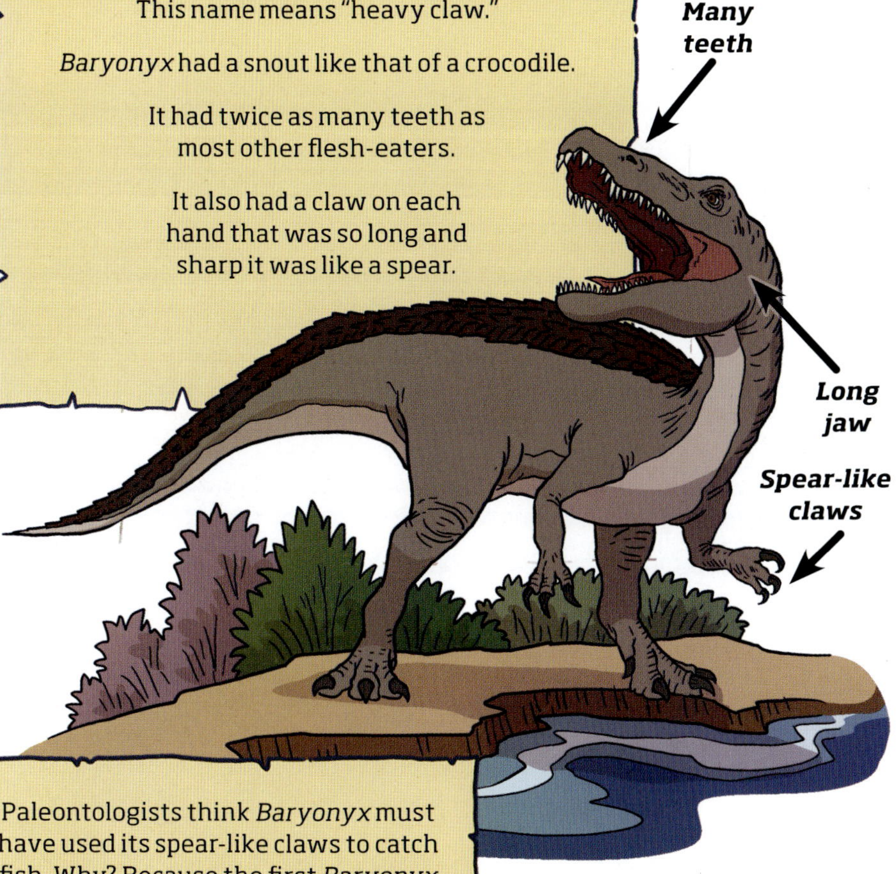

Many teeth
Long jaw
Spear-like claws

Paleontologists think *Baryonyx* must have used its spear-like claws to catch fish. Why? Because the first *Baryonyx* skeleton ever discovered had a half-eaten fish dinner in its stomach!

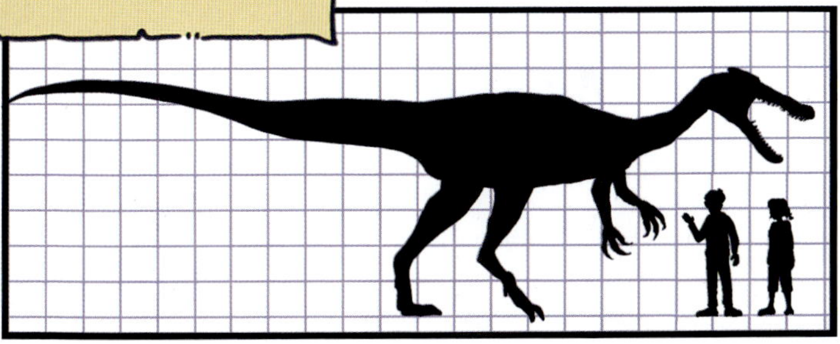

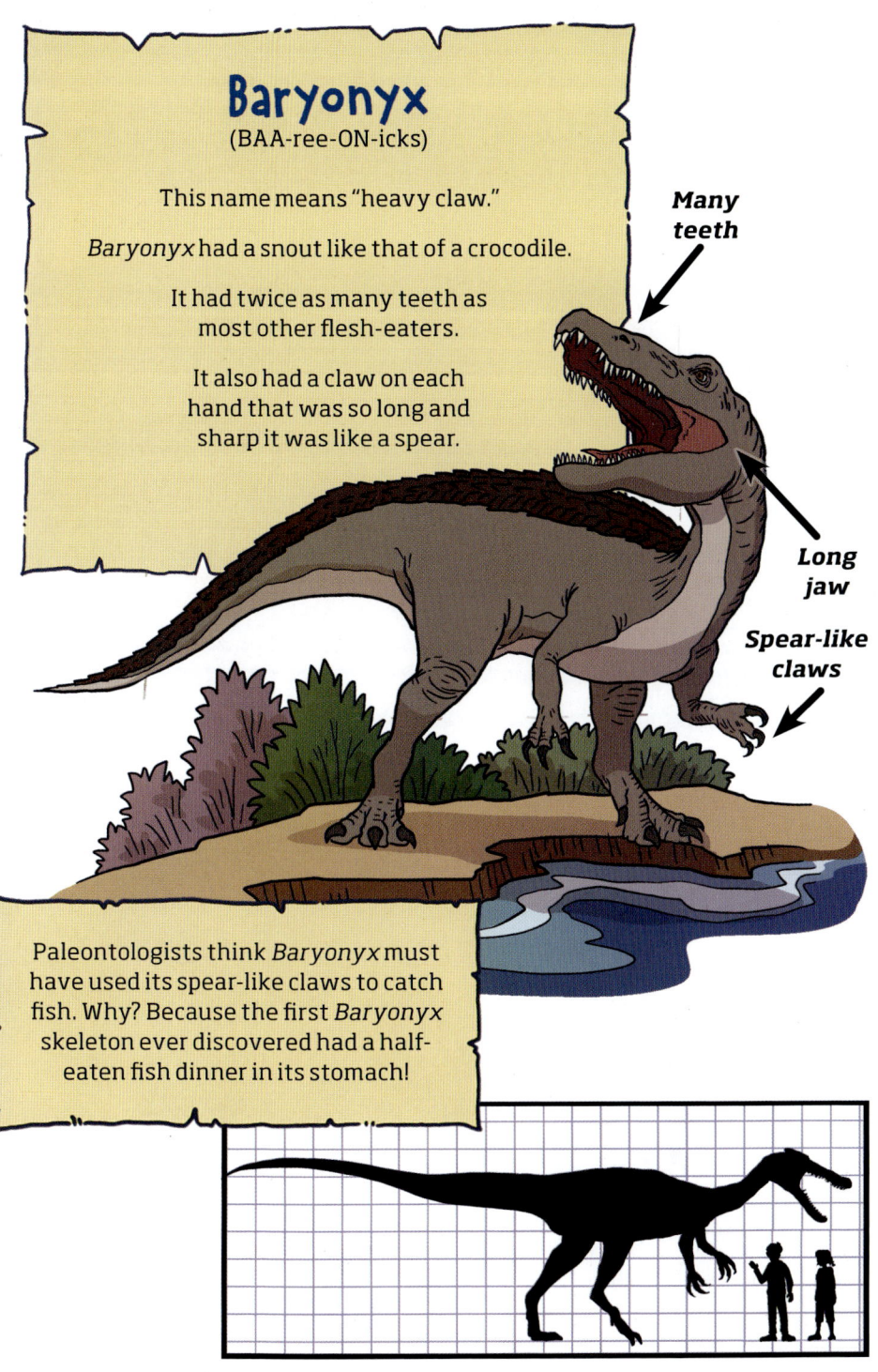

Tyrannosaurus rex

(ty-RAN-uh-SOAR-us RECKS)

This name means "tyrant lizard king."

T. rex is the most famous flesh-eating dinosaur of all time.

It had strong teeth–many were more than six inches long.

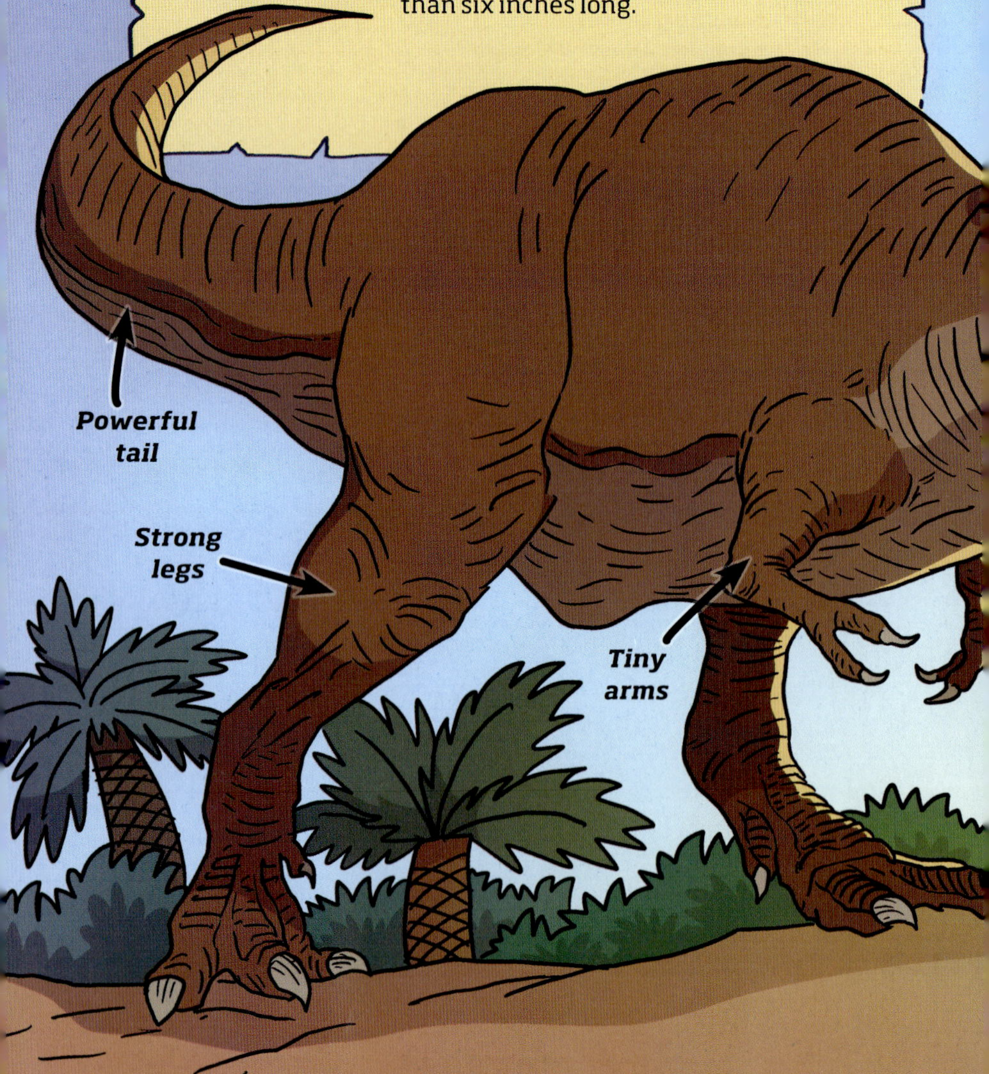
Powerful tail
Strong legs
Tiny arms

It had a head the size of a bathtub.

One *T. rex* mouthful of food could feed a whole family of humans for weeks.

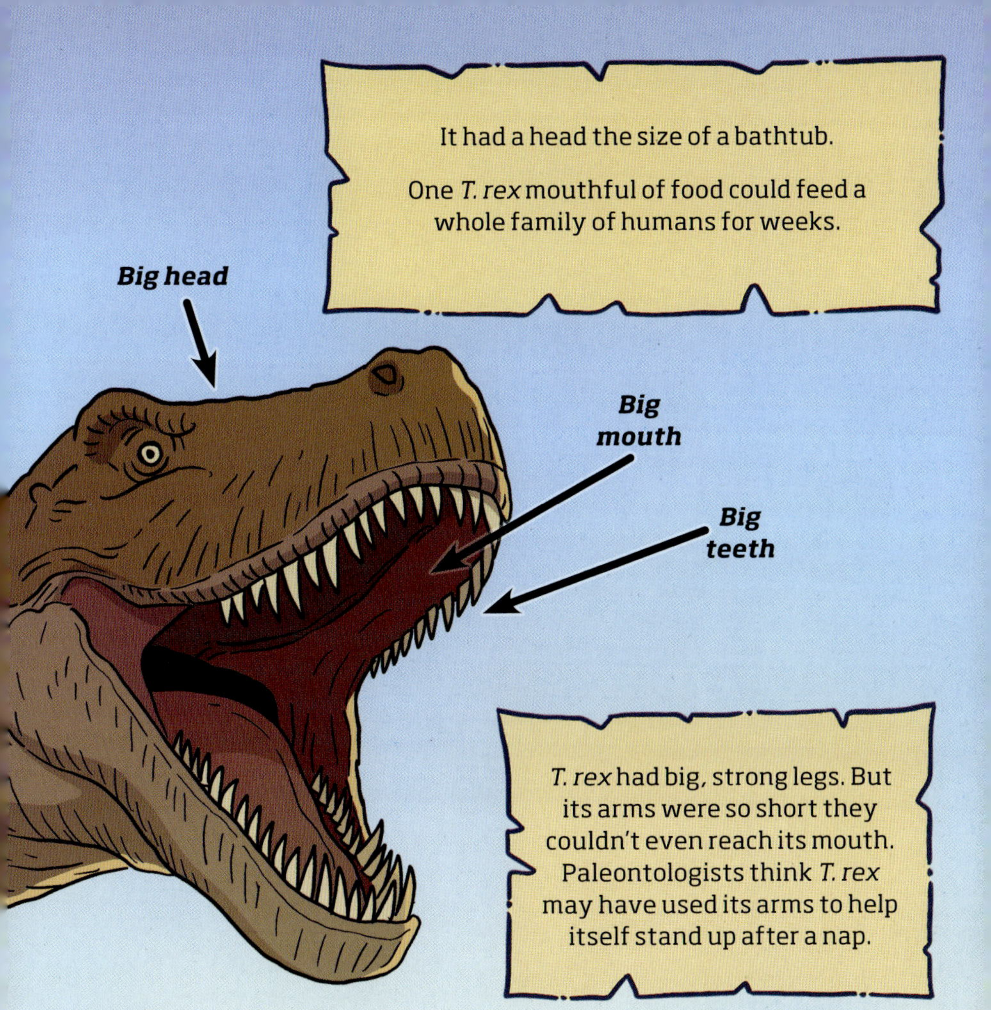

Big head
Big mouth
Big teeth

T. rex had big, strong legs. But its arms were so short they couldn't even reach its mouth. Paleontologists think *T. rex* may have used its arms to help itself stand up after a nap.

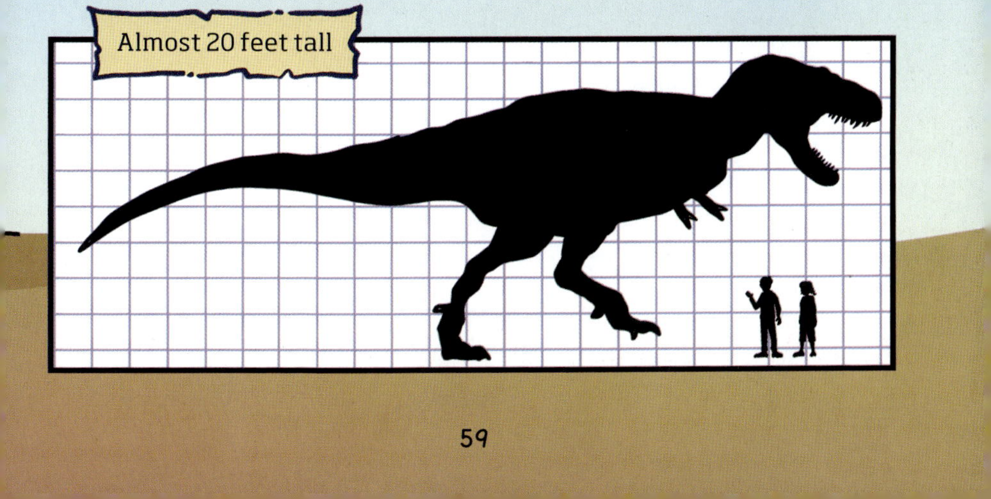

Almost 20 feet tall

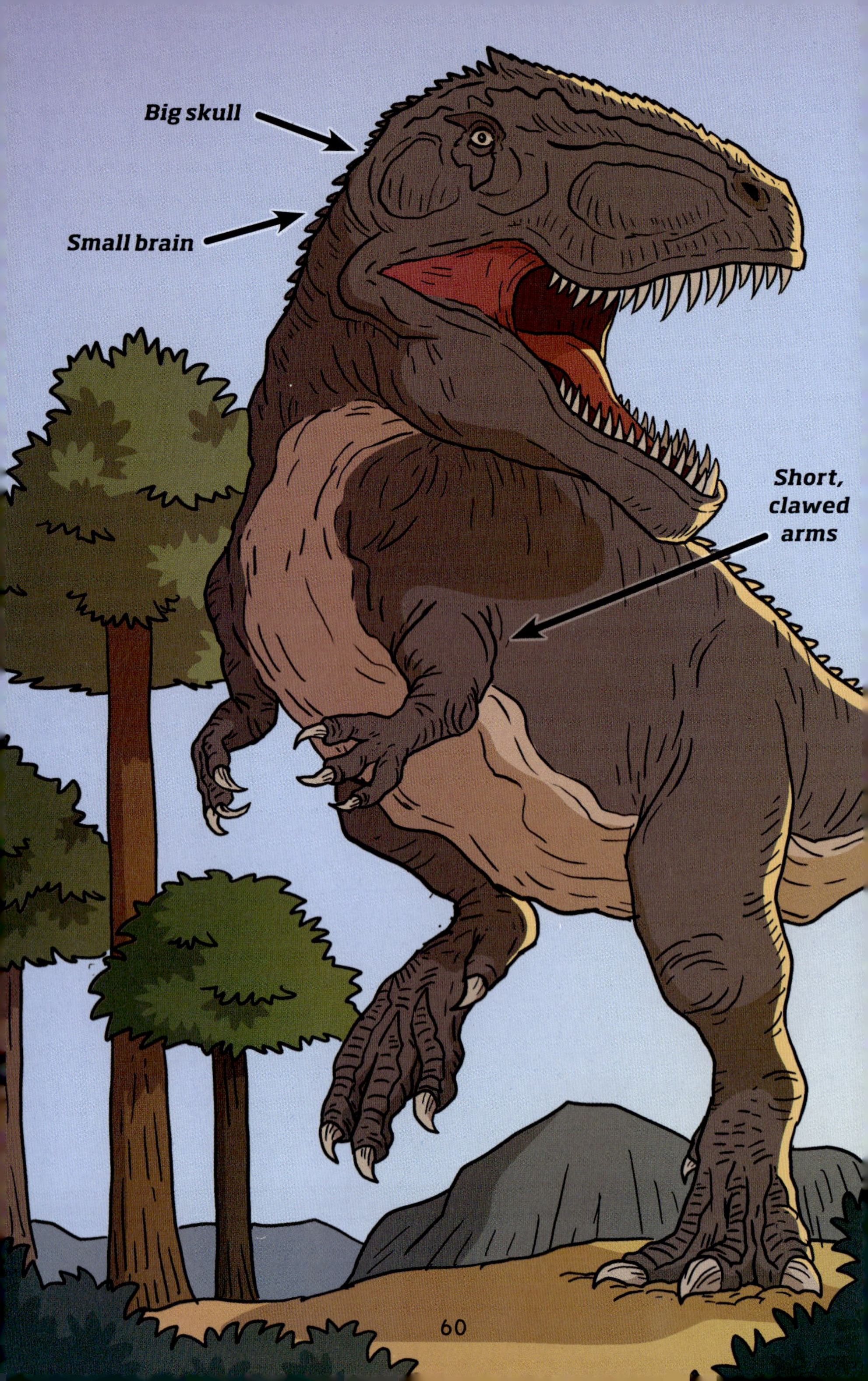
Big skull
Small brain
Short, clawed arms

Giganotosaurus
(jig-uh-NOT-uh-SOAR-us)

This name means "giant lizard of the south."

So far, only one *Giganotosaurus* skeleton has been found.

Despite its name, the *Giganotosaurus* was actually no bigger than the biggest *T. rex*.

Dinosaur hunters are looking for more *Giganotosaurus* skeletons. It's possible that when they find them, *Giganotosaurus* will replace *T. rex* as king of the flesh-eating dinosaurs.

Giganotosaurus lived about 30 million years before *T. rex*, so these two dinosaurs would never have had a chance to duke it out!

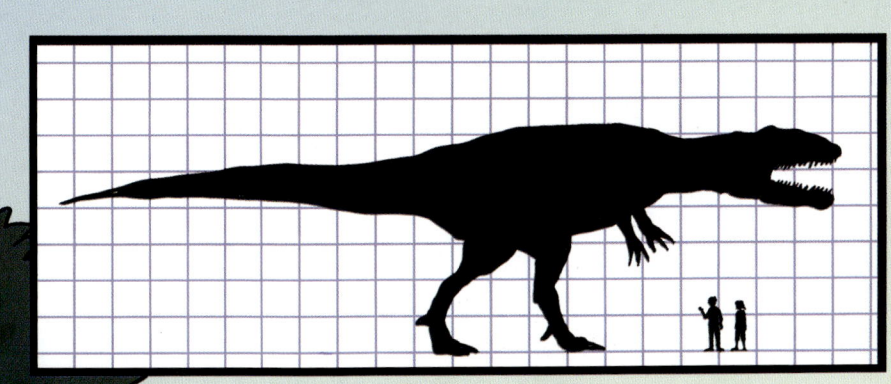

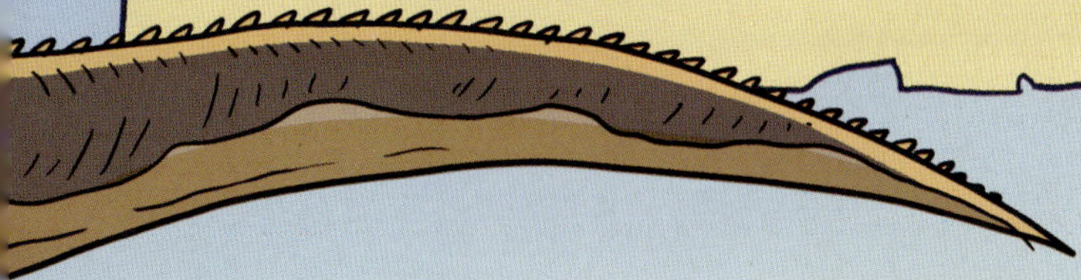

CHAPTER FIVE

Plant-eaters

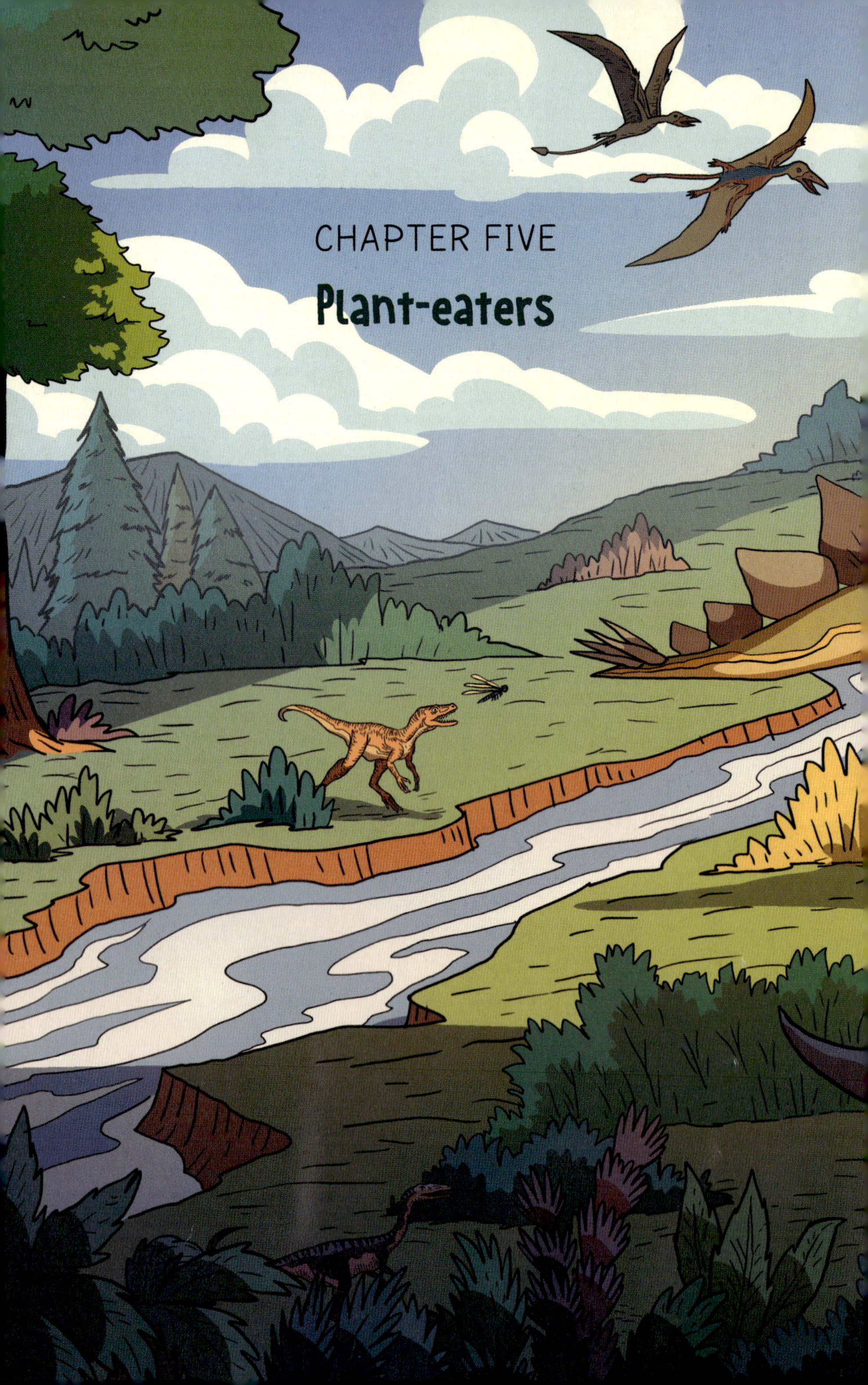

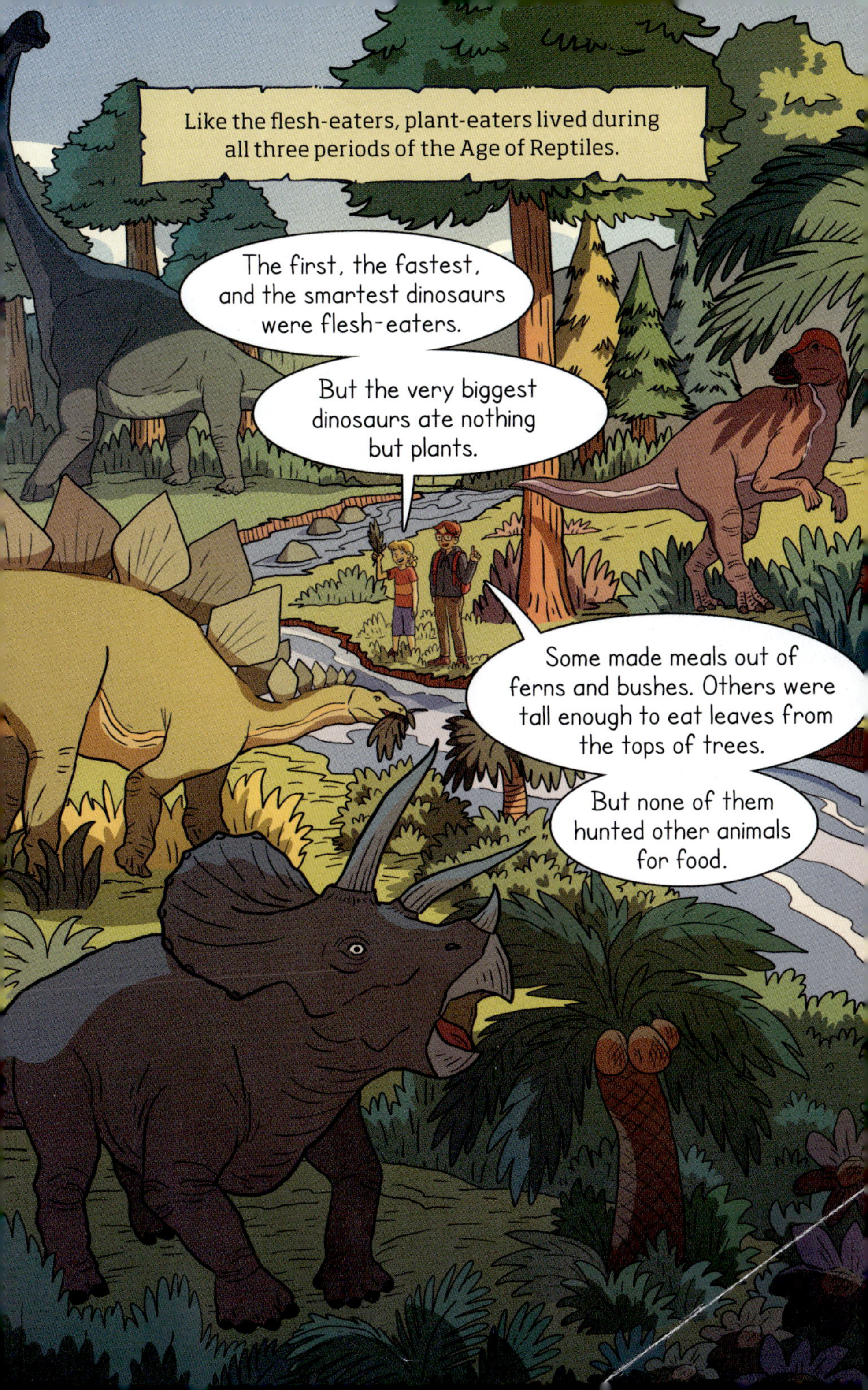
Like the flesh-eaters, plant-eaters lived during all three periods of the Age of Reptiles.
The first, the fastest, and the smartest dinosaurs were flesh-eaters.
But the very biggest dinosaurs ate nothing but plants.
Some made meals out of ferns and bushes. Others were tall enough to eat leaves from the tops of trees.
But none of them hunted other animals for food.

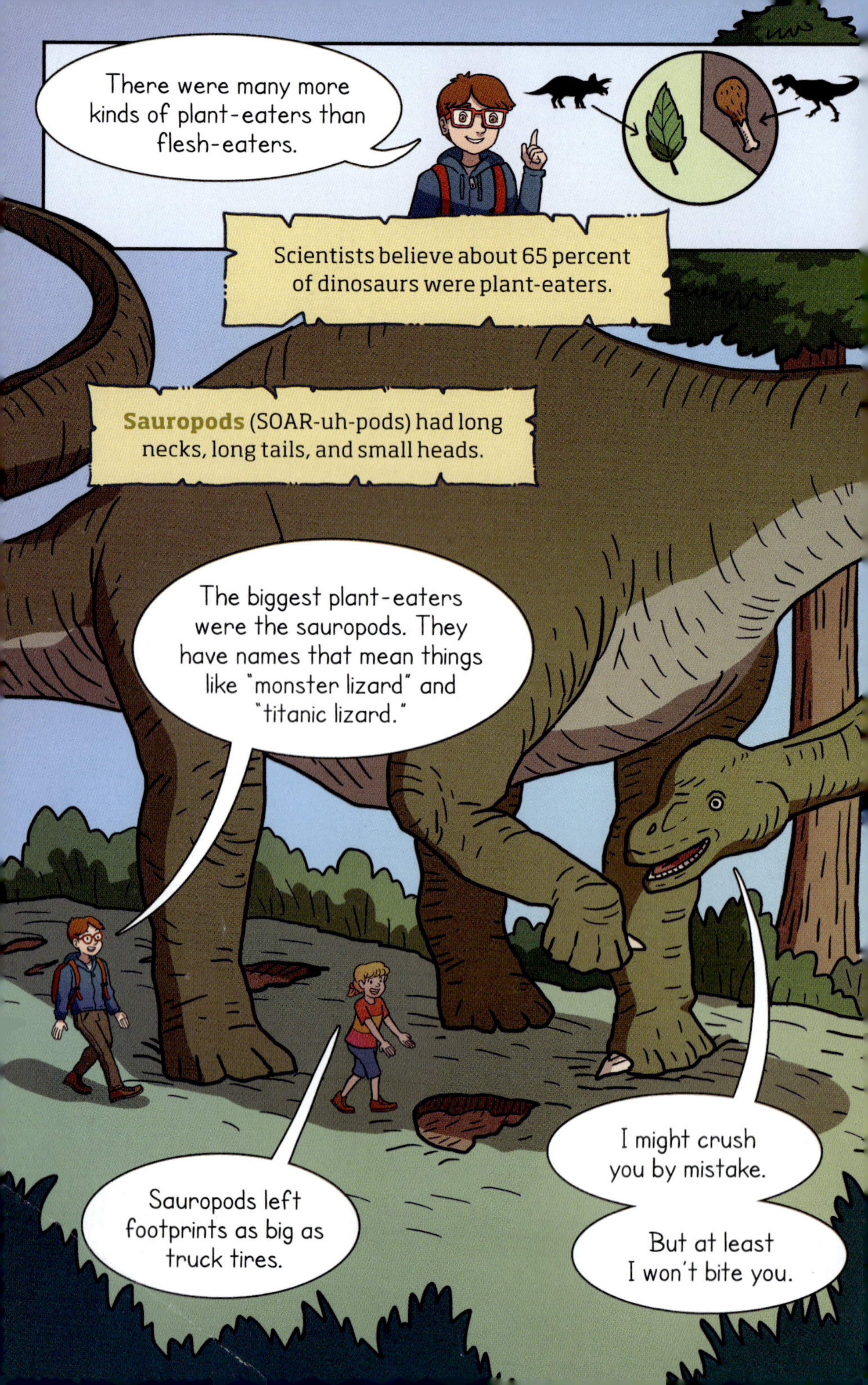
There were many more kinds of plant-eaters than flesh-eaters.
Scientists believe about 65 percent of dinosaurs were plant-eaters.
Sauropods (SOAR-uh-pods) had long necks, long tails, and small heads.
The biggest plant-eaters were the sauropods. They have names that mean things like "monster lizard" and "titanic lizard."
Sauropods left footprints as big as truck tires.
I might crush you by mistake.
But at least I won't bite you.

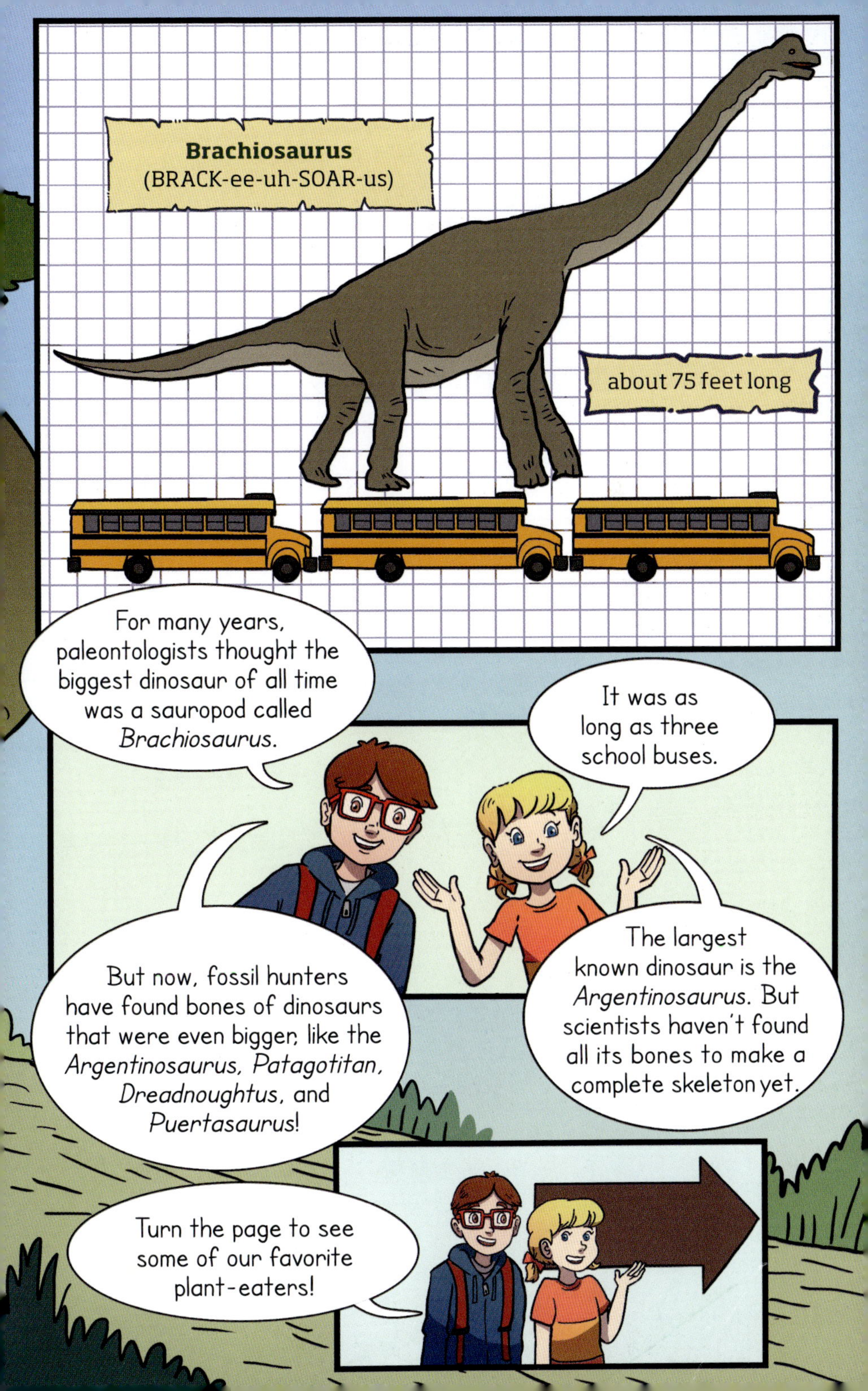
Brachiosaurus
(BRACK-ee-uh-SOAR-us)
about 75 feet long
For many years, paleontologists thought the biggest dinosaur of all time was a sauropod called *Brachiosaurus*.
It was as long as three school buses.
But now, fossil hunters have found bones of dinosaurs that were even bigger, like the *Argentinosaurus*, *Patagotitan*, *Dreadnoughtus*, and *Puertasaurus*!
The largest known dinosaur is the *Argentinosaurus*. But scientists haven't found all its bones to make a complete skeleton yet.
Turn the page to see some of our favorite plant-eaters!

Our Favorite Plant-eaters

Stegosaurus

(STEG-uh-SOAR-us)

This name means "roofed lizard."

Stegosaurus was about the size of a minivan.

It had four long spikes on the end of its tail.

It had big, flat plates growing out of its back.

Stegosaurus had a very small head.

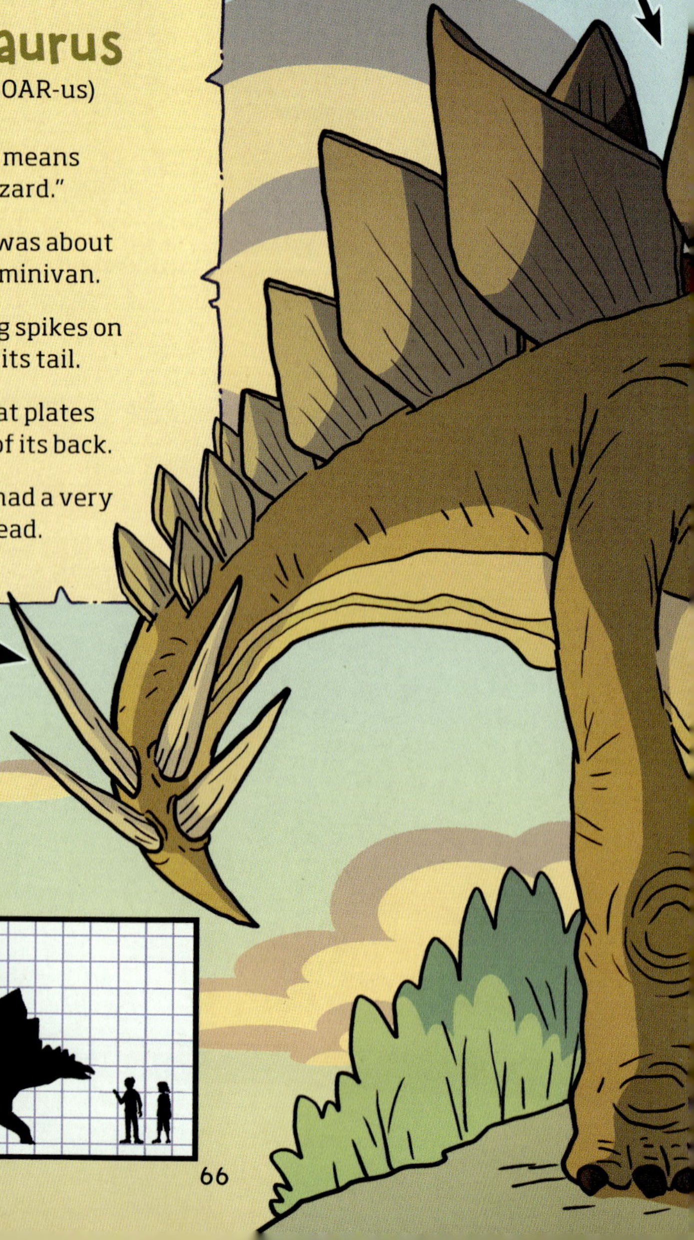
Flat back plates
Long spikes

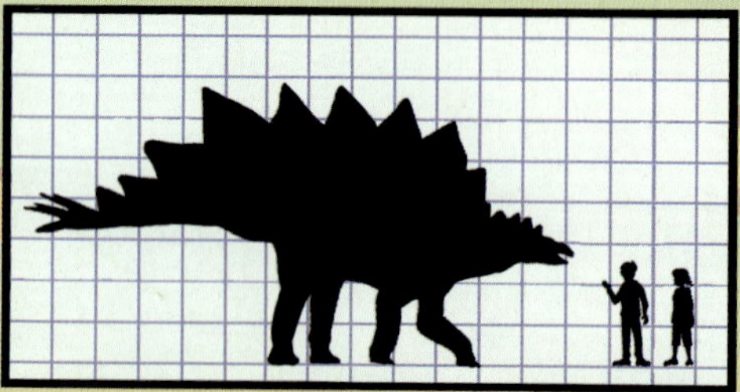

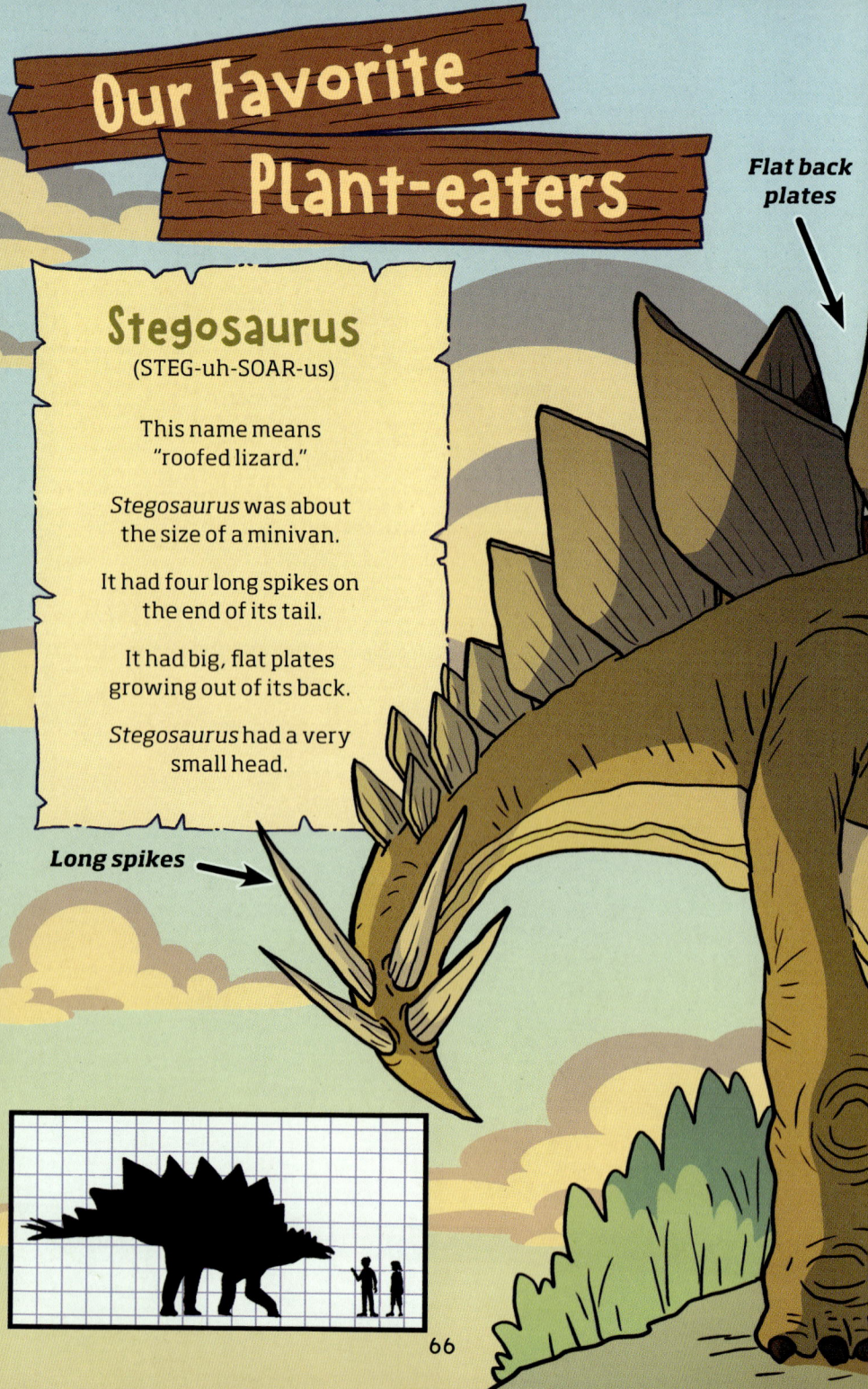

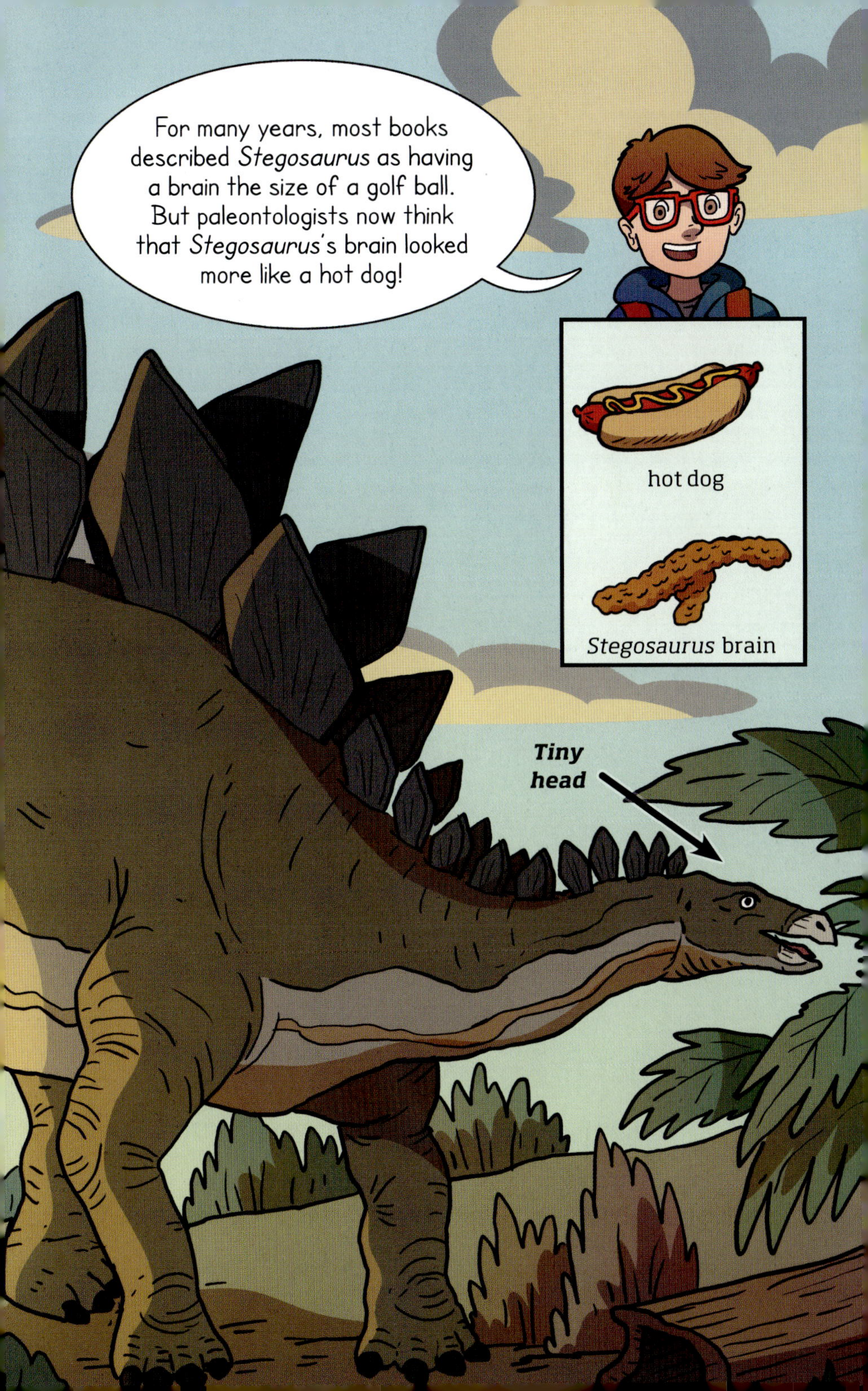
For many years, most books described *Stegosaurus* as having a brain the size of a golf ball. But paleontologists now think that *Stegosaurus*'s brain looked more like a hot dog!
hot dog
Stegosaurus brain
Tiny head

Ankylosaurus

(an-KEE-luh-SOAR-us)

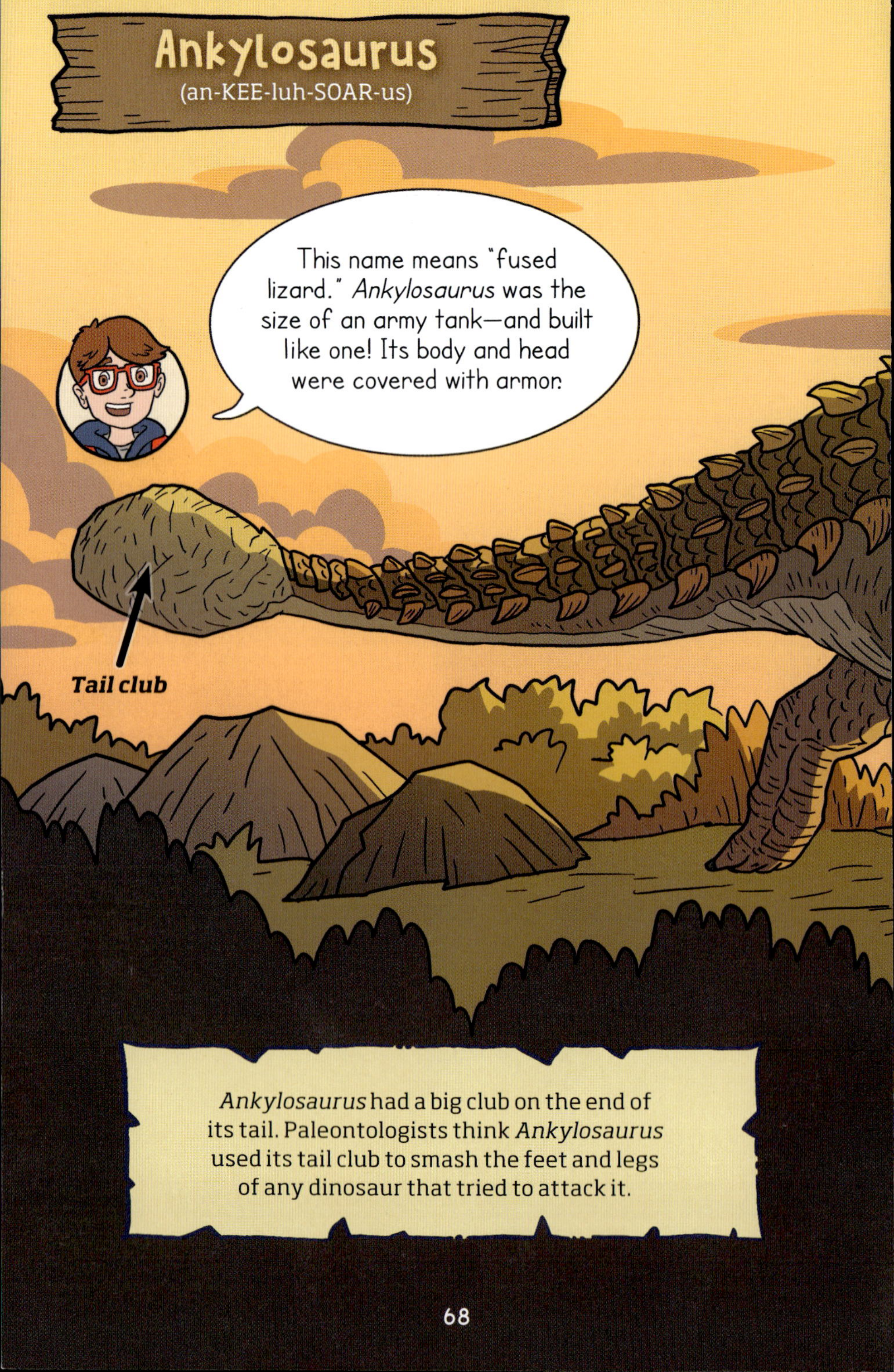
This name means "fused lizard." *Ankylosaurus* was the size of an army tank—and built like one! Its body and head were covered with armor.
Tail club

Ankylosaurus had a big club on the end of its tail. Paleontologists think *Ankylosaurus* used its tail club to smash the feet and legs of any dinosaur that tried to attack it.

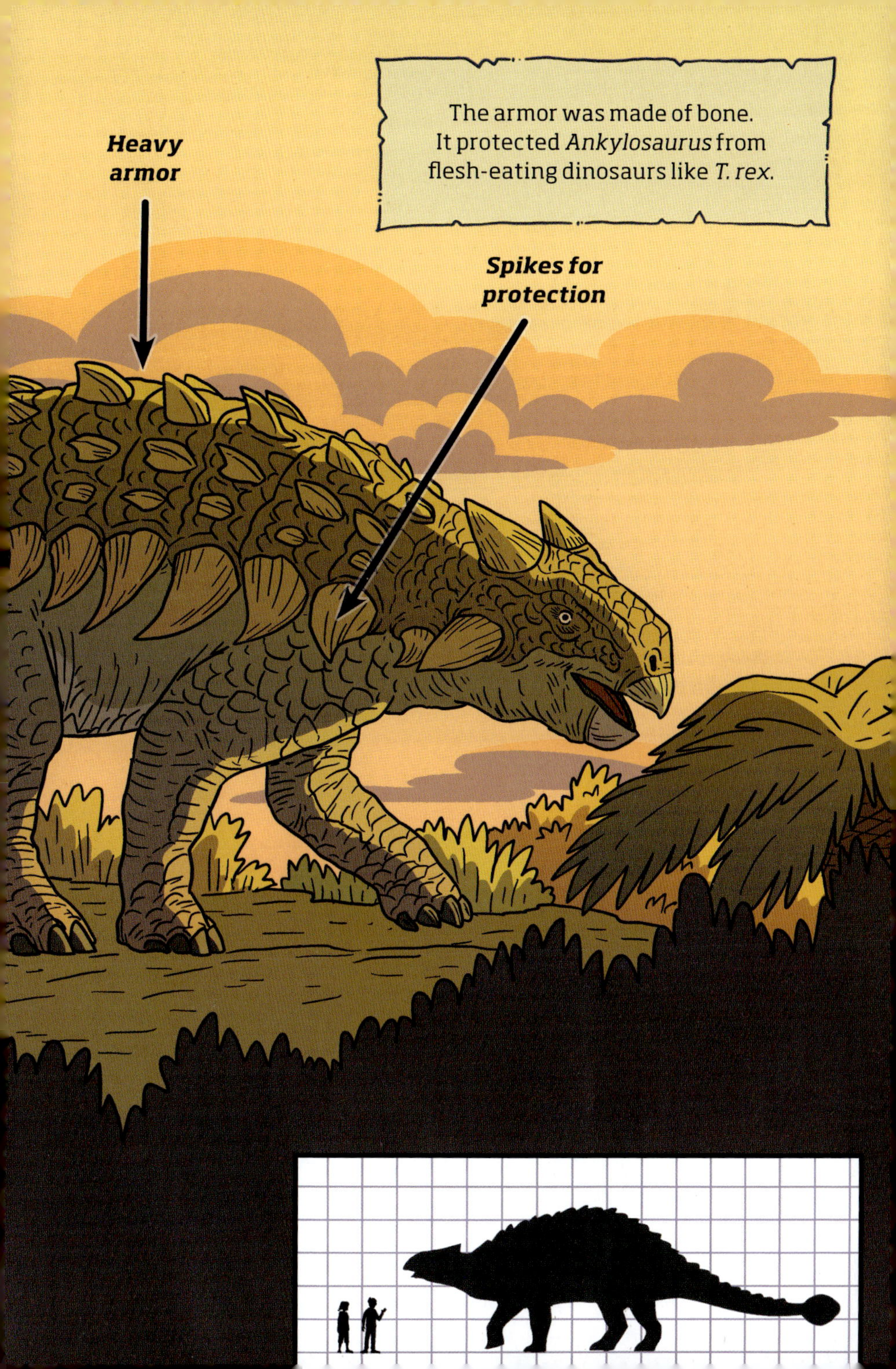
The armor was made of bone.
It protected *Ankylosaurus* from
flesh-eating dinosaurs like *T. rex*.
Heavy armor
Spikes for protection

Edmontosaurus

(ED-mont-uh-SOAR-us)

This name means "lizard from Edmonton."

Paleontologists believe that *Edmontosaurus* took good care of its babies. It protected its nest. It gathered food for the babies to eat. It probably looked after its babies until they were old enough to look after themselves.

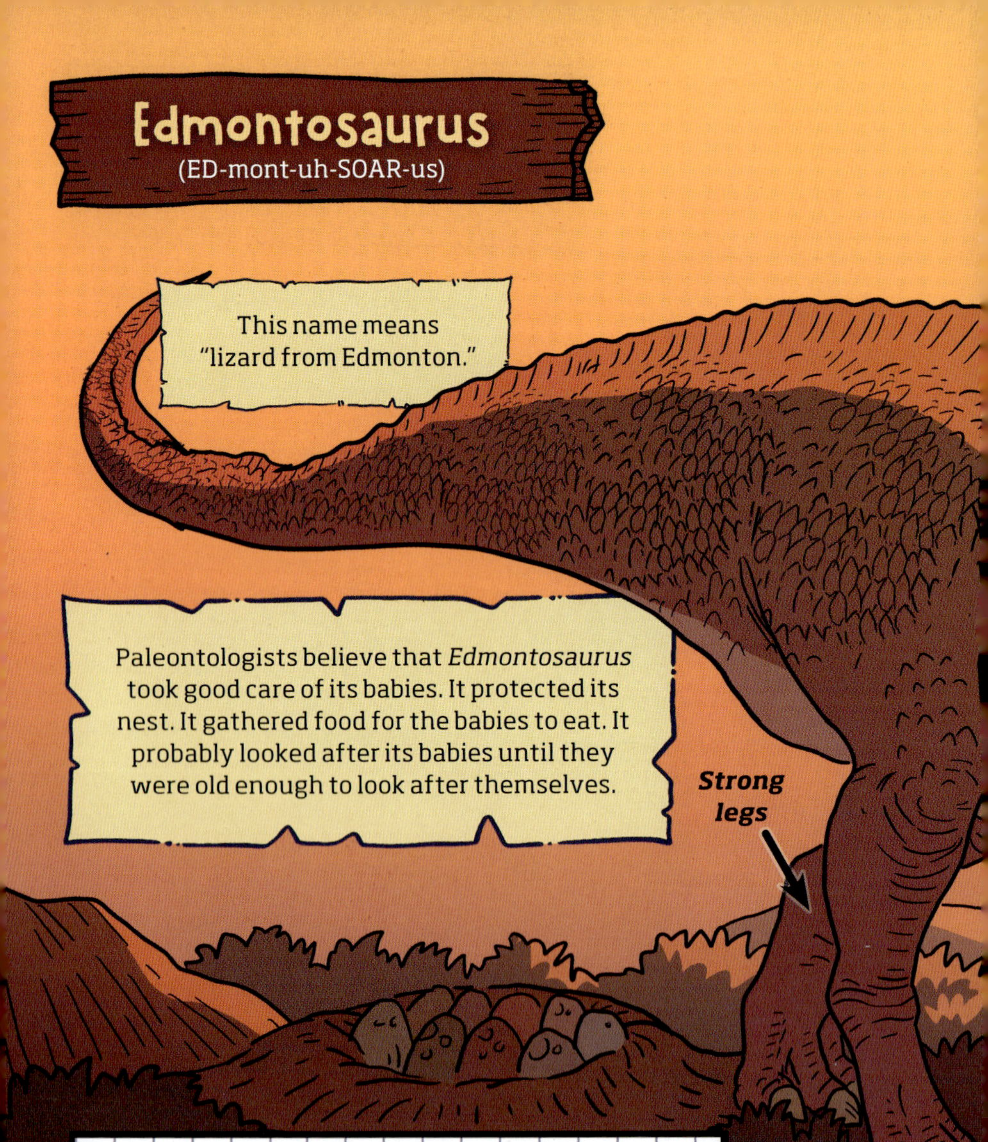
Strong legs

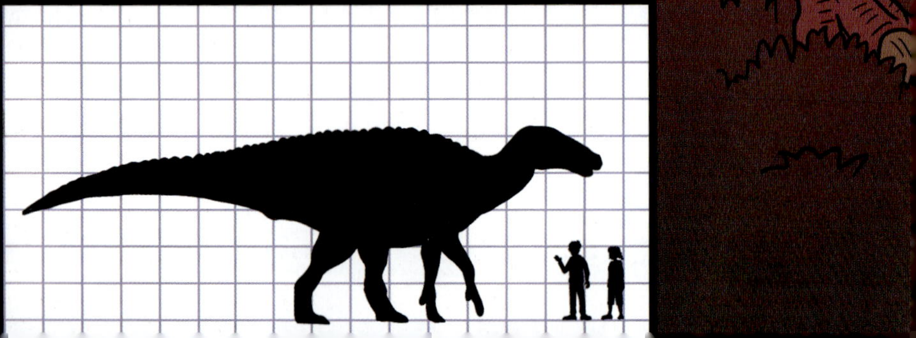

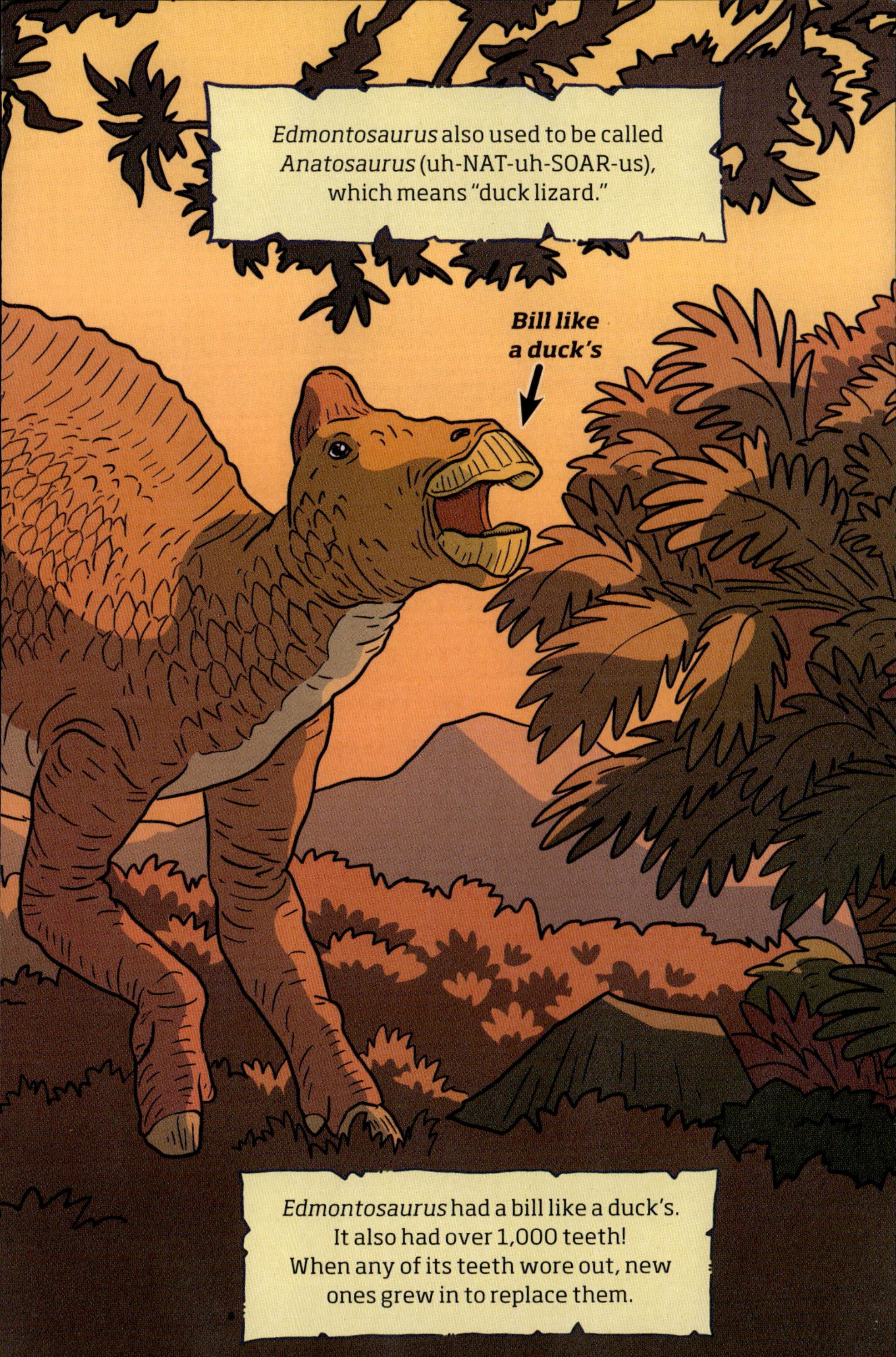
Edmontosaurus also used to be called *Anatosaurus* (uh-NAT-uh-SOAR-us), which means "duck lizard."
Bill like a duck's
Edmontosaurus had a bill like a duck's. It also had over 1,000 teeth! When any of its teeth wore out, new ones grew in to replace them.

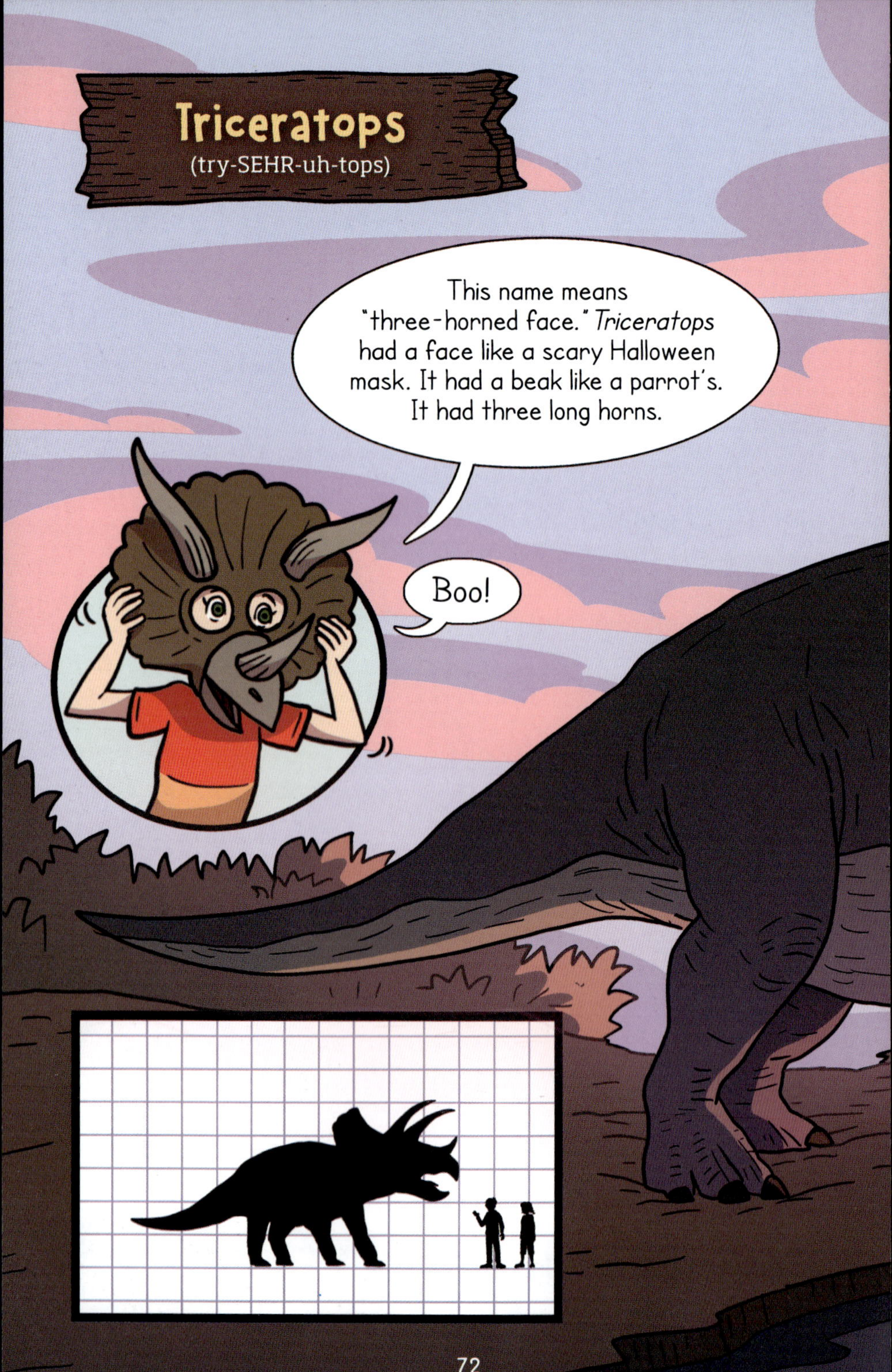
Triceratops
(try-SEHR-uh-tops)
This name means "three-horned face." *Triceratops* had a face like a scary Halloween mask. It had a beak like a parrot's. It had three long horns.
Boo!

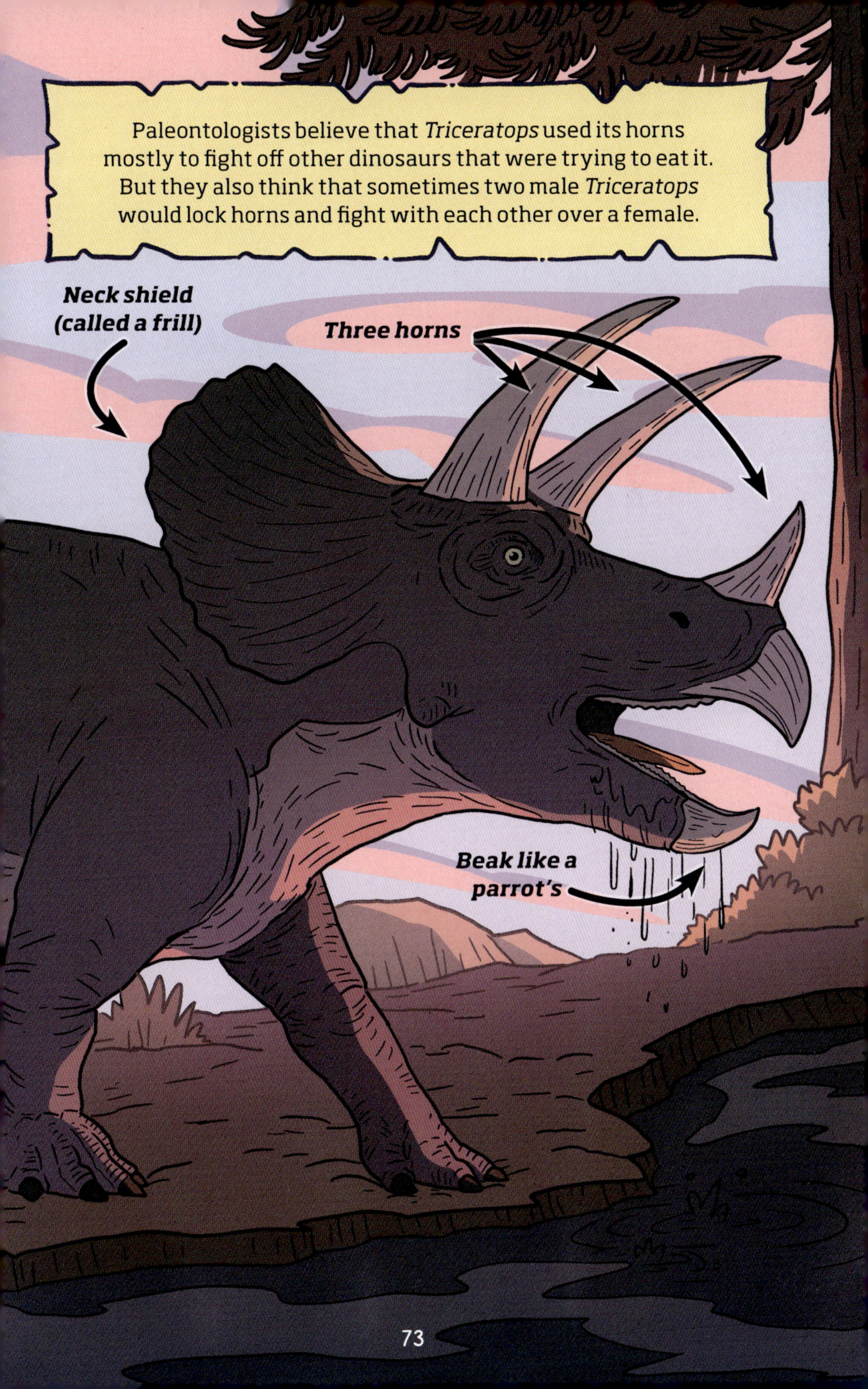
Paleontologists believe that *Triceratops* used its horns mostly to fight off other dinosaurs that were trying to eat it. But they also think that sometimes two male *Triceratops* would lock horns and fight with each other over a female.
Neck shield (called a frill)
Three horns
Beak like a parrot's

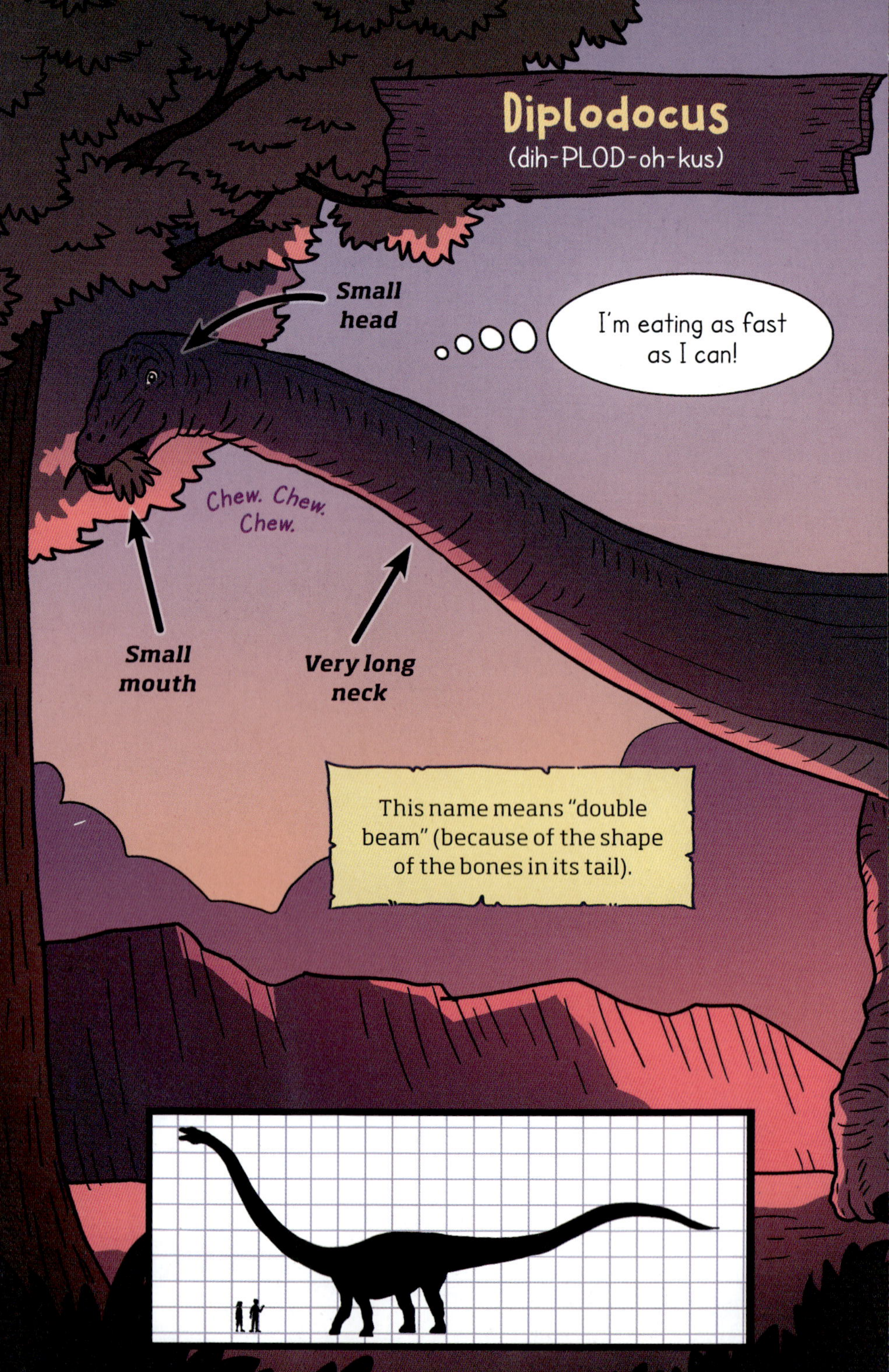

Diplodocus
(dih-PLOD-oh-kus)
Small head
I'm eating as fast as I can!
Chew. Chew. Chew.
Small mouth
Very long neck
This name means "double beam" (because of the shape of the bones in its tail).

Diplodocus was a long, skinny sauropod. It had a long tail and very strong legs.

Some paleontologists believe *Diplodocus* could balance on its back legs and its tail, then stretch up to eat from the very tops of trees.

Diplodocus ate almost all of the time! Its mouth was so small compared with its body that it had to take hundreds of bites to make a meal.

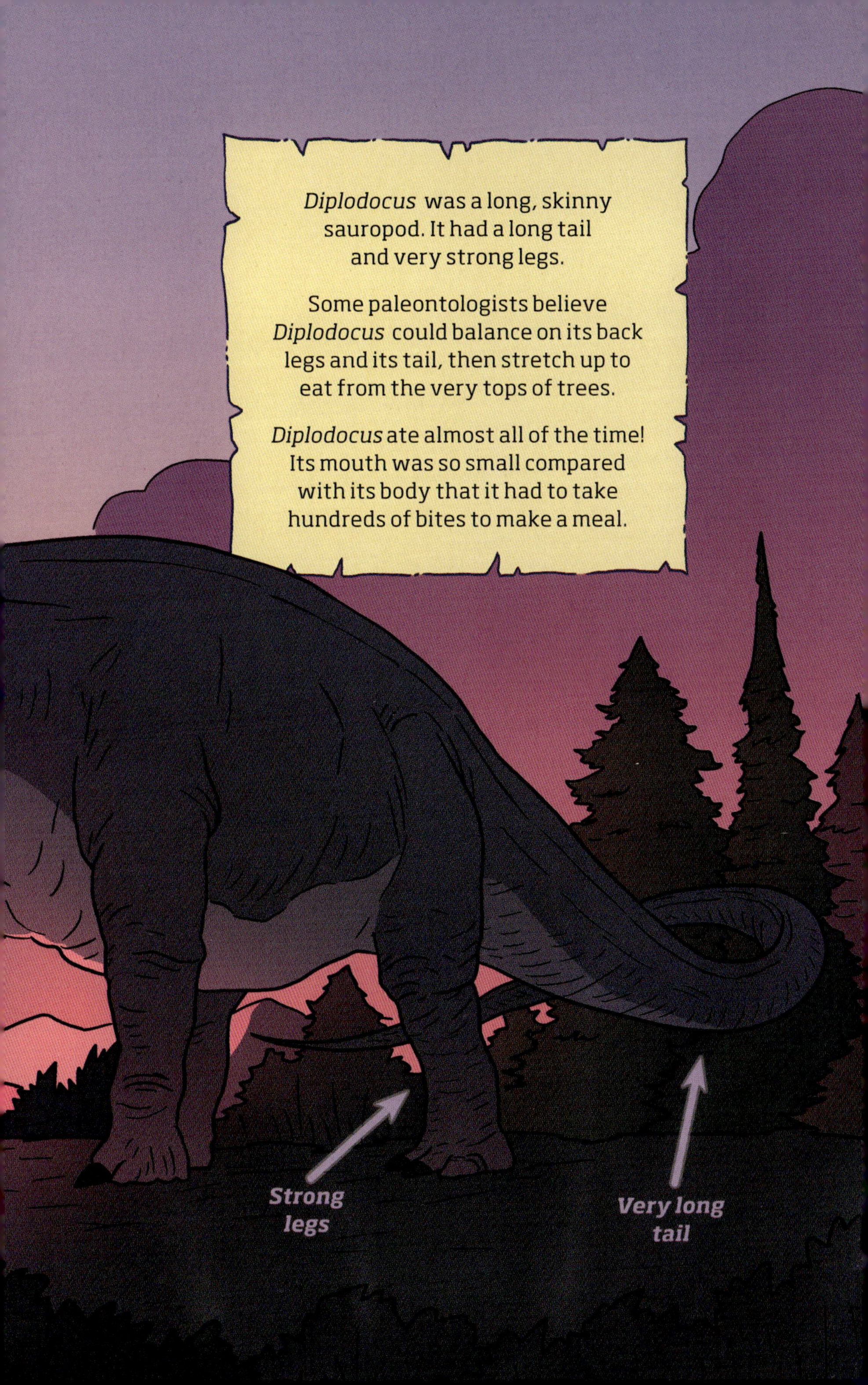
Strong legs
Very long tail

Brachiosaurus

(BRACK-ee-uh-SOAR-us)

This name means "arm lizard" (named for its long front legs).

Brachiosaurus looked a little bit like a giraffe.

It had a very long neck and a small head. It had front legs that were longer than its back legs. But *Brachiosaurus* was twice as tall as a giraffe.

And its nostrils were on the top of its head!

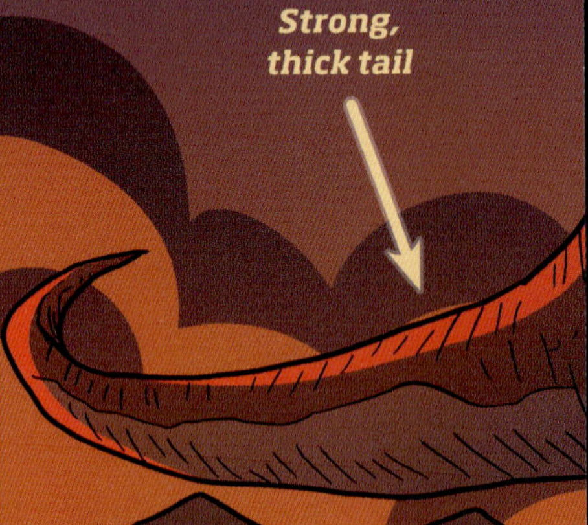
Strong, thick tail

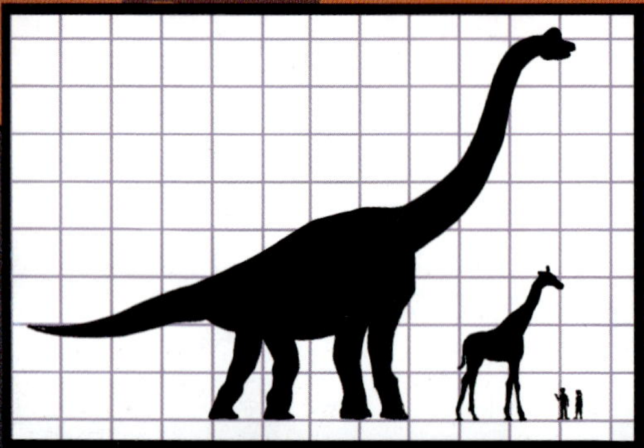

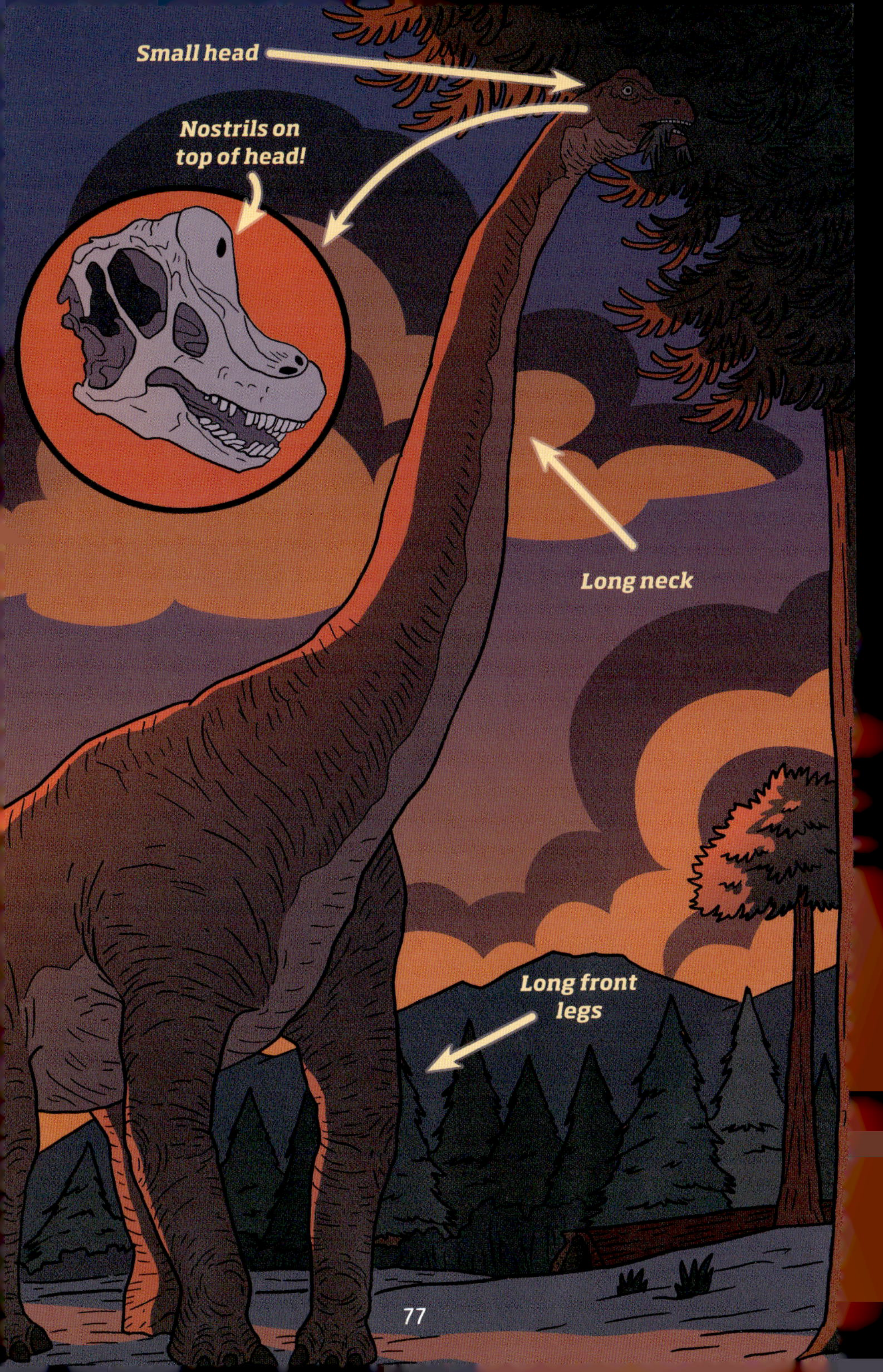
Small head
Nostrils on top of head!
Long neck
Long front legs

CHAPTER SIX

Sea Monsters and Flying Creatures

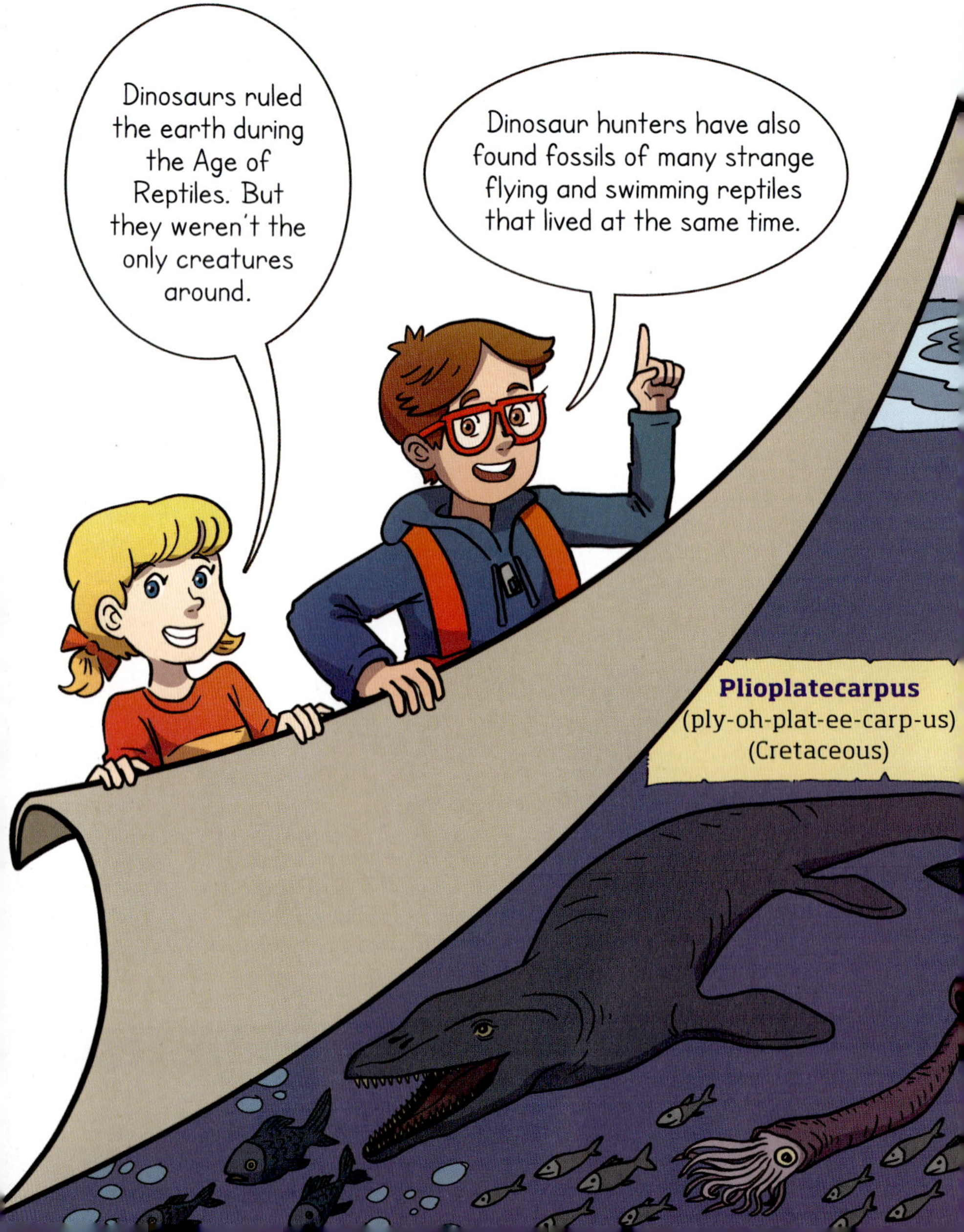
Dinosaurs ruled the earth during the Age of Reptiles. But they weren't the only creatures around.
Dinosaur hunters have also found fossils of many strange flying and swimming reptiles that lived at the same time.
Plioplatecarpus
(ply-oh-plat-ee-carp-us)
(Cretaceous)

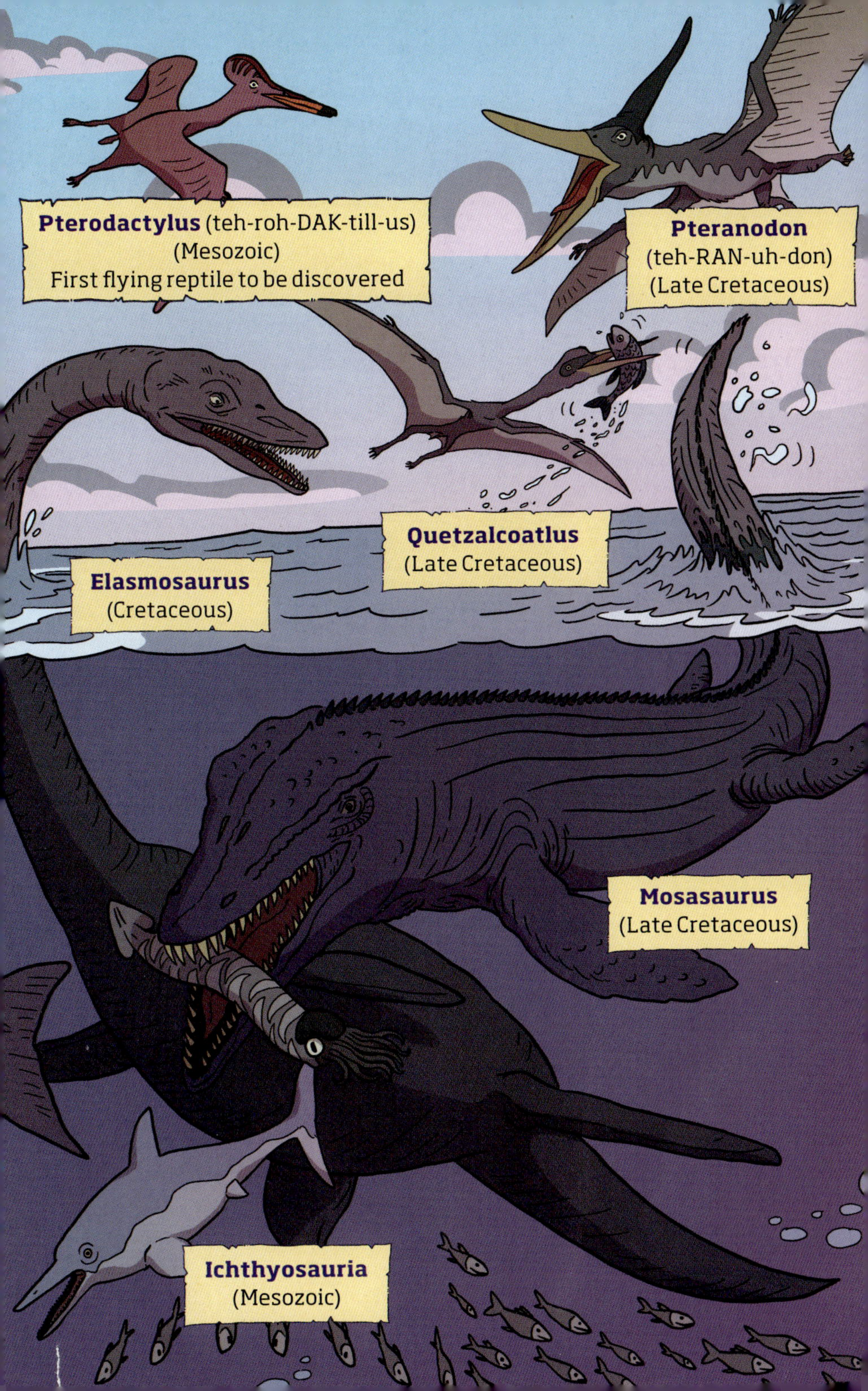
Pterodactylus (teh-roh-DAK-till-us)
(Mesozoic)
First flying reptile to be discovered
Pteranodon
(teh-RAN-uh-don)
(Late Cretaceous)
Quetzalcoatlus
(Late Cretaceous)
Elasmosaurus
(Cretaceous)
Mosasaurus
(Late Cretaceous)
Ichthyosauria
(Mesozoic)

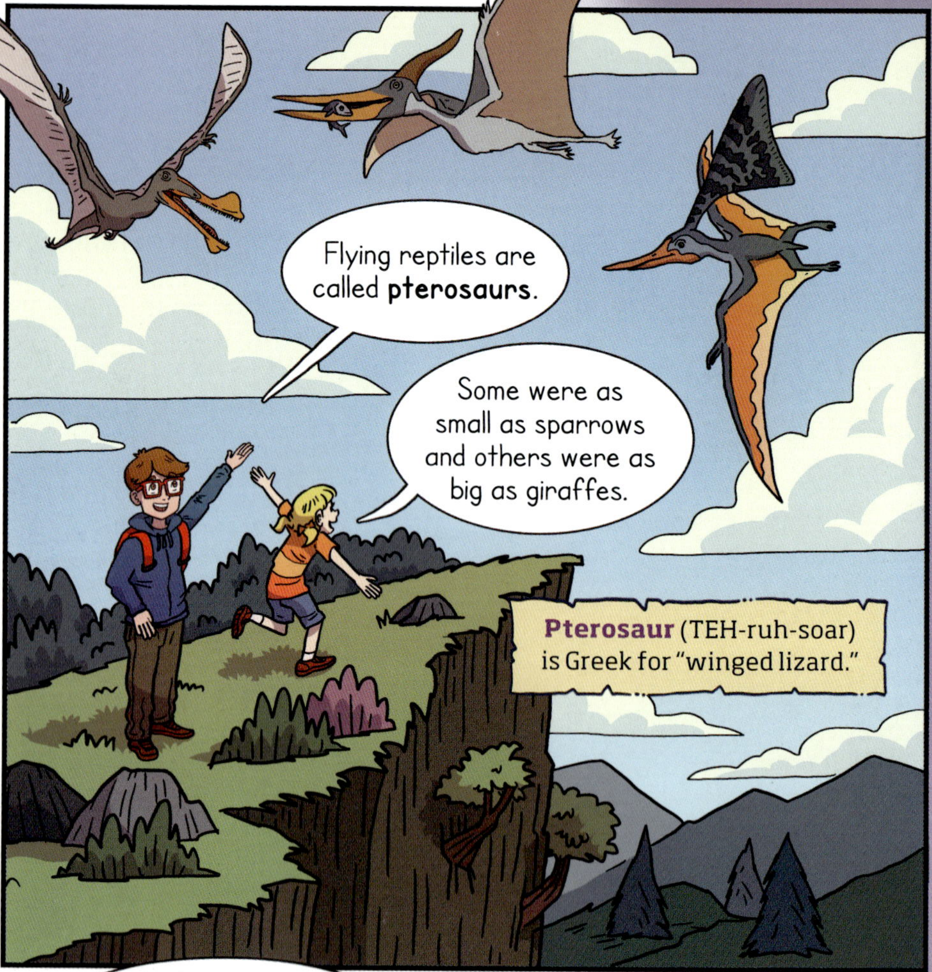

Flying reptiles are called **pterosaurs**.
Some were as small as sparrows and others were as big as giraffes.
Pterosaur (TEH-ruh-soar) is Greek for "winged lizard."

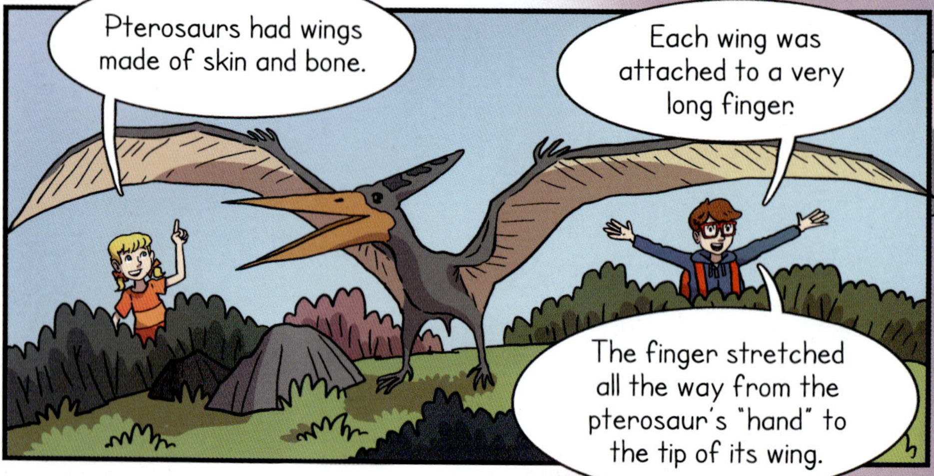

Pterosaurs had wings made of skin and bone.
Each wing was attached to a very long finger.
The finger stretched all the way from the pterosaur's "hand" to the tip of its wing.

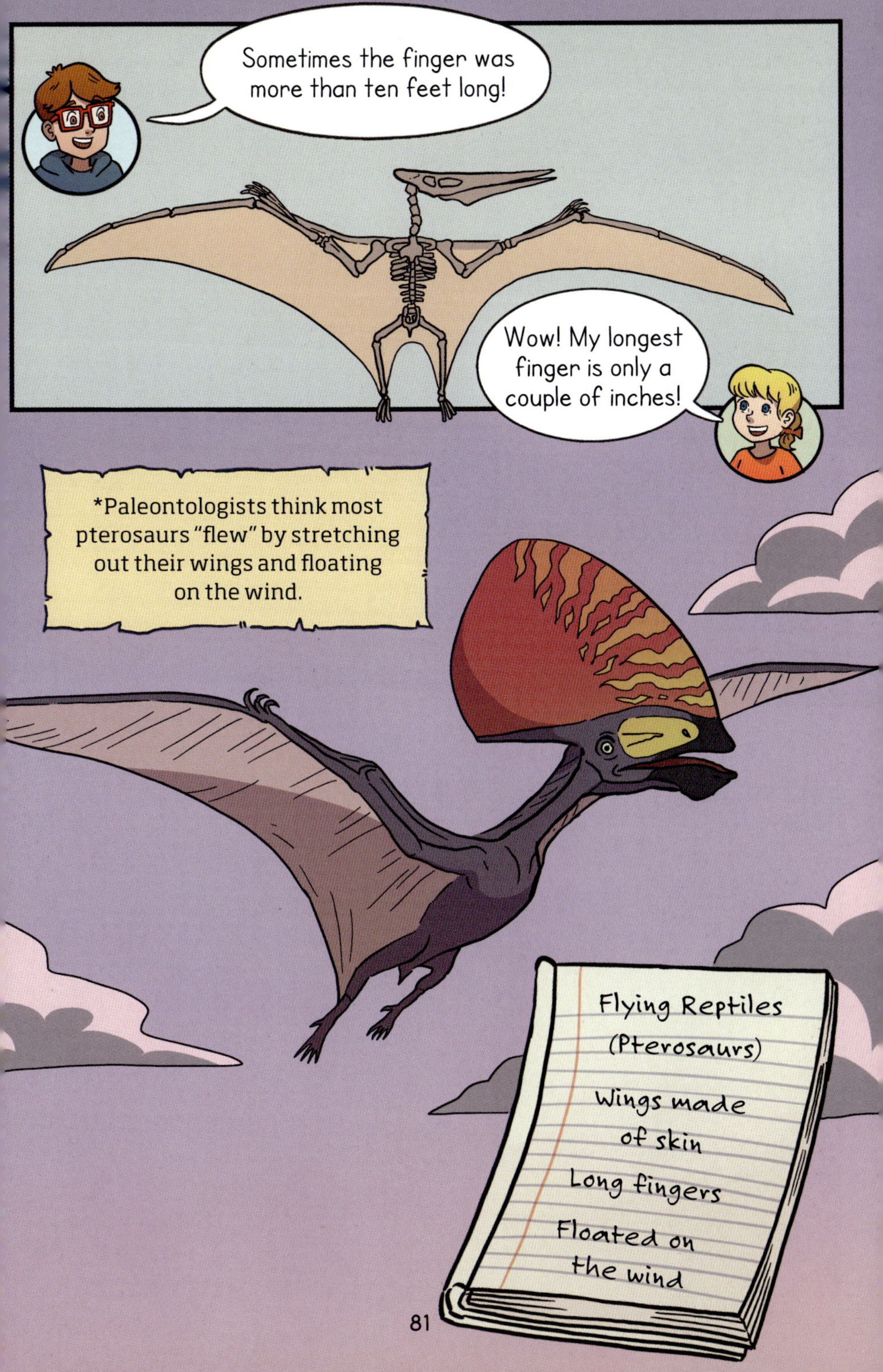
Sometimes the finger was more than ten feet long!
Wow! My longest finger is only a couple of inches!
*Paleontologists think most pterosaurs "flew" by stretching out their wings and floating on the wind.
Flying Reptiles (Pterosaurs)
Wings made of skin
Long fingers
Floated on the wind

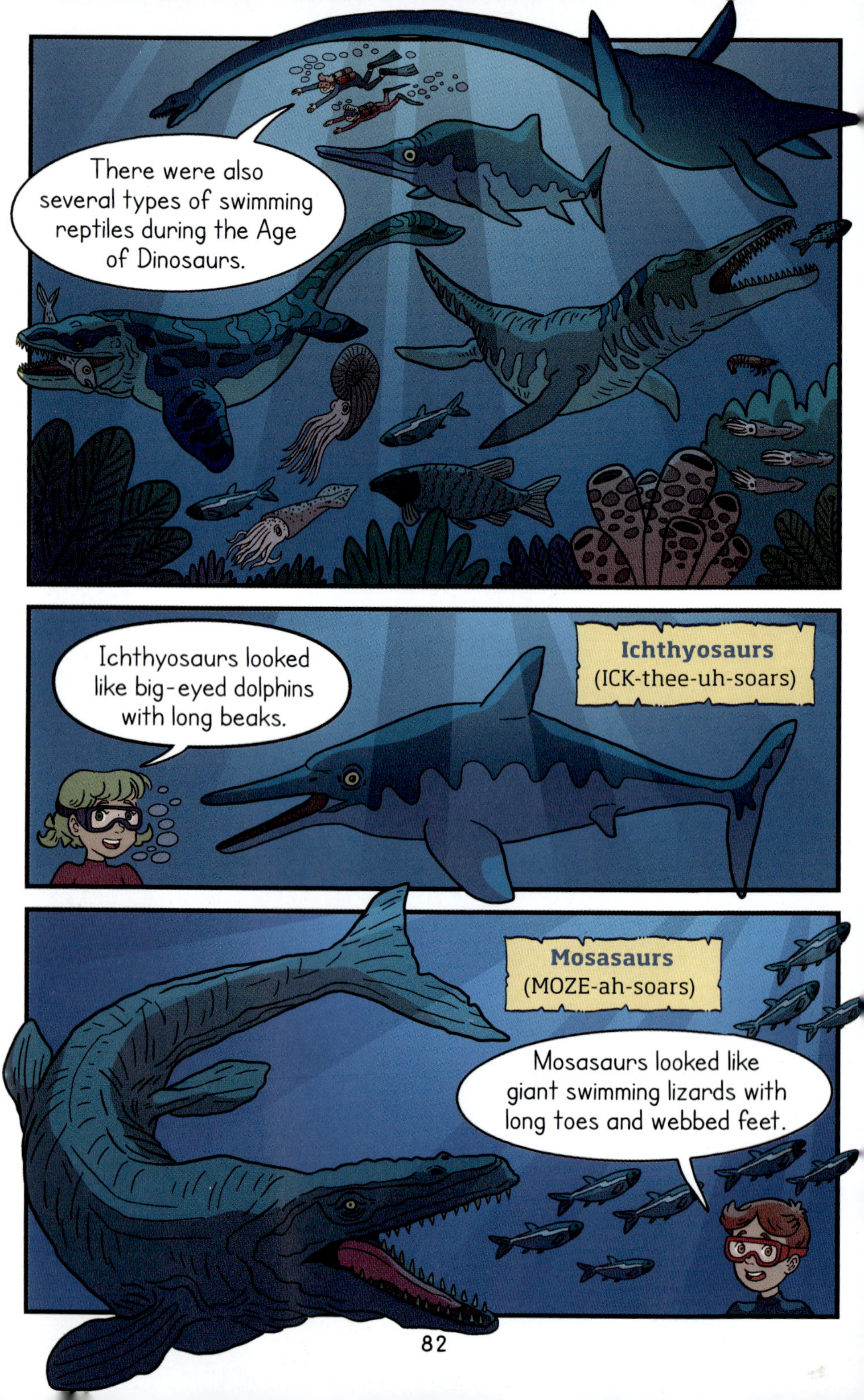
There were also several types of swimming reptiles during the Age of Dinosaurs.
Ichthyosaurs looked like big-eyed dolphins with long beaks.
Ichthyosaurs
(ICK-thee-uh-soars)
Mosasaurs
(MOZE-ah-soars)
Mosasaurs looked like giant swimming lizards with long toes and webbed feet.

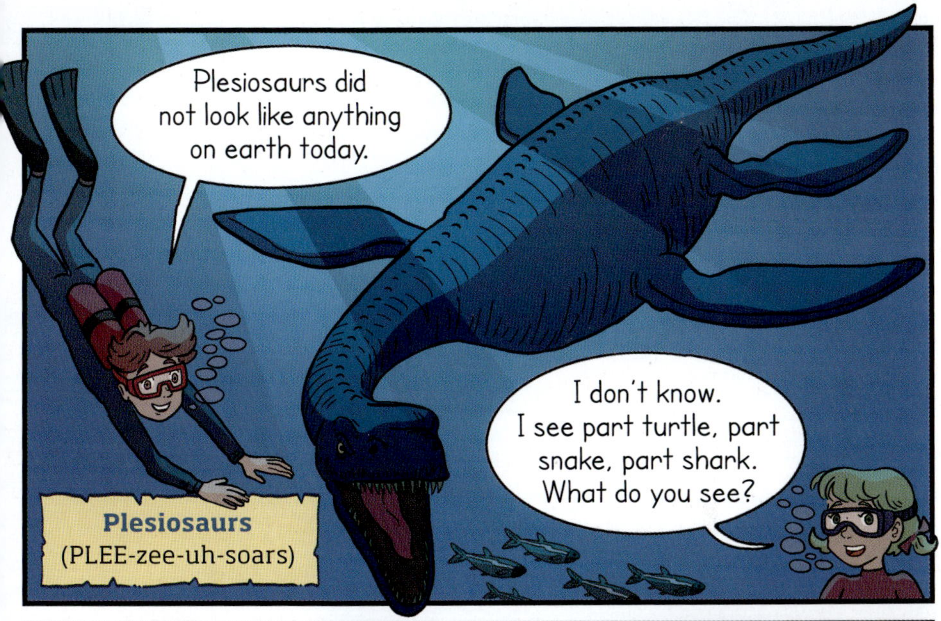
Plesiosaurs did not look like anything on earth today.
I don't know. I see part turtle, part snake, part shark. What do you see?
Plesiosaurs
(PLEE-zee-uh-soars)

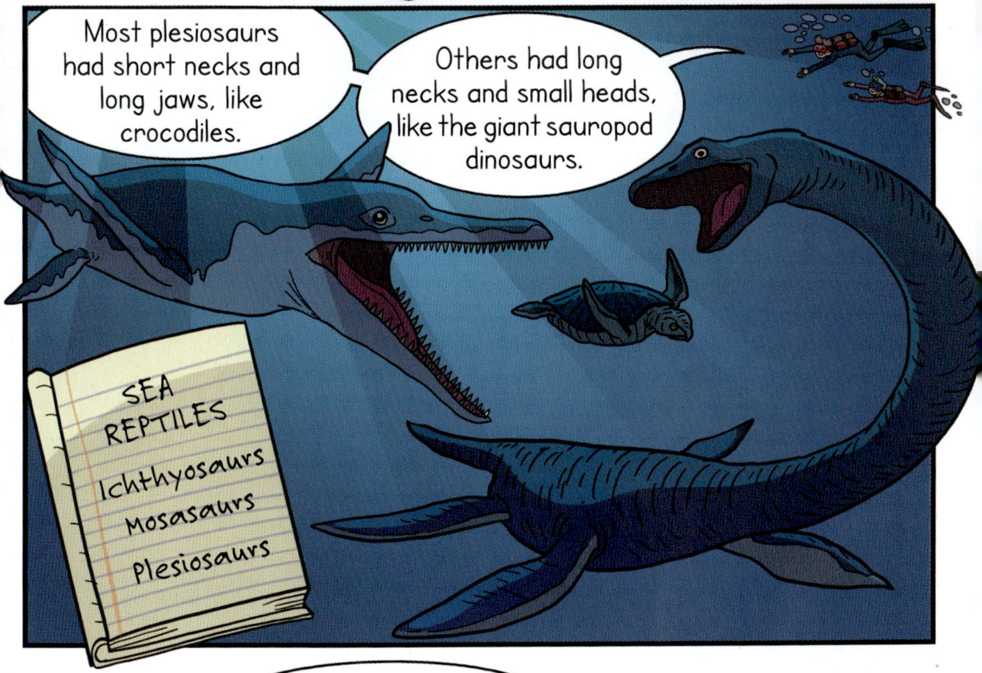
Most plesiosaurs had short necks and long jaws, like crocodiles.
Others had long necks and small heads, like the giant sauropod dinosaurs.
SEA REPTILES
Ichthyosaurs
Mosasaurs
Plesiosaurs

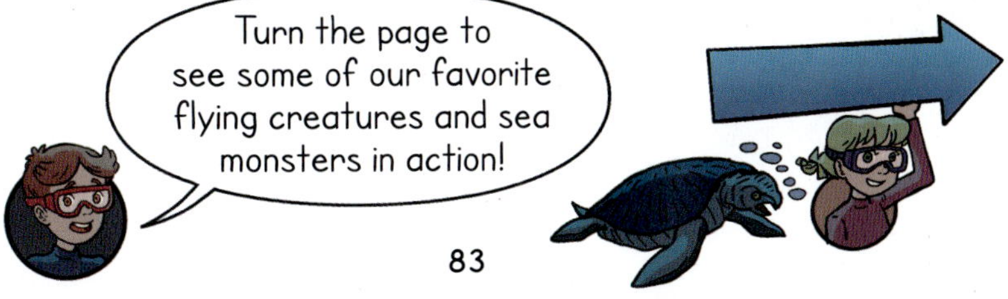
Turn the page to see some of our favorite flying creatures and sea monsters in action!

Flying Creatures

Pteranodon

(teh-RAN-uh-don)

This name means "toothless flier."

Pteranodon had a long beak and a long, bony crest on the back of its head.

It probably needed the crest to help balance its beak when it was swooping down to catch fish.

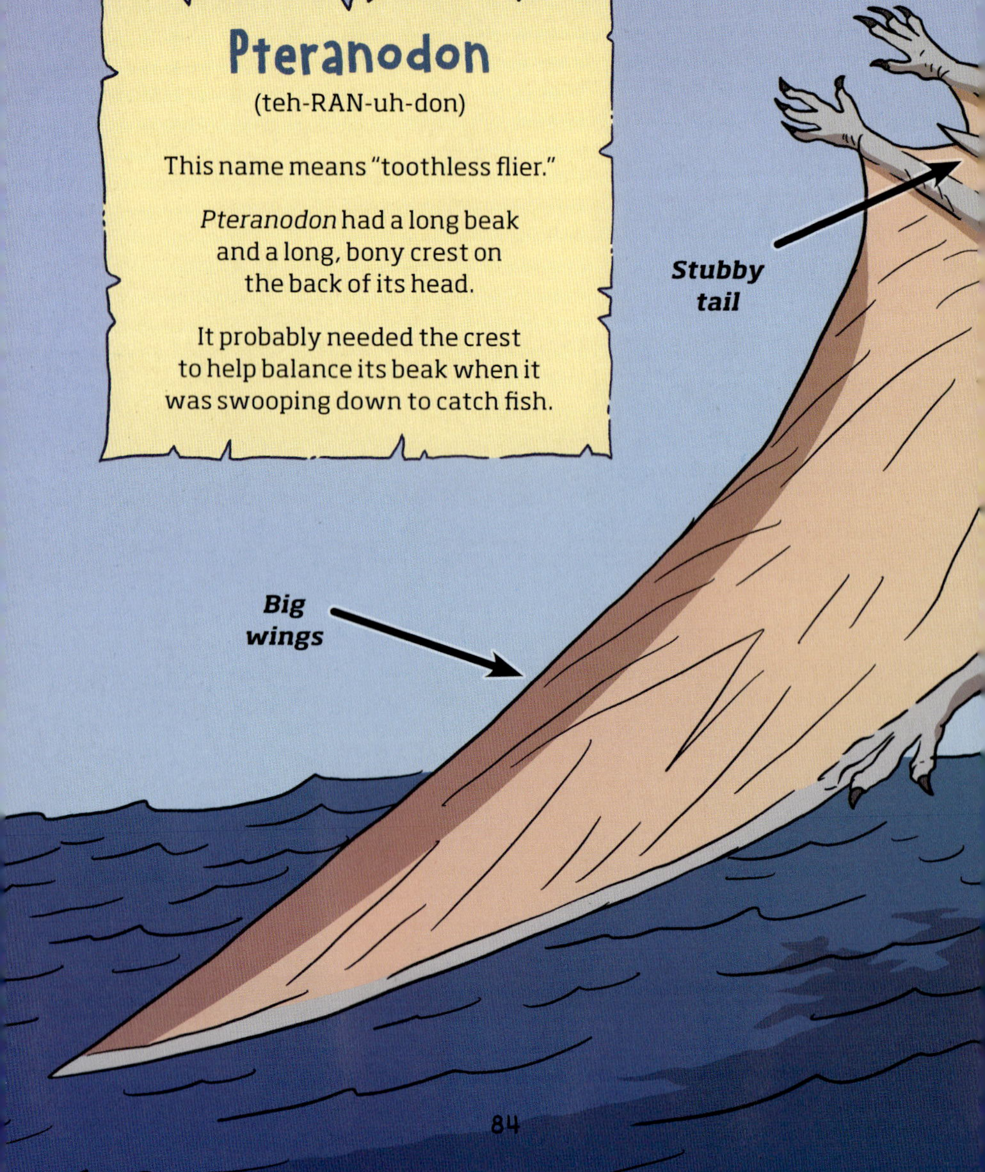

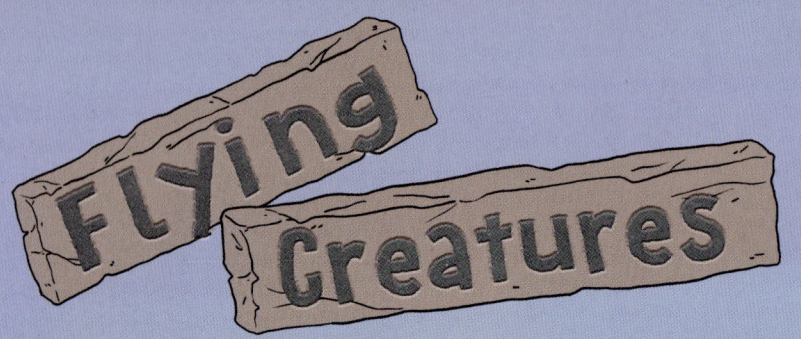

Stubby tail
Big wings

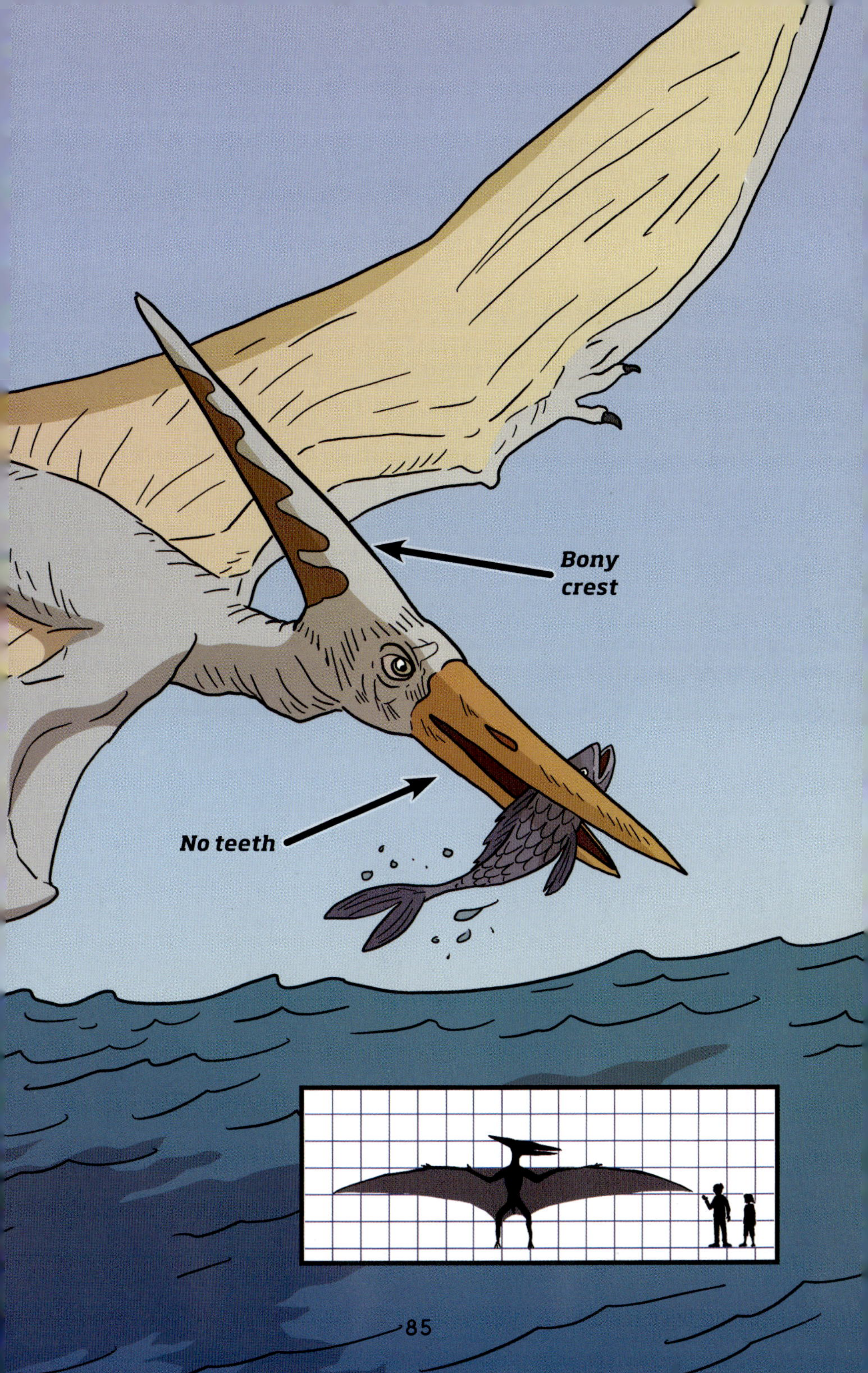
Bony
crest
No teeth

Quetzalcoatlus

(KET-sal-ko-AHT-lus)

This name means "plumed serpent."

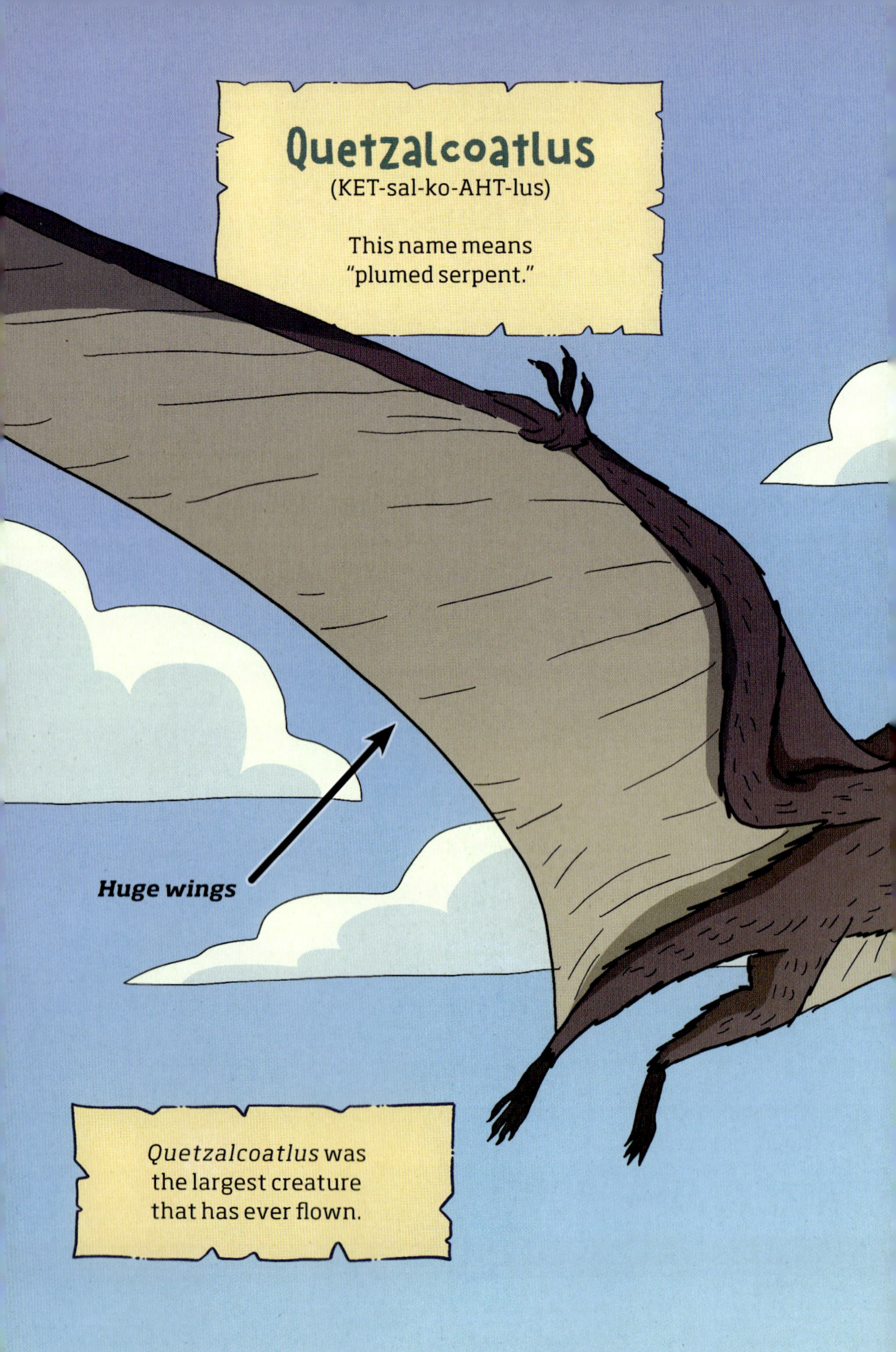
Huge wings

Quetzalcoatlus was the largest creature that has ever flown.

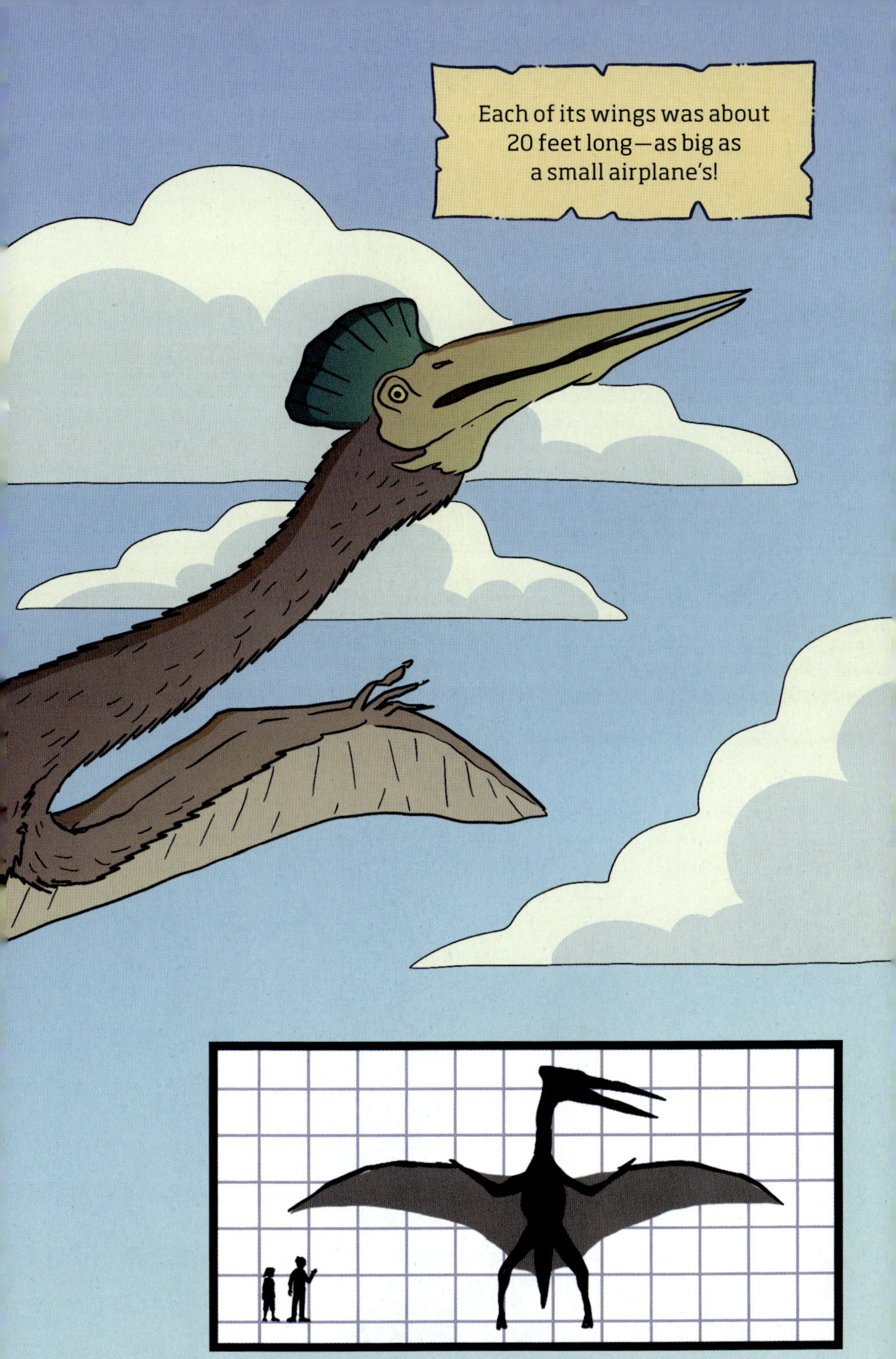
Each of its wings was about 20 feet long—as big as a small airplane's!

Swimming Creatures

Ophthalmosaurus

(ahf-THAL-muh-SOAR-us)

This name means "eye lizard."

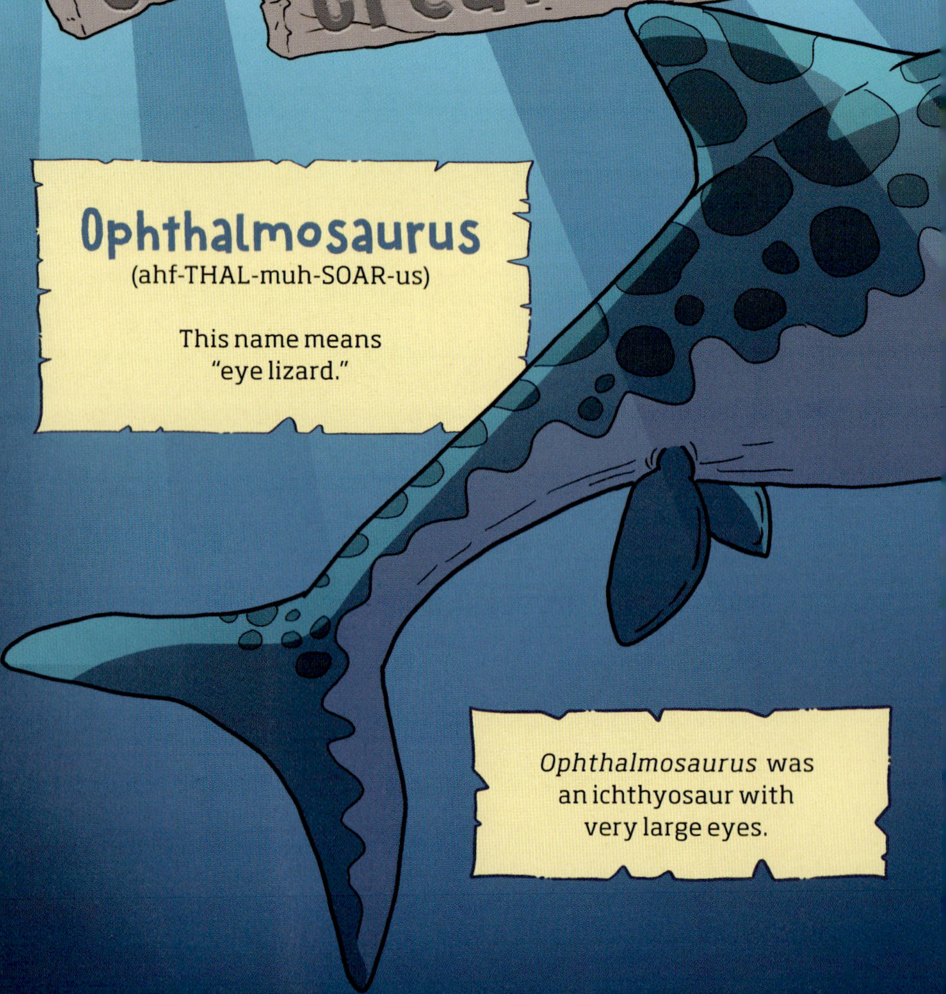

Ophthalmosaurus was an ichthyosaur with very large eyes.

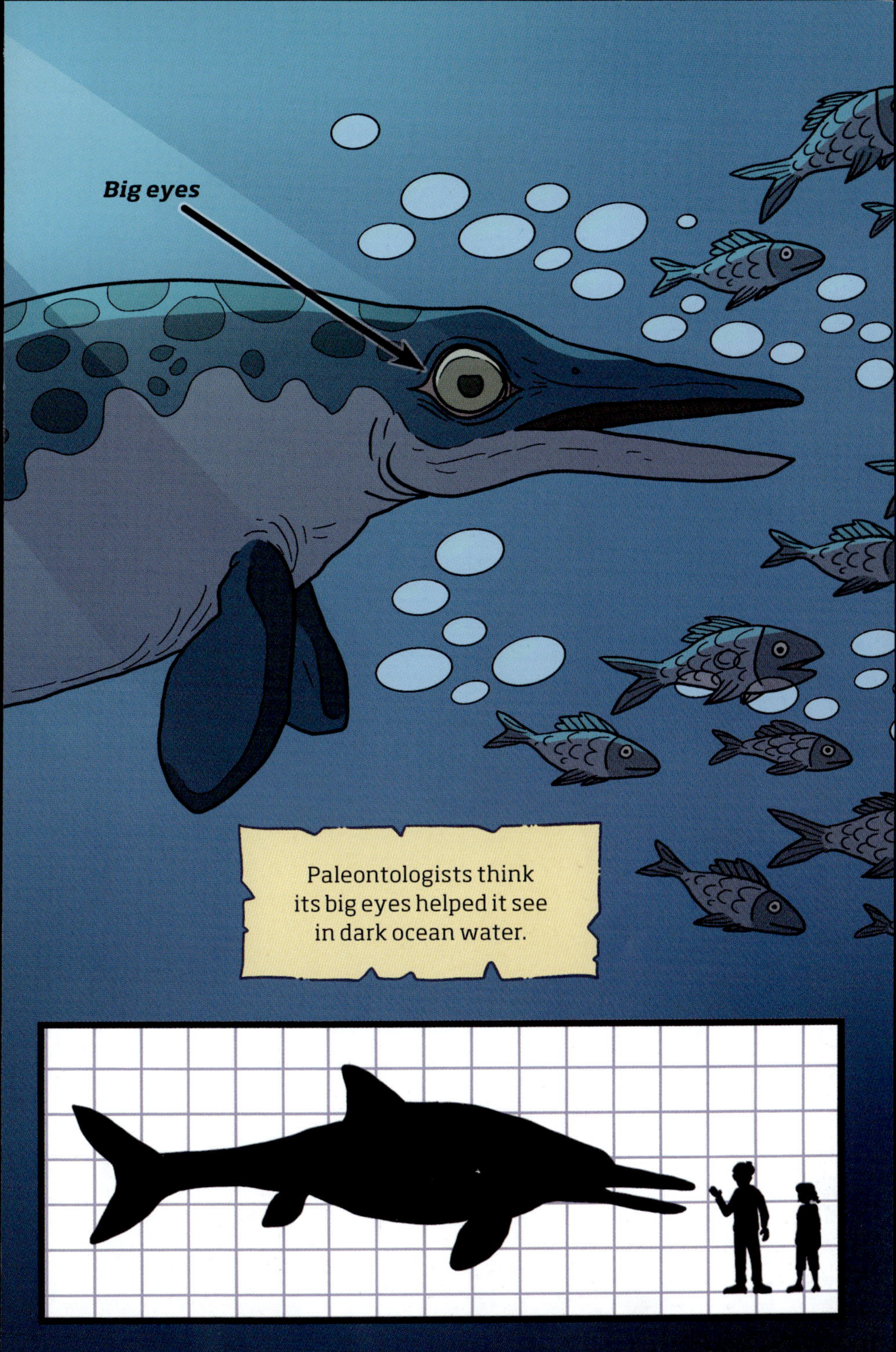
Big eyes
Paleontologists think its big eyes helped it see in dark ocean water.

Elasmosaurus

(ee-LAZ-muh-SOAR-us)

This name means "plated lizard."

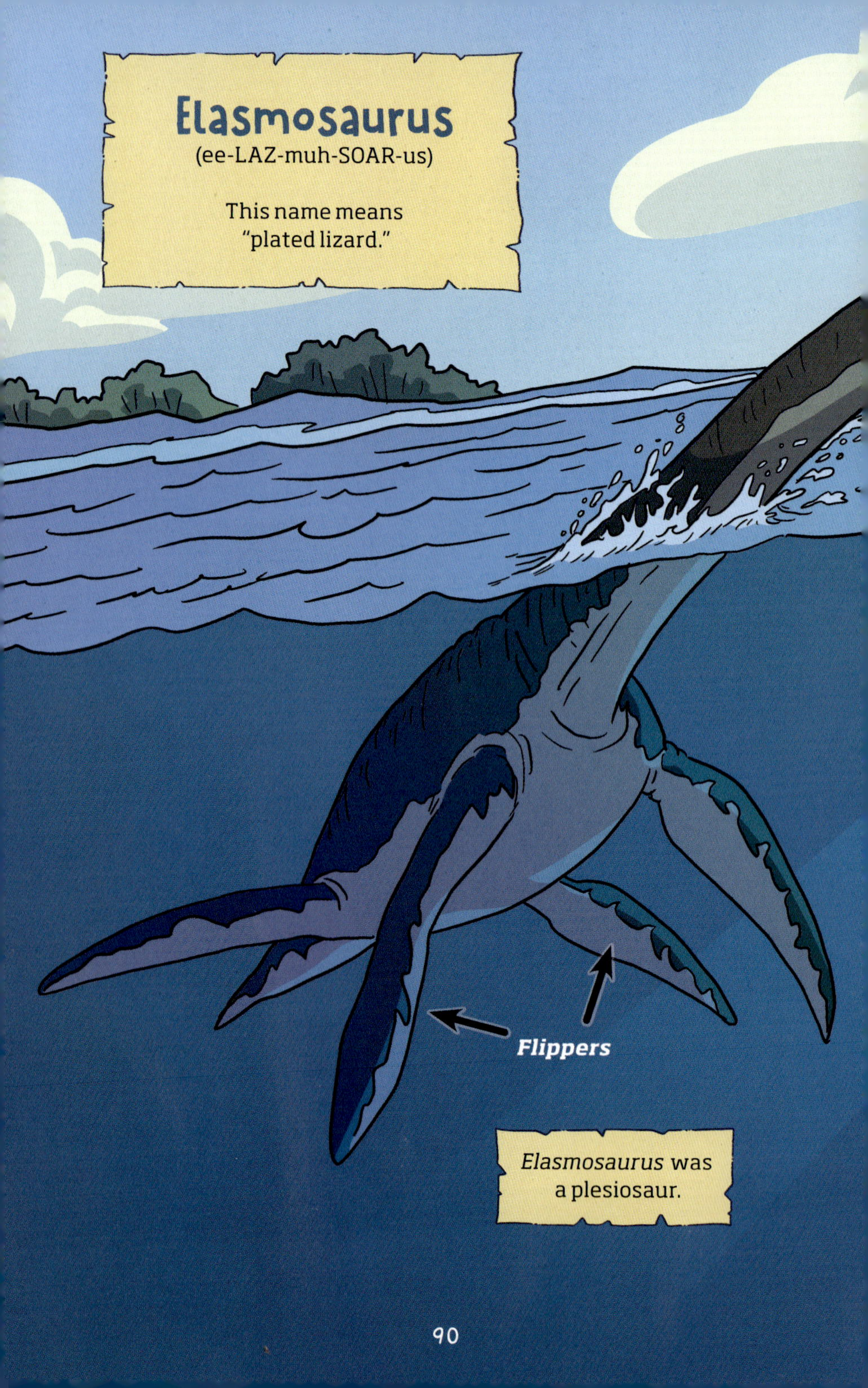
Flippers

Elasmosaurus was a plesiosaur.

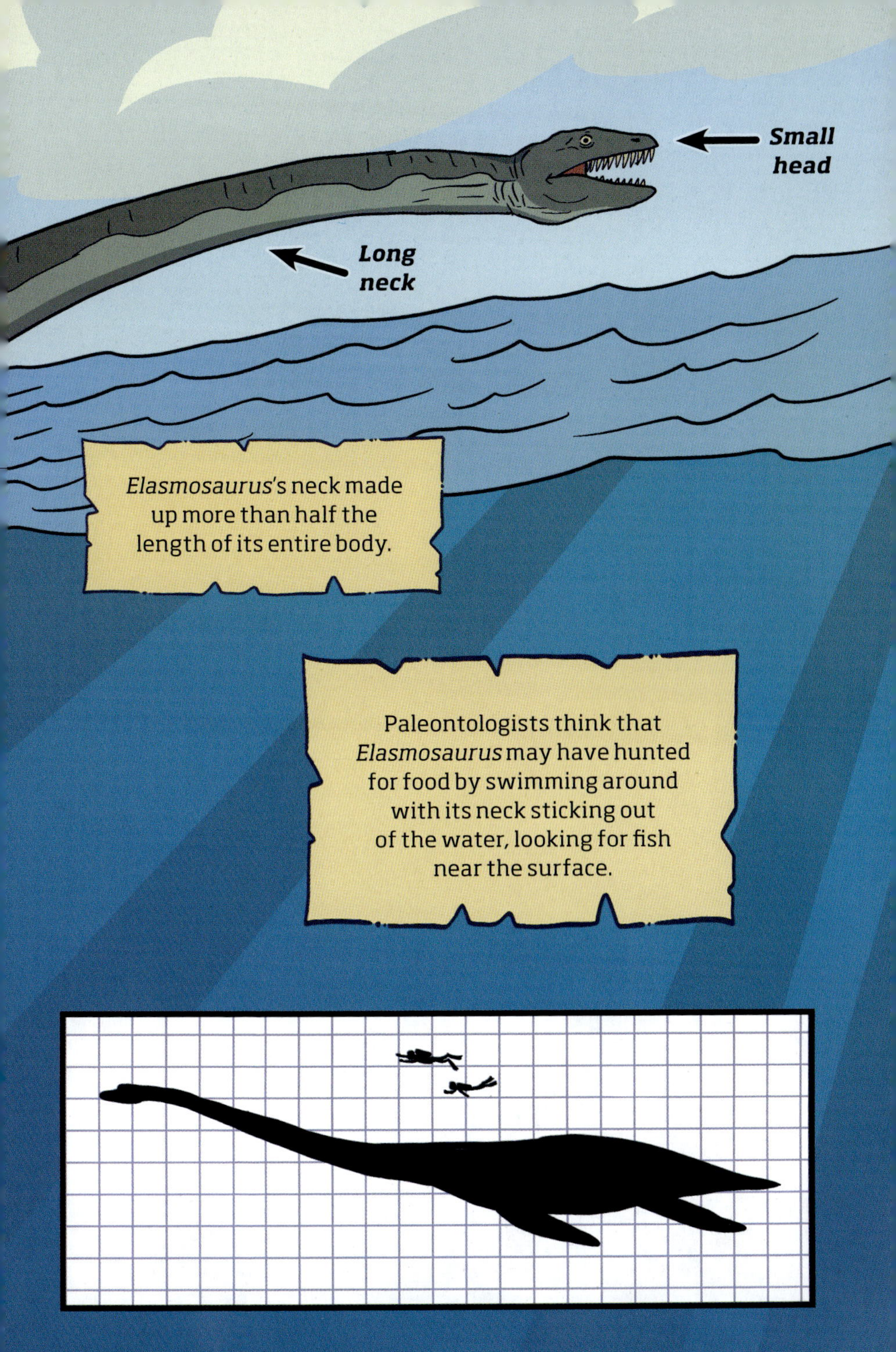
Small head
Long neck
Elasmosaurus's neck made up more than half the length of its entire body.
Paleontologists think that *Elasmosaurus* may have hunted for food by swimming around with its neck sticking out of the water, looking for fish near the surface.

CHAPTER SEVEN

What Happened to the Dinosaurs?

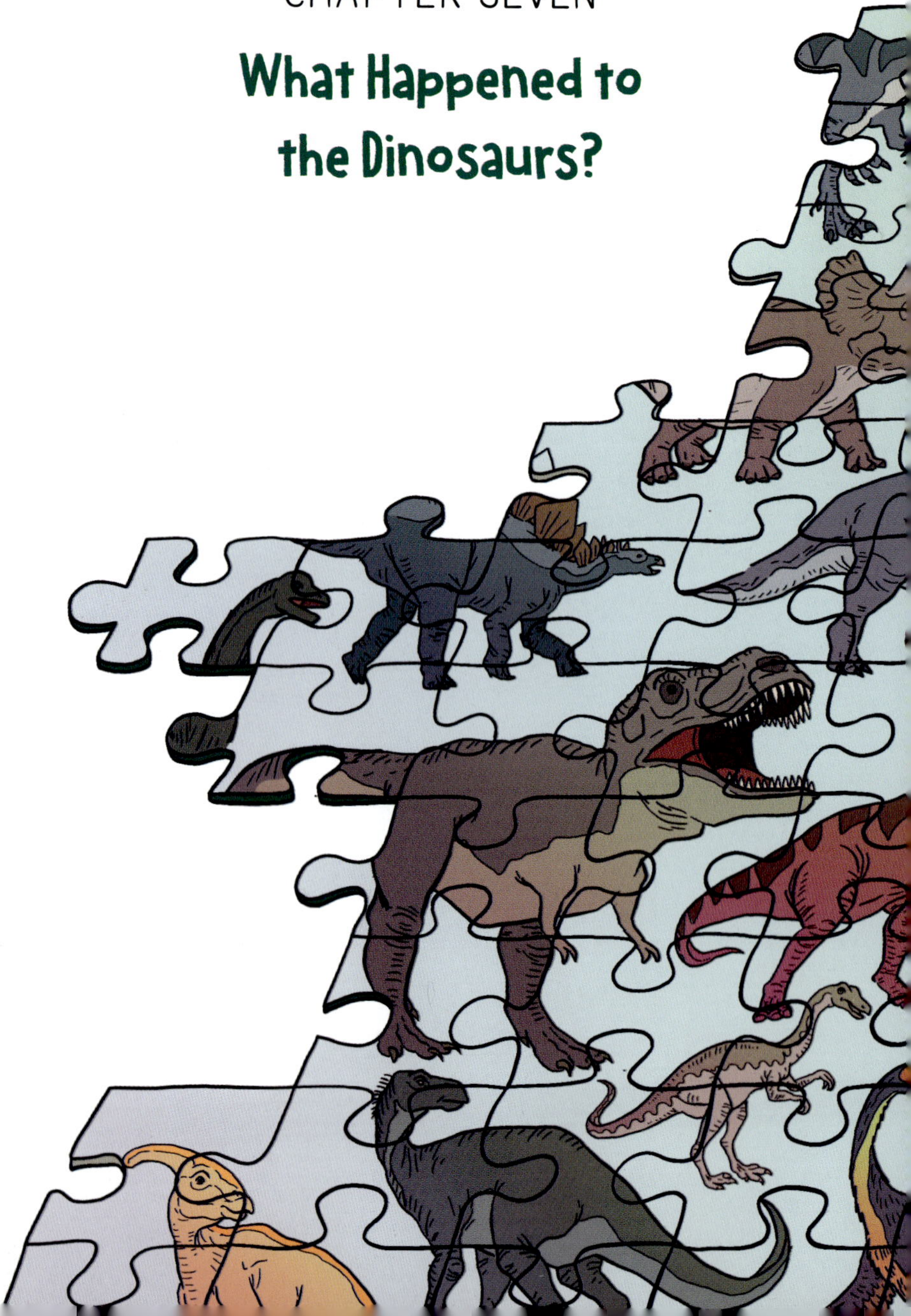

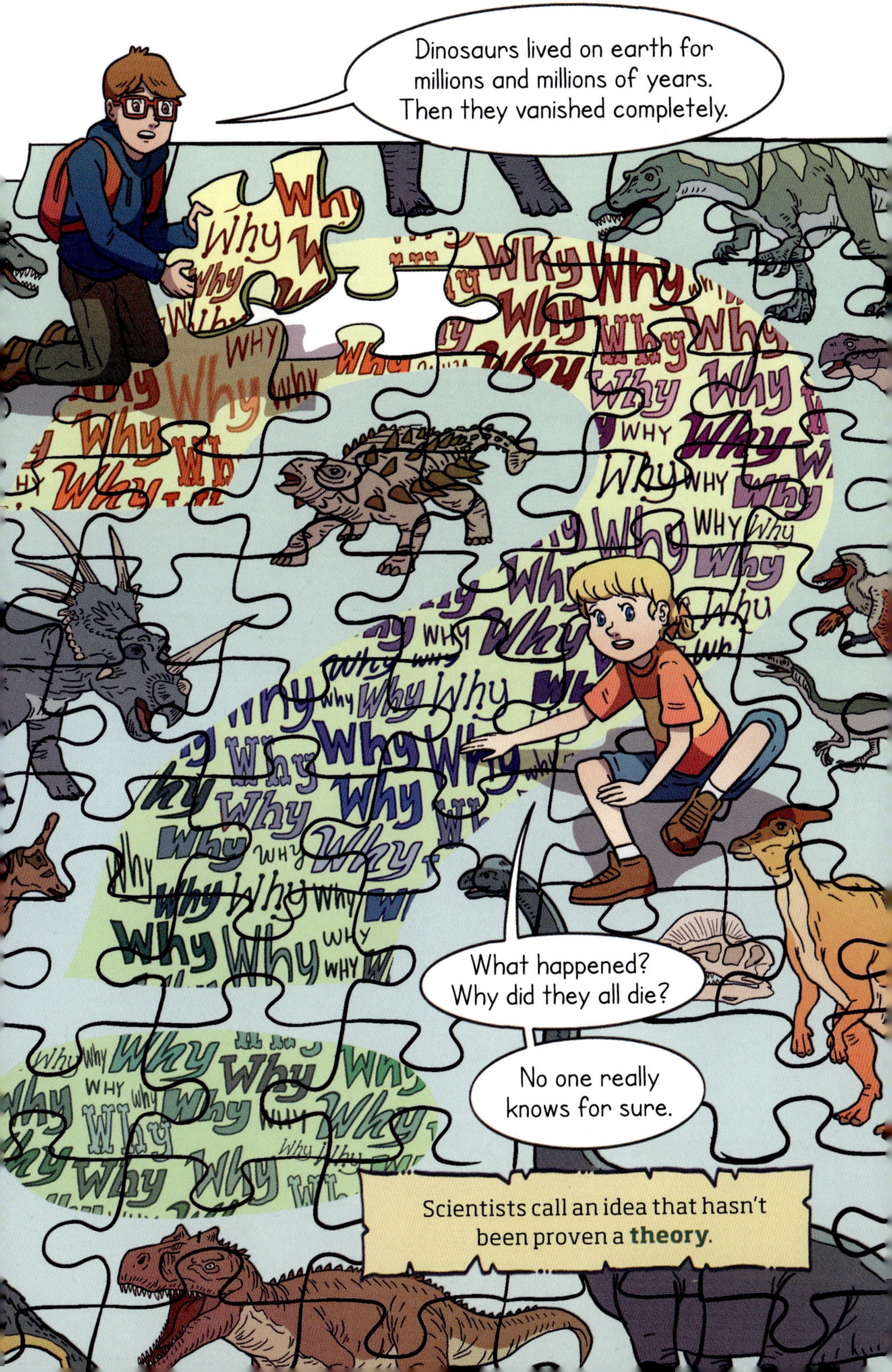
Dinosaurs lived on earth for millions and millions of years. Then they vanished completely.
What happened? Why did they all die?
No one really knows for sure.
Scientists call an idea that hasn't been proven a **theory**.

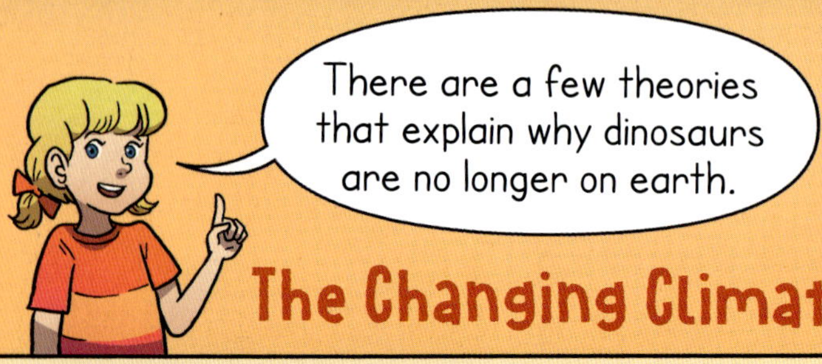
There are a few theories that explain why dinosaurs are no longer on earth.

The Changing Climate Theory

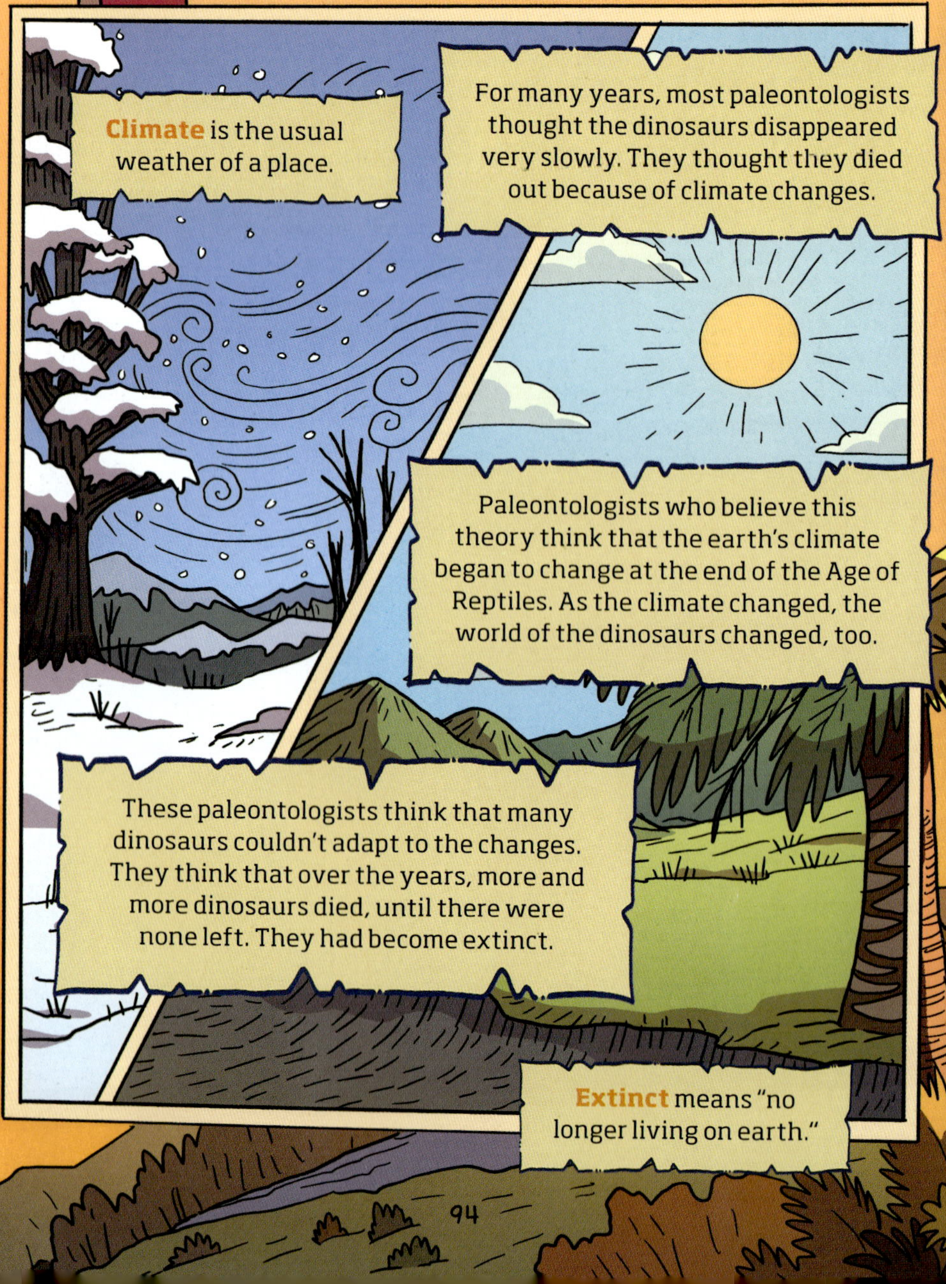

Climate is the usual weather of a place.

For many years, most paleontologists thought the dinosaurs disappeared very slowly. They thought they died out because of climate changes.

Paleontologists who believe this theory think that the earth's climate began to change at the end of the Age of Reptiles. As the climate changed, the world of the dinosaurs changed, too.

These paleontologists think that many dinosaurs couldn't adapt to the changes. They think that over the years, more and more dinosaurs died, until there were none left. They had become extinct.

Extinct means "no longer living on earth."

The Asteroid Theory

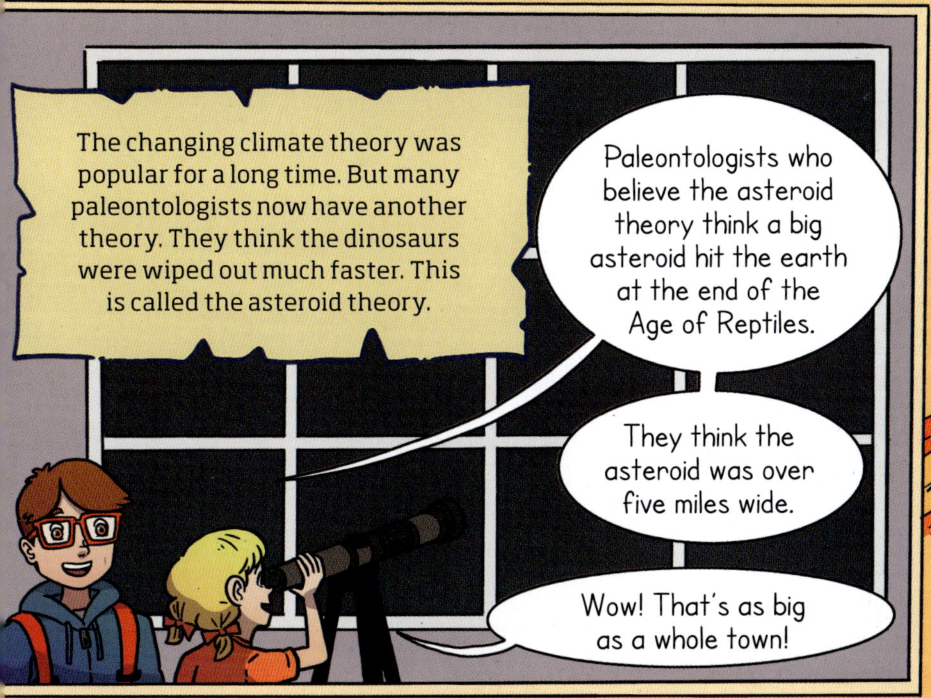

The changing climate theory was popular for a long time. But many paleontologists now have another theory. They think the dinosaurs were wiped out much faster. This is called the asteroid theory.
Paleontologists who believe the asteroid theory think a big asteroid hit the earth at the end of the Age of Reptiles.
They think the asteroid was over five miles wide.
Wow! That's as big as a whole town!

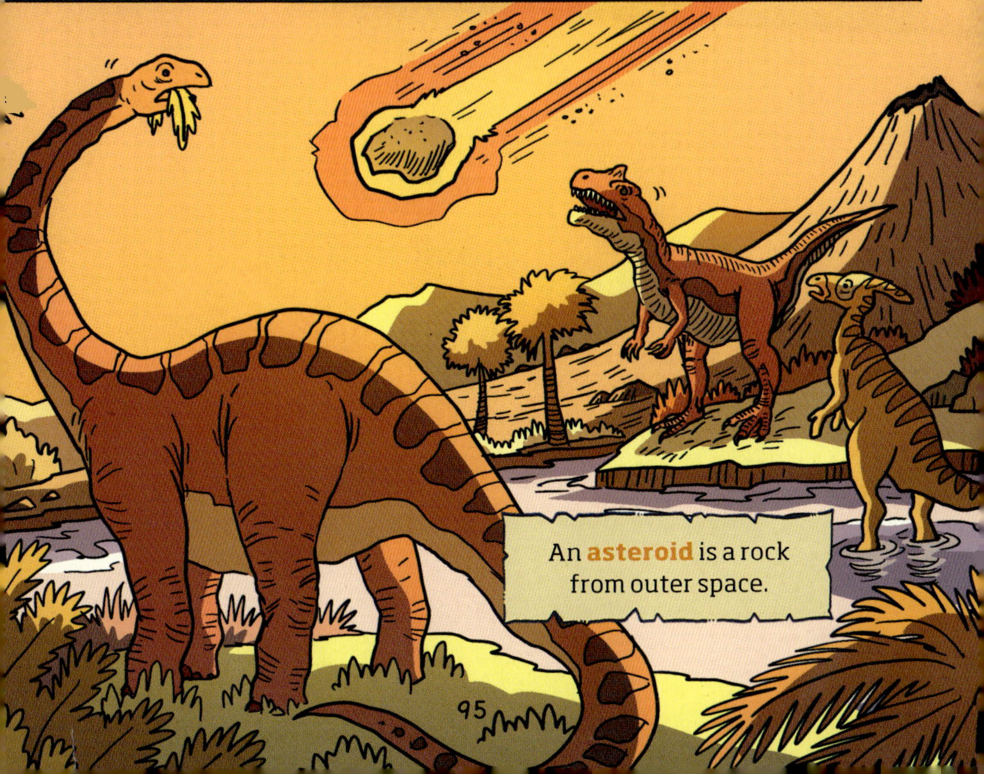

An **asteroid** is a rock from outer space.

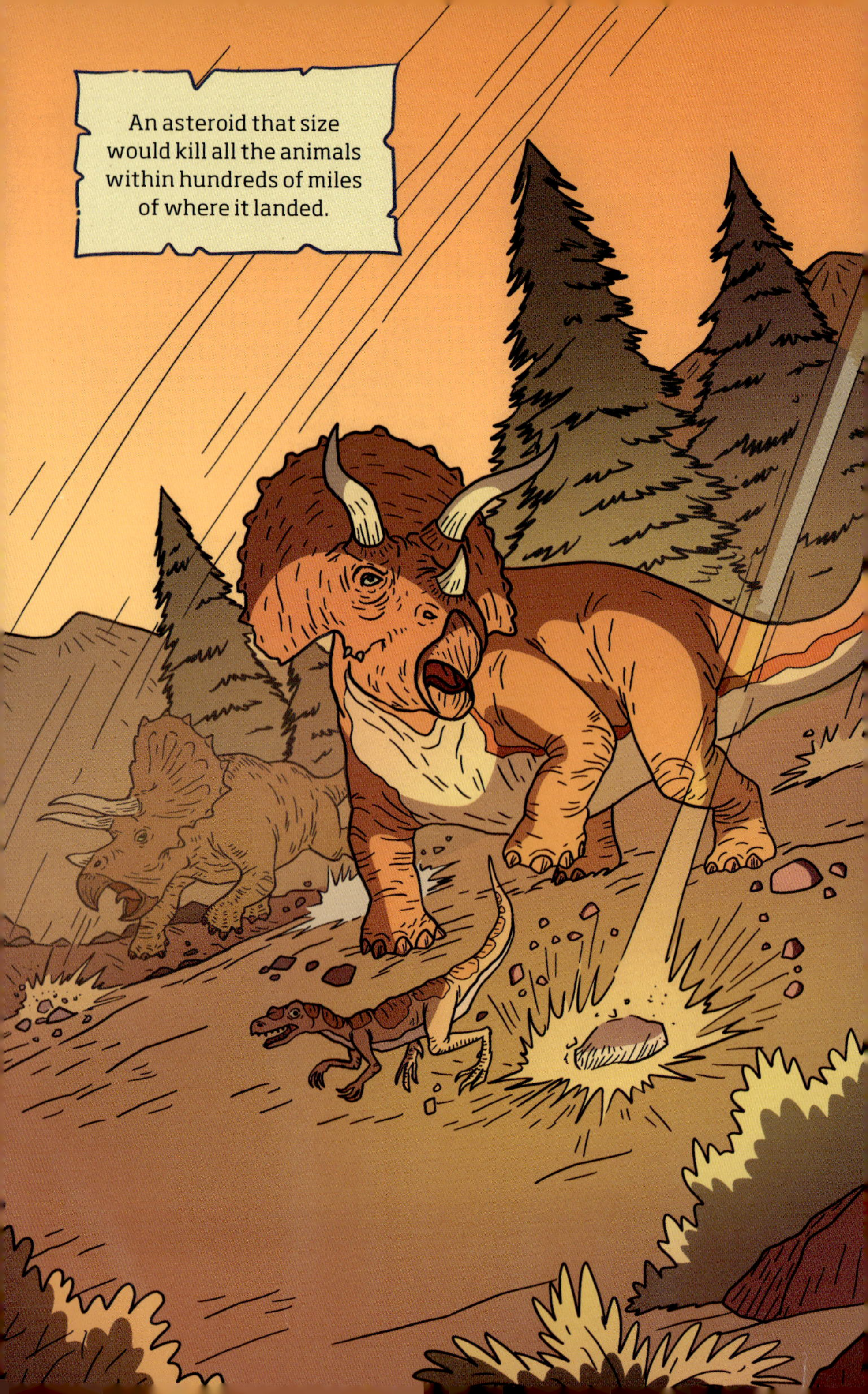
An asteroid that size would kill all the animals within hundreds of miles of where it landed.

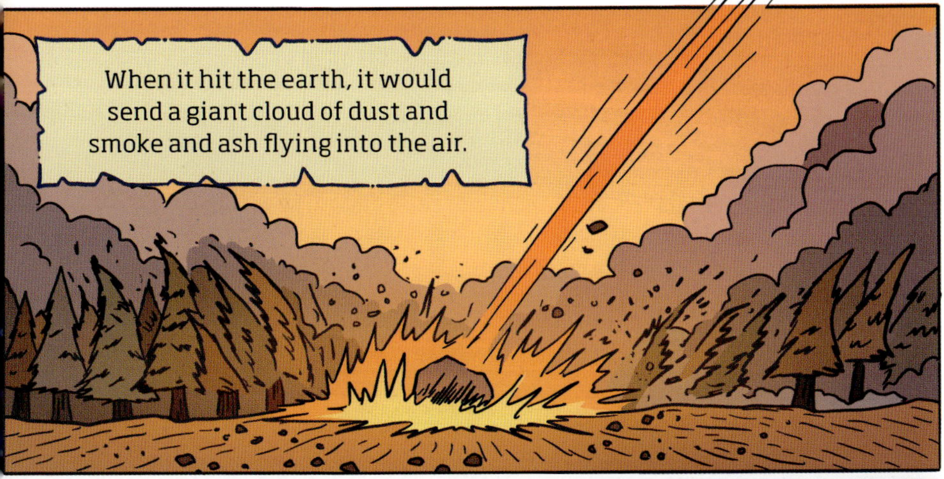
When it hit the earth, it would send a giant cloud of dust and smoke and ash flying into the air.

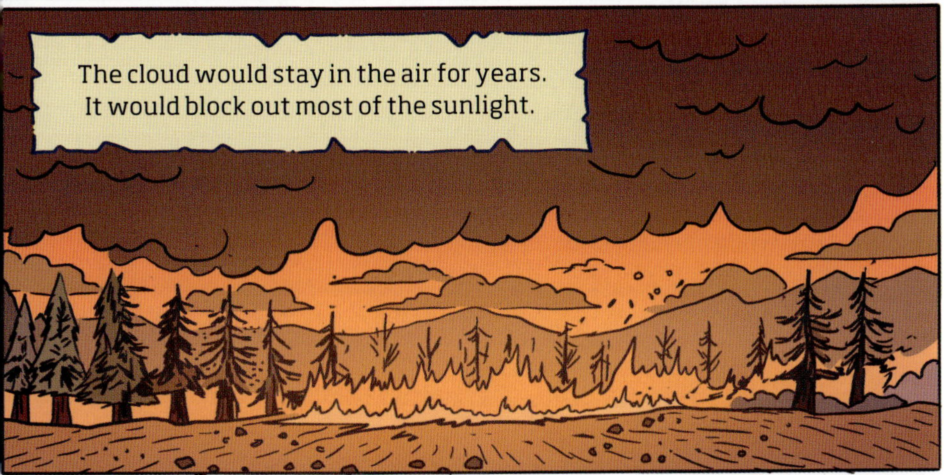
The cloud would stay in the air for years. It would block out most of the sunlight.

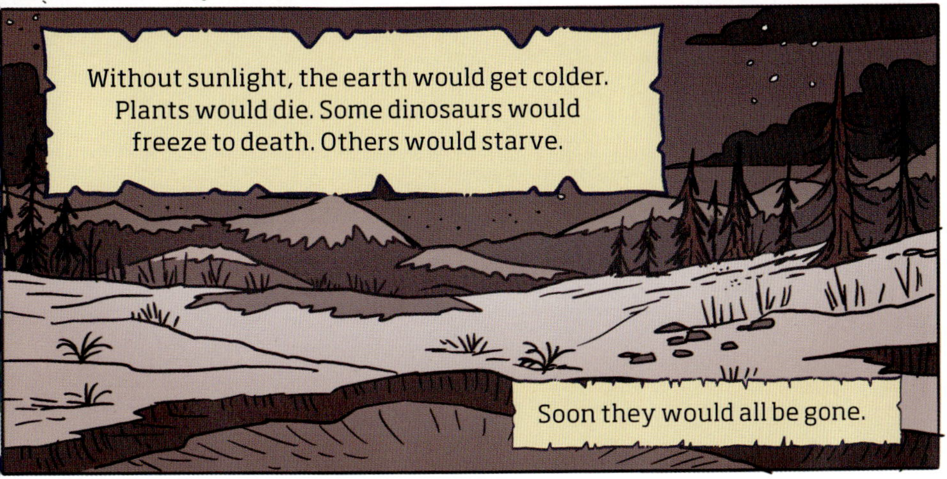
Without sunlight, the earth would get colder. Plants would die. Some dinosaurs would freeze to death. Others would starve.
Soon they would all be gone.

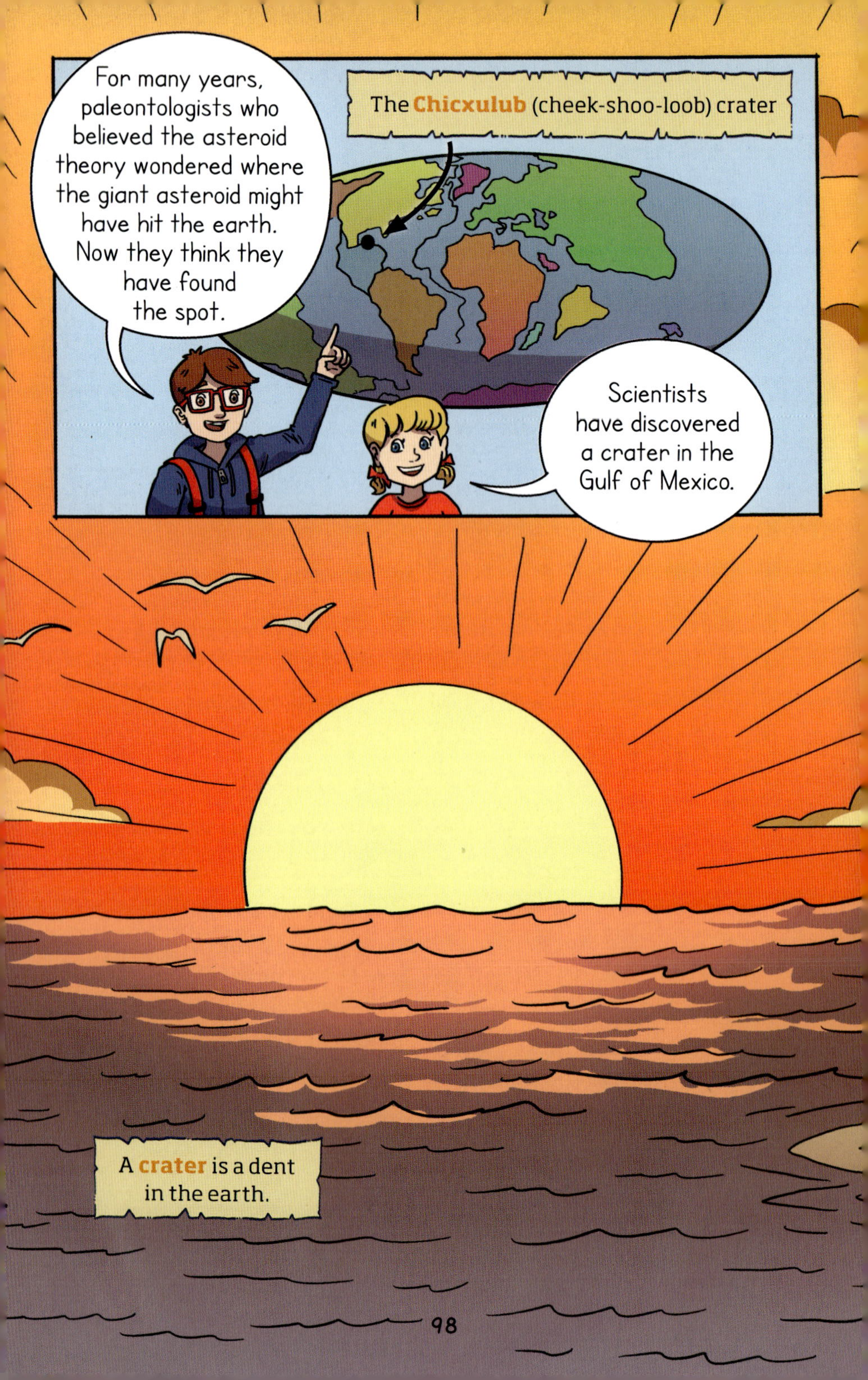
For many years, paleontologists who believed the asteroid theory wondered where the giant asteroid might have hit the earth. Now they think they have found the spot.
The Chicxulub (cheek-shoo-loob) crater
Scientists have discovered a crater in the Gulf of Mexico.
A crater is a dent in the earth.

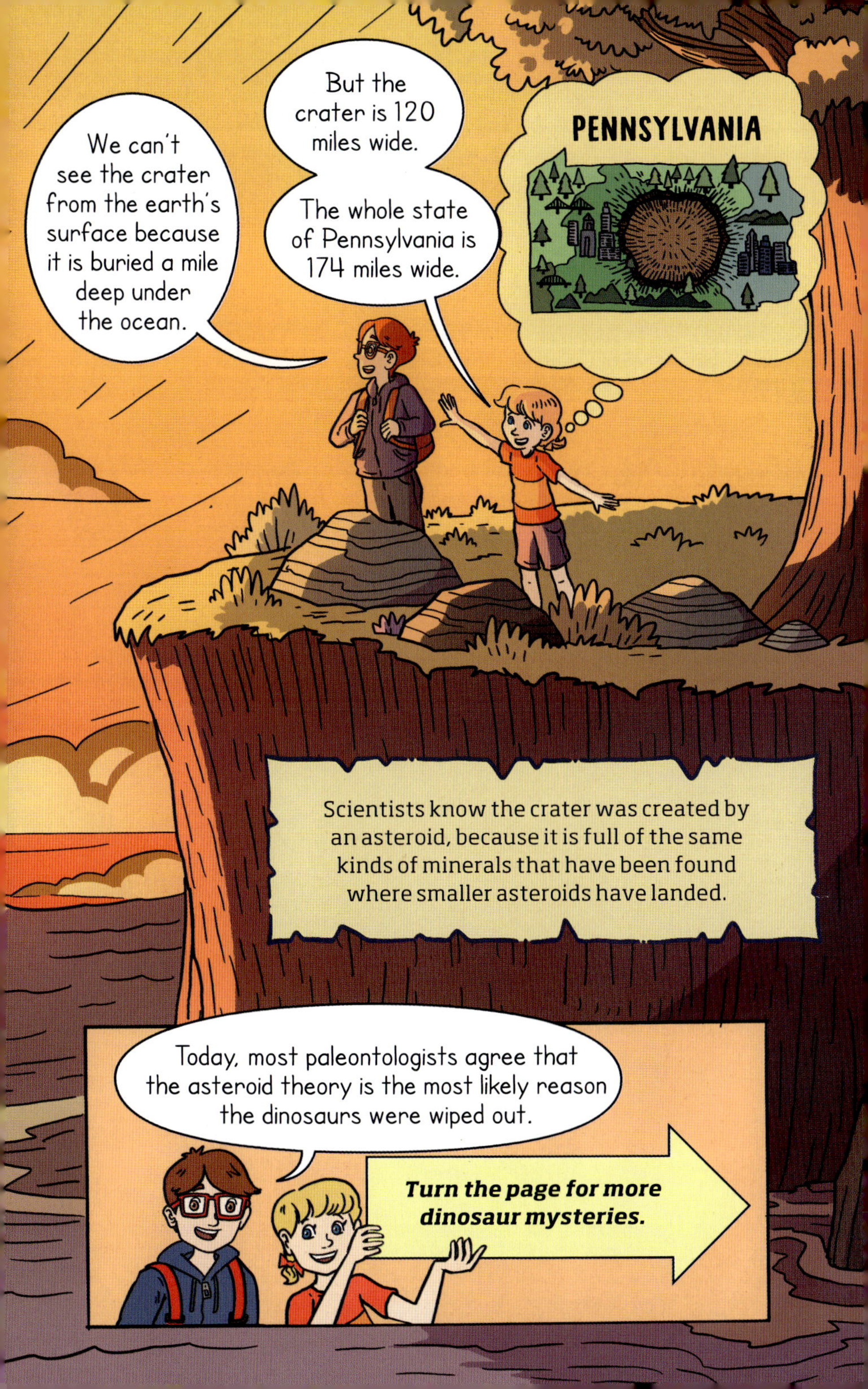
We can't see the crater from the earth's surface because it is buried a mile deep under the ocean.
But the crater is 120 miles wide.
The whole state of Pennsylvania is 174 miles wide.
PENNSYLVANIA
Scientists know the crater was created by an asteroid, because it is full of the same kinds of minerals that have been found where smaller asteroids have landed.
Today, most paleontologists agree that the asteroid theory is the most likely reason the dinosaurs were wiped out.
Turn the page for more dinosaur mysteries.

More Dinosaur Mysteries

Paleontologists have been studying dinosaur fossils for almost 200 years. But they still have lots of questions. . . .

Case #1

A Dinosaur of a Different Color

What color were dinosaurs?
Were they brown and gray?
Or were they bright red?
Green? Yellow?
Were they spotted?
Did they have stripes?

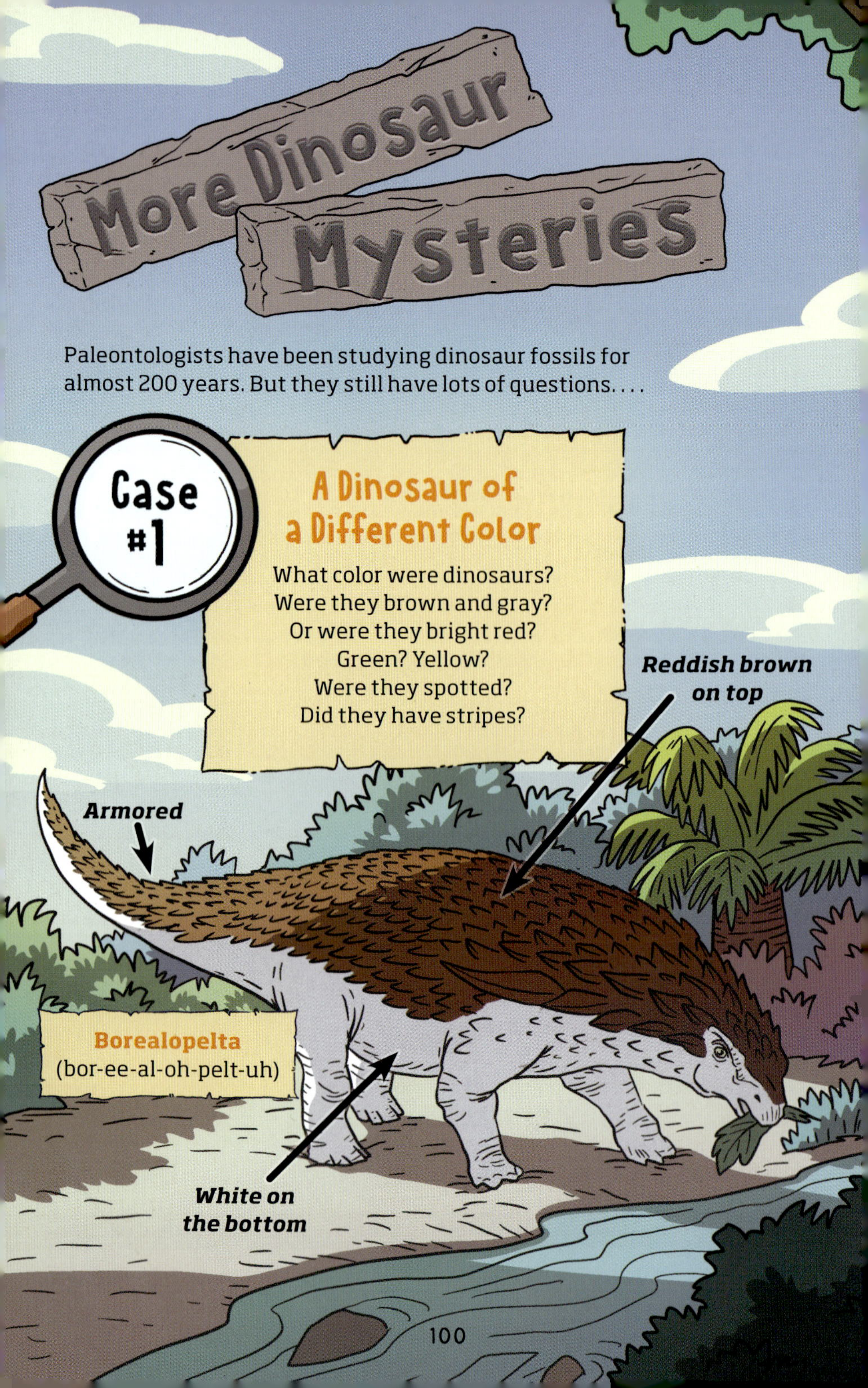

Reddish brown on top
Armored
Borealopelta
(bor-ee-al-oh-pelt-uh)
White on the bottom

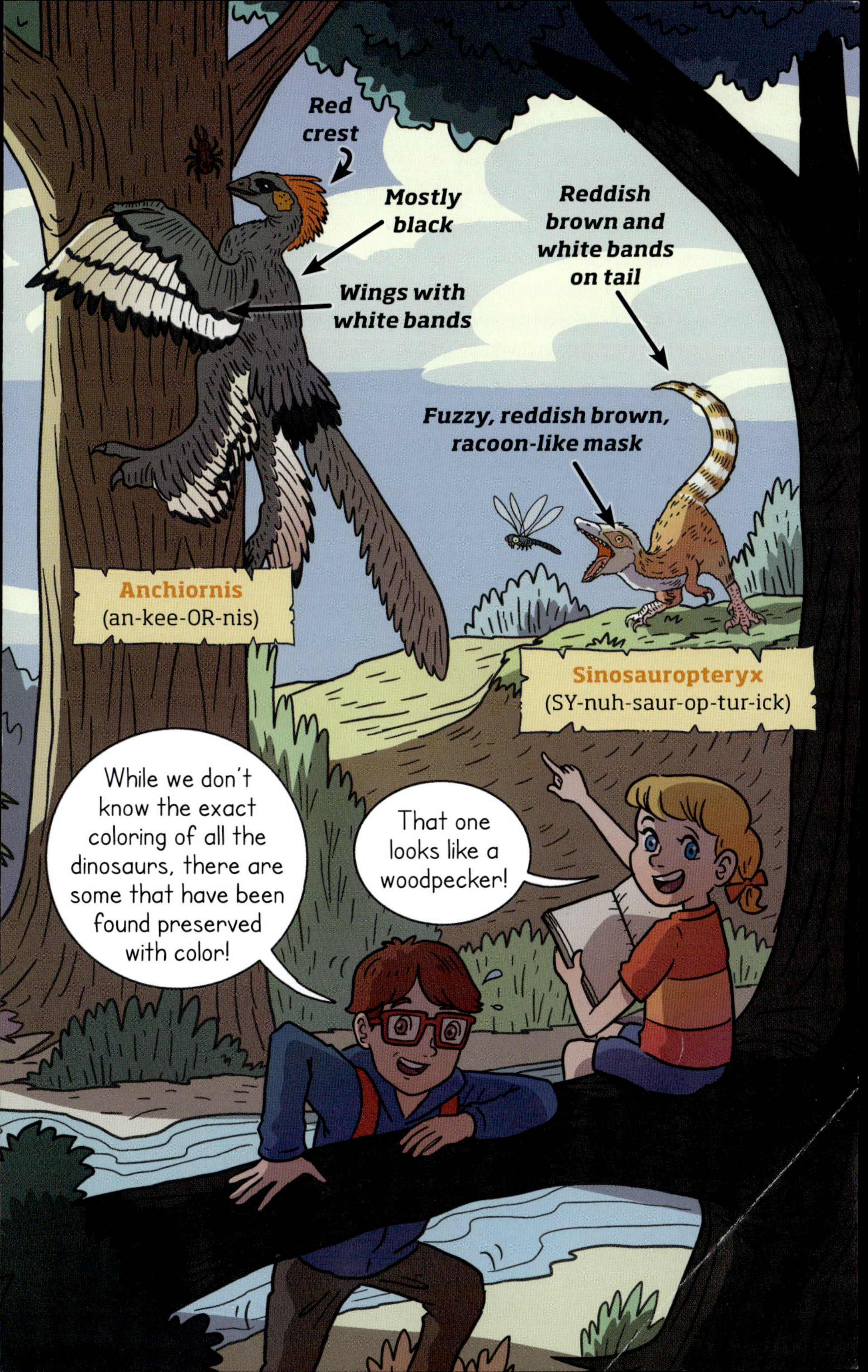

Red crest
Mostly black
Wings with white bands
Anchiornis
(an-kee-OR-nis)
Reddish brown and white bands on tail
Fuzzy, reddish brown, racoon-like mask
Sinosauropteryx
(SY-nuh-saur-op-tur-ick)
While we don't know the exact coloring of all the dinosaurs, there are some that have been found preserved with color!
That one looks like a woodpecker!

Case #2

An Age-old Riddle

How many years did a dinosaur live?

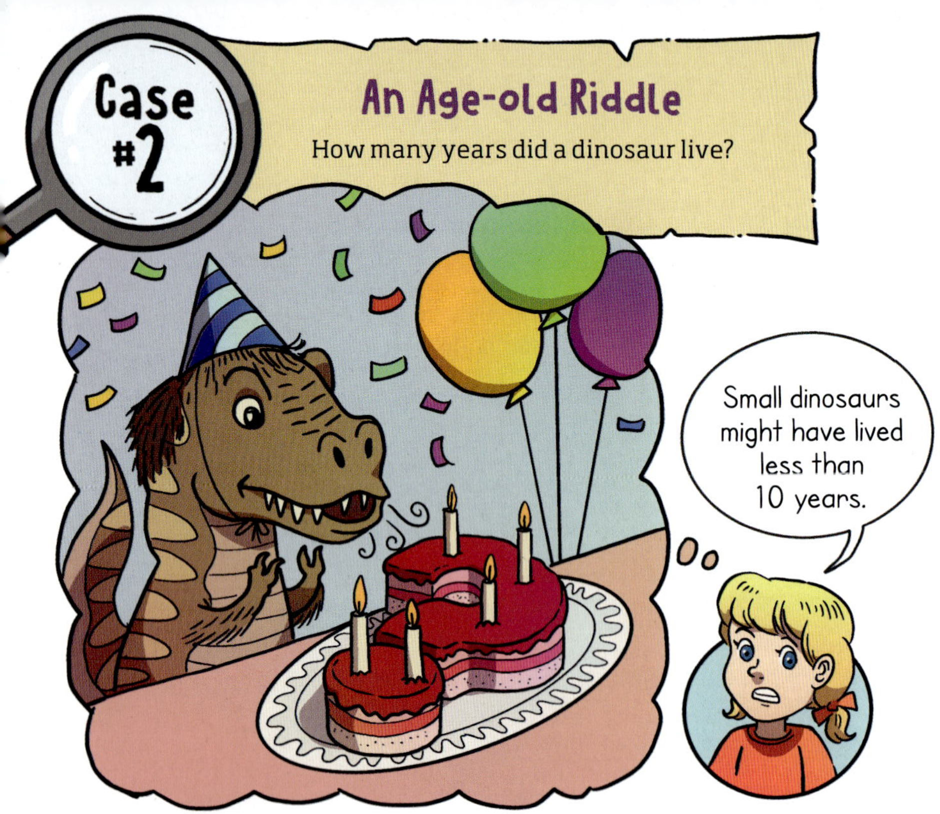
Small dinosaurs might have lived less than 10 years.

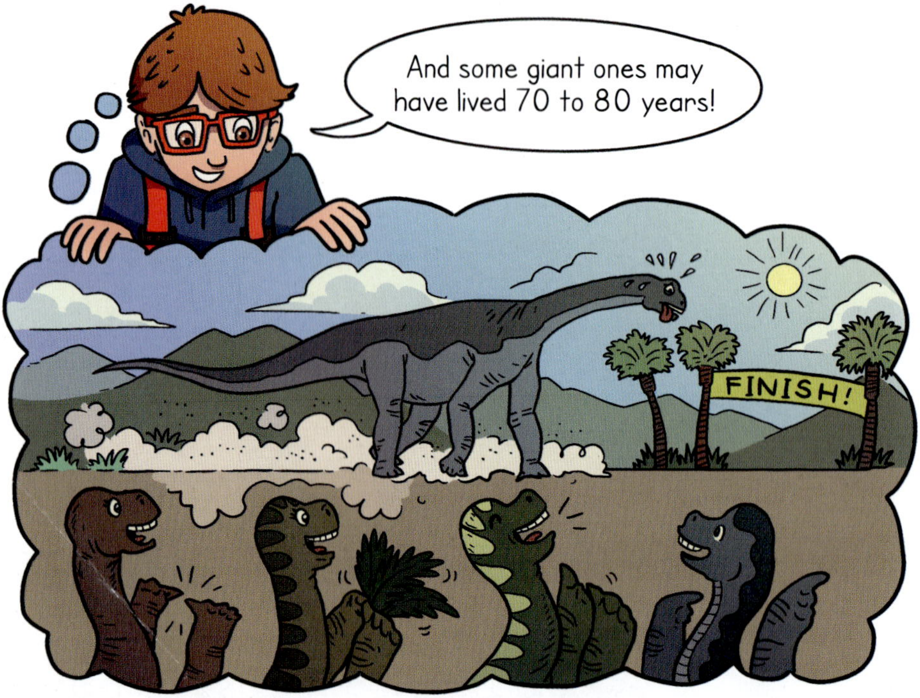
And some giant ones may have lived 70 to 80 years!
FINISH!

Two-ton Tooters

What kinds of sounds did dinosaurs make?

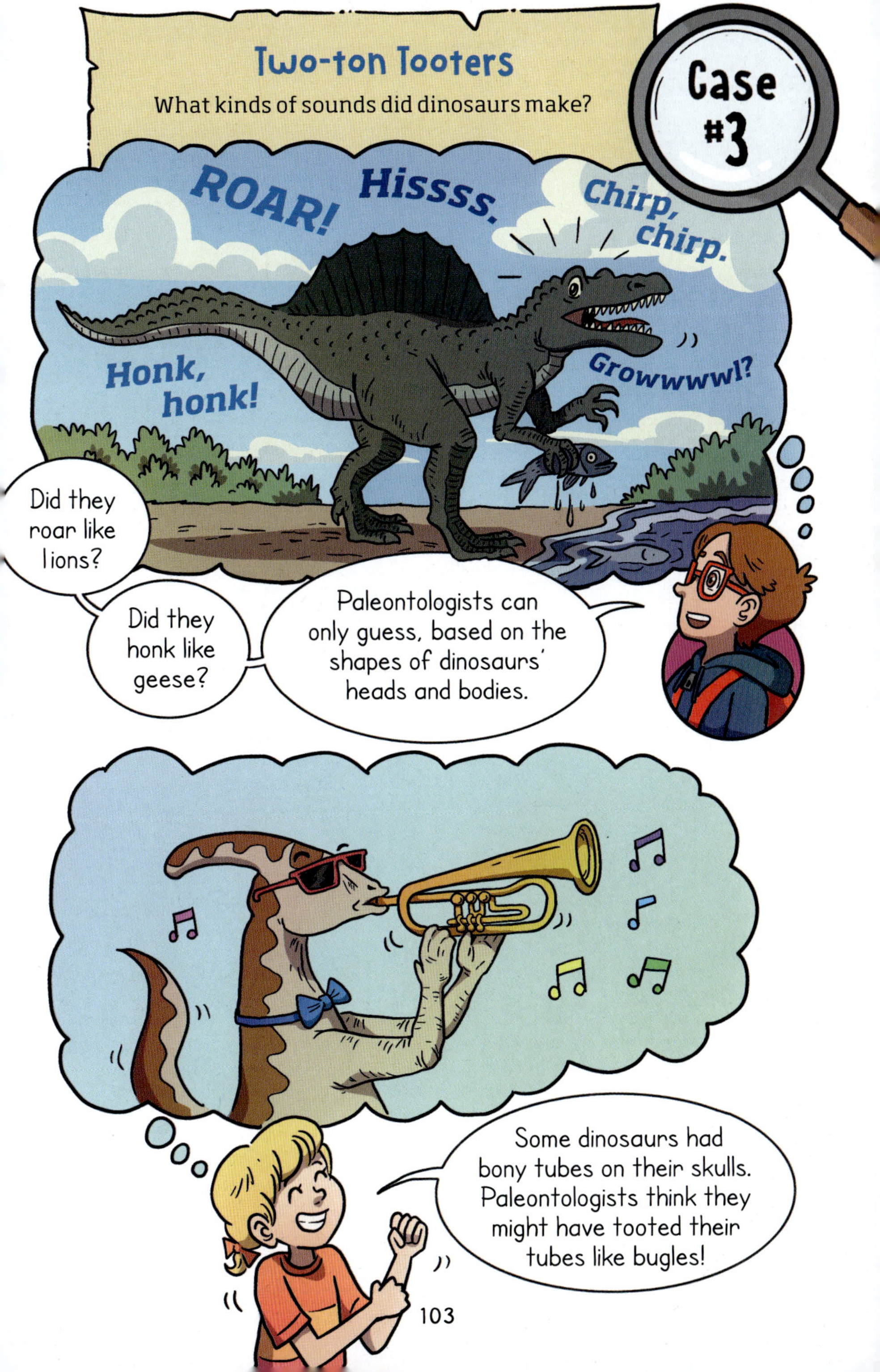
Case #3
ROAR!
Hissss.
Chirp, chirp.
Honk, honk!
Growwwwl?
Did they roar like lions?
Did they honk like geese?
Paleontologists can only guess, based on the shapes of dinosaurs' heads and bodies.
Some dinosaurs had bony tubes on their skulls. Paleontologists think they might have tooted their tubes like bugles!

CHAPTER EIGHT

Dinosaur Neighbors

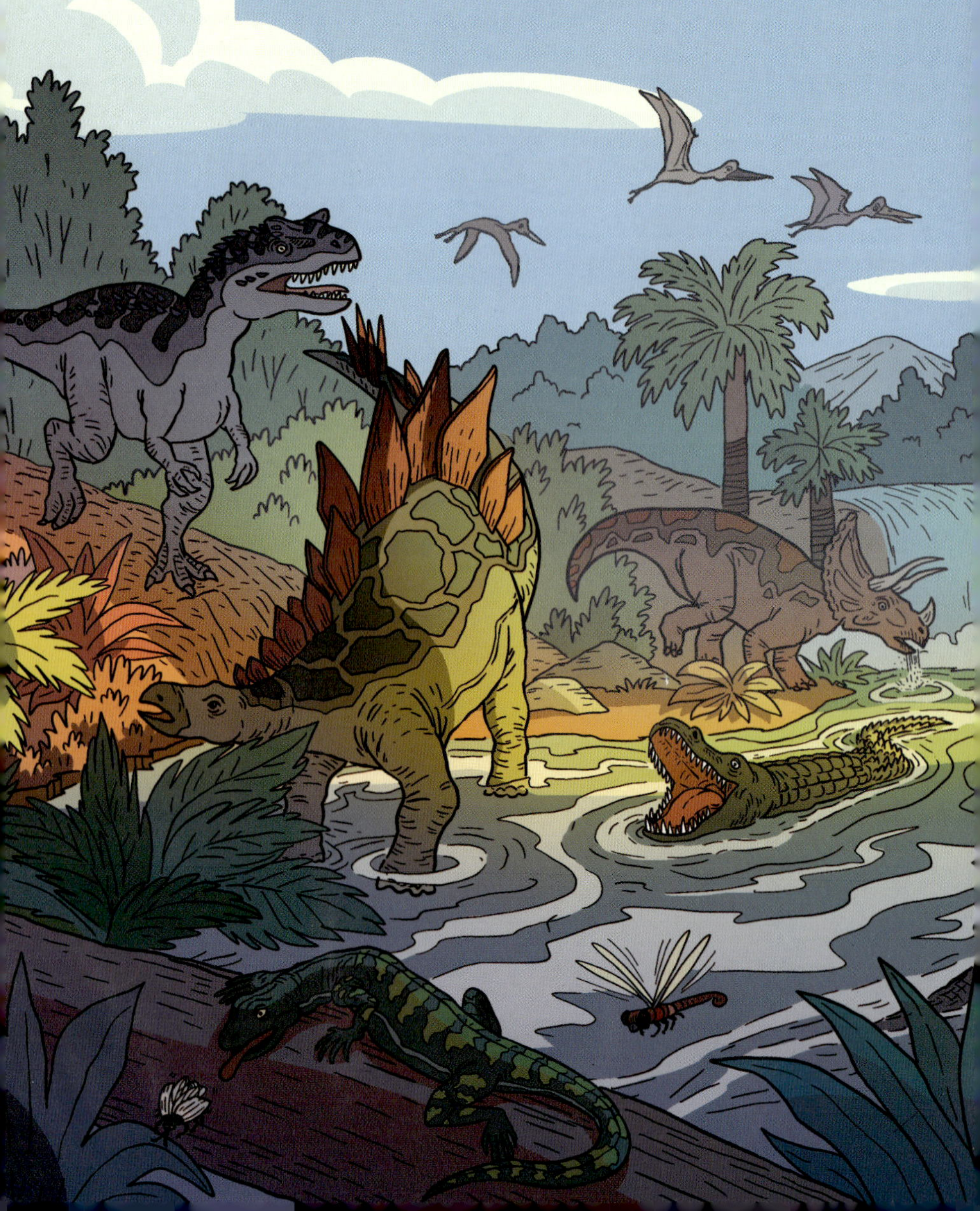

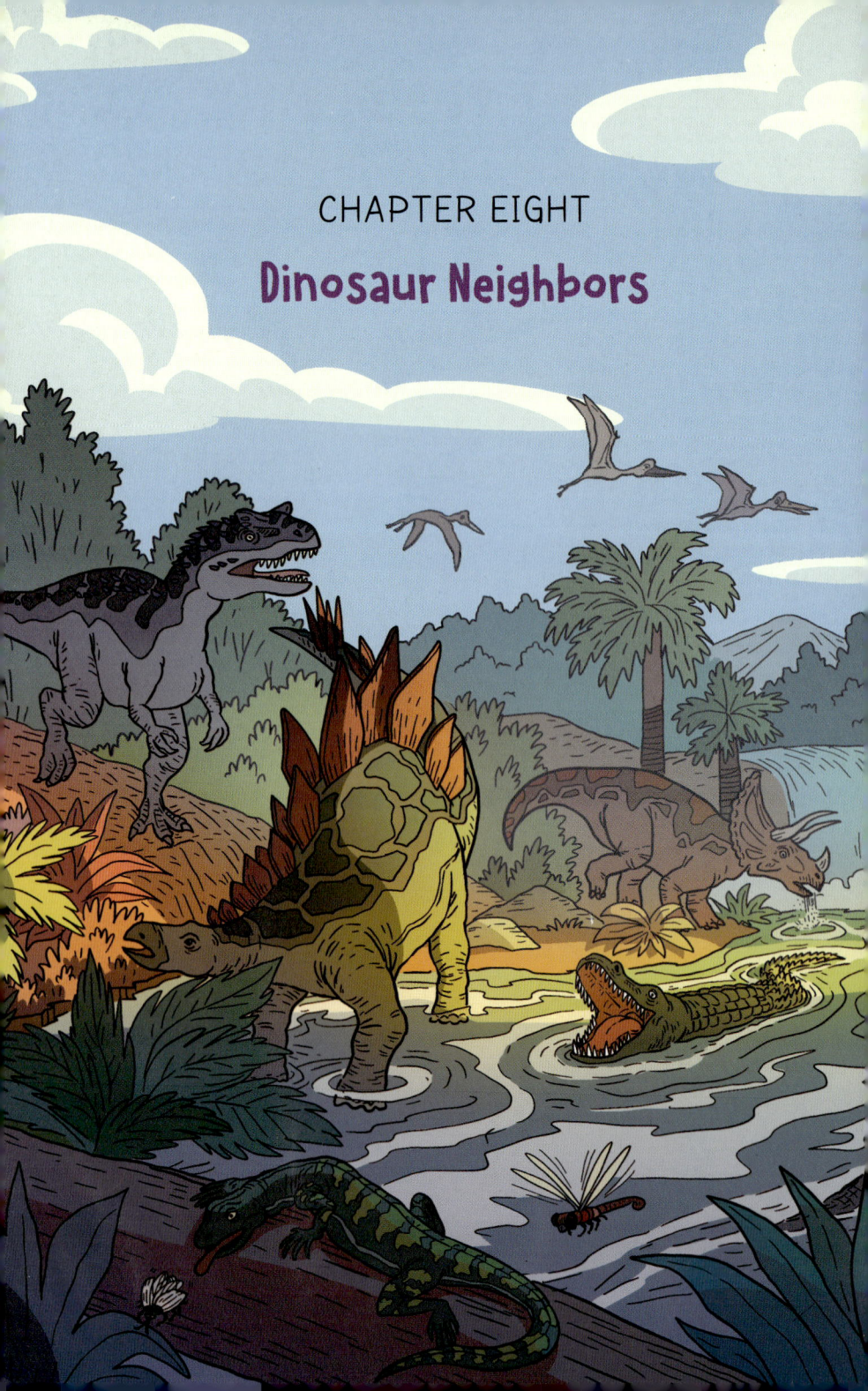

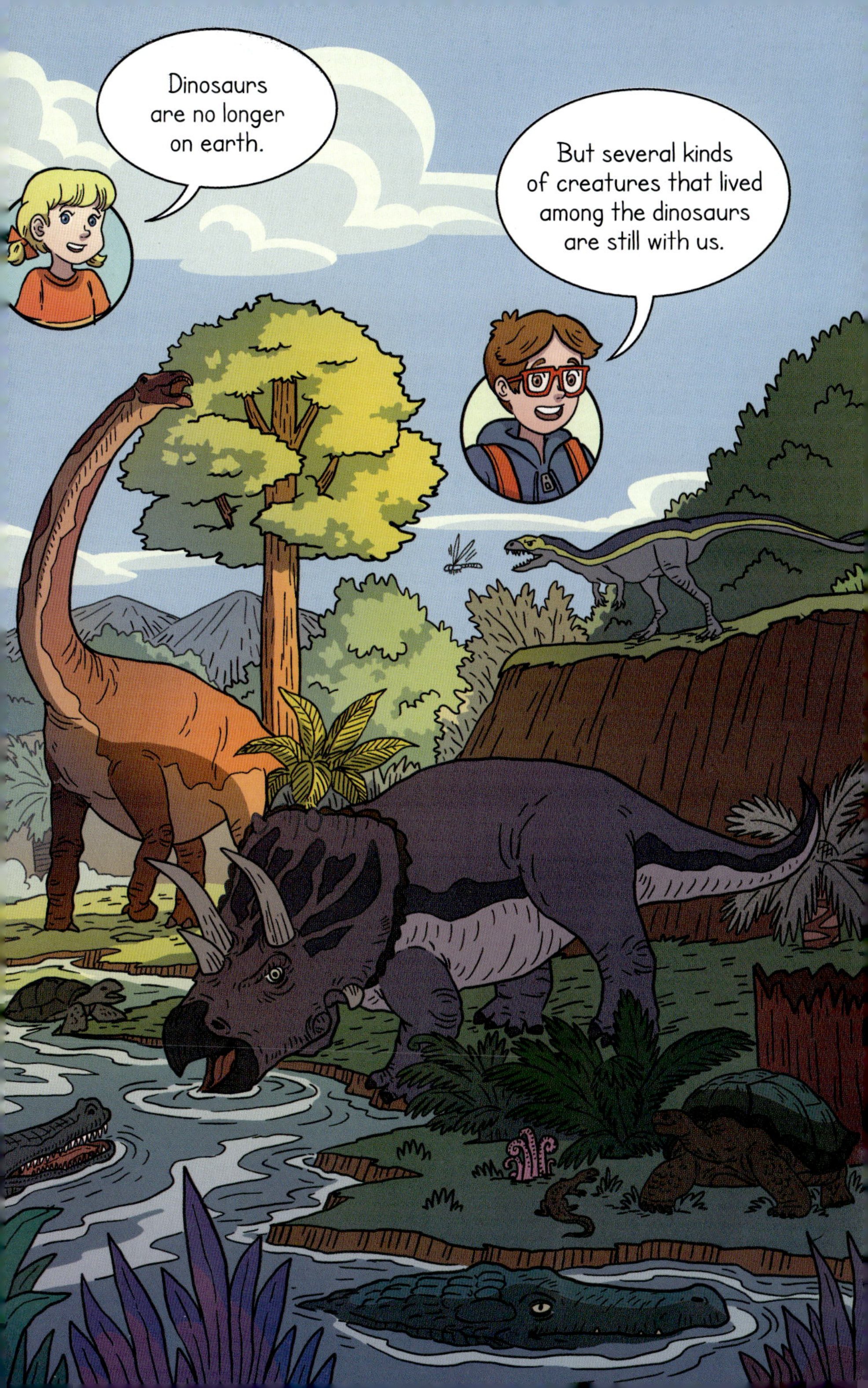
Dinosaurs are no longer on earth.
But several kinds of creatures that lived among the dinosaurs are still with us.

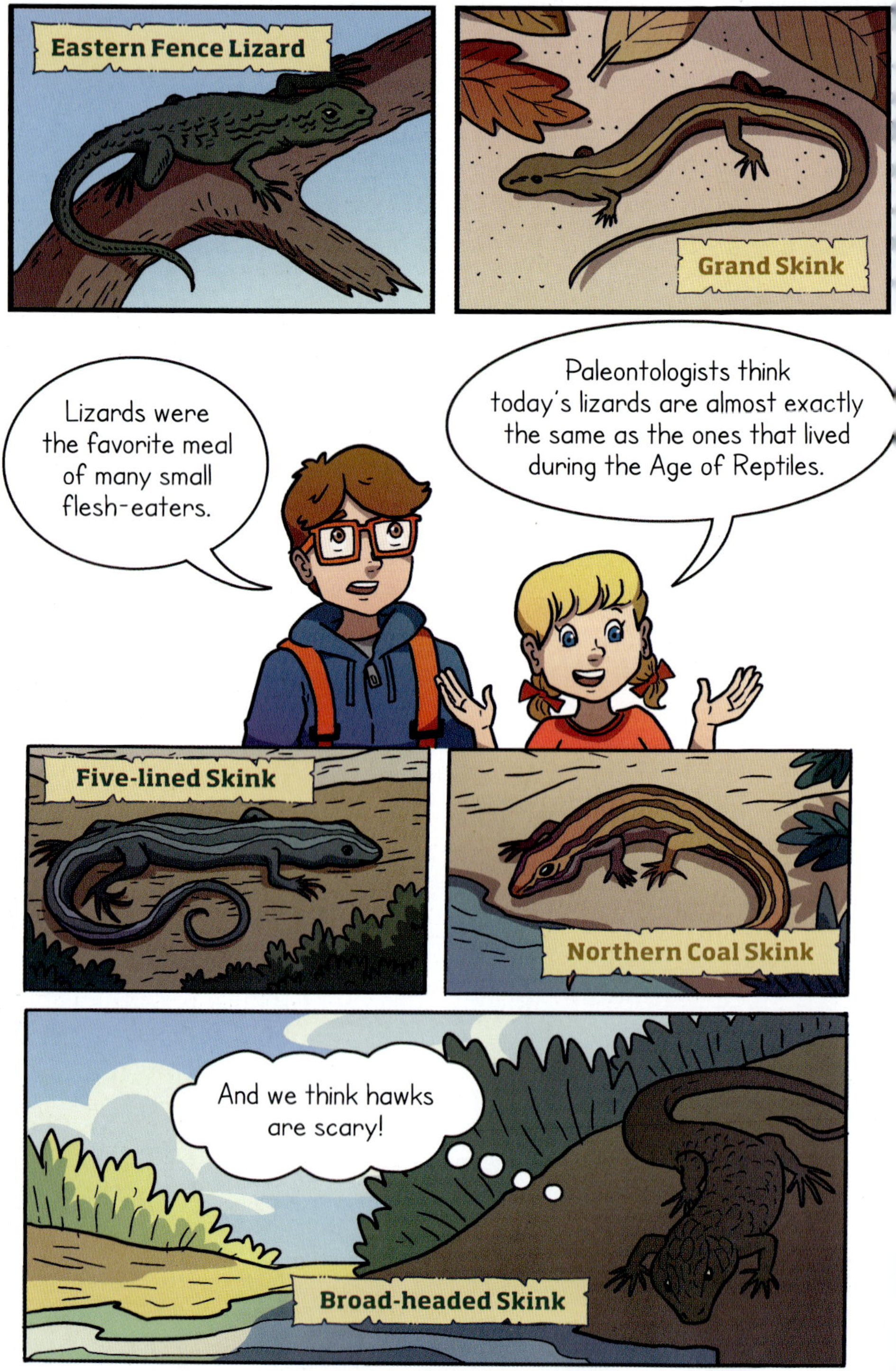
Eastern Fence Lizard
Grand Skink
Lizards were the favorite meal of many small flesh-eaters.
Paleontologists think today's lizards are almost exactly the same as the ones that lived during the Age of Reptiles.
Five-lined Skink
Northern Coal Skink
And we think hawks are scary!
Broad-headed Skink

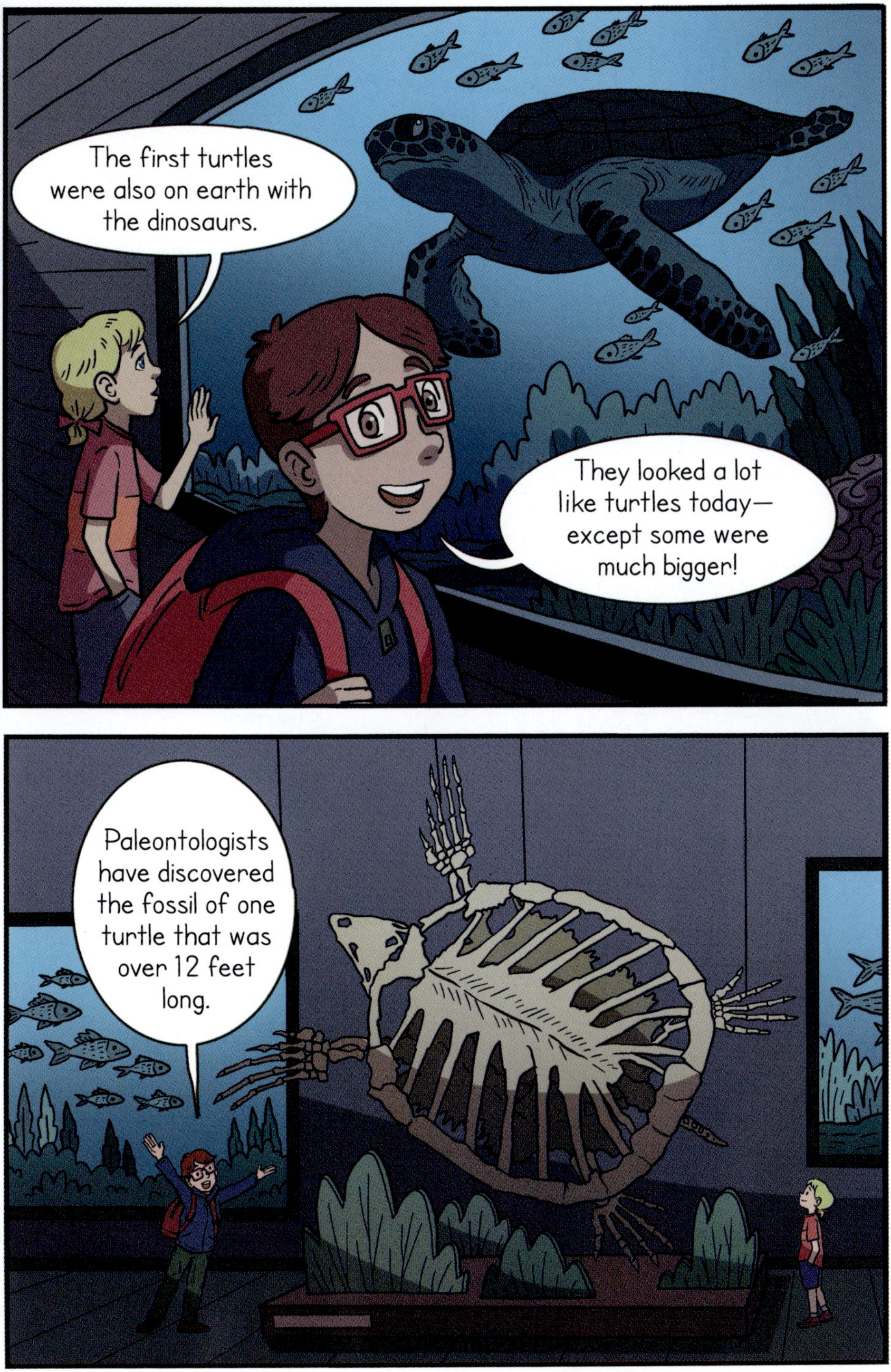
The first turtles were also on earth with the dinosaurs.
They looked a lot like turtles today—except some were much bigger!
Paleontologists have discovered the fossil of one turtle that was over 12 feet long.

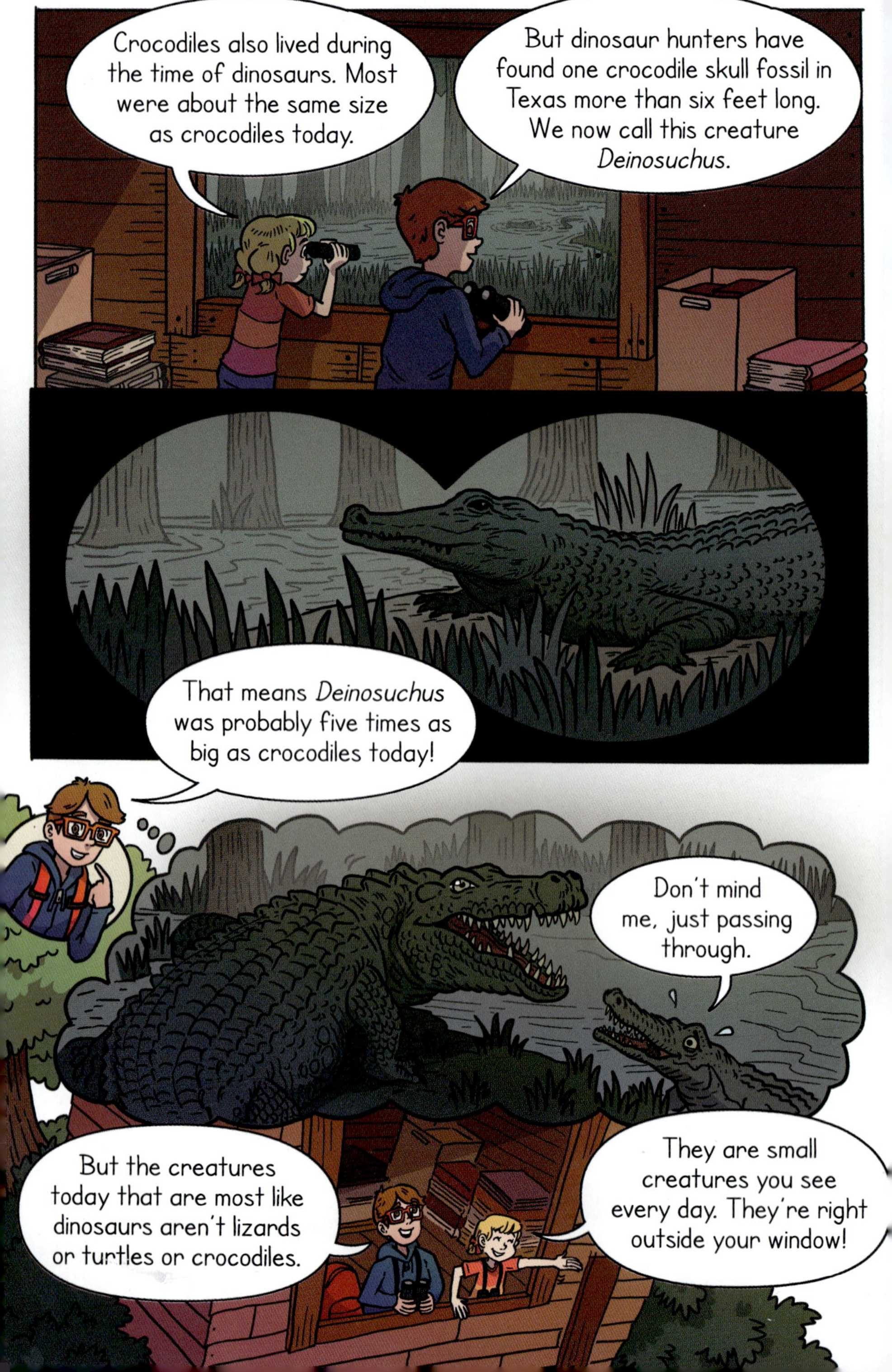

Crocodiles also lived during the time of dinosaurs. Most were about the same size as crocodiles today.
But dinosaur hunters have found one crocodile skull fossil in Texas more than six feet long. We now call this creature *Deinosuchus*.
That means *Deinosuchus* was probably five times as big as crocodiles today!
Don't mind me, just passing through.
But the creatures today that are most like dinosaurs aren't lizards or turtles or crocodiles.
They are small creatures you see every day. They're right outside your window!

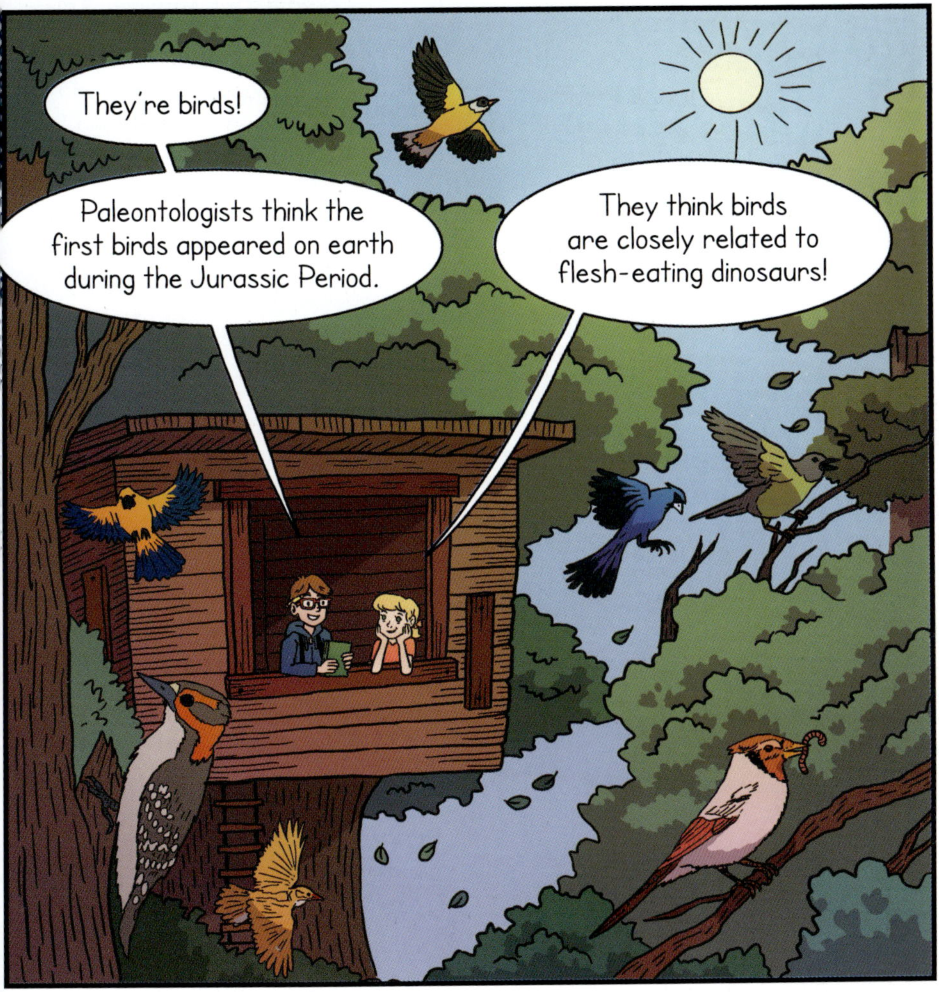
They're birds!
Paleontologists think the first birds appeared on earth during the Jurassic Period.
They think birds are closely related to flesh-eating dinosaurs!

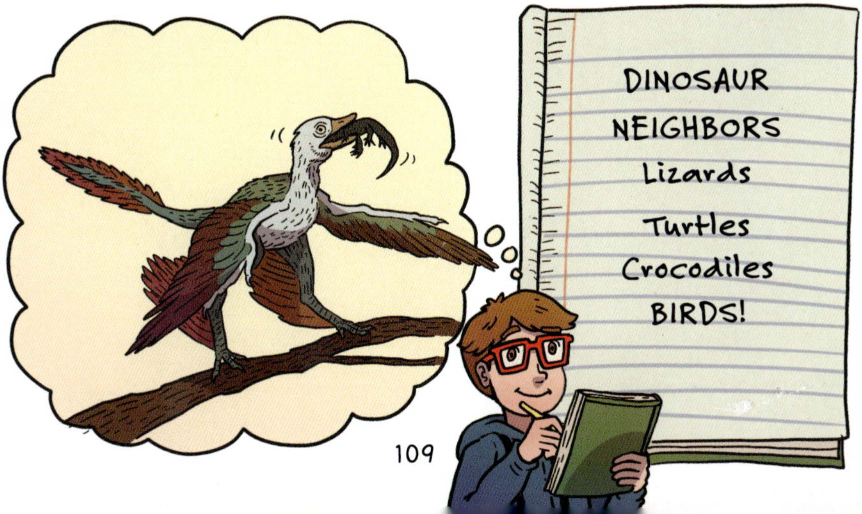
DINOSAUR NEIGHBORS
Lizards
Turtles
Crocodiles
BIRDS!

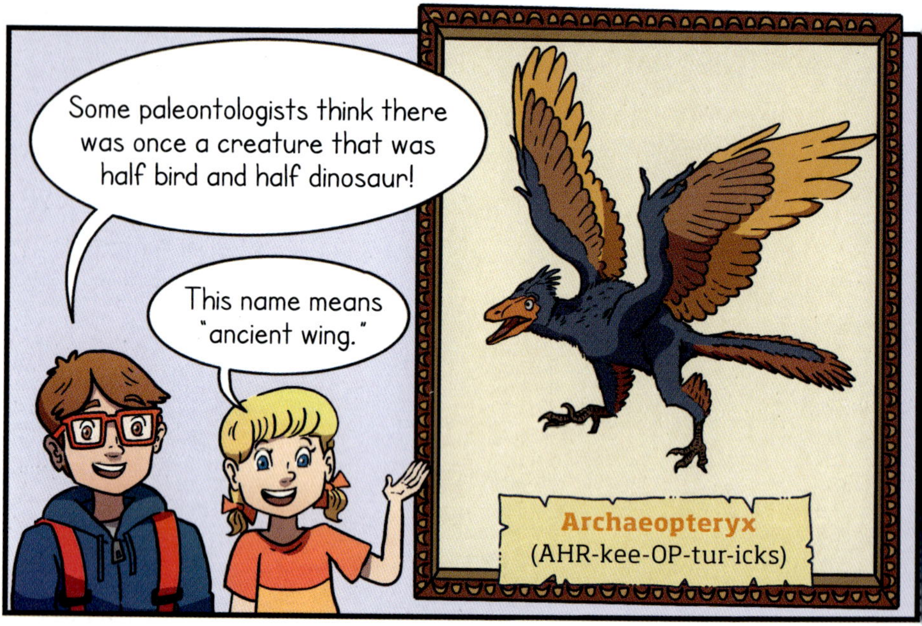
Some paleontologists think there was once a creature that was half bird and half dinosaur!
This name means "ancient wing."
Archaeopteryx
(AHR-kee-OP-tur-icks)

Archaeopteryx fossil

In 1861, workers in Germany dug up the fossil of a small skeleton. The skeleton looked as if it belonged to a flesh-eating dinosaur. But when they looked closely at the stone around the fossilized bones, they saw imprints of feathers. The dinosaur had wings!

Today, the *Archaeopteryx* fossil is one of the most valuable fossils in the world.

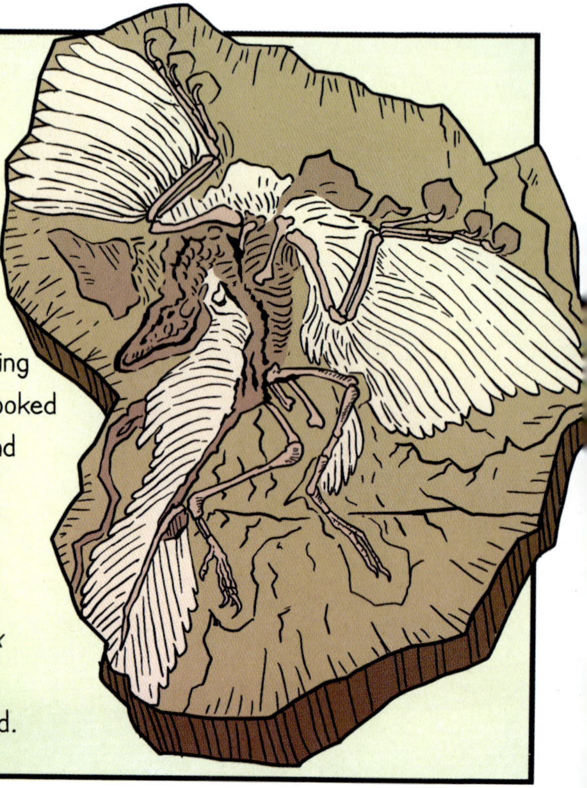

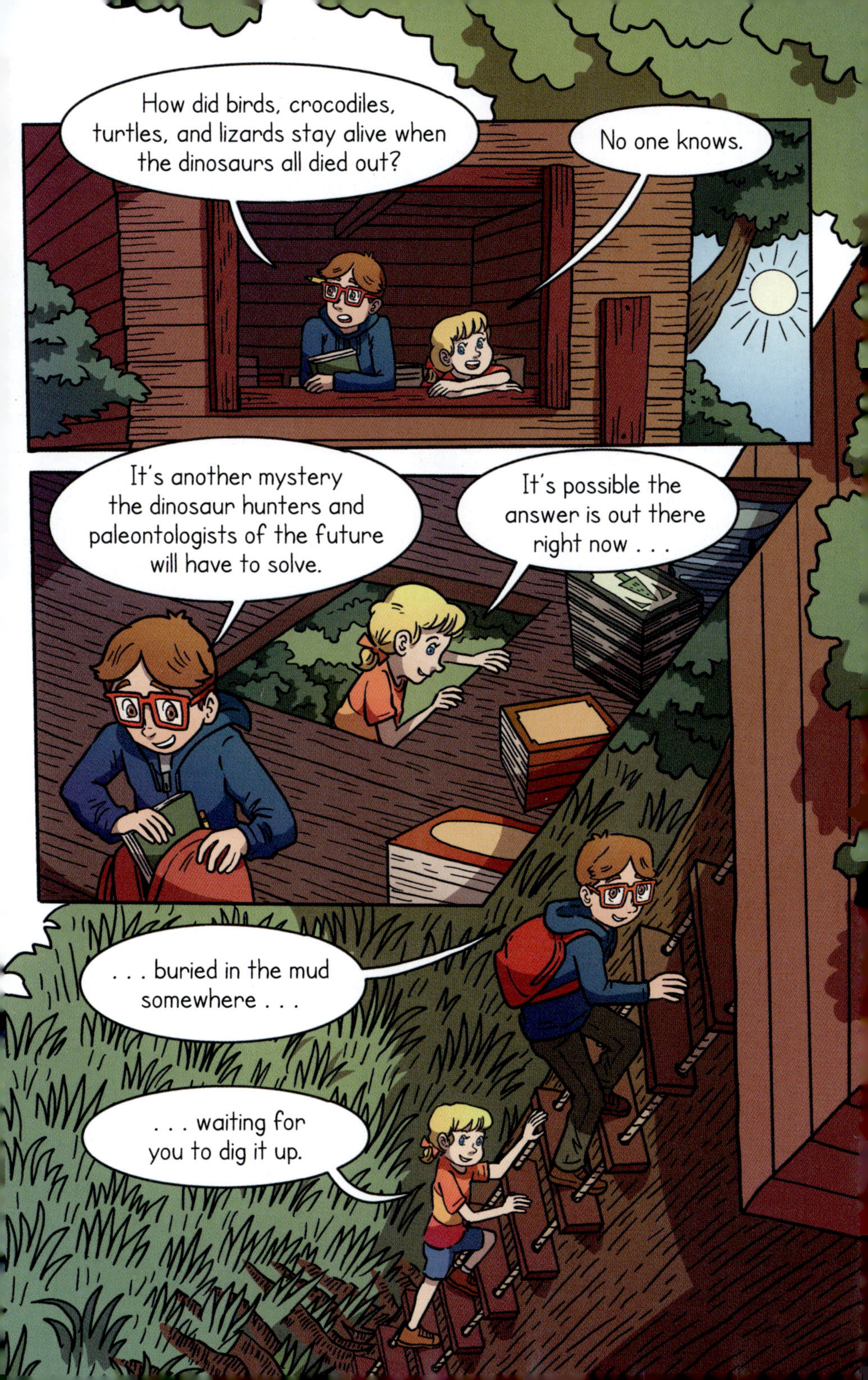
How did birds, crocodiles, turtles, and lizards stay alive when the dinosaurs all died out?
No one knows.
It's another mystery the dinosaur hunters and paleontologists of the future will have to solve.
It's possible the answer is out there right now . . .
. . . buried in the mud somewhere . . .
. . . waiting for you to dig it up.

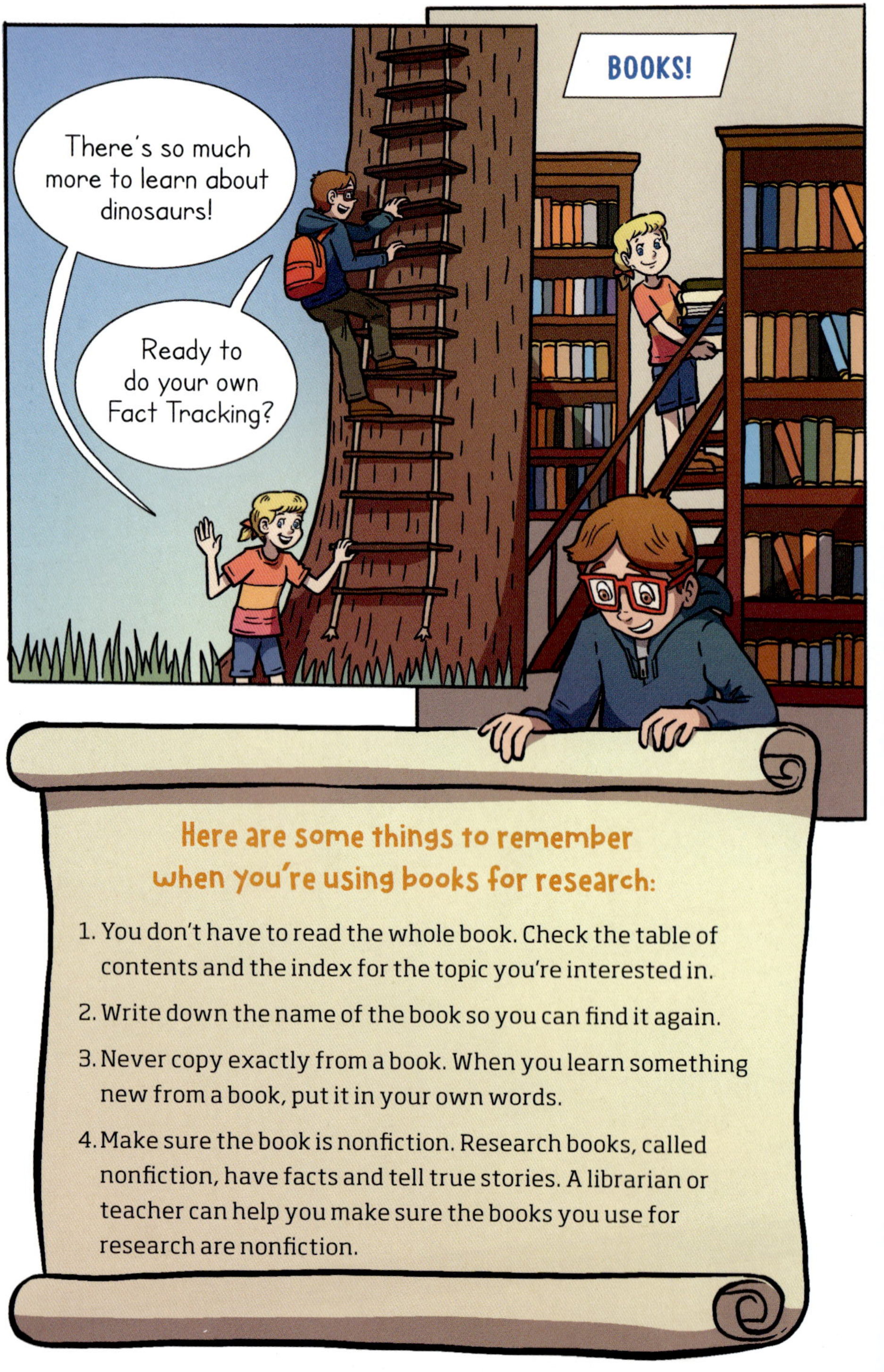
There's so much more to learn about dinosaurs!
Ready to do your own Fact Tracking?
BOOKS!

Here are some things to remember when you're using books for research:

1. You don't have to read the whole book. Check the table of contents and the index for the topic you're interested in.
2. Write down the name of the book so you can find it again.
3. Never copy exactly from a book. When you learn something new from a book, put it in your own words.
4. Make sure the book is nonfiction. Research books, called nonfiction, have facts and tell true stories. A librarian or teacher can help you make sure the books you use for research are nonfiction.

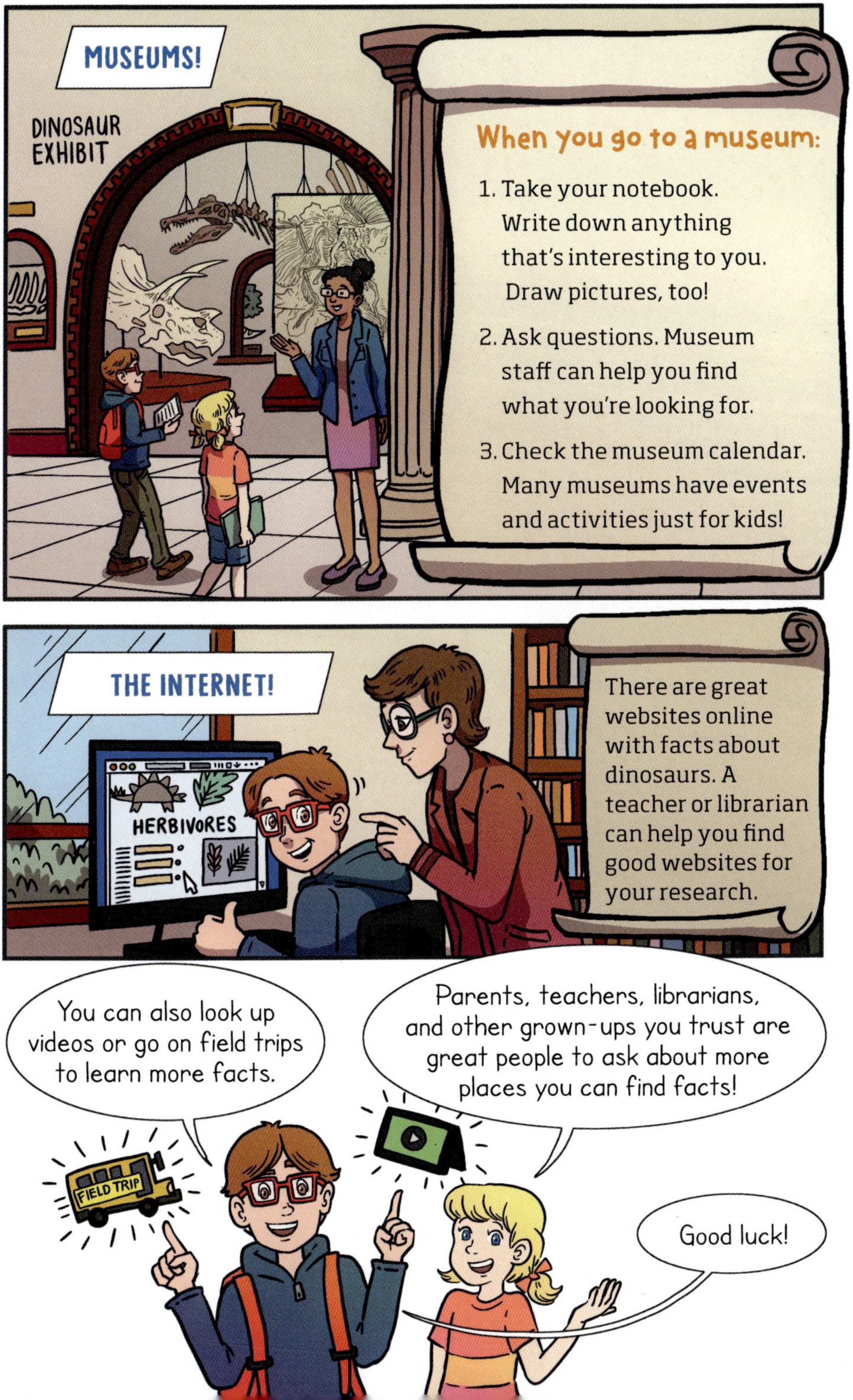
MUSEUMS!
DINOSAUR EXHIBIT
When you go to a museum:
1. Take your notebook. Write down anything that's interesting to you. Draw pictures, too!
2. Ask questions. Museum staff can help you find what you're looking for.
3. Check the museum calendar. Many museums have events and activities just for kids!
THE INTERNET!
HERBIVORES
There are great websites online with facts about dinosaurs. A teacher or librarian can help you find good websites for your research.
You can also look up videos or go on field trips to learn more facts.
Parents, teachers, librarians, and other grown-ups you trust are great people to ask about more places you can find facts!
FIELD TRIP
Good luck!

Glossary

Asteroid: a rock from outer space

Climate: the usual weather of a place

Continent: a large land mass found on earth

Cretaceous Period: the time period from about 145–66 million years ago

Extinct: no longer living on earth

Fossils: any traces of life from a long-ago age

Jurassic Period: the time period from about 201–145 million years ago

Mesozoic Era: the Age of Dinosaurs, which is divided into the Triassic, Jurassic, and Cretaceous Periods

Minerals: natural substances in the earth that do not come from plants or animals

Paleontologists: scientists who study fossils

Pangaea: one big, ancient continent that existed 300–200 million years ago on earth

Predators: animals that hunt other animals for food

Prey: animals that are hunted by other animals for food

Pterosaurs: flying reptiles, like *Pteranodon*, that are not considered dinosaurs

Reptiles: cold-blooded, usually scaly-skinned animals

Sauropods: dinosaurs with long necks, long tails, and small heads

Triassic Period: the time period from about 252–201 million years ago

Don't miss the adventure that inspired this book!

Available now!

TRACK THE FACTS WITH JACK & ANNIE!

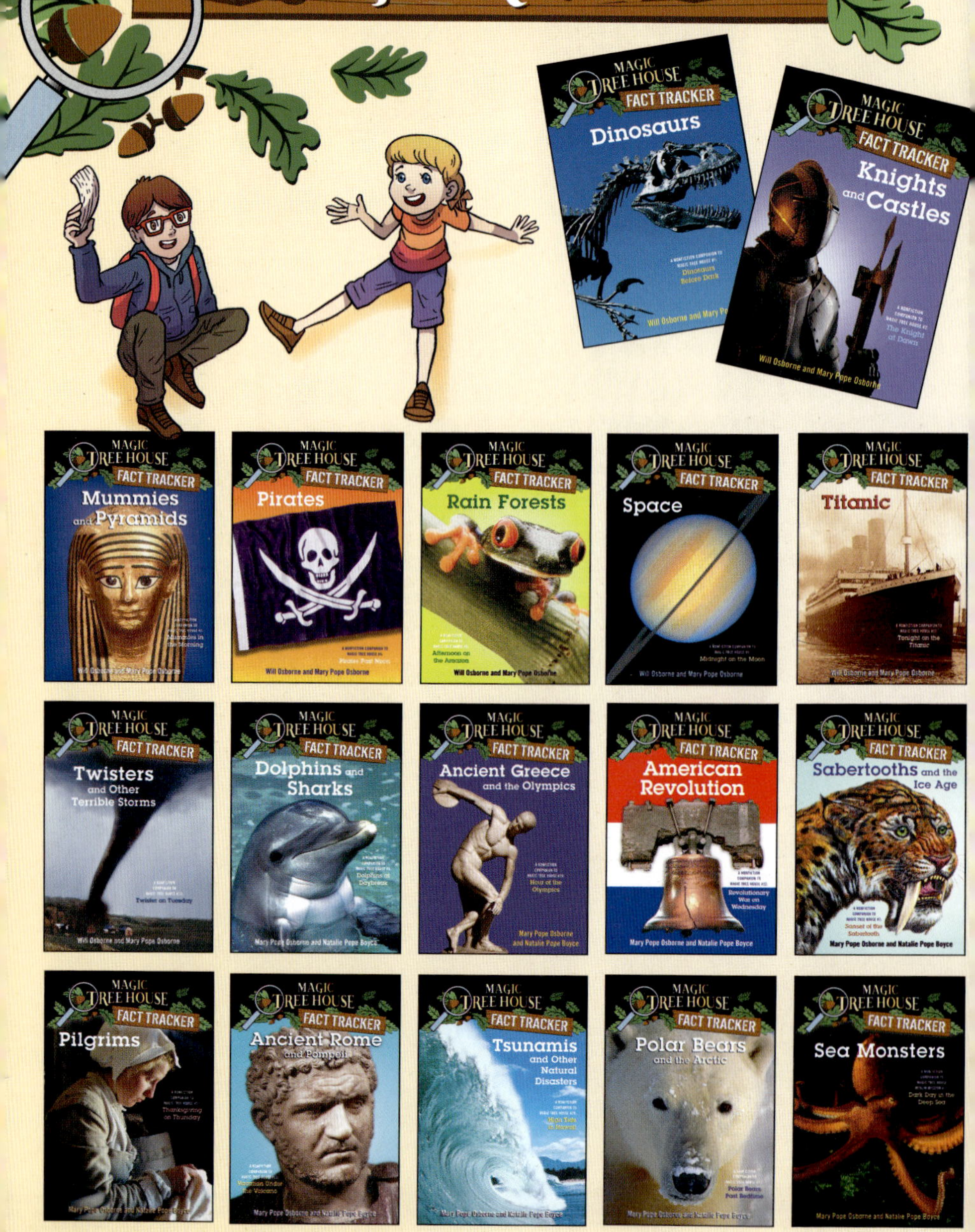

MAGIC TREE HOUSE FACT TRACKER
Dinosaurs
Will Osborne and Mary Pope Osborne
MAGIC TREE HOUSE FACT TRACKER
Knights and Castles
Will Osborne and Mary Pope Osborne
MAGIC TREE HOUSE FACT TRACKER
Mummies and Pyramids
Will Osborne and Mary Pope Osborne
MAGIC TREE HOUSE FACT TRACKER
Pirates
Will Osborne and Mary Pope Osborne
MAGIC TREE HOUSE FACT TRACKER
Rain Forests
Will Osborne and Mary Pope Osborne
MAGIC TREE HOUSE FACT TRACKER
Space
Will Osborne and Mary Pope Osborne
MAGIC TREE HOUSE FACT TRACKER
Titanic
Will Osborne and Mary Pope Osborne
MAGIC TREE HOUSE FACT TRACKER
Twisters and Other Terrible Storms
Will Osborne and Mary Pope Osborne
MAGIC TREE HOUSE FACT TRACKER
Dolphins and Sharks
Mary Pope Osborne and Natalie Pope Boyce
MAGIC TREE HOUSE FACT TRACKER
Ancient Greece and the Olympics
Mary Pope Osborne and Natalie Pope Boyce
MAGIC TREE HOUSE FACT TRACKER
American Revolution
Mary Pope Osborne and Natalie Pope Boyce
MAGIC TREE HOUSE FACT TRACKER
Sabertooths and the Ice Age
Mary Pope Osborne and Natalie Pope Boyce
MAGIC TREE HOUSE FACT TRACKER
Pilgrims
Mary Pope Osborne and Natalie Pope Boyce
MAGIC TREE HOUSE FACT TRACKER
Ancient Rome and Pompeii
Mary Pope Osborne and Natalie Pope Boyce
MAGIC TREE HOUSE FACT TRACKER
Tsunamis and Other Natural Disasters
Mary Pope Osborne and Natalie Pope Boyce
MAGIC TREE HOUSE FACT TRACKER
Polar Bears and the Arctic
Mary Pope Osborne and Natalie Pope Boyce
MAGIC TREE HOUSE FACT TRACKER
Sea Monsters
Mary Pope Osborne and Natalie Pope Boyce

Magic Tree House Fact Tracker
Penguins and Antarctica
Leonardo da Vinci
Ghosts
Leprechauns and Irish Folklore
Rags and Riches
Kids in the Time of Charles Dickens
Snakes and Other Reptiles
Dog Heroes
Abraham Lincoln
Pandas and Other Endangered Species
Horse Heroes
Heroes for All Times
Soccer
Ninjas and Samurai
China
Land of the Emperor's Great Wall
Sharks and Other Predators
Vikings
Dogsledding and Extreme Sports
Dragons and Mythical Creatures
World War II
Baseball
Wild West
Texas
Warriors
Benjamin Franklin
Narwhals and Other Whales
Mary Pope Osborne and Natalie Pope Boyce

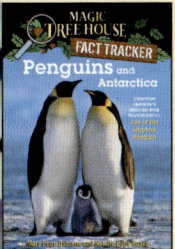

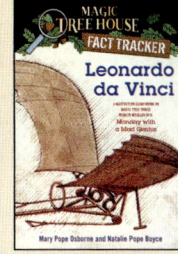

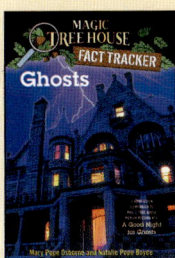

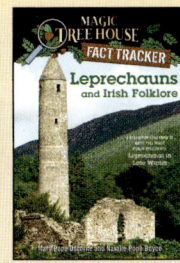

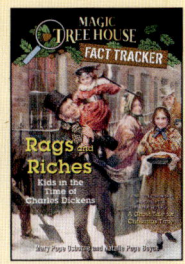

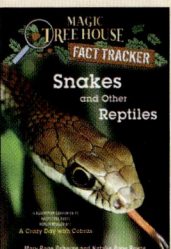

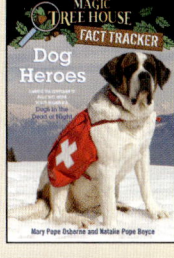

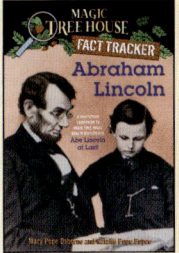

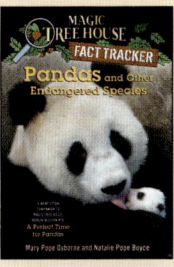

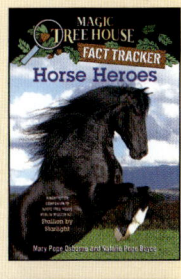

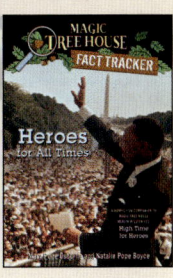

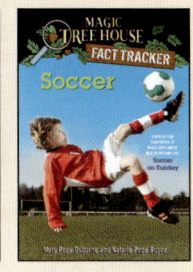

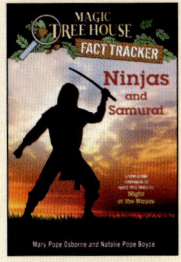

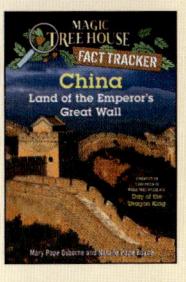

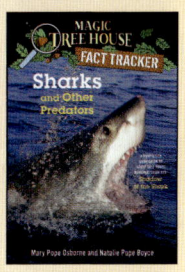

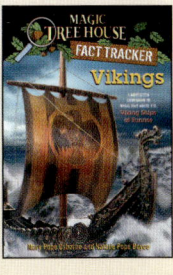

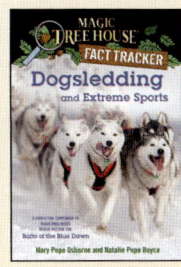

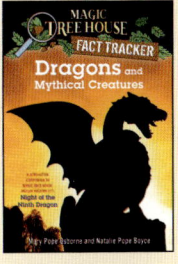

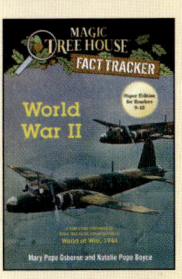

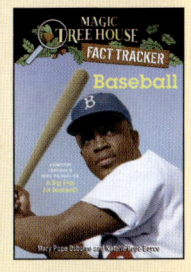

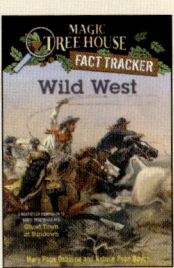

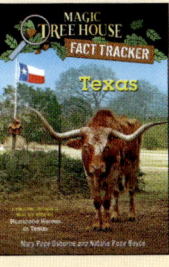

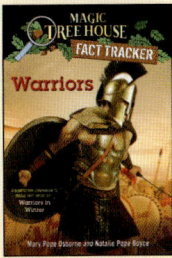

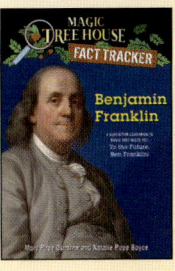

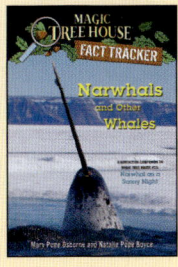

MARY POPE OSBORNE and **WILL OSBORNE** are the authors of several Magic Tree House® Fact Trackers. Mary is the author of more than a hundred books for children, including novels, picture books, biographies, and retellings of fairy tales and world mythologies. Will has worked for many years in the theater as an actor, director, and playwright.

JENNY LAIRD is an award-winning playwright. She collaborates with Will Osborne and Randy Courts on creating musical theater adaptations of the Magic Tree House® series for both national and international audiences. Their work also includes shows for young performers, available through Music Theatre International's Broadway Junior® Collection. Currently the team is working on a Magic Tree House® animated television series.

JOMIKE TEJIDO is an architect, artist, and award-winning illustrator and author who has made over a hundred children's books in his hometown of Manila, Philippines. When not making books, Jomike builds kinetic sculptures and paints on canvas. His art has been featured in twenty solo exhibitions and counting!